RULES OF ENGAGEMENT

Rules of the Game: Evanston River Otters

BRIGHAM VAUGHN

Two Peninsulas Press

AUTHOR'S NOTE

I hope you enjoy Kelly and Anders' story. Since I began this series a year ago, I've been intrigued by Anders and his devastating loss.

It took me a little longer to figure out that Kelly was who he was meant to be with, but once those pieces came together, I've been eager to tell their story.

The series is best read in order so if you haven't read Zane and Ryan's story yet, *Road Rules* is available for FREE through Prolific Works as part of a huge giveaway.

The rest of the *Rules of the Game* series is available here.

Writing about NHL players and pro hockey certainly comes with its own challenges but I've really enjoyed the research and have accidentally became a big hockey fan in the process!

Thank you to Helena Stone, DJ Jamison, and Allison Hickman for your excellent beta feedback. I appreciate you all so much. Thank you to Lynnette Brisia for your hockey-specific feedback as well. I really, really couldn't do this without you. lol.

AUTHOR'S NOTE

Huge thanks to Rebecca Fairfax for your fantastic edits, thank you to Melissa Womochil, Julie Fouts Hanson, Rebecca Fairfax, and Sandy Bennett for your amazing proofreading. Thank you to Marie-Pierre D'Auteuil for your expertise on everything French-Canadian.

I would be a disaster without all of your hard work!

As always, huge thanks to DJ Jamison for helping me stay on track (seriously don't know what I'd do without you). You're the best!

And most of all, a big thank you to all of you readers who make this possible. Without you, I wouldn't be living my dream of being a full-time author.

Happy Reading!

BOOK BLURB

Rule #1: Don't fall in love with your best friend's brother

After Anders Lindholm lost his wife and baby daughter in a car accident, he knew he'd never find love like that again.

Hockey, routines, and his team are all that have kept him going since.

But as he approaches forty, an injury makes him consider what life after retirement will be like.

And when his teammate, who just so happens to be his best friend's brother, offers him a helping hand—in more ways than one—it reawakens something in Anders he can't deny.

Rule #2: Don't let anyone know the real you

Kelly O'Shea has been in love with Anders since he was fifteen. He's been hiding the fact that he's gay for just as long.

He loves his family, but their over-protective meddling is what made him move halfway across the country and hide who he was.

Although Kelly and Anders both agreed it would stay casual, Kelly begins to hope that maybe they'll eventually be more than just friends with benefits.

And the more time they spend together, the faster the ice around Anders' heart melts.

But with a playoff spot to clinch, fractures within the team, and overprotective brothers to worry about, Anders' fear of letting go of the past isn't the only challenge they'll have to overcome.

———

Trigger Warning: *Rules of Engagement* includes off-page and non-graphic mentions of death of secondary characters, including a child. Grief. Brief and non-graphic mention of suicidal ideation. Talk of homophobia and homophobic slurs.

Non-graphic mentions of sexual harassment and sexual assault.

TEAM INFO & GLOSSARY

The *Rules of the Game* Series is set in a fictional universe.

Although real life hockey teams and players are mentioned in passing, all of the teams shown on page are fictional.

While I have done my very best to stay true to the rules and schedules of professional hockey, some minor creative license was taken writing these stories.

While not an exhaustive list of hockey terms and slang by any means, here are some used in the series that you might not be familiar with.

Biscuit - A slang term for the puck.

Black Ace - Extra players added to a roster for a team's playoff run after their own season is over in the minor-leagues or elsewhere. The Black Aces practice with the team and are expected to be ready to step into the lineup if any of the regular players in the lineup are unable to play.

Breezers - Hockey pants. Knee-to-waist protective gear that carry a variety of padding depending on whether they are worn by goaltenders or skaters. The pants are traditionally a one-piece garment with a lace-up fly augmented by a strap belt. This slang term is most commonly used in the Midwest.

Celly - Slang for "celebration". The expression of joy after a player scores a goal. Often unique to each player/team.

Corsi - An advanced statistic used to provide an indication of the time a team spends in the offensive zone, versus time spent in their defensive zone. This includes shots on goal, missed shots on goal, and blocked shot attempts towards the opposition's net minus the same shot attempts directed at your own team's net.

Crease - The shaded area directly in front of a hockey goal is called the crease. This is where a hockey goalie stops goals, and where opposing players are prohibited from interfering with the goalie.

Deke - A deke feint or fake is a technique where a player draws an opposing player out of position or is used to skate by an opponent while maintaining possession and control of the puck. The term is a Canadian abbreviation of the word decoy.

EBUG - Emergency backup goaltender. The NHL

requires its clubs to have an emergency back-up in attendance at every home game in case either team loses both of its goalies to injury or illness. If both goaltenders on an NHL roster are unavailable, the designated EBUG will dress for the game and either sit on the bench or, more rarely, play.

Fluff(ed) - Miss a shot.

Hatty (Hat Trick) - When a player scores three goals in a game, usually earning him a cascade of hats thrown onto the ice by fans (especially if the player is on the home team).

A natural hat trick is when a player scores three consecutive goals in a game.

A Gordie Howe Hat Trick is when a player gets a goal, an assist for a goal, and participation in a fight, all within a single game.

KHL - The Kontinental Hockey League is an international professional ice hockey league founded in 2008. It comprises member clubs based in Belarus, China, Finland, Latvia, Kazakhstan, and Russia for a total of 24. Based in Moscow, Russia.

Liney - An affectionate term for a player's linemate. Also sometimes used to refer to the linesman who works along with the referee calling offsides and icings and dropping the puck for face offs.

Pipes - The pipe-like bars that make up the frame around the goal.

Poke Check - When a player uses his stick in a poking fashion to knock the puck away from an offensive player. The most commonly used of all the stick check techniques and can be used by any player in any zone of the ice.

Rocket - An extremely good looking woman.

Salary Cap/Cap Space - The NHL salary cap is the total amount that NHL teams may pay for players. The amount set as the salary cap each year depends on the league's revenue for the previous season. The cap space is the amount of money that a professional team has available to spend on players' salaries.

Spitting Chiclets - Spitting out teeth that have been knocked loose in a fight.

Tape - A slang term for video footage of a hockey game.

Tendie - Goaltender. Also known as a goalie.

TOI - Time on Ice. The minutes and seconds a skater plays during a game or season.

Two-Touch - a common warmup before a hockey game. Players stand in a circle and the goal is to keep a soccer ball up in the air. The ball can be touched once or twice on each attempt, but should be passed in the air to a teammate. Players are eliminated until there is one final winner.

RULES OF ENGAGEMENT

ANDERS & KELLY

"The day I stop giving is the day I stop receiving. The day I stop learning is the day I stop growing."

-Wayne Gretzky

PROLOGUE

FOUR MONTHS PRIOR

"You should slow down, Kelly," Anders Lindholm said softly.

Kelly O'Shea squinted at his teammate, wondering why there were two of him. One was bad enough. "It's fine. I'm fine."

He proved it by tossing back another shot.

"That's my boy." Jack Malone pounded him on the shoulder, sending him slumping into Lindy, who caught and steadied him by wrapping an arm around his back.

The weight of it made the floaty feeling inside Kelly settle and his skin go hot.

Mmm, fuck. How does Lindy always smell so good?

Okay, maaaybe not deep in the postseason at the end of a game that went into double overtime when Anders' pads were all nasty and gross. Though Kelly still spent a lot of time in his bedroom with his underwear shoved down and his hand on his dick, thinking about licking the sweat that trickled down Anders' neck.

When they hugged on the ice, sometimes Kelly buried his head in the crook of Lindy's neck and breathed, let himself enjoy those fleeting seconds of Lindy's arms tight around him, pretending it was something he got to keep.

"Hey, you still alive in there, Irish?" Ryan Hartinger hollered across the table.

Kelly forced himself to straighten, though Lindy's arm remained draped over the back of the booth, fingertips brushing Kelly's shoulder.

"Still alive! Still partying!" Kelly shouted, his tongue thick in his mouth.

"Fuck yeah!" Malone shouted. It was a raucous club, and they were in the VIP section, so no one cared how obnoxious they got but Kelly still winced. One of these days someone would record their antics and blow it up on social media.

And with the ring on Malone's finger and the random girl draped half on top of him, someone would post the damning evidence and land the team in hot water.

Kelly swallowed, sick with the realization that if he wasn't careful, someone would also notice the way he looked at Lindy.

Maybe they already had.

Malone glanced at him. "Hey, you know what? We need to get you laid, Irish."

"Yeah?" Kelly asked, trying not to grimace. Or sway. Was he swaying already? Or was it the room?

"Been a while, huh, bro?" Malone asked with a smirk.

Kelly shrugged. "I do all right." The lie tripped off his tongue with ease because he'd said it so many times now.

Malone snorted. "You could be gettin' it every night of the week, even with your stupid red hair." He turned to the girl on his lap. "Hey, you got any friends?"

She smiled coyly. "Why, what do you have in mind?"

"Oh, well … how about you find someone who might want to hook up with us?" He palmed the curve of her ass. "And see if you have another friend who's into fire crotches." He nodded at Kelly.

Heat built in Kelly's cheeks until he was probably as red as his hair. Yes, the carpet matched the fucking drapes. He'd been chirped enough times about *that* growing up. But what Malone suggested made cold dread build in the pit of Kelly's stomach.

He shoved at Lindy's shoulder. "Hey. Get up," he yelled.

Lindy raised an eyebrow, but obediently shifted to let Kelly out from behind the table.

"Bring shots," Malone hollered when Kelly finally staggered out of the booth. "I don't know where the stupid waitress is. For what we're paying, she should be living at this fucking table."

"Gotta piss," Kelly shouted. "And besides, I got the last round. C'mon, Coop. You're up. This one's on you, man."

Brett Cooper grumbled but he got up. "Fine. What do you assholes want?"

"Eh. Whatever. If it's got alcohol in it, I'm good." Kelly waved vaguely at them before he turned to find the bathroom, stopping when someone grabbed his upper arm.

"You sure you're okay, Kelly?" Lindholm asked, sliding his big hand up Kelly's back, sending sparks dancing across his skin.

"Lookin' for the bathroom."

"Okay." Lindy squeezed his neck and Kelly stifled the urge to sigh and press into the touch.

"Maybe take it easy on the drinks when you get back. And grab some water. You're not as big as those guys and it always hits you harder."

"Not *small* either," Kelly squawked, offended. "Just not a friggin' giant like the rest of you."

Kelly eyed Lindy up and down, liking the way he had to tip his chin up to look him in the eye. God, he looked *so good* right now.

"I'm only looking out for you," Lindy said, a faint smile appearing at the corner of his mouth. Kelly wanted to press his lips to it.

Knowing he couldn't made Kelly's words come out snappish and short. "I can take care of myself."

Lindy pulled Kelly in for a second, not quite a hug but close enough to speak without shouting. "I know. But your brothers would murder me if I let anything happen to you."

Kelly stiffened and pulled away, blindly striking out for the bathroom. He stumbled, turned around and unsure which direction to go, and felt a soft pat on his hip, guiding him toward the rear of the club.

Thankfully, Lindy didn't follow him down the hall or into the bathroom, but Kelly's guts still twisted with shame and arousal.

Sometimes he hated the way Lindy made him feel.

If only he didn't look so good. Didn't play hockey so well. Wasn't the nicest goddamn person on the planet.

Kelly had no idea how everyone in the universe wasn't in love with Anders Lindholm.

Kelly's fingers were clumsy as he unzipped and pulled his cock out, aiming at the urinal. He braced himself against the wall, his eyes half-closed. The room spun but he was still half-hard from the warm brush of Lindy's breath against his cheek.

"Stupid," he muttered.

A guy a few urinals away shot Kelly a look but he didn't respond.

How could Kelly explain *this*?

How could he put into words how desperate he was to have his teammate's big hand wrapped around his cock, stroking? If Lindy touched him, Kelly would press up on his toes and push his head into the warm space at the crook of Lindy's neck, panting against his skin as Lindy worked him over. Kelly wanted his big rough hands and his soft words, tinged with faint traces of his Swedish heritage.

Kelly shuddered, realizing he was more than half-hard now and his bladder fucking hurt. He needed to stop thinking about Lindy or he'd never go soft enough to piss.

Instead, Kelly thought about a guy he'd played with in college who'd had nasty toenail fungus. Kelly's dick finally softened and he was able to let loose. He sighed as the pressure in his bladder dissipated and when he was done, he shook off to dry.

Probably the most action his cock would get all week. Or all month or all year. Because Kelly was sad and pathetic. Red hair or not, he could pick up girls fine, but he didn't want them, never had.

Kelly's stomach churned at the thought he'd have to fake it soon. It had been a while since he'd gone home with anyone. He fucking hated it but it was expected and Kelly always did what was expected of him.

Except moving to Illinois and being straight, and he might not be entirely happy about the whole being gay thing but even he knew he couldn't change it.

Maybe someday he'd have what his teammates had, he thought blearily as he washed his hands, splashing cold water on his face in an attempt to sober up.

Maybe someday he'd be brave like Hartinger and Murphy and kiss someone he loved on the ice. Maybe he'd hoist the Cup and pose for pictures draped in rainbow flags for the local magazine. But for now, he wasn't out, and he was sad and lonely and afraid of disappointing everyone.

He stared at himself in the mirror, the low light of the bar bathroom making his stupid red hair darker and less obnoxious, water glittering on his lashes like he'd been crying.

Something hurt right there in the middle of Kelly's chest, and he let out a weird noise. The guy washing his hands—was he the same one who'd been by the urinal?—looked over.

"You sure you're okay, man?"

"Yeah." Kelly smiled at his reflection in the mirror. "I'm okay."

He'd never be okay about Anders but some stranger didn't need to know that. He didn't need to know Kelly was in love with the one man he could never have.

"You look kinda familiar," the guy said, narrowing his eyes. "Do I know you?"

"I play hockey," Kelly said, but he left the bathroom before the guy could ask any more questions.

Rather than go to the table, Kelly headed straight for the bar, ordering two shots, which he downed in quick succession.

They had two nights in Pittsburgh before their next game and he was determined to get obliterated enough to forget how pathetic he was.

———

Muffled swearing outside Anders' door pulled him out of bed. He should have been asleep hours ago but he'd only just dropped into a drowse. He checked the peephole in time to catch a flash of red hair. He had the chain unhooked and door open before the next heartbeat.

"What're you doin' in my room?" Kelly slurred, slumping against the doorframe as he squinted at Anders.

"This is my room," Anders gently pointed out.

"Oh." Kelly stared at his keycard, freckled nose scrunched in confusion. "Guess that's why this didn't work."

"I guess so. Do you need help getting into your room?"

"Umm." Kelly looked up and down the hall. "I think maybe yes."

Anders plucked the keycard from Kelly's loose grip, slipped an arm under his shoulder, then steered him toward the room next door. "This is you."

A single swipe of the card let him in the room and Kelly let out an excited whoop. "Hey, it worked!"

"Shh. Don't wake anyone else up."

"Oh, right." Kelly giggled and turned his head, burying it against Anders' shoulder. "Sorry."

Anders focused on getting Kelly into the room and closing the door behind them. He gently deposited Kelly on the bed, where he continued giggling.

"You are going to feel it in the morning, aren't you?" he asked under his breath. Thankfully they didn't have a game until the day after tomorrow.

Anders coaxed Kelly into sitting upright long enough to drink a Gatorade, then set the trash can beside the bed. He removed Kelly's shoes and, with Anders steadying him, Kelly stripped down to boxers, kicking his clothes away from the bed. He stumbled, lurching against Anders' chest.

"C'mon. Into bed with you."

"You could join me." Kelly gave him an impish grin, locking his arms around Anders' neck and tilting his head back.

Anders froze, staring at Kelly's heavy-lidded gaze, his mouth stained redder than usual from the sports drink.

Absently, Anders brought his thumb up to wipe at the corner of Kelly's lips.

Kelly giggled and nipped at his finger, the gesture so playful it felt alien to Anders. It had been years since he'd been this intimate with anyone, felt bare skin against his in a dim room, desire blooming through him until every little hair stood on end.

"You need sleep," Anders said hoarsely, loosening Kelly's tight grip. "You're very drunk and very tired."

"Kiss me, Anders," Kelly begged. "Please." He dug his fingers into Anders' hair, the clumsy tug of it sending a wave of sensation through Anders, his body flushing hot before turning cool and clammy.

He *felt* feverish and dazed with Kelly's lips close to his, begging him for the one thing he could never give him.

"I can't," he finally rasped.

Kelly pursed his unnaturally bright lips. "But—"

Anders pressed his finger to Kelly's pout. "Don't ask me to, Kelly. Please."

"You're no fun." Kelly stuck his lip out further.

"Yeah." Anders sighed. "Wouldn't be the first time I've heard that. C'mon. You need to lie down, okay?"

Kelly gripped his hand. "Don't go ... stay with me for a bit."

"Of course," Anders promised him. "Of course I will."

Because although he couldn't be with Kelly the way he wanted, he would always look out for him. He would have done it even if Kelly's brothers hadn't made him swear to it.

Anders coaxed Kelly to roll onto his side, then pulled the covers over him. Kelly let out a sleepy murmur of thanks and quickly slipped into dreamland.

Perched on the edge of the mattress, Anders stared at Kelly a moment, smoothing his damp hair off his forehead, watching the flutter of his lashes against his freckled cheeks. He looked achingly young.

Twenty-two felt like three lifetimes ago to Anders.

Twenty-two was long before he'd met Astrid and fallen immediately head-over-heels in love. Before they'd married. Before they'd had Elia.

Before Anders had lost them both.

Anders closed his eyes, throat going too tight at the memory of the twisted, mangled scraps of metal left after the car accident.

He reached up, gripping the chain holding two wedding bands, one large enough to fit the smaller one straight through. He brushed his thumb over the warm metal, the gesture as familiar as breathing after four years of loss.

Kelly let out a sleepy sigh and Anders shook off the past long enough to tuck the blanket more firmly around him, then retreated to the chair on the far side of the room to watch over him.

The seat was large and plush, comfortable to sink into. The lamp beside it spilled light across the room, illuminating Kelly's bare shoulder and arm, muscular but not bulky, his body lean and tight, sprinkled everywhere with freckles.

Anders closed his eyes, remembering the sound of Kelly begging for a kiss.

Despite what his wife used to say sometimes, Anders wasn't an idiot.

"Kelly is in love with you," Astrid had announced one night after a team event. She'd pushed her headband up to get her blonde hair off her face and she looked at his reflection in the mirror, expression unusually grave.

Anders liked watching her go through her nightly routine, washing her face, brushing her teeth, smearing on various lotions. He liked it so much that when they'd remodeled the bathroom, she'd worked with the designer to pick out a chair suited to his large frame.

That night, Anders had looked at his wife in the mirror, thinking about her words.

"No," he'd protested automatically. "Surely it's hero worship. He's straight. I've seen him leave bars with women."

She gave him a pointed look before splashing water on her face, her voice slightly muffled as she patted dry. "As far as your teammates know, you're straight too. You're married to a woman."

"True." He gave her a rueful smile when she lifted her head.

When they met, he'd been upfront about his previous involvement with men. She'd merely nodded and treated it exactly the way she'd treated his obsession with Scandinavian military history. She didn't fully understand it herself but offered him a casual but loving acceptance that it was simply a part of who he was.

He hadn't expected anything else, in part because Sweden was generally much further ahead than the United States when it came to these things, but also because it was very *her*.

"I suppose Kelly could be bi as well," Anders had admitted. "Are you sure he has serious feelings for me though? It's probably just a minor crush."

"Don't be an idiot, Anders," she'd tartly corrected him. "Kelly O'Shea is in love with you. It's sweet. He's absolutely devoted to you."

Anders had thought about their previous interactions and nodded, his throat thickening. "He is."

She'd met his gaze again. "Be kind. Don't break his heart."

Astrid had been a smart woman. Frighteningly so.

Not perfect. God no.

She'd left her toenail clippings on the bathroom floor and absentmindedly wiped her dirty fingers on her jeans when she snacked and read. She had the most appalling habit of kissing him when her tongue tasted of the salted licorice he detested, and she left a trail of belongings in her wake wherever she went.

But she'd been the love of his life. His breath of fresh morning air and his nighttime sigh of contentment and now she was gone, and he couldn't breathe any more.

She'd left him in the blink of an eye and yes, Kelly loved Anders, and maybe Anders felt something for Kelly as well but it wasn't fair to taunt him with something Anders couldn't give him.

Tonight, he'd hated to see Kelly's worshipful gaze and bright smile dim when Anders had denied him but no matter how much he cared for Kelly, Anders wasn't the man for him.

Anders wasn't whole and Kelly deserved someone who was.

Someone who would kiss every freckle and delight in his sense of humor and love him for all his imperfections the way Anders had loved his wife.

But losing her and their baby daughter had broken Anders in a way that would never heal, and Kelly deserved better.

The problem was, Kelly O'Shea was like a toothache.

The pain of having him around was almost pleasurable. Every time Anders bumped up against it, he flinched. But he found himself poking at it again, just to feel the sharp zing mellow to a sweet ache.

Just to feel anything at all.

CHAPTER ONE

CURRENT DAY

Anders Lindholm played *filthy* hockey. Nothing was hotter than watching him on the ice, and being on the same power play unit this season made it even better for Kelly.

Sitting on the bench while he skated was equally good though.

Watching Lindy on the breakaway, dangling the puck as he glided between the opposing team's D-men and smacked the rubber into the back of the net, never failed to raise Kelly's heart rate.

Lindy was fast and fluid with a powerful slapshot and he'd dominated the league in points for years, winning the Art Ross Trophy multiple times.

Tonight was no exception. He pulled the puck out from behind the Otters' net and tore up the ice through the neutral zone, parting Buffalo's players like it took no effort at all. He passed to Murphy on his wing, who kept the puck in play while Lindy got into position. Murphy passed it back to Lindy, who then placed it neatly on Underhill's tape in the slot, where he smacked it into the net before Buffalo's goaltender could blink.

Kelly hollered his appreciation, tapping his stick on the boards in front of the bench as the guys celebrated their early 1-0 lead.

"Fuck yeah! That's how we start a fucking *game*, boys!" Underhill yelled, skating by for glove taps.

Kelly grinned down the length of the bench, watching his teammates celebrating. It was good to have The Undertaker back in the game.

Trevor Underhill wasn't typically a huge two-way defenseman though. He was known more for his role as a wily agitator with a knack for getting their opponents to draw penalties than his scoring ability.

But maybe the time away had been good for his offensive game.

Underhill was paired with Cory Burgess, one of their rookies, and Kelly was psyched about the rest of the season.

The team now had three tight D-pairs. With Hajek in goal and Dixson as backup, this was the deepest the team had been defensively since Kelly joined them. Their bottom two lines of forwards were solid, their top two lines were incredible, and no one critical was out with any long-term major injuries. For once, the entire team was in good shape.

And then it was Kelly's shift, and he was over the boards, flying on happiness and adrenaline when he hit the ice and got into position.

He was right where he needed to be when Lindy won the face-off.

Kelly kept Buffalo's forward occupied while Lindy wove around their opponents, deking so expertly the puck was in the back of the net before the goalie could react.

During the first intermission, Kelly guzzled Gatorade, crammed down a protein bar, and tapped his fingers against his stick while he listened to Coach Daniels talk about their plan of attack for the second period.

The play went exactly like planned, with Underhill targeting one of Buffalo's players and getting him riled up until he snapped and got sent to the penalty box for two minutes for slashing.

Kelly charged in with their power play unit and Murphy took a hit in the right corner but managed to win the puck. He sent it flying to Hartinger near the top of the left circle. Hartinger dished it to Lindy at the goal line, then circled toward the slot for a gorgeous give-and-go pass. Kelly could practically hear the opposing team's teeth grinding as Hartinger and Lindy lazily passed it back and forth a few times while Kelly and Gabriel Theriault kept their other players occupied.

Then with a quick snap of his wrist, Lindy buried it in the right corner of the net, giving them a 3-0 lead.

Kelly tore across the ice to Lindy, shouting his appreciation. He leapt on him, wrapping his legs around Lindy's waist. Laughing, Lindy held onto Kelly for a moment, thunking their helmets together in celebration as Kelly slid down his body.

"Fucking beauty!" Kelly shouted. "Goddamn."

"Couldn't have done it without you," Lindy said, his smile wide and free.

Their teammates crashed into them, hollering their appreciation too, Theriault babbling something in French and shaking Lindy by the front of his jersey.

Moments like this were Kelly's favorite, where Lindy looked carefree and easy. Light-hearted and happy, with the grief of his past temporarily lifted.

Kelly vowed to do whatever he could to keep a smile on Lindy's face for the rest of the game and beyond if he could.

The third period started well. A Buffalo player took a tripping penalty a few minutes in, and the Otters added a second power play goal, bringing them to 4-0.

Up until that point, the Otters had barely given Buffalo a chance to get any shots on goal, but it got heated as Malone took a penalty and their PK unit wasn't enough to keep Buffalo's center from scoring.

Kelly gnashed his teeth on the bench, but Buffalo's success was short-lived when they quickly got two penalties called after a skirmish in front of the net and left the Otters with a 5-on-3 power play opportunity.

Buffalo managed to kill half of it but Lindy snagged a pass from Murphy on the goal line and sniped a top-shelf rocket over Buffalo's goalie for a 5-1 lead *and* a hat trick for Lindy.

Caps came flying toward the ice as the crowd and team celebrated. Kelly buried his head against Lindy's neck and shook him as hard as he could, too happy for him to say much of anything.

But when Lindy turned away, looking toward the stands, and searching for something, Kelly wondered why his smile fell and his happiness faded. He should be more excited, and Kelly wondered why he'd been so fired up to play tonight anyway.

God knew the team needed the points if they were going to clinch a playoff spot but it seemed like more than that. It was mid-March and—

Oh. Kelly's heart sank.

It was Astrid's birthday.

When she was alive, Lindy had always scored goals for her on special occasions and Kelly had several achingly sweet memories of her jumping up and down in the stands, screaming her head off, so thrilled for Lindy and his success she couldn't contain it.

Lindy had continued the tradition after her death, quietly marking those moments the same way, only now when he turned to look for her in the stands, there was no one there.

Kelly swallowed hard, throat aching with grief for his teammate.

The man he loved.

Anders skated to the bench, dodging the people clearing the ice of hats, wondering if his pasted-on smile was fooling anyone.

The instinct to search for Astrid was so ingrained he was always surprised when he looked and she wasn't there. It wasn't like she'd been at every game he'd played but she'd been there as much as she could. As often as she could work it into her busy schedule as a mother and emergency room doctor.

He'd never begrudged her the time she spent with their daughter or her patients, simply been grateful that an amazing woman was a part of his life.

But there was no time for reminiscing now, not with eight minutes left in the game. Anders shook his head to clear away everything but hockey. The chance of them losing this lead was slim but not impossible. He'd seen stranger things before, so he listened intently to Coach Daniels diagram the next play on the iPad.

"I like what I'm seeing, boys," Coach shouted when they went over the boards for the next shift. "Keep it up."

And then there was only the give and take of the game, the laser-sharp focus Anders had perfected for the two decades of his NHL career serving him well as they prevented Buffalo from scoring until it was the next line's turn.

It was only when he was on the bench that thoughts returned, his gaze drifting for a few moments to Kelly, remembering how happy Kelly had been for him earlier. Anders' chest warmed at the memory of Kelly wrapped so tightly around his body.

Kelly did nothing any of their teammates, past or present, hadn't done before. Anders had celebrated as enthusiastically with Kelly's brother Pat when they played together in Boston, but it always felt different with Kelly.

Now, Kelly's warm brown eyes narrowed as he stared out at the ice with grim determination, absently chewing on his mouthguard.

Anders was never sure if it was a nervous habit or something else, but Kelly did it constantly. He sat on the bench, flipping the guard from one side of his mouth to the other. Chewed it on the ice too. Someday Kelly would bite his tongue or lose teeth because he couldn't keep the protection in place but Anders had long ago stopped nagging him about it.

Kelly bristled at the idea of anyone telling him what to do.

When Kelly left Boston University to play for the Evanston River Otters, Anders had made a promise to Kelly's brothers—all three of them—that he'd look out for Kelly.

Anders had been drafted by the Boston Harriers and had stayed with them until the league expansion that created the Evanston River Otters. He was an unprotected high value center the Otters had snapped up in the expansion draft.

Anders had meshed with Zane Murphy from the beginning and when Ryan Hartinger joined the team two years later, the three of them had locked into place like they were always meant to play together.

The other pieces of the team had come together more slowly, and it had taken a decade to nail the right overall lineup and find their rhythm. After years of making it to the playoffs and being knocked out in the early rounds, the Otters had finally clinched the Cup two seasons ago.

Anders ached for it again. At thirty-nine, the window of how long he could play at this level was rapidly narrowing and if they didn't get it this year, it might be his last shot.

So tonight, when he went out on the ice for another shift and quickly spotted an opportunity to set Theriault up for a goal, he took it, knowing their French-Canadian defenseman would be ready to snap the puck in.

After that, it was just the team allowing the final few seconds on the clock to run out, then celebrating their 6-1 blowout win.

Anders accepted the congratulations for his hatty and the nomination as one of the stars of the game. He waved to the crowd as he took his celebratory lap, then skated off and thanked his team. Kelly looked distracted, doing something on his phone, but Anders supposed he probably had plans tonight.

Anders suddenly wished it had been an away game so he wouldn't have to go home and rattle around his large empty condo.

He liked riding the bus with the guys to the airport. He usually read on the plane, but the distant trash-talking of his teammates playing poker or video games filling the air with background noise was comforting. He like the quiet murmurs of the coaching staff, breaking down plays and discussing strategies for the next game. The soft snores of Brett Cooper, who'd had his nose broken and poorly re-set in the Alberta Junior Hockey League.

Anders liked the bland impersonality of hotel rooms, carefully wiped clean. Blank but never lonely. The occasional slam of a door a few rooms down or hastily quieted conversations in the hall were comforting. When he was with the team, the ache didn't feel so overwhelming. It wasn't all-encompassing the way it was at home.

So tonight, Anders dawdled when he stripped out of his gear and took his time with the media. He leisurely shampooed his shoulder-length hair and dried it carefully before dressing in his game day navy blue suit, pale blue shirt, and buttery yellow tie. He neatly folded the patterned pocket square, tucked it into his jacket, and studied himself in the mirror.

Samantha, the team's Director of Marketing and Digital Media, had given him a big thumbs-up as he'd come in for the game tonight. He enjoyed dressing well and he'd developed a reputation as a stylish dresser, which pleased his tailor, Omar.

But it all seemed pointless when Anders would go home to eat dinner alone at his too-large table.

Sometimes Anders wished he had more vices. More excuses to kick back and let loose. But that was never who he'd been, and it had only gotten worse with time. The more he thought about retiring, the tighter his throat got and the more rigid his routines became.

Without hockey, he had nothing. He had no plan for his future. No career to pursue after. He enjoyed golf and history but had no intention of making either of them a career. He didn't want to become a coach or work in a front office, and he was terrified of the day an injury would sideline him and force him into retirement.

He'd been lucky so far. He'd worked hard to keep going so long. The healthy diet and the rare indulgence in alcohol helped. He did yoga and meditated and used the sauna and drank water, trying to eke out a few more years from his career. But he could feel himself slowing, some of the explosiveness he'd always relied on fading.

Guys were getting faster and faster and eventually, he wouldn't be able to keep up.

He stared at himself in the mirror and wondered when he'd gotten old. Astrid had liked the creases forming at the corners of his eyes and the occasional silver strand threading through the gold ones.

She'd teased him about how distinguished he'd look in his later years. They'd talked of retirement in Sweden and a quiet life together once their daughter was an adult and off on her own.

"C'mon, Lindy," Hartinger said, slapping him on the shoulder and pulling him from his ruminations. "Stop admiring yourself in the mirror. We already know you're a handsome fucker. You don't need to show us all up more."

Anders managed a chuckle and shook himself out of his stupor. He followed Hartinger into the dressing room where Murphy waited for his boyfriend to finish so they could drive home together.

He was surprised to see Kelly, still on his phone, fully dressed in a sharp charcoal suit and ready to go. Kelly had been an appallingly bad dresser when he'd joined the team, wearing too-big off-the-rack suits until Anders finally dragged him to Omar's shop where the tailor had let out a series of distressed clucks like he didn't know what to do with Kelly.

Thankfully, Kelly took it with good humor and had turned over all his game day clothing decisions to the genius with a needle. Kelly might not enjoy fashion the way Anders did, but he no longer made the worst dressed in the NHL blog lists.

Anders gathered his belongings but when he turned to go, Kelly stood nearby, staring at him.

"So, what do you have planned for tonight?" Kelly asked, shoving his phone in his pocket.

Anders sighed. As much as he didn't want to be alone, he didn't feel much like celebrating. "Nothing. I'm going home."

"Then I'm going home with you. I don't want you to be alone."

Anders managed a small smile. "I'm alone every night. I know how to handle it."

"That's why I won't let you do it *tonight*. I know it's Astrid's birthday."

Anders tensed, wondering if Kelly put it in his phone, little calendar reminders of when to look out for him, or if he could sense the heaviness in the air around him.

With a sigh, Anders draped his arm across Kelly's shoulders. "I appreciate what you're trying to do but you don't have to wallow in grief with me."

"Of course I do. You need me," Kelly said stubbornly. "Now, c'mon. I have a plan."

CHAPTER TWO

Lindy's place was immaculate. It always was. Kelly had been there dozens of times. Hell, maybe more at this point.

But it always surprised Kelly how perfect it was. How everything was in place. Elegant and tidy. In fact, it seemed like everything in Lindy's life was neat and perfect.

Except the single gaping hole of what was missing.

The one thing Kelly couldn't fix for him, no matter how hard he tried.

"You didn't have to do this, you know?" Lindy said as Kelly placed a hand on his back to push him deeper into the pristine kitchen.

Kelly thought guiltily of the wreck of his place. The junk strewn on the kitchen counter, the unopened mail, and the overflowing trash can. The smear of grape jelly on the refrigerator door handle he kept meaning to wipe off.

Even placing the large brown paper takeout bag on the counter looked out of place here, too messy and real and human.

"I didn't have to. I wanted to," Kelly retorted.

"Kelly ..."

"Shut up and say thank you."

Lindy's lips twitched in amusement. "Thank you, Kelly."

"There. Was that so hard?" Kelly shrugged out of his suit jacket and tossed it onto the stool.

Lindy immediately picked it up, carrying it to the entryway to, presumably, hang it perfectly in the closet by the door. Because he was neurotic like that.

Kelly shouldn't find it endearing.

But rather than sigh about how much he wanted Lindy, he got plates out. He'd be perfectly happy eating out of the containers but that made Anders cranky so he pulled out two real plates— not even paper!—and forks and stuff.

"By the way, I got you your nasty-ass pickled herring, you Swedish freak," Kelly said when Lindy returned.

He smiled a little, which was exactly why Kelly had said it.

"Eggs for me." Kelly pulled another container out. He looked forward to the deviled eggs with dill on top. That shit was delicious.

He unpacked a couple more containers. "Beetroot and apple salad for you, fresh cucumber salad for me."

Kelly still wasn't sure why the Swedes pickled everything, but he could totally handle the excessive dill.

"The rainbow trout with almonds is yours." He pushed that container toward Lindy and set another in front of himself. "Meatballs for me."

Lindy's eyes brightened. "You *have* to share."

"I do not." Kelly hugged the container close. "It's mine and you can't make me."

Lindy actually laughed and it made Kelly feel so good he was almost tempted to share them. But no, he was fucking starving tonight and the meatballs with creamy gravy and mashed potatoes were so delicious he wanted to lick every last drop. "Eat your gross fish and be happy I brought you anything."

Lindy chuckled again, rolling up the sleeves of his pale blue button-down and Kelly had to force himself to focus on spooning food onto his plate instead of staring at the muscles of his tan forearms and the sprinkle of gold hair there.

In the summer, it turned nearly white.

After Kelly piled his plate with heaping portions of everything he'd ordered for himself, he pulled out the final clincher.

Aquavit.

The sound of the bottle clinking on the marble counter made Lindy look up from his careful plating of his food.

"Kelly …" He gave him a fond but slightly exasperated look. Which was pretty much the permanent expression Lindy directed at him.

Kelly rather liked it.

He'd prefer if Lindy looked at him with hunger or need but clearly that wasn't happening, so he'd take what he could get.

"You need this," Kelly told him as he walked to the freezer and pulled out two glasses. Thin, fancy ones shaped like tulips. For as little as Anders drank, he did like to be prepared and the icy glasses were supposed to improve the taste of aquavit or something.

Nothing in the world could do that. The liquor tasted like strange bitter herbs and rye bread.

Lindy loved it.

Kelly had learned to tolerate it.

"This is way more than a cheat day meal, Kelly," Lindy said mildly. He reached for the bottle.

"It's all I can do for you. Please. Let me *do* this."

Lindy reached up and squeezed his shoulder, his hand warm and big, lingering there a moment. "Thank you."

"Sure." When he finally let go, Kelly smiled brightly. "Help me carry this into the living room."

"You know I don't eat in there."

"You do when you're with me!" Kelly countered, which was absolutely true.

It took a couple of trips to get everything spread out on the coffee table but once it was, Kelly nodded toward the TV. "Wanna watch the west coast game?"

"Okay."

Kelly reached for the clicker, relieved. The game was easy. They could always talk hockey and watching LA play Vegas was usually entertaining.

"So how is the food?" Kelly asked after he devoured half his plate.

Lindy ate more slowly. His shoulders were still tight but his gaze was soft as he looked at Kelly.

"It's perfect. Thank you."

"As good as your mother's?"

Lindy's smile turned crooked. "Well, I don't know. Better than anything I've had in a long time though."

"Good." Kelly bumped shoulders with him. He tried not to read anything into it when Lindy kept his shoulder pressed against his, not moving away after. It was dumb to read into things. He'd done it over and over. Thinking that maybe …

But no. He'd gotten nowhere with that shit.

Lindy had even come out to the team recently. He was bisexual, something Kelly had barely dreamed could be true.

But he'd only done it in support of Jamie Walsh, their second line forward. Nothing had changed.

Lindy was definitely bi; he just didn't want Kelly.

The thought burned in Kelly's chest, and he poured himself another shot of aquavit and tossed it back, remembering at the last second not to slam the delicate glass onto the table because he'd broken one that way last year.

Lindy looked at him out of the corner of his eye. He sipped his own drink more slowly. "Are *you* okay?"

"Sure," Kelly said, spearing another meatball. "I'm always okay."

"You seem rather tightly wound tonight. You should have been out with the guys instead of hanging out with me."

"You yell at me when I get too drunk with them."

"There's something called moderation."

"Eww." Kelly wrinkled his nose. "What fucking fun is that?"

Lindy shook his head, the same fond but exasperated look crossing his face again. "Kelly …"

"What?" He shrugged. "I knew you wouldn't go out tonight, and sitting at home and wallowing about Astrid's birthday wasn't going to do you any good."

Lindy flinched, his gaze drifting to the wedding photo in a silver frame on the sleek mantel.

"Sorry."

Lindy let out a sigh. "No, you're right. It wasn't. Thank you."

"What are friends for?" Kelly asked, though the word burned the way it always did. It was never going to change but that didn't stop him from *wanting*. Nothing stopped that.

When Kelly's plate was clear, he stood. "Want anything else? I'm going to get seconds."

Lindy looked pointedly at his plate, which still had food on it.

"What? I'm a growing boy!" Kelly tossed over his shoulder as he walked toward the kitchen.

"Moderation!" Lindy fired back.

Kelly snorted and piled more meatballs and mashed potatoes on his plate, then snagged the paper bag still containing their desserts.

When Kelly plunked the bag on the floor between them, Lindy raised an eyebrow at him. "What's that?"

"Open it and find out."

"Let me finish eating first." Lindy reached out with his fork and neatly speared two meatballs from Kelly's plate.

"Hey!" he squawked, laughing when he pulled his plate away. "What happened to moderation?"

"I'm helping you learn." Lindy flashed a rare off-ice smile at him, his teeth gleaming white as he sank them into the first meatball. His eyes closed with pleasure while he chewed and swallowed.

Kelly wanted to protest but it was way too hot watching Lindy enjoy himself.

"I would have gotten you your own if I'd known you were going to resort to thievery," Kelly countered, pretending to be crabby but secretly enjoying the playfulness of it.

He'd stabbed Underhill with a fork at the hotel the other morning for trying the same shit with his sausage links.

"What fun is that?" Lindy set down his empty plate, carefully wiped his fingers on a napkin, then opened one container from the paper bag. "Strawberry cream cake? Hmm. That must be yours."

"Yes. Gimme." Kelly snatched it from his hand.

Lindy smiled again and ducked his head, reaching into the bag to pull out the other container. He stared at it so long, Kelly wondered if he'd made a mistake.

"You got me *Risgrynsgröt,*" Lindy finally said, his voice soft.

"With lingonberry jam because you're a fucking weirdo."

"It's not weird to want jam on rice pudding, Kelly."

"No, but it's weird to want mushy, sweet rice."

Lindy shot him a look. "I have seen you eat pizza that's been sitting out on your counter for three days. You are not allowed to talk to me about food choices."

But something around his eyes had gone tight again.

"Something made you sad," Kelly asked. "What was it?"

Lindy's lips twisted in a humorless smile. "Elia ... we gave her rice pudding for the first time a few weeks before—before the accident."

Kelly sucked in a sharp breath. "Oh, God. I'm sorry."

"No need to be sorry. It just hit me. She smeared jam on her nose and Astrid laughed so hard at the sight. All the photos turned out blurry because she couldn't stop giggling. I ran across them the other day on my computer, and this brought me back."

"I'm sorry," Kelly repeated automatically but Lindy shook his head and took a deep breath.

"You have nothing to be sorry for. You brought me my favorite dessert, and it was a very thoughtful gesture. You didn't know it would bring things up." His sigh was so weary, it made Kelly ache. "Then again, what doesn't?"

Kelly reached up to rub Lindy's shoulder blade, his hand ridiculously undersized against the broad expanse of his back, though Kelly had long fingers.

Kelly wasn't the biggest guy out there. Most people thought he was too small for a defenseman. Even Theriault was bigger than him and Lindholm was huge by any standards. Tall, broad-shouldered, long legged. Everything Kelly had ever dreamed about.

Kelly sighed internally.

He couldn't be sure exactly when he'd fallen in love with Anders Lindholm.

He did know it wasn't the first time he'd met him. He'd been a little kid then. It might have been watching him play gorgeous hockey for the Boston Harriers and then the Evanston River Otters. Growing up, Kelly'd had a few inklings he wasn't straight like his brothers.

But it was probably when Kelly was fifteen.

Finn and Connor had brought Anders to their parents' house. Anders had already moved to Chicago to play for the Otters but he often stopped by when he was in Boston for a game or visited during the off-season.

That day certainly wasn't the first time Kelly had seen Anders up close, but it was the most memorable.

As Kelly finished snarfing down the final bite of his second peanut butter and jelly sandwich of the day, he'd heard loud voices in the hall and knew he needed to leave. His dumbass brothers made no secret of the fact they found their little brother annoying for hanging around when they brought their friends over.

How could Kelly forget the moment he walked out of the kitchen, licking grape jelly from his fingertips, and saw God?

Kelly had stopped in the hallway, mesmerized by the tall man haloed by the sunlight coming in from the window over the door, turning Lindy's hair molten gold.

Kelly drank in his deep laugh and his long legs and in that moment, Kelly knew with a bone-deep surety he was gay. He'd tried to ignore it, tried to deny it, tried to pretend he wasn't the *thing* that nobody in hockey talked about then. But one look at Anders Lindholm and he could no longer deny it.

His whole body had flushed even while his stomach dropped to his toes. He'd known no matter what happened, he'd spend his whole future career as the closeted guy in the league.

What he hadn't known was that he'd never *stop* loving Anders.

Not even when Anders met Astrid Sjöberg and married her.

Their wedding had taken place in Sweden in the off-season a few months later, but they'd held a big reception in Chicago before training camp to celebrate with Anders' teammates and their North American friends.

Including the O'Shea family.

Kelly had begged off and made excuses about why he couldn't go but he couldn't avoid it completely. Anders was a high-profile NHL player and there were pictures all over the internet. Video clips everywhere.

In the privacy of his bedroom, Kelly had watched them all, torturing himself, knowing Astrid was perfect for Anders.

That was the worst of it. Because Kelly had liked her too. He had wanted to hate her but no one could resist her smile. Sly and a little teasing. Kelly had fallen under the spell of her dry wit. He'd loved the way she made her little jokes and Anders laughed his big, booming laugh every time.

And Kelly had been realistic enough to admit that whether Anders married Astrid or some other gorgeous, brilliant woman, he would never love Kelly—the scrawny, freckled little defenseman. The youngest of the O'Shea boys.

An annoying pipsqueak brother who Anders looked out for like they were related too.

And when Elia came along, Kelly had fallen in love with her too. He'd been Uncle Kelly and he loved being called that, even though it burned.

When Astrid and Elia had died in the car crash, Kelly had cried hot, fat, angry tears because he loved them too and he didn't understand how God could take away people like them and leave someone like Anders howling with grief.

Now four years later Anders was still in mourning.

And the best Kelly could manage was some Swedish meatballs and a bottle of aquavit.

He was a goddamn joke.

———

Anders glanced away from the TV to look at Kelly. He'd gone quiet, slumped against the arm of the sofa, knees splayed wide. For a small guy, he took up a lot of space.

Anders didn't mind. His condo was far too big and empty when he was here by himself. Still better than the house he'd had before though. It had been spacious, lovingly designed for their family. Rattling around in it alone had been torture, the air filled with memories so tangible he'd barely been able to draw in breath.

Two years ago, he'd sold it and bought this place, but he hated it too. Hotels were better but there was nowhere on earth he could go where he could forget the soft touch of Astrid's lips against his and the slight weight of Elia's head on his chest.

There were times he wished he'd been in the car with them. Not because he thought he could have saved them—no one could have, the vehicle had come out of nowhere on a slick, rainy night —but because he would have gone with them.

"What?" Kelly wiped at his face. "Do I have food on me or something?"

"No. Sorry. I zoned out." He tapped his foot against Kelly's. "Are you going to eat your cake or not?"

Kelly glanced at the table and groaned. "I'm too full. I overestimated the size of my stomach."

"Like you do every time?"

He shrugged lazily. "Gimme a minute to digest and I'll be ready for it."

"I'm not hurrying you," Anders pointed out. "I'll put it in the refrigerator before the whipped cream melts and makes the cake mushy."

"Yeah, okay." Kelly patted his stomach and Anders had the oddest urge to rub his palm across the slightly curved swell until Kelly felt better. "It might take until the end of the game before I'm ready for it."

Anders glanced at the screen. "Looks like they might be going to overtime."

"Yeah, it does. Huh. Glad Vegas wasn't playing that well the last time we faced them."

Anders snorted. "No kidding."

He carried the leftovers into the kitchen, stowed them in the refrigerator and grabbed bottles of water. He cleared the dishes off the coffee table too, ignoring Kelly's guilty expression when he declined his help.

"You bought dinner," Anders reminded him. "I can put a few things in the dishwasher."

"You're so good to me," Kelly said with a sigh.

Good to Kelly? Hardly.

Anders often felt guilty. He wondered if he was keeping Kelly from a real life and relationship.

Anders certainly wasn't trying to string him along and he'd tried to gently urge him to date numerous times, though Kelly wasn't usually overt about his interest in Anders, except for the drunken night in Pittsburgh last fall when he'd begged Anders to kiss him.

Anders knew Kelly remembered. For days after, he'd flushed red every time their gazes met and they'd had a verbal spat in the visitors' dressing room before the game when Kelly had lashed out and accused him of still living in the past. It was true but it had hurt to hear those words viciously flung at him from someone he cared about.

But Anders tried to remind himself how painful unrequited love could be.

Since then, they'd put that night behind them but Anders was reasonably certain he was the only one on the team who had figured out Kelly was attracted to men. He'd never fully understood why he was secretive about it. As far as Anders was aware, even his family didn't know.

Then again, Kelly had always been overlooked. He wasn't the biggest or the strongest or the fastest skater. And with a father and three brothers who'd made their name in the league, the O'Shea legacy had created some enormous skates to fill. Kelly had made up for it by being scrappy and fierce on-ice and accommodating off it. He was the guy who helped out his teammates and cracked jokes and lightened the mood in the locker room. The one who got along with everyone, made the rookies feel like they belonged.

Anders had watched him do something similar in his own family.

But no one really knew who Kelly was.

Not even Anders.

He wanted to know him better but the risk of breaking his heart was too high, so he was hesitant to do anything to lead him on.

Anders didn't know how to tell Kelly he deserved more. Deserved better. That he had a right to ask for it.

Especially when all Kelly seemed to want was *him*.

"Hey, are you coming back?" Kelly hollered. "You missed a sick goal and there's only three minutes left in the final period."

"Yeah, give me a moment." Anders closed the dishwasher door and took a deep breath before he walked into the living room.

Kelly looked up at him. "You don't mind that I bullied my way in here tonight and brought dinner and stuff, do you?"

"No." Anders gave him a soft smile. "It was kind of you. I—I didn't want to be alone. I just hate bringing everyone down."

"You're allowed to be sad, Lindy."

"Four years later?"

"There's no time limit for grief."

Anders smiled. "Wise words."

Kelly jabbed his foot into Anders' thigh. "Hey. I went to college for a couple of years and everything. BU is a good school and I'm smart."

Anders chuckled and tweaked his big toe, making Kelly squawk. "I know you are."

"Promise you'll tell me if I get annoying," Kelly said earnestly. "I don't want to bug you."

There were many things Anders wanted to say.

I like having you here, Kelly.

My life is better with you in it.

You could never annoy me.

But he couldn't—*shouldn't*—say those things so he settled on, "I'm lucky to have a friend like you."

Of course, then the guilt came when he spied the flicker of hurt in Kelly's eyes.

That's the problem. Anders turned back to the television and let the sounds of the game wash over him. *Everything I do hurts Kelly.*

Anders reached for the bottle of aquavit, filled his glass, then held the bottle over Kelly's in question.

"Yeah," Kelly said absently. "Another would be good."

"Do you like this liquor?" Anders asked doubtfully.

"It's growing on me," Kelly said, and Anders was certain he was lying but he didn't call him out.

They turned their attention to the game because hockey was easy.

Hockey was the language they both spoke, and it wasn't fraught with complicated feelings and longing looks. There was no grief in hockey—not in that way, at least—only the ice and the vibration of Anders' stick hitting the puck.

Team and friendship and uncomplicated love.

Kelly held a role that didn't confuse Anders. He knew where he and Kelly stood when they played.

Outside of hockey, everything was fraught and weighted.

But in the game, there was peace.

CHAPTER THREE

"I'm fine, Ma." Kelly grimaced and poked his rubber glove at something fuzzy growing on the rim of a bowl.

"I worry about you, honey. Did you *have* to go halfway across the country to play hockey?"

Kelly tipped the bowl to empty it and tried not to gag at what came out. There weren't supposed to be thick, gelatinous things growing in his sink.

"We've talked about this a billion times, Ma," he said as patiently as he could manage. He'd joined the River Otters at the end of his sophomore year of college and this was his third full season with the team. This wasn't *new*.

"Are you eating your vegetables?"

"I had cucumbers last night."

She squawked. "That's barely a vegetable. It's mostly water. You need something green."

"They're green. Ish." Then again, so was some of the stuff growing in his sink.

"Kelly!"

"What?"

"I don't know what I'm going to do with you. You have a nutrition plan; I know you do. Evanston may not be *Boston* but I know there's a nutritionist on staff and you can't tell me they approve of your all-pizza and PB&J diet."

"I'll have you know I ate deviled eggs, Swedish meatballs, and strawberry cake last night," he said defensively. "Oh, and mashed potatoes. Those are a vegetable for sure, even if they're not green."

"Well, I'm pleased you had some variety to your diet at least. I worry about you being regular with all that cheese."

On the sofa, Underhill let out a muffled snort. Kelly flipped him off, but this was what he got for putting his mother on speakerphone.

"Ma, I eat vegetables. I swear. I had chicken and broccoli pasta before the game two days ago."

"Well, that's something." Her sigh was weary. "So, what else is new? You never tell us anything about your life."

"What is there to tell?" he asked. "I play a lot of fucking hockey."

"Your brothers managed to have full social lives while they played."

"And now they have eighty-seven children apiece," he pointed out.

"Oh, speaking of which, did I tell you about the cute thing Rose did the other day?"

"No. Tell me about it," he said. It would be a long story. They always were. But he'd happily listen to every word about his niece if it kept his mother off his back about his personal life.

He hummed encouragement as she relayed the story, his attention half on her and half on the memory of sitting on Lindy's couch, their knees pressed together in companionable silence.

"Are you listening to me, Kelly?" she asked.

"Yes," he said, snapping to attention. "Just multitasking and loading the dishwasher."

"I suppose it's been a while?"

"Um, a little bit." Like maybe a week where gross dishes piled up in the sink because neither he nor Trevor could be bothered to unload the dishwasher after they ran it and they were out of paper plates. But Kelly felt too guilty at making the cleaning person tackle the mess in the sink, so he usually did it the day before they were scheduled to come in.

"Hey there, Mrs. O," Trevor said. He dropped a bowl in the sink Kelly had emptied.

Kelly shot his roommate an angry finger again but he grinned and opened the refrigerator, pulling out a beer.

"Trevor! How are you? How's the ankle?" she asked.

"Solid," he called out. "Feels good to be back on the ice."

"Oh, I bet. You looked great the other night. by the way. Nice goal against Buffalo."

"Thanks!"

That was maybe the widest Kelly had ever seen Trevor smile. Then again, he had pretty much been adopted by the O'Shea family.

They sort of did that to people. Kelly's childhood had been a never-ending revolving door of his brothers' teammates coming in and out of the O'Shea's Charlestown-neighborhood home for meals or a place to relax and get some motherly attention.

Catherine O'Shea had never once hesitated to set an extra plate or three at dinner and they'd been a billet household, taking in junior league hockey players who'd moved across the country—or sometimes the continent—to play.

The minute Kelly's mother learned his roommate didn't have much family to speak of, she'd immediately taken Trevor under her wing. And given what a shitheap Trevor's family was, Kelly wasn't surprised he'd loved every minute of it.

"Kelly? Are you listening to me?"

"Just wasn't sure if you were done talking to Trev," he lied, stuffing the bowl into the overpacked dishwasher.

Kelly tossed one of the little detergent pods in, closed the door, and hit the Start button. He grimaced at the sink. That was definitely too gross to leave to the cleaner. He squirted too much soap in, then sprinkled in some of the gritty powder stuff for good measure and attacked it with a sponge that he needed to toss after this if the smell was any indication.

"Your father says you need to work on your gap control."

"Why doesn't he tell me himself?" Kelly asked, frowning at a particularly stubborn spot.

"He sent you a text last night but you ignored it."

"Oh. Whoops." He vaguely remembered getting it on the drive home from the restaurant where he'd picked up takeout. "I was hanging out with Lindy last night. It was Astrid's birthday, and I didn't want him to be alone."

"Thinking of his loss just breaks my heart sometimes." His mom's voice went soft.

"It's awful," Kelly agreed.

"It's nice the team looks out for him."

"We try."

Though these days it was mostly him. Their captain, Zane Murphy, was usually on top of it for the big anniversaries, like the date Astrid and Elia had died, but the smaller ones were beginning to fall by the wayside.

Even Kelly had nearly forgotten Astrid's birthday last night.

They should be good until the summer though, when Anders' wedding anniversary hit.

"Tell Dad I'm sorry and I'll reply to his text once I'm done cleaning the kitchen," Kelly said.

"I will. Oh!" His mother sounded startled. "Look at the time. I should get going. I need to do the grocery shopping before the hordes descend."

"Okay, Ma. Thanks for calling."

"Love you, Kelly."

"Love you too." He ended the call with his elbow, then attacked the sink until the sludge was gone and it was shiny silver again.

He tossed a few old pizza boxes, took out several bags of trash, then finally flopped onto the couch next to Trevor. "Okay, that's enough cleaning. *Call of Duty?*"

"I'm in. Want a beer?"

"I think I'll stick to Gatorade today," he said. "Fucking aquavit, man."

"That is some nasty-ass shit. I don't know how you stand to drink it."

Kelly shrugged. "Ehh, it made Lindy smile."

"It's about time something did."

Kelly frowned at him. "Yeah."

"I know you get all protective of him, but I don't mean anything bad, you know?" Trevor said a little defensively. "I do feel terrible that he's like, in such a rough place or whatever."

"Wouldn't you if you lost the love of your life?"

Trevor snorted. "Dude, I've never found anyone I can stand for more than a few weeks."

"Yeah, true. You are kind of a man whore."

"Fuck you," Trevor said. "You wish you got half the tail I did."

"I dunno, I'm pretty good with not having to tell the team doc I need a dose of antibiotics," he chirped.

"That was once," Trevor protested, but he was laughing. "And it was *meningitis,* you fuckface. My dick was fine."

"Well, if you didn't stick your tongue down strangers' throats six days a week ..."

"It's not my fault something got fucked up with the records from my doctor's office and I didn't get the vaccine like I was supposed to."

"You keep telling yourself that, Slutty McSlutterson," Kelly teased.

"Hey! No slut-shaming." Trevor knocked their shoulders together like they were out on the ice. "Now, are we gonna play, or what?"

"Yeah, yeah." Kelly picked up his controller.

"Anyway, what were we talking about before you pathetically attempted to chirp my undeniable sexual prowess?"

Kelly toggled through the options for his character. "Lindy's broken heart."

"Kinda makes you wonder if he'll ever move on, you know?"

"You never know," Kelly said.

"Man, I can't believe he fucking came out too. How did we not know he was bi?"

Kelly's pulse leapt. Trevor didn't usually talk about this stuff.

"Well, I mean he was with Astrid fucking forever and he hasn't been with anyone else since."

"Wait. You mean he hasn't even gotten head or anything since then?" Trevor looked absolutely horrified.

"Well, I don't know. I haven't *asked* him," Kelly said, staring straight ahead. "He's pretty private. But it sure doesn't *seem* like he's interested in anyone else."

"Yeah, but a guy can't go four fucking years with only his hand, right?"

Kelly shrugged. He'd spent a lot of time thinking about what Lindy would be like in bed, but for his own sanity, he'd never thought about his teammate's jerk-off habits.

Kelly's heart clenched at the idea of Lindy being with someone else.

Lindy was a classy guy who wouldn't want to hook up with someone from a bar in front of the team, but for all Kelly knew, Lindy had someone discreet who looked out for his needs.

Maybe he had a friend who helped him out or something.

Or maybe Lindy was so loyal to his wife's memory that he hadn't touched anyone since her death.

It shouldn't make Kelly feel better to think of Anders being celibate for all this time but guiltily, he admitted it did.

———

Anders slowed to a walk as he approached his building, wiping the sweat from his brow. He was drenched, though it was only March. Today was unseasonably warm and he hadn't quite acclimated yet. The weather could be extreme here, though usually the breezes off Lake Michigan cooled him.

It had been a pleasant run overall. His knees and hips felt solid, thanks to the exercises the team's strength and conditioning coach had suggested, and it was always good to build up a sweat. The endorphins helped too, shaking off the lingering sadness from last night until it returned to the usual low-level hum that never truly went away.

Anders was surprised he hadn't felt more hungover. He and Kelly had put away quite a bit of aquavit before he sent Kelly home in a cab. Kelly had been drunk, pink-cheeked, and staring at Anders with worshipful eyes.

Anders had been far more sober, thankfully, but now, as he nodded at his building's doorman in greeting and took the stairs to the sixth floor, he couldn't forget the feel of Kelly tucked against him while they waited on the sidewalk last night.

Even as Anders walked into his bathroom and stripped off his sodden workout gear, placing it in the hamper, he remembered the whoosh of Kelly's liquor-laced breath against his cheek and the heat of his body as he clung to Anders.

Guilt nagged at Anders. He stepped under the hot spray, trying to ignore the insistent rise of his cock. He soaped his body efficiently and when he was clean, he closed his eyes and braced a hand on a large marble tile.

He tried to empty his mind while he used the slippery body wash to stroke, forcing himself to think of nothing and no one as he worked his shaft over. He tried to keep his own touch as impersonal as possible, satisfying a basic biological urge rather than making it something to linger over.

He panted lightly by the time he was done, watching his release wash down the drain, oddly empty.

He ate after his shower, allowing his hair to air dry, disliking the long-wet strands against his neck but too hungry to wait.

Most of his meals came from a meal service approved by his nutritionist and he tried not to think of the partially eaten container of *risgrynsgröt* still in the refrigerator, the same way he'd tried not to think of Kelly's warm brown eyes and freckled shoulders in the shower.

Anders should throw the dessert out. He certainly didn't need it. He stood, intending to be rid of it once and for all, but he hesitated, holding it over the trash can, oddly conflicted. Kelly's gesture had been kind. Thoughtful.

A few years ago, they'd gone to the Swedish restaurant in Chicago's Lakeview neighborhood. Ever since then, Kelly had sporadically ordered his favorites for him from there for takeout. The gesture was too much but it was difficult for Anders to complain when it was done with such stubborn surety it was what Anders needed.

And it was.

The food wasn't as good as his mother's in Sweden. The fish was never as fresh as the ones his father had caught in the stream a few kilometers from their home on the outskirts of Karlstad, but it still filled the longing for familiar flavors, the ones he'd grown up with.

Anders had been happy to leave home at sixteen to play for a Canadian Junior League team in the hopes of getting noticed by the NHL. And he'd been happy to move to Boston when he was finally ready to play for the Harriers at eighteen.

But the longing for home never quite faded.

The problem was, when Anders was home in Sweden, he missed the Chicago area. He hadn't expected that, but after two decades living in North America, he'd grown to love it. There were things he missed no matter where he was.

This summer, he'd go home for a few months like usual. His parents were getting older and though they typically traveled to visit him once or twice a year, his father had fallen and broken his femur last winter. He'd healed well after surgery but it was doubtful they'd be able to fly that distance before the end of the season, even if the Otters made it to the playoffs.

Anders reached out and gently rapped his knuckles against the face of the pale wood cabinet, muttering the Swedish phrase that roughly translated to "pepper, pepper, knock on wood" to dispel the bad luck from tempting fate.

The first time he'd done it in front of Kelly, he'd given Anders a curious look, asking what the words meant. Anders had explained the pagan origin, that it was done to awaken the spirits and creatures inhabiting the tree trunks in the forest to protect him. Kelly had smiled, seeming delighted by the folklore.

It was a shame Kelly hadn't been able to finish his college career. He'd left BU early to play in the NHL. Anders certainly couldn't blame him, not when a team like the Otters had come calling. He was shaping up to be an excellent defenseman, especially now that he was paired with Gabriel Theriault. This season, Kelly was flourishing.

But Kelly was smart too. Much brighter than he gave himself credit for, and the way he soaked up knowledge made Anders wonder what his life might have been like if he'd been born into another family. One where hockey wasn't the beginning and end of everything.

Anders loved the O'Sheas. They were a loud, gregarious family who truly cared for everyone they adopted into their fold. But they were also an intimidating bunch, and he wasn't surprised Kelly had been happy to move out from under the weight of their expectations.

Anders could see why Kelly hadn't come out to them. He probably hadn't wanted to feel like the odd man out.

Sometimes Anders wished Kelly would do something solely for himself though. Something to make him happy, rather than worrying about what everyone else thought of him.

What kind of future did Kelly see for himself?

Did he want a family? Did he enjoy being single?

It seemed a shame he wasn't at least out to the team. Certainly, there was no better organization to come out to.

Anders had winced at the barbed words Malone had thrown at him when Jamie Walsh came out. Anders had never told the team he was bi before then, but if Jack Malone wanted to claim that being anything but straight would have a detrimental impact on a man's ability to play hockey, Anders knew he could prove him wrong.

He'd half-expected Kelly to chime in too but he'd only made a strange, startled sound, his eyes widening.

After, it had hit Anders that Kelly had probably always assumed *he* was straight.

Why wouldn't he?

But it had left Anders feeling oddly guilty, like he'd inadvertently lied to a friend.

CHAPTER FOUR

"Motherfucker!" Kelly swore, his cheek stinging as he skated toward the bench, heart thudding after the scrap he'd gotten into with Matty Carlson.

Jesus Christ, he was a beast. According to everyone who knew him, he was a big teddy bear off-ice, but Jesus, on-ice, he was fucking massive and *mean*.

Kelly was usually wily enough to stay out of range of the big guys or at least get his shoulder down and knock them off balance when they were least expecting it, but he'd been off tonight or something because Matty had gotten in a couple of good hits during the puck battle. He'd caught Kelly's cheek with his stick as Kelly tried to steal the puck from him.

Now, he could feel blood trickle down, dripping onto his white jersey. Oh well, at least Matty was currently cooling his heels in the sin bin thanks to the high-stick penalty the ref had called on him.

Of course, now Kelly would miss the power play because he had to get his stupid face looked at.

In the dressing room, he allowed Cameron Ward, the assistant athletic trainer, to clean the wound.

"It's not bad," Cameron said. "I'll slap a butterfly bandage on now and you'll only need a couple of stitches after the game. Don't worry, you'll still be as pretty as ever after this, O'Shea."

Kelly chuckled. "Not like it's the first time I've taken a stick to the face."

After Cameron was done applying the bandage, Kelly walked to the bench to wait for his next shift.

"You okay?" Lindy asked with a concerned frown. "No dizziness or anything?"

Kelly nudged him with his elbow. "You taking over as a trainer, Lindy?"

"No. Just worried about you." Lindy's eyes looked bluer than usual, shadowed by his helmet.

"I've already been over this with the actual training staff. I got cut, not concussed."

"Okay." But Lindy's gaze was still concerned, and Kelly had to look away and focus on the game.

Not that it did them any good, since they lost the game to Toronto in a shootout.

Anton Makarov was in net and even Lindy's gorgeous, clever shots couldn't fake him out. Toronto had struggled after Noah Boucher retired last season, but Makarov was quickly becoming a formidable starting goaltender.

The Otters' goalie, Hajek, was good too, but Dustin Fowler's five-hole shot against him was better and the Otters left the ice in defeat.

A single-point loss wasn't the worst they'd walked away with but this late in the season, every point could make or break their playoff dreams and Kelly was annoyed at himself for not playing better.

Maybe if he hadn't had that turnover in the second period …

In the training room, Kelly kept his eyes closed as Cameron gave him a quick numbing shot, then stitched the small cut, the tug of the needle and thread uncomfortable but not painful.

The team went through the usual postgame routine, then headed for the airport. It had been an afternoon game and they had a quick flight to Montreal. On board, Kelly wolfed down his dinner, then joined Underhill and Walsh in playing *Legend of Zelda* on Trevor's Nintendo Switch.

The mood wasn't somber—not the way it was after a big loss— but the guys were less boisterous than usual as they walked off the plane to catch the bus to the hotel, the weight of the season pressing on them.

Kelly had just arrived in his room when there was a knock on his door.

The moment he opened it, Anders pushed his way inside. "Are you sure you're okay?"

"Jesus Christ, Lindy," Kelly snapped. "I'm fine. I've seen you take way worse hits. I swear to God, it's a little fucking cut."

"I worry about you."

"Yeah, well, you can tell my brothers I'm fine. I assume they texted you?"

Lindholm's silence spoke volumes.

"Yeah, that's what I fucking thought. I'm not a goddamn kid."

"Carlson is a big guy, Kelly. We're all concerned. It was a hard check."

Kelly shrugged out of his suit jacket and unbuttoned his shirt with sharp, jerky movements, pushing one side of it open. "Look, he caught my hip and my ribs, but it wasn't that bad. I'm barely going to bruise."

Lindy stared at his bare chest and Kelly froze, heat creeping up to fill his face as Lindy reached out, gently skimming his warm fingertips across Kelly's ribs. Soothing and ticklish all at once, making Kelly's dick chub up at the touch.

Fuck.

He cleared his throat and turned away, blindly doing up his buttons again. "See? You don't have to worry about me," he said shortly.

"Kelly—"

"Why do you care?" Kelly snarled. He turned back, hoping the trembling in his hands wasn't visible. "Why, Lindy?"

"I'm your friend," Lindy said, gently batting away Kelly's hands and tugging at his shirt.

Kelly looked down in shock when Lindy undid the top two buttons, but his heart sank when he realized it was only to fix the ones Kelly had lined up wrong. He'd skipped a buttonhole in his haste.

"Jesus Christ, I can do it myself." He pushed Lindy away.

Lindy held up his hands. "I apologize if I overstepped."

"Right," Kelly said tersely. "Well, you can run along now that you've verified I'm alive and in one piece and can dress myself like a big boy."

Another knock came on the door and Kelly grumbled under his breath, assuming it was their captain coming to check on him.

"Murph, I'm *fine*—" he said as he yanked the door open, startled to come face-to-face with their teammate Jack Malone instead. "Oh, hey."

Malone pushed his way inside too, but stopped in his tracks at the sight of Anders. "Oh. What are you doing in here, Lindholm?"

"Lindy was just checking up on me." Kelly couldn't quite hide the venom in his voice. "What do you need, Malone? Did you lose your charger again?"

"No. I was thinking about getting a drink. Want to join me?" Malone leaned against the dresser, glancing between him and Lindy.

Kelly snuck a peek at his phone. *Hmm.* They didn't have practice until the afternoon tomorrow, then a game the following day before they flew home.

"Yeah okay. I'll go out."

"You in, Lindholm?" Jack's voice held a sneer that had been there since Anders came out.

Kelly didn't want to think about how Malone would feel if he knew about *him.*

"No thank you," Anders said politely. "I'm quite tired."

"No surprise at your age."

It wasn't much of a chirp as far as they went but Lindy's gaze held real loathing when he passed Malone and walked to the door. Then again, most of the guys didn't like Malone much. Kelly always felt sort of guilty for his friendship with him. It wasn't like he admired Malone. He didn't look up to him or anything or think he was a particularly good guy.

But sometimes it was hard for Kelly to separate what Malone meant to the team—or had in the past anyway—and what he was like outside of that. And Kelly had been so damn lonely when he joined the Otters, living half the country away from his home and playing on a team where Anders was the only teammate he knew.

At Boston University, Kelly had played with a few guys he'd come up through hockey with and when he left BU to play for the Otters, he'd missed that connection.

Malone had taken Brent Cooper, Trevor Underhill, and Kelly under his wing, and the four of them had been tight from the beginning.

It had been nice to have guys to go out to the bar with, and it was easier to go with the flow and enjoy the nights out and camaraderie even when Kelly knew underneath that Malone was a piece of shit in his personal life. Kelly didn't *want* to be like him. He just wanted to belong somewhere that was totally independent of his stupid and wonderful family who took over everything.

He wanted something that was his and his alone.

As a nineteen-year-old NHL rookie, Kelly hadn't had much in common with Lindy, who was a decade and a half older.

He'd had a huge-ass crush, sure, and they'd known each other decently well because of Lindy's friendship with Kelly's brothers, but it had taken a while for a true friendship to develop.

So Malone had been one of Kelly's closest friends when he was a rookie.

"Cool," Malone said with a nod. "Meet you in the lobby in ten, Irish?"

"Sure," Kelly said, vaguely annoyed Theriault's nickname for him had stuck. "See you then."

"Are you sure you should drink tonight?" Lindholm asked as Kelly turned and stripped off the shirt again, exchanging it for something better for going out.

"I didn't fucking get a concussion, Lindy," he barked. "I got smacked into the boards a bit and I have a tiny little cut. We've all had way worse in our careers. Why are you being so overprotective now?"

"Why are you in such a mood?" Lindholm asked.

"I don't know. But let me go drink it out of my system and leave me the fuck alone about it."

Lindholm sighed heavily. "Okay. If that's what you want."

It *wasn't* what Kelly wanted. What he wanted was to have Lindy grab him by the shoulders, kiss him hard, and tell him he had a better way to let out his frustration. But that wasn't going to fucking happen so Kelly would have to take what he could get.

"Yes," he said between clenched teeth. "It's what I fucking want, okay?"

"Okay. Good night, Kelly."

"Night." He didn't look back as the door quietly closed behind him.

Kelly stood in the middle of his hotel room, clenching the clothing in his bag, trying to breathe through the weird shaky sensation inside him. He rarely got mad at Lindy. He hadn't been mad at him since the morning after that stupid, embarrassing night in Pittsburgh where he'd begged Lindy to kiss him and join him in bed.

God, he'd never been so humiliated in his life to wake up hungover to those memories with Lindy asleep in the chair on the other side of the room, watching over him.

Kelly was a grade-A fucking idiot.

And he'd felt like an asshole when he'd snapped at Lindy in the visitors' locker room about not being willing to let go of his past. That had been cruel and horrible, and Kelly still regretted it.

But how long could Kelly keep pining and pining and never getting anywhere with someone who clearly wasn't going to return his feelings?

Determined to get Lindy out of his mind, Kelly gathered his things, checked for his key card, and left his room. In the swanky lobby, Malone was easy to find, sprawled on a couch like he owned the place.

"The other guys'll be down in a few minutes," he said.

"Okay." Kelly dropped into a nearby chair and pulled out his phone.

"What was up with you and Lindy, earlier? Was he hitting on you?"

Kelly choked on air. "*What?*"

Malone glanced up. "I dunno. He stares at you a lot, you know? It was fucking weird to find out he's into guys too. What is up with this fucking team?"

Kelly held up a hand. "Dude, he's my friend. My brothers texted him all worried about me when they heard I tangled with Carlson, and Lindy checked on me for them. It's not like that or anything with him."

Much to Kelly's chagrin.

Malone seemed to relax. "I'm just saying. If he ever makes you feel weird or tries something—"

"Dude, he's still in love with Astrid. He's not going to come on to anyone on the team. Pretty sure he's never moving on with anyone new anyway." He couldn't hide the trace of bitterness in his tone but Malone didn't seem to notice.

"Yeah. True. Fucking pathetic, right?"

Anger flared hot inside Kelly but he forced himself to take a deep breath. "She was an amazing woman," he said aloud. "I can understand it."

Malone grunted.

Then again, Jack Malone had a sweet, gorgeous wife he regularly cheated on. Kelly didn't know Carlie well, but she was definitely too good for the shit Malone got up to.

Kelly had asked once if they had an open marriage or something and he'd had the gall to laugh.

"Fuck no, nobody else is touching her. But c'mon, I have needs, man." He'd actually fucking winked as he said it, like he was totally justified in screwing around behind her back. Kelly had called him an asshole to his face but it hadn't made any impact.

Jack Malone would do whatever he fucking pleased. He wasn't the first NHL player to cheat on his wife and he wouldn't be the last, but he was definitely one of the most blatant. And the GM and owner of the franchise clearly didn't care. They kept cleaning up the messes he left in his wake. Why, Kelly didn't know, but that was way above his pay grade.

"Where are you thinking about going tonight?" Kelly asked, because if he spent any more time thinking about what a shitty person Malone was, it would put him in a worse mood.

"The bar we went to last time we were in town," Malone said, not glancing up from his phone. He was probably either on his Tinder profile or sending out some bat signal on social media to announce he was in Montreal and looking to hook up. Gross.

"Oh, the one with the club upstairs?" Kelly asked.

"Yeah."

"Sure, that'll work," Kelly said. It wasn't his style but whatever. They had booze and Malone was usually generous about picking up the tab.

"You gonna pull any girls tonight or are you going to be totally lame like usual?"

"You know, you seem pretty concerned with my love life there," Kelly joked. "Are you sure *you* don't want in my pants?"

Malone visibly recoiled. "Fuck no. Just like looking out for my boys. The rest of the guys are tied down and boring as shit now so it's you, me, Underhill, and the rookies."

"Yeah," Kelly said absently as some of their teammates walked across the lobby to meet with them. "Sure, I mean, it has been a while since I've hooked up with anyone, I guess."

Christ, this was the last thing Kelly wanted tonight but he was running out of excuses.

———

"Hey," Anders said, frowning at the clock on the hotel nightstand as he answered a call from Patrick O'Shea. Anders had just left

Kelly's room and while it wasn't incredibly late, it was much later than Pat usually called.

"How's Kelly doing?" Pat asked without any preamble.

"Nice to hear from you too," Anders said drily, the pieces slotting together in his head. The late-night call made sense now. "Kelly is fine."

"No worries about a head injury?"

Anders stretched out on the bed, feeling the tug of sore muscles from the game. "No. It was a small cut on his cheek. He only needed a couple of stitches."

"I don't like the way Carlson went after him."

"Kelly's tougher than he looks," Anders reminded his former linemate mildly.

"I know. But Carlson's got what, nearly fifty pounds on him? Why the hell is Kelly even tangling with him?"

"They were battling for the puck! Would you rather Kelly had let them score?"

"No, of course not."

"That's how the game goes. You can't protect him from *that*. Besides, Kelly is *good* at toppling those bigger guys. They always underestimate him."

"Yeah, well, one of these days that's going to come back and bite him in the ass."

"I think you worry unnecessarily. Kelly is one of our most skilled D-men."

"He should have been a forward like the rest of us in the family," Pat grumbled. "He's more suited to it at his size."

Anders rubbed the spot where his browbone and nose met, a headache beginning to form there. "Do you think maybe that's exactly *why* he chose a different path?"

Pat scoffed. "Why? Because he's a stubborn little shit?"

Anders laughed. "I believe that trait runs in the entire O'Shea family."

"Yeah, maybe, but at least the rest of us have the good sense to not put ourselves in a situation where we're in danger of being smeared across the ice."

"Do you hear yourself, Pat?" Anders said, shaking his head. "Every single one of us could have something go wrong in a game. Carlson's the one who needs to learn to control his stick better. Why do you act like Kelly is inherently more helpless than anyone else? He *isn't*."

Pat let out an annoyed-sounding grunt.

"You know he's playing well this season," Anders pointed out.

"He is."

"Have you *told* him that?"

"No." Pat's tone was grudging.

"Well, maybe you should. I think it would do him good to hear it."

"You know we don't talk about our feelings much in this family."

Anders rubbed his forehead again. "Then maybe it's time you started."

"Why are you getting all worked up about this, Lindy?" Pat asked, sounding confused. "I think I know how to handle my brother."

"Well, he's annoyed I'm constantly checking up on him on your behalf and I'm annoyed you've made me an intermediary."

"Ooh, fancy word there."

"Shut up," Anders said with a laugh. "You know what it means, you asshole."

They moved onto other topics, though Pat didn't apologize for the position he put him in or promise to tell Kelly he was proud of him. Anders let it slide for now and asked about Pat's wife and kids.

"Aubrey's good and so are the kids. Did I tell you we're having a girl in August?"

"Congratulations," Anders said. He meant it sincerely. He *was* genuinely happy for his friend but there would always be a sting of pain when he remembered sharing the happy news about Elia with Pat. "I know you've always wanted a little girl."

"Yeah." Pat's voice softened. "We're pretty excited."

"How are the boys taking it?"

Pat chuckled. "Theo, Noel, and Cory are pretty excited. Brendan isn't happy about the idea of not being the baby anymore."

"I would imagine."

Originally, Anders had wanted two children. Astrid had been strongly in favor of one. Since she would be the one carrying them and she had to juggle her own challenging career, motherhood, and him being on the road nine months out of the year, he could hardly argue.

Anders had been content with Elia, never feeling like he'd missed out on anything.

But he felt a sudden ache knowing he'd never again sit in a doctor's office and experience the joy of hearing the heartbeat of his future child. He'd never cradle an infant, moments old, in his arms, and promise them he'd protect them with his last breath.

Then again, he'd never have to admit to himself that he'd failed at his one job as a parent.

Anders was happy for Pat and Aubrey. He was happy for his teammates and their children. But the pain of the future he'd lost never faded.

"Hey, you doin' okay, Lindy?" Pat asked, suddenly serious.

"Yes." Anders cleared his throat. He didn't need another O'Shea fussing over him and wallowing in Anders' grief with him. "Please tell Aubrey how happy I am for both of you."

"Of course. Hopefully you can tell her yourself this summer. You are coming for a visit, right?"

"I am. We'll see when that ends up being though."

"Yeah, I hear you. I'm not sure how far we're going to make it into the playoffs either," Pat said with a sigh.

The Boston Harriers and Evanston Otters were each sitting squarely at fourth in their respective divisions and if they didn't pull it up soon, they'd be lucky to snag a wild card spot, much less earn a guaranteed berth in the playoffs.

"We have to get our scoring up, that's for sure," Anders said.

"Same here." Pat sighed again. "Anything new with you?"

"No," Anders said. "I'm just focused on getting through the rest of this season."

"You have to have something in your life that isn't hockey," Pat said. "Maybe it's time you think about dating again."

Anders blinked. For once, Pat wasn't being aggressive. His tone had turned uncharacteristically gentle, in fact, but Anders still had to take a few deep breaths before he could continue.

"That wouldn't be fair to anyone," Anders said tightly. "You know my heart is still with Astrid and I'm not … I have nothing to give someone new."

Pat scoffed. "That's a bunch of bullshit and you know it, Anders. Love isn't like that. Did I love Theo less because I had Cory?"

"Children are different."

"I disagree but fine. Do you honestly think the woman you married would want you to bury yourself in grief for the rest of your life?"

Anders winced. "No, I don't. But I also know she'd respect my choices."

Pat hooted. "When did Astrid ever sit quietly when you were being an idiot? That wasn't the kind of woman you were madly in love with and that's exactly *why* you were so crazy about her. She kept you from being a miserable fuck and you know it."

Anders winced again. Pat wasn't wrong.

"I can't risk it again." Anders dragged in a deep breath. "How can I put myself out there when I already lost everything once?"

"I don't know, man." Pat sighed. "I'm not saying it's easy or that you don't have a tough road ahead of you, but come on. You deserve to have love again, *that* I'm sure of."

"If you lost Aubrey, would you give it a shot again?"

"Jesus, don't tempt fate like that." Anders didn't have to see Pat to know he'd made the sign of the cross. "But if it ever happened, yeah, I'd like to think I would. I can't imagine spending the rest of my life alone."

"And if you lost your children too?"

"I'd put a fucking gun in my mouth."

Anders swallowed. "Don't say that."

"Sorry, man. It's ..."

"Yeah." Anders thought of his baby girl again and grief rose in his throat, sharp and fast, his eyes stinging.

"I really am sorry, Anders." Pat's earnest sincerity sounded so much like Kelly that for a moment it was spooky. "I shouldn't have said what I did. I didn't mean to say anything hurtful, man."

"I know you didn't."

But there wasn't much more either of them could say after that and Anders told Pat he needed to get some sleep. They said goodbye and after Anders ended the call, he stared at his lock screen.

It displayed his favorite picture of Astrid and Elia. They had cat and mouse ears on—it had been taken on Halloween—and they were making the most ridiculous faces.

Astrid's cheeks were puffed out with air until they were as wide as a chipmunk's and her eyes were crossed. She looked ridiculous and beautiful, and Anders' heart ached remembering how hard he'd laughed at her antics. She'd been so vibrant and alive, and it still seemed impossible she was gone. It was like he'd blinked, and four years had passed with no end to the pain.

The grief seemed to have no time. No ending in sight. Just endless loneliness stretching before him.

Maybe Pat was right. Maybe it *was* possible for Anders to love again, but how could he risk it? What if he hurt someone in the process?

Anders thought of Kelly and his naked longing for whatever Anders would give him. Kelly was the only person he'd consider it with, but how could he do that to someone he cared about so much? If he dated someone—anyone—and let them get their hopes up for a future Anders wasn't ready for, he'd feel terrible when he left them heartbroken.

And the thought of doing that to Kelly was unbearable. It was wrong to promise someone a future he couldn't give them. Kelly deserved so much better.

Thinking of Kelly made Anders feel guilty for how he'd spoken to him earlier. Anders would need to apologize tomorrow.

With a sigh, he sat up to plug in his phone, then trudged to the bathroom to get ready for bed. After he was done, he turned out the light, closing his eyes despite knowing sleep remained hours away.

After ten minutes of lying there restlessly, he flipped onto his other side and reached out, patting his hand against the bare sheets beside him, the faint scent of hotel laundry rising to his nostrils.

He was exhausted but his mind was too filled with the thoughts Pat had put in his head to rest.

He had a long, sleepless night ahead of him.

CHAPTER FIVE

An hour later, Kelly was well on his way to drunk while a blonde giggled beside him. He didn't hate it. He wasn't repulsed by women or anything. They could be great friends but he'd never met a single one who got a rise out of his cock.

Why couldn't I have been bi? he thought bitterly. It would have been so much easier than having to fake interest in the girl beside him.

Kelly should probably remember her name too. Sasha? Shannon? Something like that. He tossed back another shot.

"You wanna get out of here, Sarah?" one of her friends yelled across the table a few minutes later. "We were supposed to be at the club across town half an hour ago."

Oh, *Sarah*. Kelly needed to remember that.

"I thought maybe I'd stick around here." She glanced at Kelly, and he tightened his grip on her, because all the other guys were looking at him expectantly.

"Definitely," Kelly said with a smile at Sarah.

"I'll meet you guys at the apartment later?" she said to her friend.

The girl nodded and winked. "Okay. Have fun, girl!"

Sarah grinned at Kelly. "Oh, don't worry. I think I will."

Guilt washed through Kelly. He fucking hated this.

He pretty much had hooking up down to a science now. He liked kissing, even if the person wasn't necessarily his ideal choice, and he had good hands. He knew how to get a woman off, and one had told him he was the best orgasm she'd ever had, which had made him both oddly proud and a little queasy because it felt wrong to lie to people he was fooling around with.

But when the girl would smile and reach for his cock, expecting to find him hard under the boxers he wore, he'd roll away. He'd sit on the edge of the bed and reach for his pants before she could see he was totally limp.

"Sorry, I can't," he'd lie. "Big game tomorrow. You understand."

The girl would nod and drape herself over his shoulder and kiss his neck as she told him to call the next time he was in town.

But he never did.

Kelly had always half-expected there to be some weird fan message board or something floating around the internet discussing his lack of interest in sex but if something like that existed, he'd never seen it.

He'd been drunk out of his fucking mind and curious, so he'd googled it once.

He'd nearly had a panic attack when his name and gay had come up on the same page, but it had only been a hockey fan site run by some gay guys.

Apparently, a lot of them were into gingers which was flattering and all, but it wasn't like Kelly could take advantage of it.

Besides, he'd always had this stupid fantasy about Anders being the one he lost his virginity to, which was as dumb as it got, but here he was.

"You want to get out of here?" Sarah shouted in his ear.

"Um, sure," Kelly said, shaking off the dread about what was to come.

Just because he was good at faking it didn't mean he *liked* it.

Kelly nudged the rookie beside him out of the booth, then got out, holding a hand out to Sarah because he was a horrible person for lying but he tried to be a gentleman whenever he could.

Sarah giggled as she took his hand and flipped her long hair over her shoulder before tugging down her short dress. She was pretty and seemed sweet and goddamn it, he wished he *wanted* to take her to bed.

Kelly was too warm and feeling a little sick as he wove through the noisy, crowded club, Sarah trailing in his wake, her hand clutched tightly to his.

The cooler spring air was welcome when they finally made it to the sidewalk, and Kelly felt a little steadier, despite the alcohol swimming in his veins.

Sarah snuggled up against his side and smiled at him as she teased at the waistband of his trousers. "Wanna head to my place? My roommates are out, and we'd have some privacy."

"Um." Kelly had been fully prepared to say yes but something in him rebelled at the thought of faking his way through the next hour or so.

Sarah seemed way too fucking nice and God it made him feel shitty to lie to people to cover up what he was too cowardly to admit aloud.

"Oh." Her face fell and she stepped away. "Never mind. If you're not interested ..."

"I'm sorry," Kelly said miserably. "You're gorgeous and you seem amazing, and I wish I could, I just ..."

But how could he finish that thought without making her feel worse?

"You don't have to lie about it. I know I'm nothing special." To Kelly's horror, tears welled up, spilling down her cheeks.

"Oh God no." He wrapped his arms around her and pulled her close again. "Seriously, I *like* you."

Or he'd liked the short conversation they'd had earlier about Boston and the way she'd clearly known nothing about hockey and chatted with him because she thought he was attractive. She was the kind of girl he'd *want* to get to know better if he was into girls. At the very least she seemed like she could be fun to be friends with.

Sarah tipped her head back and looked at him. "What is it then?"

"I'm kinda in love with someone else," Kelly admitted with a sigh. It was the closest to the truth he'd ever come. "My friends were encouraging me to uh, hook up tonight and you're *great* but my head's not in it. I'm sorry."

"Oh." Her expression softened. "Well, that sucks but I get it."

"So, this is totally cliché, but it really is me, not you."

She gave him a wobbly smile. "That's what they all say."

"No, I *mean* it," Kelly said forcefully. "It wouldn't be fair of me to go home with you when there's someone else in my head, you know?"

"You're way too nice," she muttered as she gently disentangled their bodies and stepped away, grasping her elbows as she hugged herself.

"Better than me being a dick, right?" he said weakly.

"Sure." Her smile was half-hearted, and he hated that she obviously felt shitty about being rejected.

"Want me to call you a ride?" he asked.

"Um, sure," she said. "Or you could come to my place with me, and we could hang out and watch a movie if you want. I promise, I'll keep my hands to myself. I just don't feel like being alone tonight, you know?"

Kelly was half-tempted but didn't want to lead her on. He glanced at his watch. "It's getting pretty late. The team does have a curfew."

That was kind of a lie. They'd have one tomorrow night but Daniels was more lenient when they had two nights between games.

"Oh. Okay." She gave him another weak smile but he was pretty sure she'd easily seen through the lie.

They stood in awkward silence while they waited for the car to pull up and Kelly helped Sarah in and wished her a good night.

He'd turned to walk back to the hotel when loud shouts made him whirl to face the bar.

Malone, Underhill, and the gaggle of rookies tumbled out of the front door, along with a couple of people Kelly didn't recognize.

"Keep your fucking hands off her, you creep!" a guy shouted.

"She was all over me. It's not my fault your girl's a fucking whore," Malone yelled.

The first guy's punch landed on Malone's nose with a sickening crunch and Malone let out a bellow of rage, charging the guy. They grappled, the crowd around them surging as Underhill and the rookies tangled with the guy's friends.

Kelly jogged toward them, shouting at them to stop. He pulled people apart as best he could, ducking flying fists and shoves the whole time, but it wasn't until a couple of large men joined in the fray that the groups were finally pulled apart and Kelly recognized the people helping him as club security.

"Keep your fucking hands off me, you asshole," Malone shouted, struggling against the bouncer's tight grip, his face a mask of rage. "Don't you fucking know who I am?"

"I don't fucking *care* who you are," the guy growled. "Get the hell out of here or we're calling the cops."

"What the hell is going on?" Kelly demanded.

Underhill stood there, dabbing at his split lip, an annoyed expression on his face. "Malone got handsy with the wrong girl. Her boyfriend took exception to it."

"Jesus Christ," Kelly muttered. He glanced around and caught a glimpse of people waiting in line to get into the club staring at them, half a dozen of them with their phones out, expressions rapt as they recorded everything.

"C'mon, Malone," Kelly hissed. "Let's get the fuck out of here. Coach is going to be pissed if this ends up all over social media."

"Go on with your friends," the bouncers said, shoving Malone in Kelly's direction.

Malone shot a baleful glare at the guy but he joined Kelly and Trevor on the sidewalk.

With a sigh, Kelly rounded up the rookies who were in various stages of disarray.

"C'mon, guys," Kelly said when they were all accounted for. "We need to get out of here."

He herded his teammates in the direction of the hotel while Trevor nudged Malone along. He still looked mad enough to spit nails, his hair disheveled and his nose dripping blood onto his suit. He'd have some wicked black eyes tomorrow.

"Fucking pussy!" the boyfriend shouted at their backs as they walked away.

Malone turned and lunged for him, but Kelly and Trevor grabbed his arms and stopped him in time.

"It's not worth it," Kelly snarled, gripping his bicep. "Jesus Christ, we have to *go*."

Together, Kelly and Trevor strong-armed Malone into walking toward the hotel, Kelly's stomach sinking as he thought about the fallout from this mess.

They were going to be in so much shit.

Malone had mostly calmed down by the time they reached the hotel, though he muttered under his breath the whole time. Kelly ignored his drunken little rant about how he would have kicked the guy's ass given the chance. Kelly got Malone into his room and ordered him to shower. The rookies had scattered for their rooms too, and when it was just him and Trevor in the hallways, Kelly turned to him with a tired sigh.

"What the fuck do we do now?"

Trevor grimaced. "I don't suppose we can hope this all blows over without making it on social media?"

"Dude, we're in *Montreal*. It's not as bad as Toronto but it's pretty bad. We might have gotten away with this somewhere else but there is no way this is flying under the radar. At least six people in line were filming it. Someone will recognize one of us and it'll be on *JockGossip* in the next twelve hours, I guarantee it."

"Fuck." Trevor poked at his split lip with the tip of his tongue. "Um, I guess we better let Murph and Daniels know about this then."

Kelly blanched. "Ugh, not looking forward to that."

"Seriously."

They stared at each other a moment, as if waiting for the other one to crack first.

"You were in the middle of this shit," Kelly finally said. "*You* can wake Coach. I'll get Murphy."

Trevor grumbled but he nodded. "Yeah, okay."

Kelly had taken a few steps toward the other end of the hall where their captain's room was when Trevor said, "Hey, what happened to the girl you were with? I thought you were going home with her."

"Uh, she wasn't feeling great. I sent her home in a cab," he lied.

"Oh damn. Looks like a shitty night all around, huh?"

"Seriously," Kelly muttered. He raised his hand to knock on the door and wake up Murphy.

Kelly should have fucking listened to Lindy when he told him he should stay in tonight.

———

Anders swam out of the haze of sleep, blinking tiredly as he registered the buzz of his phone on the nightstand beside him. A glance at the clock told him he hadn't been asleep long.

He swore in his native tongue and fumbled for his phone. Who on earth would call at this hour? The sight of Zane Murphy's name on the screen woke Anders quickly though and he answered as soon as his tired fingers could manage to hit the right combination of buttons.

When their captain called at this time of night, they had a big problem.

"Lindholm," he answered.

"Murphy. We have a situation."

Anders grimaced. "Malone?"

"How'd you guess?"

"I assumed any situation urgent enough to address in the middle of the night would involve him."

"Yeah, fair."

"What do you need from me?"

"We're meeting in Daniels' room to discuss it. Be there in ten?"

"Okay."

Exhausted, it took Anders a few minutes to pull on clothing, then splash his face with some cold water. His hair was tangled so he pulled it back in an elastic, then grabbed his phone and key card.

Coach Daniels' door was propped open a few inches, so Anders slipped inside without knocking. Murphy and Hartinger were already there, along with Coach Tate, Coach Horton, Trevor Underhill, and Kelly.

Anders frowned at the sight of Underhill's split lip and bruised knuckles but when he searched Kelly's face and body, he looked no worse for wear than he had after the game.

"You okay?" Anders asked quietly. He took a seat beside Kelly on the bed, their knees brushing.

"Yeah. I'm fine." Kelly wouldn't meet his gaze.

"Okay, we're all here now," Daniels' said. "Want to repeat what happened earlier, O'Shea?"

He shrugged. "Well, like I said, I only caught the tail end because I was outside on the sidewalk about to head to the hotel but when I looked over, Malone was yelling at some guy and they started trading punches. Underhill and some of the rookies ended up in the mix and there were fists flying everywhere. It took a while for the bouncers and stuff to get everyone separated."

"Underhill, you said it started because the guy claimed Malone groped his girlfriend without her consent. Is that true? Was she unwilling?" Daniels sounded disgusted.

Underhill sighed, dragging a hand through his light brown hair, long on top with a buzzed undercut on the sides. "Honestly, I'm not sure. At one point, I saw Malone talking to a woman. There was no guy around and she seemed into it, but all they were doing was having a conversation. When the shouting started, I was talking to someone at the bar. I had my back to them, so I didn't see any of it go down."

"Damn it," Daniels muttered. "Murphy, I'd like you to discuss this situation with the rookies in the morning. Get their opinion on it. See if any of our guys saw *anything*."

"Knowing Malone, it wouldn't surprise me if he did grab someone," Hartinger muttered.

"No, it wouldn't surprise me either," Daniels said. He scrubbed a hand across his face. "Christ. Okay, I'm going to have to call Cliff and James, along with the PR department and get them all looped in on this situation so they're ready to roll."

Lindholm winced. Their GM and owner were going to be pissed and no matter what happened, the franchise would have a messy situation to deal with.

For better or worse, Jack Malone was the recognizable face of the franchise. With Kelly's red hair and Underhill's extensive tattoos, they were both easily identified as well. They could pray no one filming outside of the club would post it on social media but Anders wasn't hopeful.

They woke the head of PR and spent the next half an hour discussing various contingency plans with her via video chat before finally breaking up for the night so Coach Daniels could call the owner and GM.

"Okay, guys," Daniels said tiredly as they trooped out. "Get what sleep you can."

As they walked to their respective rooms, Anders looked at Kelly. "Are you okay?"

"I'm fine. Just exhausted and annoyed by the whole thing."

"I'm sure." Anders rubbed a hand over his face, weariness catching up with him. "I'm glad you weren't hurt."

Kelly stopped so quickly Anders did too, and when he met Kelly's gaze, it was filled with confusion. "Why are you always more worried about me than anyone else?"

Anders stood in the hallway, staring after Kelly as he turned and walked down the hall and disappeared into his room, trying to digest what he'd said.

The truth was, Anders had no idea how to answer.

CHAPTER SIX

"What the fuck?" Malone hissed to Kelly as they got on the bus to go to the practice arena the following afternoon. "Why didn't you back me up about what happened last night? I got my ass chewed out all morning."

"Back you up about *what?*" Kelly snapped as he dropped into a seat. He was tired and annoyed. He'd managed a few hours of sleep but he'd spent most of last night and this morning talking about what happened at the club and he was seriously over it. "I didn't see what happened inside and all I told them was what I witnessed on the sidewalk."

"You could have had my back."

"I told the truth," Kelly insisted. "That's all. Nothing more or less. I have no idea what happened, but I honestly wish I hadn't been a part of it at all."

Though Kelly knew the situation would have escalated if he hadn't. Underhill had a temper, and he probably wouldn't have broken up the fight without Kelly there to pull him away.

The police probably would have been called too.

Kelly liked Trevor—way more than he liked Jack at this point—and he didn't want to see him get tangled in Malone's mess. God, it was fucking scary when *Kelly* was the voice of goddamn reason.

Malone scowled. "How the fuck was I supposed to know this would go viral?"

"Really?" Kelly snorted. "How could you think anything else? In this day and age, some dude coming out of a club that's known as a hangout for athletes and getting accused of sexually harassing a woman is going to get noticed. There were like six or eight people filming."

"I didn't fucking sexually harass anyone." Malone glowered. "She was into me, dude."

"Yeah, well, she better have been, or this is going to get a lot worse," Kelly said shortly.

"The franchise already fined me and Underhill for fighting, and I'm scratched tonight. What the fuck is that bullshit?"

Honestly, Kelly had been surprised they'd benched Malone. This late in the regular season with their playoff chance still so uncertain, they needed as many healthy, talented players on the ice as possible. In the past, their GM and owner had seemed to have no interest in keeping Malone in line but maybe this time it had blown up too big for them to ignore.

A two-game scratch for bad behavior wasn't much, but the league had said they were investigating. That was something. God knew what they'd find. Malone didn't strike him as the kind of guy who spent any time thinking about what other people wanted. If he'd thought the woman in the club was hot, would he have listened too closely if she tried to tell him she wasn't into him?

A cold feeling settled in the pit of Kelly's stomach.

God, this situation could get ugly.

At least for once, it wasn't the team's dating life in the news. They'd had plenty of that this season as guys came out. Kelly didn't blame Coach and Gabriel for getting caught by some overzealous fan with a camera or begrudge Jamie for professing his love for figure skater Taylor Hollis.

But sometimes Kelly tired of all the drama.

He wanted to think about hockey, not that everyone and their brother was coming out of the fucking closet.

Especially when it left him bitter that he still hadn't.

———

Evanston River Otters' Defenseman Jack Malone Accused of Sexual Harassment

Following a loss against Toronto, a handful of players for the Evanston River Otters drowned their sorrows at an upscale nightclub on Boulevard Saint Laurent in Montreal.

The night concluded when a fight in the VIP section spilled out into the street in front of the club.

Club patrons maintain that the argument began when the veteran D-man groped a woman. Reportedly, her boyfriend went after Malone and several of Malone's entourage retaliated. Footage from the night is available, but none of it shows the initial incident.

Although this is likely to turn into a 'he said, she said' situation, events like this need to be taken seriously by the team and the league. After years of them turning blind eyes to rumors of his drunken antics and cheating, it would be nice to see Jack Malone held accountable for his actions.

The two-game suspension and fine are the usual pathetic attempt at looking like something is being done about problematic players. The announcement that the incident is 'being looked into' is cold comfort. How many times have fans been told that only for nothing to come of it?

People are increasingly sick of watching powerful men get away with terrible behavior and it's time the franchise and the league step up and deliver more than a slap on the wrist.

Cliff Hines, the team's General Manager, and James Franklin, the majority owner, have shown they value their bottom line above all else.

Just remember who attends the games and pays for the tickets. Supporting your LGBTQ+ players isn't enough. Fans expect better from the team than sexual assault allegations and drunken brawls.

The writing on the walls is becoming clear: do better or be prepared to lose fans.

CHAPTER SEVEN

"You're better than that, you know?"

Kelly lifted his head at the softly spoken words and stared at Lindy as he walked into the slightly hazy air of the steam room. He took a seat beside Kelly on the bench. Nearly forty years old and he looked like he was carved from granite.

Kelly looked at his own body, wincing at his pale, freckled chest. He was fit but he was maybe half Lindy's size. Nearly half his age too.

But somehow Kelly doubted he'd be anywhere near as built as Lindy—or playing half as well—when he was his age. That was a depressing thought.

"Huh? Better than what?" Kelly finally asked, shaking himself out of his Anders-induced daze.

"Better than letting Malone pull you into trouble. I hate your name being dragged into this mess on social media."

Kelly grimaced. He and Lindy had hardly spoken about anything except the game in the past few days. He'd been waiting for this. He hadn't expected to be ambushed in *here*, however.

It made sense though. They were back in Evanston, and the steam room was private enough for a serious conversation. It was his own fault for coming in when Lindy would probably be right behind him.

"Is that an 'I told you so?'" Kelly asked tiredly. It had been a long, rough game against Montreal last night and he hadn't slept well for two nights in a row now.

"No. I just worry you're going to end up in a bad situation. Worse than what happened in Montreal."

"Yeah well, I wasn't *with* the guys when the argument began," Kelly pointed out. "I was on the sidewalk, about to return to the hotel. I told you I tried to break the fight up."

"I know. I watched the footage. Besides, I believed you when you told us that the other night."

The trace of Anders' Swedish accent wrapped around the words and for the thousandth time, Kelly wondered what it would sound like whispering softer words. Right in his ear.

But that was dumb, stupid fantasy on his part. Why couldn't he just stop imagining things like that?

"Is this because my brothers are worried about me?" Kelly asked bitterly. His phone had been flooded with messages from his family since the news broke. He'd ignored them all.

"No. You asked me the other night why I worried more about you than anyone else on the team and the truth is, I care because you're a talented player, Kelly. You love the game, and I don't want to see you ruin your career over a friendship with someone who isn't worth it."

"Right." Well, those weren't the words Kelly wanted to hear but it wasn't like he expected Anders to confess his undying love or something. He didn't know why he'd asked. "I'm an okay D-man, I guess." He leaned his head against the wall and closed his eyes.

"You're talented already and you have the potential to be a *great* defenseman if you're willing to put in the work. You'd be even better if you didn't look to Jack Malone for guidance. You've done so well this season. I don't want to see you backslide."

As much as it annoyed Kelly to be told what to do, maybe he had a point. It wouldn't do him or his career any good to get a reputation as a problematic player. His game was improving and had been since he'd been paired with Gabriel Theriault at the beginning of the season.

Theriault had cleaned up his act when he was picked up by the Otters last summer and he'd been invited to the All-Star game and the Olympics this year. If Kelly wanted to be better, if he wanted to prove his brothers weren't the only ones with talent, maybe he *should* be more careful of who he associated with.

"Okay. I'll try to distance myself," he promised with a sigh.

"Good." Lindy smiled at him, and Kelly's internal temperature rose in a way that had nothing to do with the heat of the steam room.

God, he couldn't count the number of times he'd imagined dropping to his knees and crawling to Lindy. He'd pictured parting the towel and taking Lindy's cock into his mouth and getting him hard. He wanted it so bad his mouth watered and he shifted, realizing his dick was getting hard and he needed to stop thinking about it before he embarrassed himself.

They lapsed into silence and Kelly wiped at the sweat on his forehead, wondering how red he was. Lindy faintly glowed with sweat but Kelly was probably the color of a tomato. Which went so fucking well with his carroty red hair.

Supposedly, gingers were dying out of the population or something but the O'Shea family seemed to be determined to fix that. And the way Kelly's brothers were knocking up their wives, they were looking to create the first all-ginger hockey team in the NHL.

Kelly idly wondered what they'd call them. The Cleveland Carrots, maybe.

Nah, he couldn't picture the O'Shea brothers leaving the Boston area except in a body bag, so maybe the Charlestown Carrot Tops.

"What are you chuckling to yourself about there, Kelly?" Lindy asked, his voice slow and lazy like the heat of the sauna had done its job and relaxed him.

Kelly repeated his thoughts about his brothers and their future NHL team. Lindy chuckled. "Sounds about right."

"What about the Roslindale Redheads?" Lindy asked after a while and Kelly snorted.

"Southie Spitfires," he offered, and Lindy's laugh filled the air.

"I like that. I'll have to text it to your brothers in our group chat."

"Ugh. Leave me out of it. They'll find reasons to chirp me about not being in a relationship or something. Letting down the family honor by not spreading the O'Shea genes far and wide."

His words came out more bitterly than he'd intended.

"Is that why you don't date?"

Kelly blinked at him. "Um, because my family's on my case about it?"

Lindy nodded.

"Well, it doesn't help," Kelly admitted.

"But it's not the main reason?" Lindy shifted, the towel he wore around his waist parting to reveal a muscular thigh. The muscle was sprinkled with the same golden hair that covered his forearms and trailed down from his navel across the flat planes of his lower abs before disappearing under the edge of the towel.

"No." Kelly's heartrate picked up and he breathed shallowly, forcing himself to glance away before he made Lindy uncomfortable. "I, uh, it's complicated."

His smile was faint. "If you aren't ready to say it out loud, you don't have to. But you know *whatever* you tell me, it'll stay between us, right? I wouldn't spread your private confidences to anyone else."

Kelly swallowed hard and he licked his lips. "Why didn't *you* tell anyone you were bi until now?"

The words left Kelly's mouth before he could stop them. Before it hit him that asking that question was nearly the same as admitting he was, in fact, hiding something about his sexuality too. Then again, Lindy had been stone-cold sober last year when Kelly had humiliatingly begged him for a kiss. He was a smart man. He'd obviously put most of the pieces together already.

Lindy sighed. "Because for most of that time, I was married to the love of my life, and it seemed unimportant."

He reached up, almost absently, to touch his bare chest where the rings he wore on a chain usually rested. Metal got scaringly hot in the steam room but as far as Kelly knew, this was the only situation where he took the wedding bands and chain off.

"Was it unimportant for La Bouche to come out?" Kelly argued. "For Murphy and Hartinger and Coach and Gabriel, or Jamie when he said he was in love with Taylor?"

"Of course not," he protested. "I suppose it sounds hypocritical of me because being married to Astrid didn't make me any less bi, but I felt I wasn't the right choice to be the first in the league."

"Yeah, fair enough," Kelly said, considering the idea.

"But it's true I could have said something before now to the team." He looked at Kelly.

Kelly shrugged. "I don't want you to feel bad or anything. I was curious is all."

"I know." Lindy looked him in the eye. "And I'm not trying to make you feel obligated to say something, if you don't want to."

"I'm not bi," Kelly blurted out.

"No?" Neither Lindy's voice nor his gaze held any judgment, but Kelly still had to look away.

"No," he whispered. "I'm gay."

"Oh, Kelly." The soft sympathy in his voice made Kelly's chest hurt.

"Yeah." He scuffed his sandal along the floor of the steam room, nearly kicking the slide off. "I've never told anyone until now."

"I'm honored you told me."

"Why?" Kelly's eyes burned. "I'm not brave like the rest of you. I'm just a coward pretending to be something I'm not. I've lied to everyone for years."

He sniffled, trying to push away the encroaching emotions and he suddenly felt too hot all over, like his blood was boiling and his skin was going to melt off.

"I've—I've gotta go," he managed.

He stood, then fled out the door of the steam room and into the cool training room. He brushed past a startled athletic trainer on his way to go hide in the showers, small and ashamed of himself without knowing exactly why.

————

Anders remained in the steam room a little longer, knowing Kelly wouldn't want him to follow. He regretted pushing Kelly to admit anything about his sexuality. He'd only wanted to give him a safe space to do it, but he shouldn't have pressured him that way.

He'd never considered the idea that Kelly wasn't attracted to women at all. He'd played the part so well Anders had assumed the women he'd taken home with him were people he was genuinely interested in. Poor Kelly, feeling so much pressure to pretend to be someone he wasn't. That was a miserable way to live, though with guys like Jack Malone for friends, Anders couldn't blame him.

He had no doubt Kelly's family had played a part in that too. Coming out wouldn't be easy in a family of staunch Irish-American Catholics.

Anders didn't believe they'd be the type to shun Kelly but the nagging doubt about if they would accept him must be crippling. It would take a tremendous amount of courage for Kelly to risk their disapproval.

When Anders finally left the steam room, the locker room was empty of players and Kelly nowhere in sight.

Anders felt soft and relaxed as he rinsed the sweat from his skin, then patted dry. He dressed in workout clothes, then went to the fitness room to do some yoga. That was nearly deserted too. Gabriel Theriault was on a bike across the room. He held up a hand in greeting, though he didn't take out his earbuds.

Anders left him to it and walked to the mats. He took a deep breath, trying to quiet his mind while he flowed through a yoga sequence. He'd arrived this morning for video review, though he'd skipped the skate in favor of working with the trainer on some hip and knee stabilization workouts and the steam.

Anders liked doing yoga after, something gentle and restorative to increase his flexibility and wind down.

Anders went home after and ate, sitting alone at his large dining room table. He wondered if the melancholy inside him was because of his earlier conversation with Kelly. He thought about texting him, reaching for his phone half a dozen times to send a message, but decided against it every time.

Anders still wasn't sure what he should say and whatever it was, it was much better done in person.

Anders took his usual pre-game nap but was restless and unable to sleep. The bed felt too wide, the sheets rough on his skin, though they were high quality and usually very comfortable.

He still felt restless as he dressed for the game, something itching under his skin while he went through his routine.

Malone would be watching the game from the team box, clearly pissed off that for once he'd been held accountable for his actions. Underhill was angry at the fine he'd been given for fighting but he was at least playing that night.

Kelly was quieter than usual, not participating in the banter flying through the air.

Anders went through warmups like usual, and when it came time to line up, he and Kelly did their usual pre-game ritual.

Anders still didn't feel quite settled by the time they skated onto the ice and lined up for the national anthem.

As a Swede, he found the ceremony of it before every game odd, especially with so many international players, but North Americans did love the spectacle of their anthems.

Anders used the time to quiet his mind, lifting the rings he wore to his lips, quietly thinking of Astrid and the words she'd always spoken to him the morning of every game, whether he was on the road or at home.

"You can do this, Anders," she'd always told him. If they were together in person, she'd cup his cheeks in her palms and stare him straight in the eye. "You are a talented player and you are going to lead your team to victory. Now, go win me a game."

She'd end it with a butt slap like she was one of his teammates and he'd shake his head and kiss her like she wasn't.

Now, he felt the brush of Kelly's upper arm against his elbow, and he wondered what it would be like if he allowed himself to be with Kelly. What would it be like to merge his life with Kelly's until no separation existed between his team and his personal life?

The thought felt both tempting and alien and Anders felt a flash of guilt for thinking of someone other than his wife.

After the anthem ended, he gave the rings one final kiss, then tucked them safely beneath his jersey before he skated to take his place in the face-off.

Right now, there was no Astrid, no Kelly, no past or future.

Only the game ahead.

———

"You doing okay, Irish?" Gabriel Theriault asked after the game.

Anders looked up from the cuff he'd been buttoning in time to see their D-man drape an arm over Kelly's shoulders.

Kelly let out a tired sigh. "No. My head's not in it tonight, Frenchie."

Kelly hadn't had a great game. He hadn't played badly but he hadn't contributed much. Anders worried it was because of the conversation they'd had earlier. Had he pushed Kelly too hard? Had it interfered with his focus?

The team itself had done well tonight though. They'd won 4-1 against Arizona and those points would be crucial. Hopefully they could do as well against San Jose and L.A. in the next two days. They *had* to clinch a playoff spot. Anders hated the summers where they were knocked out early and he was without the routine of games, forced to occupy himself other ways for months on end.

Theriault continued. "Why don't we go out tonight and grab a bite together and talk about what's on your mind?"

Kelly blinked at him. "Don't you have plans with Coach?"

"Oh, I think he'll survive an evening without me, *non?*" Gabriel gave him a crooked, captivating smile.

It hit Anders then how good-looking Gabriel was, how charming. Something flared within Anders, the sight of their teammate so casually touching Kelly making irritation rise in him.

"Yeah, I guess you guys do live and work together, huh?" Kelly commented. "I'm surprised you don't get sick of each other."

"We balance each other in many ways."

"Must be nice."

"*Oui.* But we can talk more about this at dinner. Go finish getting ready, Irish, and I'll meet you here in twenty." He tapped Kelly's flank, nudging him toward the showers. Kelly had dawdled in the weight room, spending more time on the bike for his cooldown than usual tonight.

"Yeah, okay." Kelly slipped his feet into his slides, then disappeared into the wet room.

Anders slowly finished packing his bag, trying not to think too much about why he felt so off-kilter.

On his way out of the locker room, Gabriel stopped him. "A moment, Lindholm?"

Anders paused, allowing Gabriel to tug him into the hallway where they'd have some privacy.

Anders frowned. "Everything okay?"

"I was about to ask you the same thing. You looked concerned earlier."

"Me?" Anders blinked at him.

"Concerned about O'Shea, maybe?"

"Ahh. Yes, well, I can't help but worry about him given the situation he found himself in the other night." Anders tweaked his shirt cuff where it bunched under his suit jacket.

"He's a good kid."

"He is," Anders agreed, although something in him bristled at the idea of Kelly being called a kid. He wasn't. He was young, yes, but he wasn't a child.

"I thought I'd take him out tonight. Get him to talk." Gabriel let out a quiet laugh. "I've tried to mentor him on-ice and I thought I might do the same off it."

"That's kind of you."

Gabriel shrugged, the gesture as eloquent as any words. "No one who knew me in Toronto would believe I did anything out of the goodness of my heart." He let out another laugh, this time far more self-deprecating. "No one would have believed I was trying to be a good influence."

"You are though," Anders insisted. Whatever his earlier irritation had been about, Anders could see that this would be a good thing for Kelly. Someone like Gabriel who had gone down a path he didn't like and changed his life was exactly who Kelly needed to talk to. "Kelly gets touchy about me offering advice, so it's good he has someone else to turn to."

Gabriel leaned against the wall, casual despite his well-tailored suit, shirt open at the throat, tie forgone. "Why is that?"

"I'm friends with his brothers," Anders said with a sigh. "He thinks I'm only doing it because they want me to."

Gabriel's glance was searching. "Ahh. And why *are* you doing it?"

"I care for Kelly. He's a good teammate and friend."

"Is that all though?" Gabriel probed and Anders could only shrug helplessly.

That was the question, wasn't it?

CHAPTER EIGHT

The San Jose game two days later was chippy from the start.

Anders won the initial face-off and after that no one was in a mood to play nice. Both teams racked up penalties like they were going out of style, and they'd barely get a play going before the refs were blowing their whistles again.

Anders rarely had penalties called on him—he was more of a finesse player than an agitator—but even *he* spent two minutes cooling his heels in the penalty box after an elbowing call, tired of the way the San Jose player kept trying to trip him.

Their opponents were relentless throughout the first period and the game was tied 1-1 as the final minutes of the period ticked down.

Anders finally managed to get the puck away from one of San Jose's defensemen and shot it to Murphy. Anders skated past the neutral zone, building speed as he entered the offensive zone. Murphy shot to Theriault, who tipped the puck back to Anders. He shifted his weight to fire it off through the slot and his skate went out from under him.

A bolt of pain shot through his ankle. He went down, swearing as he slid across the ice toward the boards, too fast to stop. Instinctively, he covered his helmet with his arms and twisted, barely managing to hit with his shoulder instead of headfirst.

It was a tooth-rattling collision and he groaned and lay on the ice a moment, trying to gather his thoughts and assess how bad it was.

"Anders!" Kelly shouted, on his knees beside him. "Talk to me."

"I'm fine, Kelly," he managed through gritted teeth. He got to his hands and knees, head hanging low as he breathed through the pain. His shoulder smarted and he could feel a headache forming but it was his ankle he was most concerned with.

"What did you hit?" Kelly carefully patted his back, as if checking him for injuries. "Is your head okay?"

"Head's fine. It's my ankle." It hurt like the devil.

He lifted his head to see Kirk, their head trainer, hurrying toward him. Anders' teammates circled them, staring at him with worried frowns.

"You lost a blade," Kelly explained, his brown eyes filled with concern.

"Well, that explains why I lost my edge," Anders said with a sigh. "Okay, help me up."

Kirk did a quick evaluation before he and Kelly helped Anders to his feet. With their assistance Anders gritted his teeth and skated off the ice on one foot.

The assistant trainer, Cameron, took over from Kelly, and along with Kirk, both trainers urged Anders through the tunnel. When Anders finally made it to the table inside the training room, his head swam with pain radiating from his shoulder and neck, his ankle throbbing in time with his heartbeat.

Dr. Gardner stepped into the training room, brow furrowed. "Do you need a minute?"

Anders nodded, wincing when the pull in his neck and shoulder made his headache intensify. He unstrapped his helmet and set it aside but after he had a moment to pull himself together, he glanced at the doctor.

"Okay. What do you need to know?"

Dr. Gardner crossed his arms, squinting as he looked Anders over. "Tell me what you're feeling."

"My ankle got tweaked when the blade came loose and I went down," he admitted. "I don't think it's a severe sprain but it's hard to tell."

"Okay, let's get the skate off and take a look."

Cameron crouched to loosen Anders' laces as Dr. Gardner stared intently at him, gaze sharp and assessing. "What about your head?"

"I didn't hit my head," he said automatically.

"Are you sure?" Kirk asked doubtfully. "It was hard to see from the bench—there were too many guys screening you—but it looked like you might have."

"It was my shoulder. The pain is radiating from there. I definitely tweaked something in my neck too. It's incredibly tight and making my head throb."

Dr. Gardner gave him an unimpressed look. "Are you *sure* you didn't lose consciousness?"

"As sure as I can be," Anders promised him.

"Hmm."

"Honestly, I had my arms up to cover my head. I hit here." He twisted to indicate the spot below his deltoid muscle, hissing in discomfort as the motion pulled at something sore toward his shoulder blade. "Everything from there on up is tight and strained."

"Okay. Well, that's encouraging but we're still going to have to do a full eval, Anders," Kirk said quietly. "If there's any chance you took a head hit …"

"I understand." Anders sighed. He didn't want to be out for the rest of the game when the team needed him but there was nothing he could do about it. Post-concussion syndrome was too serious to risk and his ankle might not be in any shape for him to skate anyway. "I'll do whatever you think is best."

Kelly and Murphy poked their heads in to check on him during intermission but Anders waved them away.

"Focus on the game, I'll be fine," he assured them. "Score some points for me, okay?"

Anders thought momentarily about his distraction during his pre-puck-drop ritual again tonight. For the past two games, he'd been unable to clear his head and think of Astrid like usual. Had his thoughts about Kelly somehow messed with his usual routine? Had that impacted his game?

He didn't want to think so but it was impossible to not let superstitious thoughts creep in.

Anders went through the testing with as much patience as he could manage, gritting his teeth through Dr. Gardner's assessment of his head. There was also an X-ray for his ankle, along with icing and splinting it. His shoulder had to be iced and worked on too and by the time he'd been cleared to go home, he was exhausted.

The game was over—they'd won, thankfully—and several of his teammates and coaching staff stood nearby, waiting to hear the results.

"Okay," Dr. Gardner said once he made sure Anders was fine with them hearing the verdict. "All things considered, you're in pretty good shape, Anders. It looks like a mild high ankle sprain. You're out for a week minimum. Thankfully, everything looks fine with your head. After reviewing the tape, it does appear you hit with your shoulder. Keep ice on that and your ankle over the next 24-hours and get some rest. Come in tomorrow and I'll do an evaluation and see how you're progressing. If anything worsens with your head, I want you to notify me immediately. Sometimes these things *can* crop up later—"

"I promise I will let you know if anything changes," Anders said with a relieved sigh. He reached for the crutches they'd given him. He rose to his feet, all his weight on his uninjured ankle.

"I'd prefer if someone could keep an eye on you overnight."

Anders tried not to let his irritation show on his face. "You said it yourself. I didn't hit my head."

"There could still have been a rebound—"

"I'm fine," Anders insisted.

Dr. Gardner huffed. "Just like every other tough guy out there. An abundance of caution is worth it. The team would rather have our top line center out for a week now than during the entire playoff run because he didn't take care of himself."

If the team didn't score more in the next few weeks, there wouldn't *be* a playoff run, Anders thought but he bit his tongue. "I'll be careful," he promised.

"Is there someone who can keep an eye on you tonight?"

Kelly stepped forward and looked Anders in the eye. "I will."

"You don't have to—" Anders protested.

"I offered. You need someone to look out for you overnight." The stubborn set of Kelly's jaw told Anders there was no use in arguing.

Frankly, Anders wasn't sure if it he had it in him to pull together a convincing case against it. His head throbbed from the tweak to his neck while he waited for the painkillers and anti-inflammatory they'd given him to kick in.

He swallowed and nodded. "That's kind of you, Kelly."

"It's what you would do for me, and we both know it."

———

Kelly tried not to hover as he followed Anders into the elevator in his building. Anders wasn't wobbly or anything on the crutches but it still made Kelly nervous. Anders *seemed* clear-headed but Kelly worried the trainers and team doctor had been wrong.

"You don't *have* to do this, Kelly," Anders said a few minutes later as they stepped inside his condo.

"Uh, pretty sure I do," Kelly argued. God, Anders could be so damn stubborn. It drove him nuts.

"No, you don't. I'll be—"

"Last fall, did you or did you not sit in my hotel room all night to make sure I didn't choke on my own vomit in my sleep?"

"Yes." Anders sounded almost resigned.

"Then I can look out for you tonight."

"I'll be fine. I didn't black out or lose memory—"

"If Dr. Gardner wants someone with you overnight, I'm going to stay with you overnight," Kelly said mulishly. Okay, maybe Anders wasn't the only stubborn one around here. "Besides, you need to stay off that ankle anyway."

"I can manage—"

"But you don't have to. Jesus, Anders, do you not want to wake up in the morning or something?" Kelly snapped.

"Of course that's not it," Anders snarled. But his refusal to look Kelly in the eye triggered an alarm.

Kelly stepped closer, worry pooling cold in his gut. "Seriously. I'm not talking about the hit to the head. Have you ever—"

"I'd never harm myself, Kelly. I promise." Anders closed his eyes a moment, drawing in a ragged breath. "But yes, there were some days where I gladly would have not woken up. If you must know, I've wished I'd died when my family did."

Kelly's throat was too thick to speak so he reached out and grasped Anders' bicep. "If it helps, I'm glad you're still here," he finally whispered.

"It does help." Anders seemed to soften. "And if you … if you want to stay tonight, I'd be grateful. I'm not good at accepting help but sometimes I do hate being here alone."

"Why do you think I have a roommate?" Kelly asked, stepping away, the intimate moment coming to a close more quickly than he'd like. "I could afford to live alone but I didn't like it. I tried it for like six months when I joined the team, remember?"

"I'd forgotten," Anders said slowly.

"Well, I'm not surprised. I got a roommate right after—"

Kelly didn't finish the thought but they both knew what time he was talking about. There was only before the accident and after.

"Anyway. I hated it so I asked Trev if he wanted to move in with me. I was fucking psyched when he said yes." Kelly shrugged. "You could think about getting a roommate or something, maybe. You could always take in a rookie."

"No young guy is going to want to live with someone so uptight and boring," Anders scoffed.

"You might be surprised," Kelly said lightly.

"Are you offering?"

Anders' words came out surprisingly flirtatious sounding and they both stared at each other a beat too long before Kelly cleared his throat. "Well, for a few days."

Because as tempting as the thought of moving in with Anders was, even if he was serious, Kelly could never do it. It would be torture to live in the same place and see Anders first thing in the morning before he'd drank his cup of coffee or sleepily turning off the lights before bed.

It would only make Kelly want Anders *more*.

What Kelly wanted was to be the one tucked into the bed beside Anders. The one who woke him with soft morning kisses and went to bed with the beat of Anders' heart against his ear but that wasn't going to happen so he might as well be smart about it.

Kelly swallowed and stepped back. "Okay, you should be sitting. Couch good for now?"

"Sure."

Kelly got Anders settled on the couch, then dragged a soft leather ottoman over so he could prop up his ankle, then handed him the TV remote. "Are you hungry?"

"Not particularly but I should eat."

"Want me to grab one of your prepared meals?"

"Yes, that would be good. You're welcome to help yourself to one too."

"Okay. Thanks."

Kelly heated the food, then carried their plates into the living room. He found Anders staring at the blank TV, sitting in silence, his forehead furrowed.

"Here's your dinner," Kelly held out a plate tentatively. Anders blinked and took it from him with a quiet murmur of thanks.

Once Kelly was comfortable, he picked up the clicker.

"Game?" he offered.

Anders winced. "Honestly, I'd rather not. I'm not in the mood at the moment."

"Okay. Want me to find something else to put on?"

"Sure." Anders smiled at him. "I have some documentaries queued up. There are a few you might like."

"Awesome. Thanks." Kelly scrolled through the offerings before spotting one he'd been dying to watch.

"Ooh," he said, excited by the sight of the American Revolutionary War documentary. "Can we watch this one? It's supposed to be wicked good."

"Of course."

Kelly pressed Play and they lapsed into silence as they ate and watched. It didn't take long before Anders had a question about something—he'd been living in the US for two decades and was knowledgeable about the country's history but there were still some gaps sometimes—and Kelly was happy to explain.

A little while later, Anders compared what they'd said on screen to something in Swedish naval history and they nerded out for a few minutes about battleships.

"Did you tour the *U.S.S. Constitution* while you were in Boston?" Kelly asked excitedly.

It was the world's oldest commissioned warship, launched in the late 1800s. Kelly had gone a couple of times growing up and he knew Anders would enjoy it.

"No, I've heard of it but I never made it there."

"Oh, I should totally take you when you're in Boston this summer."

Anders smiled at him. "I'd like that."

Anders usually flew from Chicago to Boston at the end of the season and spent a few weeks there catching up with friends before flying to Stockholm to visit family for the remainder of the summer. Sometimes he took shorter trips around Europe with friends from home during the off-season too. Kelly had always been a little envious.

"There are some things I'd like to show you in Sweden, if you want to visit," Anders added.

Kelly looked at him in surprise. He'd never offered *that* before. "Sure. I'd love to, honestly. Let me know when you want me there. I don't usually do much anyway so I'm flexible."

Kelly often spent his summers hanging around Evanston, although he and Trevor usually flew to Miami and spent some time deep-sea fishing before he let his mom badger him into spending a few weeks in Boston. This year he'd need to buckle down for training too. He'd already committed to working out with a trainer and a skills coach Theriault had lined up.

"Absolutely," Anders promised. "Let me figure out some dates and I'll let you know."

Kelly ducked his head and smiled. Anders would undoubtedly create a detailed itinerary for their trip that included historical sites *and* intensive training. Because that was the kind of guy he was.

Kelly didn't mind. He didn't mind Anders being organized and in charge of things because sometimes Kelly kinda felt like a hot mess. It would be a relief to have someone else tell him what to do.

Just as long as it wasn't his fucking family.

After they'd eaten, Kelly paused the documentary, then stood. He cleared the remnants of their meal, knowing it would bug Anders if he didn't, and Kelly didn't want him to try to get up and take care of it himself.

"Want some water?" he asked on the way to the kitchen.

"Please."

After he'd tidied the kitchen and grabbed water, he snagged an ice pack and took a detour to the bathroom for the wrap he'd seen Anders use before.

In the living room, Kelly set the water bottles on the coffee table and slipped the ice pack into the soft wrap. Anders looked surprised as Kelly held it out. "Want this?"

"Thanks. I should ice my ankle again. I didn't want to be a bother though."

"Dude, that's what I'm here for," Kelly said. "Bother me all you want."

"I'll try to remember."

"It's just a mild sprain, right?" Kelly asked. He carefully perched on the ottoman next to Anders' feet.

"The trainers think so. You know ankles can be tricky though."

Kelly gently settled the cold pack in place and secured it with Velcro. "They can. But I'm sure you'll be healed in a week or so."

Anders groaned. "I don't want to think about being off the ice so long."

"Better than being gone like Underhill was," Kelly said absently.

He stared at Anders' feet.

Huh.

They were really nice actually. Kelly wasn't like *into* feet or anything but Anders' were nicely shaped and surprisingly un-gross for an athlete. Kelly glanced up, ready to chirp Anders about getting pedicures, but he paused when Anders grimaced.

"I can't contemplate being out for most of the regular season. Half of me is afraid …"

"Afraid of what?" Kelly prompted when he didn't finish.

"Afraid this will be the end for me," he said quietly.

"Oh, no." Kelly rested a hand on Anders' shin. He'd worn shorts home, so his skin was bare, the hair under Kelly's palm soft, the muscle firm. "No, God, this *isn't* the end of your career."

"Something will be someday." Anders' mouth twisted at the corner. "And it'll be sooner rather than later, Kelly. I can't play forever."

"You're going to beat league records for career length, and we all know it," Kelly said loyally, but Anders was right.

Kelly felt hollow inside as he imagined being on the ice without Anders, but Anders was thirty-nine years old. Eventually it *would* happen.

Anders managed a weak smile in response. Kelly patted his shin again, double-checked the ice pack, then stood. "Need anything else while I'm up?"

"No. Stop fussing."

"I like fussing over you," Kelly retorted before he could stop himself. His ears turned hot when he thought about what he'd said but he caught a glimpse of Anders' small smile when he took a seat beside him again.

Kelly hit Play on the documentary and things returned to normal.

By the time it was over, they were both yawning. Kelly helped Anders to his feet and handed him his crutches.

"I hate these," he grumbled.

"Well, they probably don't like being jammed into your armpits either but you need them."

He followed Anders out of the room, turned off the lights, checked that the front door was locked, then retrieved the bag he usually carted back and forth to the practice facility. He kept a change of clothes and a toothbrush and stuff in there and it sometimes came in handy if he was out late and crashed at one of his teammates' places.

He caught up with Anders in the hall since he moved so slow.

Anders turned to look at him. "Thank you. Tonight was nice. I ... I liked having the company."

"It doesn't just have to be when it's a bad day or whatever, you know?" Kelly offered. "I mean, if you want, I'm cool with hanging out and doing this whenever."

"I'll keep that in mind," was all Anders said, but he smiled, and Kelly's heart skipped a beat.

He would swear something had felt different between them lately.

CHAPTER NINE

"Did you need something?" Anders asked, confused when Kelly followed him into his bedroom.

There was a guest room across the hall and Kelly had crashed there two years ago, after the housewarming party the guys had bullied him into hosting. Anders hadn't minded their pushiness, but he never would have held one otherwise.

"No." Kelly stared blankly. "I'm going to nap on the chair there so I'm close if you need anything."

"There's no need," Anders protested. The chair was large and comfortable—if mostly unused these days, since he had no one to watch get ready for bed at night—but it wouldn't be good for Kelly to sleep sitting up. "If you're that concerned, we can both leave our doors open so you'll hear me if I need anything, but I promise, I'm *fine*, Kelly."

"I promised I'd keep an eye on you," he said stubbornly.

Anders suppressed a sigh. He was tired and he wasn't in the mood to argue with Kelly right now.

"There's no reason for you to lose an entire night's sleep and feel like shit in the morning," he pointed out. "The team needs you fresh right now more than ever."

"I'm not budging on this, Anders." Kelly's gaze was sharp, his voice firm.

"Fine. Then sleep in my bed."

Kelly let out a surprised squeak, blinking a moment. "With *you?*"

"Well, *I'm* not sleeping in the chair," Anders said, a touch of irritation bleeding through. "So yes. We'll both sleep better and you'll be right there if I *do* need something."

Kelly's cheeks filled with color, and he opened his mouth but nothing came out.

Guiltily, Anders realized how the offer had probably sounded and that he was being a horrible tease inviting Kelly into his bed. But he was exhausted, his ankle had begun to throb again, and he still had a low-level headache threatening to make him snappish if he didn't get horizontal soon.

"We're teammates, Kelly," he said gently. "It's no big deal. If you'd prefer not to, that's your choice, but there's plenty of room for both of us. Just don't kick my ankle in my sleep and we'll be fine."

He limped to the bathroom door on crutches to brush his teeth and wash his face.

Anders wondered what Astrid would say about this situation and almost smiled. Knowing her, she'd find it hilarious. Not the idea of him being injured but ending up in bed with Kelly because both of them were too stubborn to give in.

He could hear her saying, "You brought this on yourself, *älskling*," with a smug smile, her blue eyes dancing with amusement.

"I suppose I did," he said under his breath. He used the toilet and when he could no longer delay it any longer, he went into the bedroom again.

He'd half-hoped maybe Kelly would have changed his mind but he was still there. He'd changed into team-branded shorts and a T-shirt, but he perched awkwardly on the edge of the bed like he wasn't sure what to do next.

"You're welcome to use anything in the bathroom you need," Anders offered. "The shelves next to the shower have toiletries and towels. Help yourself."

"Thanks." Kelly fled for the bathroom and Anders hobbled more slowly to the walk-in closet.

He managed to change into shorts on his own, suddenly grateful for the amount of time he spent in tree pose. Yoga came in handy for more than flexibility and mental discipline on the ice.

Still, exhaustion was setting in and he was nearly ready to collapse by the time he returned to the empty bedroom.

He leaned his crutches against the wall by the bedside table, hopped to the bed on one foot, then got into it with a relieved groan. He went through his usual nightly routine of plugging in his phone and getting out a book to wind down with, but he felt oddly fidgety as he stared at the pages.

The words swam in front of his eyes, and he knew if he told Kelly, he'd worry it was because Anders was concussed but he *wasn't*. It was the thought of sharing a bed with someone.

When Anders had blurted out the suggestion they share a bed, he hadn't considered how intimate it was to sleep next to someone but it had been *so long*.

These days he only shared a bed with ghosts.

Anders stared blankly at the first page until the bathroom door opened.

He looked up when Kelly approached the bed. When he hesitated next to it, expression uncertain, Anders took a deep breath and pulled back the covers on Kelly's side. "Well, get in then."

Kelly's cheeks were flushed as he slid into the bed but he didn't argue.

Anders belatedly wondered if he should have worn a shirt but it was too late to get one now without making the situation more awkward. He set his book aside, still not sure if it was one written in Swedish or English.

Kelly fiddled with his phone a moment, then turned it face down. "I can sleep whenever you're ready."

A twist of Anders' wrist turned off the light, plunging the room into darkness and his heart rate picked up. He shifted to lie flat on his back, trying to find a comfortable position. "Goodnight, Kelly."

"Night, Anders."

Kelly flipped onto his side, facing away. He lay quiet and still but Anders felt restless. His head still hurt, radiating from his strained neck. The exhaustion was bone-deep but an odd energy coursed through him too.

He often had trouble falling asleep but this was different than usual.

Anders shifted, trying to find a comfortable position but it made his ankle twinge and he forced himself to lie still, not wanting to disturb Kelly.

He lay there a long time, muscles screaming to move, his head whirring with too many thoughts for him to pin down. Eventually, he twitched, unable to hold still any longer. He shifted, which helped a little, but the rustle of sheets next to him indicated Kelly was awake too.

"Can't sleep?" Kelly said quietly.

"No." Anders sighed. "I'm sorry. This was probably a bad idea."

"Need something for your ankle?"

"No. I took my meds earlier. Sorry I'm keeping you awake."

"It's okay. Better than sleeping in the chair for sure."

In the dark, Anders smiled.

He was all too aware of Kelly beside him and the heat from his body. The slow, almost silent rasp of his breath.

"It often takes me a while to fall asleep," Anders admitted.

"Can I try something?" Kelly asked, flipping onto his side to face him.

Anders hesitated. What exactly did Kelly have in mind?

"It's not … I'm not suggesting …" Kelly sucked in a deep breath. "It's something my mom did for me when I was little and couldn't sleep."

"Okay." Anders' smile widened. "Do you need me to move?"

"Nope." Kelly reached out, gently settling his fingertips on Anders' forehead. "Just let me do, um. This."

Anders tensed.

Kelly paused for a second, but Anders forced himself to take a breath, then another until he relaxed, and Kelly moved again.

Kelly started at the center of Anders' forehead, gently swirling his fingertips toward his temple before returning to the center.

Anders' lashes fluttered closed. God, it had been so long since anyone had *touched* him in a way that didn't have to do with hockey. This wasn't the impersonal healing touch of a massage therapist or trainer. It wasn't a bro hug from Murphy or a slap on the butt from Hartinger.

Kelly's touch was personal. Private. Platonic but still *intimate.*

Anders hadn't noticed how much he ached for that. Hadn't realized how much loneliness had settled into his bones and taken up root.

He could easily picture Catherine O'Shea doing this for a small restless child like Kelly.

Slowly the tension faded from Anders' shoulders, and he let out a sigh, softening against Kelly's touch, the headache that had been nagging him all night fading into nothing.

"Good?" Kelly whispered and Anders hummed his agreement, too relaxed to speak aloud.

Kelly scooted closer, moving his fingertips to the other side of his forehead and Anders could feel the warmth of Kelly's arm where it gently rested against his chest.

Anders' eyelids were heavy and he blinked, feeling a bit like he was underwater. He fought sleep for a moment before he realized he didn't have to and he let out a sigh, eyes slipping closed for a final time.

Kelly let out a soft sound of approval, but he didn't stop his gentle motions and Anders sank into sleep, letting it take him into its arms, warm and sweet.

CHAPTER TEN

Kelly awoke in the morning to the vibration of his phone, his head on Lindy's shoulder, Lindy's arm curved around him, hand splayed against his back, their chests plastered together, Kelly's left leg thrown over one of his thighs.

It hit Kelly that he'd slept in Lindy's bed last night and had attached himself to his teammate like some sort of obnoxious, clingy squid or something.

He gently disentangled himself, then rolled over to grab the phone still vibrating on the nightstand.

As Kelly silenced the alarm, Lindy let out a grumbling noise and flipped on his side, spooning around Kelly. He buried his nose against the back of Kelly's neck, his warm breath sending a shiver down Kelly's spine that lit his body from the inside out.

Kelly closed his eyes, soaking in the sensation for a moment. Helping Anders relax and fall sleep last night had made him feel so good. And waking up like this was everything he'd ever dreamed about.

God, Kelly was tempted to lie here like this all morning, wrapped in Lindy's arms, enjoying the feel of being held tight.

He'd drunkenly crashed in plenty of beds with teammates before and accidental cuddling wasn't unusual, but he'd never spent the night with a guy he wanted before. And to be in *Lindy's* bed …

Kelly closed his eyes, his phone still clutched in his hand. He needed to move, needed to wake Lindy. It was the responsible thing to do. He was here to look out for him, not to act like a creep.

But it was painful to think about prying himself out of Lindy's arms and pretending like it didn't mean something to him.

"Lindy?" he croaked.

But he sighed, his arm curving around Kelly's chest and pulled their bodies more tightly together, his pelvis cradled against Kelly's ass.

Anders was *hard*.

Kelly's skin went hot all over at the feel of an erection pressed against his cheeks, the insistent nudge of it making Kelly achingly aroused too. Without thinking, Kelly ground against him and Lindy let out a sleepy sound of pleasure.

Kelly groaned quietly, gripping his phone so hard the edges bit into his palm.

This was *torture*.

The best kind of torture ever but still torture because nothing felt better than this and if he didn't put a stop to it, he would be no better than Malone, groping someone who didn't want it.

The thought of Jack Malone was a cold bucket of water over his arousal, and Kelly gently shook Lindy's arm.

"Lindy," he hissed. *"Anders."*

He jerked awake, swearing softly under his breath in what Kelly assumed was Swedish.

"I'm sorry, Kelly." Lindy loosened his grip immediately, rolling away. "I—that shouldn't have happened."

"It's uh, okay," Kelly said, dying a little inside, already missing the warmth of Lindy's arms and their bodies pressed tightly together.

"I shouldn't have taken advantage of the situation," Lindy said stiffly.

Kelly tossed his phone on the nightstand, then rolled to squint in the dim bedroom, the heavy curtains blocking out most of the morning light. *"You* didn't take advantage of anything. *I* did."

Lindy let out a heavy sigh and rubbed a hand over his face. "Let's forget it happened, okay, Kelly?"

"Sure, okay," Kelly said slowly. He sat up. "How are you feeling?"

Lindy shrugged. "Achy. Stiff. The headache is gone though."

"No nausea?"

"No." Lindy pushed back the covers and hopped on one foot until he reached his crutches.

Kelly stared at his broad back, grimacing at the nasty bruise forming between his left shoulder blade and armpit, Kinesio tape running across his shoulder and neck.

He walked slowly toward the bathroom, and Kelly looked him over carefully. He didn't seem weak or clumsy and Kelly hadn't noticed any slurred speech or confusion. He seemed clear and alert, just tired and grumpy. But maybe it was embarrassment over the position Kelly had put them in.

Before Lindy disappeared into the bathroom, shutting the door behind him, Kelly caught a glimpse of his cock pushing at the fabric of his shorts. *Oh.* Well, that hadn't gone down as quickly as Kelly would have expected if it had been sleepy confusion about who he pressed against.

What if Lindy *did* want him? Not any warm body but Kelly himself?

Kelly's heartrate spiked suddenly as the idea hit him. What if he'd been wrong? What if Anders wasn't indifferent to Kelly?

What if he was attracted to him, just not sure how to move on from Astrid? Or what if it was that he was worried about what Kelly's brothers would say? What if he was afraid of hurting Kelly?

There were a thousand reasons he might be afraid to give in to his feelings, but that didn't mean he didn't have them.

What if one of those reasons Anders hadn't said or done anything was because he wasn't sure if Kelly was still interested or he didn't know how to change things between them?

Hmm.

Kelly clicked on the light, then got out of bed and yanked open the curtains to let sunlight flood the room, a plan beginning to form in his head.

He'd never seduced anyone in his life but there was no reason not to start now.

After Anders used the bathroom and changed into comfortable clothes, Kelly insisted he get into bed, ignoring Anders' protests that he wasn't an invalid.

"Dr. Gardner told you to rest," he said. "So, you're going to rest."

Kelly practically pushed him into bed, propped several cushions behind his back, handed him his book, then went off to shower.

The book was the one Anders had unsuccessfully tried to read last night. This morning had gone better. It turned out the thriller was in Swedish.

He didn't read the genre often, but his mother was partial to them, and she often sent her favorites to him. It gave them something to talk about—she wasn't a huge hockey fan and he had little else going on in his life these days—so he made a point to read the ones she sent.

They were good escapism at least.

Anders glanced up from the pages when the bathroom door opened. Kelly walked out wearing a towel wrapped low around his waist, his red hair darkened from the water.

His body was milk-pale, sprinkled with cinnamon-colored freckles. Anders idly thought of *risgrynsgröt* and wondered if Kelly would taste as sweet as rice pudding on his tongue.

Unexpected warmth hit low in Anders' stomach, crawling up his body until he felt flushed all over. Thankfully, it wouldn't show. He wasn't prone to blushing. But it made him think of how intimate their embrace had been this morning.

How good it had felt to wake with a warm body pressed against his.

Kelly smiled at Anders as he reached for his duffel. "Whoops. Realized I forgot my clothes in here."

"If there's anything you need, feel free to help yourself to anything of mine," Anders said, though most of what he owned would swim on Kelly's smaller frame.

He tried to focus on Kelly's face and shoulders rather than tracking lower but there was something so appealing about the slope of his shoulders and the way water glistened along his collarbone. He was tightly muscled, the delineation between his pecs and upper and lower abdominals defined without being bulky.

"Thanks." Kelly flashed him another brief smile before he turned to go.

Anders dropped his gaze to the page again, desperately trying to return his attention to the story but when he didn't hear the bathroom door close, he glanced up. It was most of the way shut, like Kelly had pushed it closed but it hadn't latched and had popped open a little. The gap allowed Anders an uninterrupted glimpse into the bathroom.

From the bed, he could see a section of marble counter and the mirror framed in black metal hanging on the wall behind it. Kelly stepped into view, pacing while he brushed his teeth, humming under his breath.

Anders watched him for a moment, looking away when Kelly bent over to spit and rinse his toothbrush, the towel slipping lower.

Kelly disappeared from view again, then reappeared to fuss with his hair in the mirror. The towel sank lower on his hips, until Anders could see the hint of the cleft between his cheeks before the fabric slithered to the tile floor in a puddle.

Under any other circumstance, Anders might have been annoyed at his towel being on the floor but he was too transfixed by the sight of Kelly's body.

In the locker room, Anders saw Kelly undressed all the time, but in this very different context, it took on a whole new meaning.

Anders didn't look at Kelly and scan his body for injuries or vaguely note his increased muscular definition the way he did at the arena.

No, the way he looked at him now was *personal*. Private and intimate. There was nothing appropriate about watching Kelly this way, but Anders couldn't stop himself. Couldn't drag his gaze away from the sight of Kelly's ass. It was small but perfect, high and tightly muscled. As incredible as Anders could have imagined.

Anders held his breath as Kelly bent to retrieve the towel and only resumed breathing when he disappeared from view completely.

Surely, he'd get dressed now.

But Kelly was still nude when he walked into view, carrying his duffel. He set it on the vanity counter and rooted through it, apparently in no hurry to put on clothes, totally unaware he put on an unintentional show.

If Anders was a better man, he'd close his eyes or shut the door for him. He'd do something other than stare, breath caught in his throat, heart beating too fast.

He wasn't.

Kelly straightened, underwear clutched in his fist as he let out a triumphant noise, just loud enough to carry into the bedroom.

Kelly dragged the fabric on with a shimmy of his hips, then reached for his bag again.

It fell to the floor too and Anders' breathing went shallow when Kelly bent nearly in half to retrieve something from it. The thin gray boxer briefs he wore now were almost worse than when he was naked, drawing Anders' attention to the spot where Kelly's thigh curved to become his ass.

Suddenly aware of the hot pulse of blood in his cock, Anders shifted on the bed, drawing his uninjured leg up to hide the jut of his erection under the thin sheet.

What was he *doing*? He shouldn't be looking at Kelly this way.

Anders looked down, blindly staring at the book, the heavy, insistent need in his groin making his breath go ragged. He fought to get himself under control. He'd never thought of himself as the sort of man who was led around by his dick. He was thoughtful, measured. He made decisions based on what he knew was right, not what he wanted.

But right now, he didn't trust himself at all.

"Good book?" Kelly asked a few minutes later.

Anders jerked, blinking stupidly. "Yes, very good," he managed, his voice strained.

He was thankful when Kelly didn't ask what the story was about because in that moment, he couldn't have answered to save his life or anyone else's.

———

"So, how's the ankle feeling?" Kelly took a seat at the foot of the bed, reaching for the edge of the sheet to pull it away from

Anders' feet, but Anders slapped a hand onto the covers, barking out, "leave it" in a tone that made Kelly freeze.

"Uh, okay," Kelly said, baffled.

Anders cleared his throat. "My ankle is fine."

"I wanted to check for swelling."

A strange look crossed Anders' face and Kelly frowned. "Are you *sure* you're okay?" he asked doubtfully. "Is your head bothering you now or something?"

"No. It's *fine*. Can you give me space while I get ready?"

Kelly's frown deepened. Anders looked oddly rattled ... Kelly blinked, wondering if his show in the bathroom had worked. But if it had, was Anders upset by what Kelly had done? Had he crossed a line and made him uncomfortable?

Kelly swallowed hard. Shit, what if this had backfired completely?

"Do you need some help getting up?" Kelly rose to his feet, reaching for the crutches.

"No. Leave it," Anders barked.

Kelly held up his hands. He'd never seen Anders like this. He was passionate in a game but Kelly had never known him to fight and he rarely raised his voice, except to argue about a ref's call he disagreed with.

"Jesus. I'm sorry. I didn't mean to bug you. I'll uh, go in the kitchen if you want."

"I'm sorry, Kelly. I didn't mean to snap. I would like a few minutes alone though, please," Anders said, rubbing at his forehead. His voice sounded more normal now but he wouldn't meet Kelly's gaze.

"Sure. I'll um, leave you to it," Kelly said, fleeing with a final concerned look at his teammate.

CHAPTER ELEVEN

After the bedroom door closed behind Kelly, Anders threw back the covers. He cupped his erection in his hand, sliding his palm along the hot, hard length. He let out a quiet groan of desperation at the sensation, his skin oversensitive and tingling.

Kelly was going to kill him.

Anders wasn't surprised Kelly was so casual about his nudity. He'd yet to meet a hockey player with much modesty, but Anders had never expected to react so strongly to the sight of Kelly nude in his bathroom.

Anders closed his eyes for a moment, trying to will his erection away, but all he could see behind his eyelids was the smooth curve of Kelly's back and the quick glimpse of his pink cock, nestled in a bed of soft red hair.

With a groan, Anders got out of bed and hobbled to the bathroom. With the assistance of some cool water, he eventually managed to get himself under control.

When he could think rationally again, he was pleasantly surprised to see Kelly had cleaned up after himself. There were no toothpaste splatters on the mirrors, and his toiletries were tucked away in a kit, not scattered across the counter. The towel had been hung to dry, and Kelly draped the shower mat over the lower rung of the heated rack.

Anders had seen Kelly's hotel rooms too many times to think Kelly was naturally a neat and tidy person.

He smiled a little, wondering if Kelly had done it for him.

After Anders was dressed in workout shorts and a tee, he made the bed the best he could. His tension built as he slowly walked to the kitchen, his right crutch pushing painfully against his bruised muscle.

He wondered how awkward the discussion they needed to have would be.

But when Anders stepped inside the kitchen, Kelly was whistling tunelessly at the stove. He turned to face Anders, his lip caught between his teeth in a sheepish expression.

"Um, I tried to cook us some omelets but I'm not great at it so it's kind of more of a … scramble or whatever."

Anders smiled a little, peering into the pan. "It still looks delicious. Thank you, Kelly. That was kind of you to make it."

He shrugged. "It's fine. Why don't you go get comfortable on the couch and I'll bring it to you in a minute?"

Anders had already made Kelly feel terrible once this morning, so he merely nodded.

He'd just settled in the living room when Kelly carried in their plates. He disappeared again, then returned with cups of coffee. His final trip, he carried ice packs.

Anders allowed Kelly to secure one across his ankle and another behind his shoulder. He put the coffee within easy reach on the end table, then handed him a plate.

"Do you need anything else?" Kelly's warm brown eyes were earnest. He studied Anders' face.

"No. But thank you. You should eat before your food gets cold."

"Okay."

Kelly sat close enough their arms brushed while they ate. They weren't the best eggs or turkey bacon Anders had ever eaten but he didn't complain. He was touched by Kelly's thoughtfulness.

It had been a long time since anyone had been so ferociously protective of Anders. So single-mindedly determined to take care of him.

After Anders finished his food and coffee, he turned to see Kelly staring at him.

"What?" he asked, oddly self-conscious at the intense scrutiny.

"I'm worried about you."

"I'm fine, Kelly." He patted Kelly's thigh. "Honestly."

Kelly didn't quite look like he believed him, but he nodded. "So, we have practice this afternoon and you need to meet with Dr. Gardner, right?"

"Yes."

"And you can't drive right now, yeah?"

Anders gave his ankle a rueful look. "No."

"So, I'll drive us both there, okay?"

"Okay," Anders agreed. It was pointless to argue he could take an Uber.

Kelly looked at him through his lashes. "Could I drive the Bentley?"

Anders shook his head, chuckling a little. "Kelly …"

"What? It's a nice car."

"It's a very nice car," Anders agreed.

Most days he took his Mercedes SUV to the practice facility or arena. The roomy SUV was far more practical than his Bentley coupe but he couldn't blame Kelly for being tempted by the convertible.

"Please, Anders." Kelly fluttered his lashes and Anders wondered if he realized he did it.

"I suppose," Anders said with a soft smile, enjoying the way Kelly's face lit up with glee. "If you promise to be careful."

"I promise," Kelly said, wide-eyed. "Trust me, I'm not complaining about my contract but I'm not getting paid top line center at the height of his career money. I don't want to have to pay for the repairs if I fuck your car up."

Anders chuckled. After their Cup win two seasons ago, he'd been an Unrestricted Free Agent and his agent had been able to negotiate an excellent contract. Despite his age, the Otters had been in no hurry to let him go.

What on earth he'd *do* with all the money was still undecided, but he'd done his best to enjoy some of it by buying the Bentley.

Luxury cars were one of his very few vices.

"Hey? Are you sure you're okay?" Kelly asked with a worried tilt of his head.

"Why? Do you think I must have hit my head to hand over the keys to my Bentley?" Anders teased, his tone dry.

"Well, maybe," Kelly said with a laugh. "But I wondered why you seemed so upset earlier this morning."

"Oh." Anders cleared his throat. "I ... it was nothing, Kelly."

"Clearly it was. And I'm starting to worry you *did* hit your head. They said sudden mood swings are a sign—"

"It's not a concussion," Anders insisted, his stomach sinking as he realized he'd have to come clean about his reaction. Kelly wouldn't stop pushing if he thought Anders was hiding an injury. "It was ... I was turned on, Kelly," he said gruffly.

"Oh." Kelly blinked for a moment. "Um, I know you were this morning when we woke up but ..."

"Not just when we woke," Anders admitted, swallowing hard. "But after you got out of the shower as well."

"What? Why? Was it the book you were reading or something?"

"No. It's a thriller. There was nothing steamy about it." Anders rubbed the back of his neck. "You were ... you didn't quite close the door when you were getting ready and ..."

Anders shifted, his cock beginning to respond to the memories. Jesus, why was he reacting like this? He was nearly forty years old; he should have control of his erections. It had certainly never been a problem around Kelly before.

"So you"—Kelly licked his lips—"you liked looking at me?"

"I did," Anders admitted. "You're very attractive, Kelly."

"Oh." Kelly let out a breathy little noise, then sidled closer, his chest brushing Anders' shoulder. "How long has it been since someone touched you like that, Anders?"

"Years," he admitted, swallowing hard. "I haven't been with anyone since …"

It was much too painful to finish the thought.

Kelly nodded anyway, understanding what he hadn't said. "I wondered." He set his hand on Anders' thigh, gaze never leaving his.

His eyes were so beautiful. A clear, rich brown like good, aged whiskey, a starburst of lighter amber in the center. Freckles dotted his slightly upturned nose, and a hint of auburn stubble covered his cheeks and upper lip.

Anders could hardly draw a breath as he watched Kelly's tongue peep out, licking his pink lips. Slick and soft looking, they tempted Anders to lean in.

"Would you like someone to touch you?" Kelly whispered.

"No," Anders protested automatically. "I shouldn't—"

"I didn't ask what you *should* do." Kelly squeezed his thigh. "I asked what you *wanted*."

Anders swallowed, mouth going painfully dry. He'd built his life and career on doing what he should. Doing what he wanted had always been secondary.

But staring into Kelly's eyes, he was hit by the sudden surety that if he said no, he'd spend the rest of his life regretting it. He'd go to his grave wondering what might have been.

Anders reached out and cupped the back of Kelly's head, lightly brushing his thumb across the shell of his ear. A shudder rippled through Kelly's body. "What are you suggesting?"

"My hand or my mouth on you."

Anders sucked in a deep breath, his lungs finally working again. "Because you think I need it?"

"Sure," Kelly said, his mouth curling at the corner. "But also because I'd like to make you feel good."

"You don't—"

"This isn't pity," Kelly said earnestly. "I don't feel sorry for you or *owe* you anything. I want you to feel good. I want you to relax and—and be touched. Not be so alone."

"How much experience do you have with men, Kelly?"

"None." Kelly's cheeks went bright red but he didn't blink, his gaze almost defiant. "I've never been with another guy, okay? I've never done any of this but I *want* to."

"Sex should be with someone special," Anders argued.

"Maybe it *should* be but it never has been. I've fooled around with girls I barely knew and wasn't attracted to because I felt like I was supposed to. I hated it," he said passionately. "Let me give both of us this. You're my friend, that makes it way more special than anything I've done in the past. I swear, it doesn't have to *mean* anything serious. It doesn't have to be a promise of anything, okay?"

"I don't want to hurt you, Kelly. I know you have feelings for me."

Kelly's lashes fluttered, his swallow audible in the quiet room.

"Yeah, I do." His voice was rough. "But I know you don't want a future with me. I can accept that. I want to make you feel good this once. I'm not asking for anything else."

Kelly's hand was still pressed to Anders' thigh but he hadn't moved it a fraction of an inch, waiting for his okay.

Anders took a deep breath and slid his hand across the back of Kelly's head, the short hairs there brushing against his palm with the prickly softness of velvet.

He should say no but his excuses dried on his tongue and all he could do was nod.

"Okay," he whispered. "You can touch me, Kelly."

———

Kelly's heart felt like it might beat right out of his chest.

For one wild moment, he thought Anders might change his mind or push him away but he closed his eyes and pulled Kelly close. Kelly tipped forward, bracing himself against Anders' firm chest, palms flat against his white tee.

Kelly could barely breathe as Anders brushed their lips together softly, his beard tickling, his nose warm as he angled his head and did it again.

All Kelly could do was let out a little moan and open his lips, hoping Anders would deepen the kiss. When he did, sweat broke out on Kelly's forehead, his heart rabbiting like he'd done sprints.

Kelly slipped a hand around the back of Anders' neck, brushing against the soft strands of his hair. It was long enough to dust Anders' shoulders, soft against Kelly's knuckles when he pulled him closer.

"Oh, Kelly," Anders whispered against his mouth.

Anders' pulse thumped against the heel of Kelly's palm. He met Anders' gently seeking tongue with his own.

This close, Kelly was overwhelmed by the scent of his cologne, the strength of his arms tightening around him.

He pulled away with a gasp, resting his forehead against Anders' as he sucked in a few shaky breaths.

"You okay?" Anders whispered. He ran his hands along Kelly's back, smoothing gently along it.

"Shouldn't I ask you that?" Kelly muttered.

"I'm okay. It—it's been a long time but it helps that it's with you."

"For me too." Kelly threw himself at Anders, pulling him in for another kiss, this one rougher and needier.

Anders responded, his grip tightening. He coaxed Kelly to shift onto his lap. Kelly was careful of his ankle as he knelt over Anders' thighs, but Anders felt so big and solid Kelly wasn't worried about hurting him.

He let out a gasp when Anders gripped his ass, broad palms covering way more of his cheeks than Kelly would have expected. It was unexpectedly hot too and Kelly wound his arms around Anders' neck and kissed him more deeply.

He shifted forward, letting out a rough noise at how hard Anders was. Hard for *him*. He'd been hard all morning because of Kelly and that thrilled him in a way he couldn't put into words. Anders wanted him. Not just someone—anyone—but *Kelly*.

Anders wasn't the only one who was hard, but Kelly ignored his own cock in favor of sliding his hand between their bodies to grip Anders' shaft through the slippery fabric of his shorts.

Anders hissed and Kelly loosened his grip. "Too much?" he whispered against his mouth.

"No. It feels good. I won't last long."

"What do you want?" Kelly pulled back far enough he could look Anders in the eye. See the pale gray blue of his eyes swallowed by his dilated pupils and watch the way his lashes fluttered when Kelly dipped his fingers under the stretchy waistband of his shorts.

"Whatever you want to give me." Anders' expression was open and honest, and Kelly drew in a deep breath, considering his options.

"Okay." Kelly shimmied off Anders' lap, then reached out to tug at his waistband. "Can we pull these down?"

"Yes."

Anders lifted his hips, letting Kelly tug the shorts to mid-thigh. His underwear went with it too and Kelly stared a moment, taking in the size of him. He was … definitely not small. Anders was a large man and his cock looked intimidatingly proportional.

Kelly had seen him in the locker room often enough to know he was uncut, but his foreskin had pulled away enough to show the shiny pink head. Kelly licked his lips and when Anders let out a little groan, his cock jerking in response, it was an easy choice of what to try next.

Kelly shifted until he lay on the couch beside Anders on his stomach, his head near Anders' hip, propped on his elbows. "This okay?" he whispered, reaching out to gently close his hand around Anders' cock.

"Yes." Anders settled his hand on Kelly's back, right between his shoulder blades. "Whatever you want."

Kelly nodded and gave him a few strokes, experimenting with how tightly to grip him, knowing he'd gotten it right when Anders let out a breath like the air had been punched out of him.

His hand tightened against Kelly's back, gripping his T-shirt and Kelly scooted forward to press his lips to Anders' cock.

Anders let out another desperate noise and Kelly closed his eyes, letting his instincts take over as he licked at the tip. He'd tasted his own cum plenty of times but Anders' was less bitter than he was used to, a little sweeter.

Kelly slipped his mouth over the head, sucking, and Anders slid a hand up to cup his neck, not holding him in place, merely squeezing gently to encourage him.

"Oh, Kelly," he whispered. "Fuck, that's good."

Kelly pulled away long enough to glance at him. He licked his palm and Anders slammed his eyes shut like he couldn't watch. But it didn't feel like a rejection at all when Anders' whole body trembled.

Kelly licked his palm again and smoothed it along Anders' shaft, playing with his foreskin before he lowered his head to take him in his mouth again. The angle was still awkward but he loved this too much to stop.

He gathered as much spit in his mouth as he could, then sucked a little, trying to coordinate the movements of his mouth and hand. He was clumsy and awkward until Anders' grip tightened, guiding him gently.

Kelly let him take over. There was nothing rough or harsh about it at all, but it still felt so good to let Anders take charge and show him what he liked.

"Kelly …" Anders said, his voice going rough as Kelly took him a little deeper.

He almost gagged but he pulled off in time, coughing.

135

"Easy," Anders whispered, brushing his thumb tenderly across Kelly's cheek. "You don't have to go deep. Focus on the head. I'm almost there."

Pleased, Kelly kept working Anders with his hand, sucking harder at the tip while he bobbed over him.

"Getting close," Anders said after a minute, voice going tight and strained. "Where do you want me to come?"

Kelly sucked harder, wordlessly telling him he wanted to swallow. Anders trembled beneath him, body taut when he shot across Kelly's tongue.

Cum leaked out of Kelly's mouth but he kept swallowing, taking the last of Anders' release down his throat before he pulled off, gasping.

Anders slid his palm up to cup Kelly's head, rubbing gently with his thumb.

Kelly rested his forehead on Anders' thigh, panting a little, his cock like an iron bar beneath him as he rocked his hips against the couch cushion. He was so hard he *hurt*, and he slid a hand between his body and his shorts to grip himself.

He brushed the bare, oversensitive head with his thumb and shuddered.

"Are you going to come for me, Kelly?" Anders whispered.

"Yes," he gasped, rocking into his fist, dimly aware he probably looked ridiculous humping the couch but too desperate to care.

"Mmm." Anders let out a pleased little noise, petting the back of Kelly's head as if to encourage him. "Perfect. I want you to feel good too, Kelly. Let go for me."

Kelly cried out, cock jerking as he shot into his fist. He desperately tried to catch his release in his palm, shuddering through his orgasm.

He flipped onto his back, panting and shaking through the aftershocks, his head still pillowed on Anders' thigh. Anders reached out, rubbing his hand against Kelly's abs where his shirt had rucked up and he cried out again, a little more cum spurting from the painfully sensitive tip.

"Holy shit," Kelly gasped, eyes closed, his entire body trembling.

When the tremors finally slowed, he let out a tired noise and slumped against Anders' leg, pressing his hot cheek against the silky fabric of Anders' shorts until he could gather his thoughts.

Embarrassed but content, Kelly opened his eyes and looked tentatively at Anders. He'd been afraid he'd see disgust on Anders' face for the way he'd humped the couch, but there was none, only a soft, pleased expression that made Kelly's chest go warm.

Or maybe it was Anders' palm rubbing against his sternum.

"Thank you, Kelly." Anders shifted, brushing his thumb against Kelly's lower lip. "That was … it was …" He let out a soft laugh, shaking his head a little. "Well, it's left me speechless, apparently."

"In a good way?" Kelly asked, craning his neck to look at Anders.

"Yes." Anders sighed and brushed his thumb across Kelly's lower lip again, pressing in gently. "You were right. It's been a long time and it felt good to be touched."

"Good." Kelly twisted his neck to press a kiss to Anders' thigh. "I'm glad. Thanks for letting me give you that."

CHAPTER TWELVE

As Kelly padded softly toward the bedroom to clean himself, Anders stared blankly at the wall in front of him, head still swirling with the memory of Kelly's mouth on his cock and the desperate little sounds Kelly had made as he came in his shorts.

Anders had been selfish, watching rather than helping Kelly, but he'd been so overwhelmed by the pleasure making his head swim. He'd loved watching Kelly get himself off, turned on by giving a blowjob. Anders' spent cock twitched at the memory and he shivered and tucked himself away, lifting his hips to slide his shorts up.

He didn't know how Kelly felt about coming in his pants with no assistance but at the least, Anders should have gone to get a cloth for him instead of leaving Kelly to clean up alone.

Anders gave his sore ankle a rueful glance. Well, probably better he didn't but he still felt oddly conflicted.

He'd enjoyed what they'd done. A fleeting feeling of unease lingered but after being alone so long, the touch of someone else, the intimacy of a mouth on his cock—*Kelly's* mouth on his cock—was enough to make Anders giddy.

It had been years since he'd felt this relaxed.

He flinched at the thought of what that meant. For the first time since Astrid's death, Anders had held someone else in his arms, kissed them, shared the intensity and passion of a release with them.

Involuntarily, his gaze drifted to the framed wedding photo on the mantel, guilt teasing at the edges of his relaxation.

That perfect, idyllic day when they'd celebrated their love with their family and friends in Sweden.

He forced himself to look at the picture, to *see* Astrid in her long white lace dress, her pale blonde hair falling in loose waves around her shoulders, colorful wildflower bouquet in her hands. In the photo, she looked straight at the camera, laughing and joyous, her smile so wide it lit up her whole body.

For the ceremony, Anders had worn a pale stone-colored three-piece suit, but by the time the photo was taken, the jacket had come off to reveal his vest over a white shirt, the sleeves rolled up to reveal his forearms.

The photographer had captured him standing with his head bent, his forehead pressed to the side of Astrid's hair, smiling with his eyes closed. Blissful.

How dizzyingly happy and in love he'd been. He'd desperately wanted to breathe in every last experience, so he'd never forget a single moment of the day.

There had been so many other wonderful moments during their ceremony and reception, but *this* particular memory was the one he cherished most. If a single photo could sum up their entire relationship, it was that one.

Astrid's fierce, bright love had always radiated loudly out into the world. Anders' quieter but equally deep emotions were always turned inward, focused only on her.

Anders dragged in a deep breath, wondering how she would have felt about what he'd done with Kelly.

He chuckled humorlessly, knowing damn well how she would have responded.

"Oh, get over yourself, Anders." She would have laughed at how ridiculous he was, twisting himself into knots about this. "Are you happy? Do you feel good? That's all that matters."

And maybe to her it *was*. But it wasn't the same for him.

The only thing Anders had ever done quickly was falling in love with her. But moving forward, moving *on*, wasn't something he could rush.

He could picture her arched eyebrow as she tartly said, "It's been four years, Anders. What the hell are you waiting for? Kelly literally dropped into your lap; do you need more signs telling you it's time to live again?"

But he shrank away from the idea like he'd touched something scorching hot.

"Shit."

Anders looked up to see Kelly standing a few feet away, lip caught between his teeth, dressed in a pair of Anders' much-too-long sweats and nothing else.

Well, Anders *had* told him to help himself and from what he'd seen of Kelly's shorts on his way out of the room, he'd made a thorough mess of them.

"Shit?" Anders asked with a frown, not sure what Kelly meant.

"You regret this." Kelly took a hesitant step forward.

Anders let out a sigh. "I … I'm conflicted."

"About what?" Kelly skirted around the ottoman and coffee table, dropping onto the couch beside him.

"Well, I was selfish," he admitted. "You deserved better for your first—"

"Oh, for fuck's sake, Lindy. Don't make this a bigger deal than it is."

"After what we did, I think you can call me Anders," he pointed out.

Kelly shrugged. "Fine, *Anders*. I'm not a delicate little flower. What we did was hot. I've been wanting to suck your cock for years."

Anders blinked. "I'm afraid to ask how many."

"Yeah, you don't wanna know."

"Right." Anders rubbed his hands across his face.

He didn't like to think about the fact Kelly had been an infant when Anders played his first game with the Boston Harriers. He'd played hockey with Kelly's *father* initially, then played with all three of his brothers. He'd had an O'Shea as a teammate for most of his career in the NHL.

And now he'd had sex with one of them.

Anders felt a little faint. Four of Boston's most talented wingers were going to kill him and dump his body in the Charles River.

"Whatever." Kelly waved Anders' concern off like it was unimportant. "Look, don't get all up in your head about this. Sucking you off was exactly what I wanted. You didn't take advantage of me or whatever you're worrying yourself about. I wanted it. I loved it. And I have zero regrets now."

Anders sighed. "I could have *reciprocated* at least."

Kelly's eyes brightened. "Well, if you feel that terrible, you can make it up to me in like ten minutes."

Anders tried to hide his smile at Kelly's enthusiasm. Tempting, but he needed to find a way to gently break it to him that they shouldn't continue.

"We did agree this was a one-time thing."

"When did we decide that?" Kelly asked with a wrinkle of his nose.

"When you said something to the effect of making me feel good this once. And you weren't going to ask for anything else."

Kelly winced. "Well, that was stupid of me."

"Kelly."

"What?" He widened his eyes. "You enjoyed yourself, right?"

"I did. Of course I did." How could Kelly doubt it? Pleasure still hummed through Anders' body and lurked under his skin, singing in his veins.

"Then I don't see what the problem is. We should definitely keep doing this."

"You know I'm not—"

"I'm not asking you for a relationship," Kelly said doggedly, like he'd already braced himself for the arguments Anders might have and was prepared to rebut every single one. "I'm not asking you to move on from Astrid or anything like it. I'm saying we're two guys who are into each other. I don't see any reason we can't enjoy ourselves for a while."

"We're teammates, your brothers and father would murder me, and we could potentially ruin our friendship," he pointed out.

"I mean, that's all little stuff, right?" Kelly grinned. "Totally no big deal."

Anders couldn't quite hide his smile. "*Kelly.*"

"What?"

"Take this seriously, please."

"I *am*. I mean, yeah, I was joking about it being no big deal. I get why you're worried, but I also think you're way overthinking things. You've been lonely, right? You've missed having someone around here. You've missed sex. There's an obvious solution here."

"And what about you? Is it fair for me to use you that way?"

"Well, the thought of you *using* me sounds pretty fucking hot to me."

Anders groaned and buried his head in his hands. Kelly Michael O'Shea was absolutely going to kill him. Kelly would do him in before his overprotective family had a chance to commit homicide.

But oh, the image Kelly painted with his words sounded tempting. It was too easy to picture Kelly spending more time here. He could easily imagine Kelly in his bed, taking Anders apart with his enthusiasm, then cracking jokes after, nudging Anders out of his perpetual gloom and making him laugh.

Anders knew it would be good for him. But what would it do to Kelly? Astrid's advice rang in his ears. *"Be kind to him, Anders. Don't break his heart."*

If they continued, would he hurt Kelly when he couldn't give him more?

Anders lifted his head to see Kelly staring hopefully.

"Is it fair of me to start something with you that won't go anywhere? If you have feelings for me, then it's unkind to offer you—"

Kelly covered Anders' mouth with his hand.

"Oh my God, Anders. You are being ridiculous. It's not your job to worry about that shit. It's on *me*. I am asking you for sex. Nothing else. Well, friendship and sex, and ideally some really fucking great playoff hockey together. But that's it. I know it's not going to turn into anything else, okay? You're not going to break my heart or something."

Kelly lifted his hand and Anders licked his lips, clinging to the hope that maybe he was right. Maybe he should trust Kelly to know his own mind. Perhaps Kelly *wasn't* in love with him. Maybe it really only was attraction and hero worship.

"Are you *sure?*" Anders asked, searching Kelly's face for any hints of doubt.

"Yeah, I'm fucking sure. Now, are you going to kiss me or am I going to have to parade around naked again to get you to change your mind?"

Anders blinked. "You did that on purpose this morning?"

"Fuck yeah." With a crooked grin, Kelly pushed Anders against the couch, then swung a leg over his thighs to straddle him like he had earlier. "You were turned on but being all noble and shit. I figured it couldn't hurt to show you what you could have if you gave in."

"You—you're ..." Anders laughed, unable to help himself. "You're a little shit, you know that?"

Kelly's grin widened. "Totally part of my charm, man."

"So it appears." Anders sighed and shook his head as he admitted how much he wanted this. The threads of guilt remained but when he settled his hands on Kelly's waist, feeling his muscles flex under his palms, he couldn't deny Kelly was right.

Anders had missed this.

He'd been lonely and touch-starved, and Kelly had awakened something inside him that had slumbered for far too long.

Kelly's weight pressing against Anders' thighs, the hard planes of his chest and abs against Anders' torso, and the soft touch of his hands on Anders' hair brought something inside him to life again.

Anders rested his forehead against Kelly's and closed his eyes. "Okay," he whispered, desperately hoping he'd made the right choice. "Let's do this."

———

Kelly pressed harder on the accelerator, his heart beating faster as the engine roared and the Bentley surged forward. "Fuck this is amazing."

Anders grinned at him from the passenger seat, the wind from the open top ruffling his hair. "If you crash it, you buy it."

"I remember," Kelly grumbled. He eased off the gas, then appreciatively petted the black and tan leather steering wheel.

Kelly's Mustang was nice enough but this convertible was fucking next level.

"Someday you're going to have to let me take this out and really open it up. The roads around here aren't good for speed."

"You're going to have to prove I can trust you at high speeds first," Anders said drily. "But maybe."

"Fuck yes."

"That wasn't a yes."

"It wasn't a no," Kelly pointed out.

"What am I going to do with you?" Anders murmured but he sounded more amused than annoyed.

"Whatever the hell you want."

Kelly still felt a little pouty they hadn't had time to fool around again before they had to leave for practice. They'd made out on the couch for a while before they had to eat and get ready to leave. They'd had to swing by Kelly's place first to get some clothes for the next few days too.

"You're staying with me a while then, huh?" Anders had asked as Kelly got out of the Bentley, illegally parked in front of his apartment building.

Kelly had nodded and reached for his duffel in the back seat. "Yep. I have to keep an eye on you and you're going to need lots of help with your ankle."

"Am I?"

"Definitely." Kelly had leaned on the doorframe and winked. "You are going to fuck me stupid for the next few days."

Anders had blinked at him. "I thought I had an injured ankle."

"Then I guess you better get creative."

Now, as they arrived at the practice rink and parked beside Zane Murphy's Audi, Kelly put the car in park with a regretful little sigh. Too bad they couldn't have stayed at Anders' place and fucked.

But Anders was way too responsible.

"Top up," Anders reminded him, and Kelly grumbled. He made sure the windows were up and the top was secured.

"It's like you think the totally threatening dark cloud coming in is going to dump a bunch of rain on us or something," he teased, swinging his bag over his shoulder. "So pessimistic."

"Pragmatic," Anders countered.

"Shit, you can't use big words on me, Lindy," he joked. "I'm a hockey player, remember?"

He expected a chirp in return but what he got was Anders' suddenly stern expression and the snug grip of his hand on his bicep. "You're smart, Kelly. Don't ever tell yourself otherwise."

"Um, okay," he agreed, rattled by the sudden turn the mood had taken.

Anders softened. "I don't like to hear you put yourself down. You're smart and talented and if anyone tells you otherwise, they're wrong."

"Thanks, Lindy," he managed, not expecting the way those words made his throat go thick.

"And don't forget my bag." Anders winked at Kelly as he walked away from the car, moving pretty quickly for a guy on crutches.

"Hey!" Kelly squawked. "What am I? Your personal servant?"

"You volunteered for this position," Anders threw over his shoulder. "Now do your job."

Kelly grinned, his body fizzing with excitement at the thought of what was to come. Hockey and more sex with Anders.

Did life get any better?

Kelly dumped their bags in the dressing room, then joined Anders where he waited by the door to the video room.

"How're you feeling?" Murphy asked Anders the moment they stepped inside.

Anders shrugged and carefully took his usual seat, handing his crutches to Kelly who automatically took them and leaned them against the wall. "Fine. I don't have a concussion. My head feels good. My shoulder and neck are still painful but it's nothing they can't fix."

Ooh, maybe Kelly should offer to give him a massage later. He'd have to remember that.

"And the ankle?" Murphy asked.

"It hurts but it's bearable. I'm being careful with it."

"Good." Murphy set his hand on Anders' uninjured shoulder and squeezed. "I'm gonna miss my liney this week. You're so healthy, I'm not used to playing with anyone else. It'll be an adjustment playing on anyone else's wing."

It was true. Anders was rarely injured or sick.

"Are they moving Truro up?" Kelly asked. He dropped into his spot beside Anders. The room was only half full. They were earlier than Kelly usually arrived but later than Anders typically showed up.

Murphy nodded. "That's the plan."

"Think he's ready for it?" Kelly was kinda doubtful. Truro was a good center but Kelly wasn't sure he was first-line-center good. Not yet anyway.

"I think it's a good opportunity for growth for him," Murphy said.

Kelly snickered at the diplomatic way he'd worded that.

"I know the timing of this is terrible," Anders said with a sigh, rubbing a hand over his face.

He'd smoothed down his hair, tucking it into a loose bun. Anders and Gabriel both rocked the long-haired man-bun look but they were complete opposites otherwise. Gabriel dark where Lindy was light, compact where Lindy was big and broad.

Murphy laughed. "Yeah, the timing is fucking terrible but I don't think you loosened the skate blade on purpose, Lindy. Equipment fails sometimes, no matter how careful we all are. Jeff's already beating himself up enough."

Jeff was their head equipment manager, tasked with wrangling their gear and sharpening their skates. It was a more than full-time job, although he had plenty of assistants.

"I'd hate to see this hurt our chances of making a playoff run this year," Anders said, his tone earnest.

"We held it together the other night," Murphy pointed out. "We won. And we're so fucking close to nailing a spot. We can hang on."

"Yeah, you're good, Lindy, but you don't carry the whole team on your back, dude," Kelly pointed out.

Anders shot him a small smile. "You're right. Thanks for the reminder."

"Look at it this way. It'll give you time to rest," Murphy said. "Relax. Listen to the trainers. Take good care of yourself, and you can come back ready to push hard after that."

"Yeah, and try having some *fun*," Hartinger said with a grin. "It wouldn't kill you, Lindy."

Kelly fought off a smile. He could think of a few ways to make Anders have a lot of fun. If the look Anders shot him out of the corner of his eye was any indication, his thoughts had gone there too.

Shit, this was really happening.

A giddy thrill shot through Kelly. He felt like a kid on Christmas morning. Everything he'd ever wanted was finally here in front of him.

It wouldn't last forever but he was going to enjoy every second of it in the meantime.

The final stragglers appeared, and their video coach stepped to the front of the room.

Everyone automatically fell silent as Coach Greene spoke. "Okay, boys. We have a lot of work ahead of us today. Truro, I'm going to pick on you this morning because we're expecting a lot of you in the next few games."

Truro nodded and leaned forward. "Tell me what I need to hear, Coach."

Greene's smile turned evil. "You might regret that by the time we get done, but here goes. What the fuck were you doing at the end of the second period?"

Kelly tried to listen attentively while Coach critiqued his performance in his last game but he was distracted by the occasional brush of Anders' elbow or knee.

After they reviewed film, Anders split off to meet with Dr. Gardner while Kelly followed his other teammates to do dryland training. He tried to turn off his brain and focus, grateful Anders wasn't around to distract him.

He laughed and chirped the guys between sets, wiping the sweat from his face, unable to stop the smile that appeared every time he thought about touching Anders again.

By the time he returned to the dressing room, Anders was there.

"How'd it go?" Kelly asked.

"Great. I passed every test for my head. Everyone's in agreement that the muscle pull in my neck caused the headache. The bruising is nasty but the swelling on my ankle is way down. I need to take it easy for a little while longer to be sure it's back to normal before I hit the ice again."

"Fuck yeah," Kelly said. "We should celebrate later."

Anders shot him a look, half-amused, half-annoyed. "We'll talk about it."

Kelly laughed. He totally had Anders' number now. He couldn't go back on what he'd promised earlier.

Hartinger squinted at them. "You're both in weirdly good moods today. What's up?"

"Lindy let me drive his Bentley here," Kelly said with a grin. He really wanted to say he'd blown Lindy but *no*.

Hartinger wouldn't care. He'd totally high five Kelly and tell him good job but since Kelly wasn't out to the team and Anders wouldn't want the guys to know they were hooking up, that was a bad idea.

"Hey, I asked you if I could drive it once and you said no," Hartinger said, throwing a pair of balled-up socks at Anders. "What the fuck, man?"

"You're not responsible enough," Anders said, batting away the socks. They landed in Hartinger's bag.

Hartinger let out an outraged noise as he rummaged around for them. "Are you fucking kidding me? I am your *equal*. We're both alternate captains and that comes with a certain set of responsibilities. Irish here is way too young to be trusted with that beautiful piece of machinery."

"I've already warned him if he breaks it, he buys it," Anders said evenly but Kelly could have smacked Hartinger for the *young* comment. Damn it, Anders didn't need the reminder.

"You couldn't have given me the same deal?" Hartinger protested, expression outraged.

"No. Go test drive a Bentley if you want to get behind the wheel."

"I don't think I like you anymore, Lindy," Hartinger made a huffing noise and took a seat in his stall, pulling up his sock.

"Big loss, huh?" Kelly teased.

"I don't think I like either of you today," Hartinger protested, but he laughed too hard for them to take him seriously. "I thought you were supposed to be injured, Lindy. Instead, you come in all smiles and sass this morning. If I didn't know better, I'd say you'd gotten laid last night."

"It's probably the painkillers," Kelly said before Anders had a panic attack about the team accidentally guessing the truth. "Maybe we should start slipping them into his sports drinks on the reg."

"Is there a reason you're not all out on the ice yet?" Coach Daniels asked, clomping into the dressing room with a scowl on his face. "Because you're already five minutes late and if you don't get your asses out there in another five, you're all getting fines and doing suicide sprints."

Kelly scrambled to finish dressing, then followed his team to the ice for practice.

Not even the threat of sprints and the reminder that Anders would be watching from the bench instead of skating could dim Kelly's smile today.

CHAPTER THIRTEEN

"I think we should go to bed," Kelly said. He'd been restless all day, ever since they returned from practice.

Anders looked away from the television. "It's seven in the evening. Are you that tired?"

"No." Kelly gave him a long look like he was especially stupid. "But I do want you to fuck me."

Anders choked on air. "Have you ever heard of subtlety?"

"Um, no," Kelly said. "It's not gonna get me what I want so it seems like a waste of time. I want your dick in me. The sooner the better."

Anders glanced at the screen, realizing he'd never be able to focus on what they were watching now that his head was filled with those images.

"I don't have supplies—"

"I do." Kelly nudged a little closer, his knee pressing against Anders' thigh. "Lube, condoms. I think they're even big enough to fit your dick."

Anders' neck went hot. "I'm perfectly average."

Kelly gave him an appraising look. "Shit, if you're average, I'm *definitely* taking a trip to Sweden this summer."

Anders cleared his throat, annoyed by the flash of irritation at the thought of Kelly sleeping with another man. He had no right to feel that way at all. If anything, he should be encouraging it.

"I'm not sure this is a great idea," Anders said, gesturing to his ankle. "I *am* injured."

"But you said you were feeling much better after the trainer worked on you."

"Still, I don't want to risk a setback."

"Oh, come on, Lindy," Kelly teased. "You can't think of a single position we could safely manage?"

"I'd like to do it right."

"Pfft." Kelly made a dismissive noise. "There's no wrong way to have sex."

Anders bit back a retort asking him how he knew that since he'd apparently never experienced it before. There was no reason to be cruel. "I just—"

"If you don't want this, say so," Kelly said with a frown. "I'm not gonna sit here and beg. I want you and you said you were good with us hooking up. If you changed your mind or whatever, that's fine, but I need you to tell me and not throw a bunch of bullshit excuses in my face, okay?"

Without another word, Anders hit the Power button on the remote, chastened. Kelly was right. Anders respected his forthrightness. He was acting more like an adult than Anders. Kelly was being clear about what he wanted and asking Anders to do the same.

The least Anders could do was return the respect Kelly had given him, so he looked Kelly in the eye. "I want you. I'm nervous about this, but you're right, I shouldn't invent excuses."

"Why are you nervous?" Kelly settled a hand on his thigh, stroking the length of the muscle through the fabric of his shorts. "It's just me."

"Exactly," Anders said, surprised by how rough his voice had gone. "It's *you*. And there's no one in the world I want to protect more."

Surprise flickered across Kelly's face before he cupped Anders' cheek. "You could never intentionally hurt me, Anders. There's no one in the world I trust more."

Anders' breath caught, the words eroding every last bit of hesitation he had.

"Come here," he whispered, and Kelly leaned in, his lips soft and gentle. He seemed content once he was in Anders' arms. More patient than Anders could have imagined.

They kissed deeply for a long time, Kelly sifting his fingers through Anders' hair as Anders traced his palms along Kelly's back, occasionally dipping down to tease at the smooth skin below the waistband of his shorts.

Kelly was fairly quiet, letting out soft noises of pleasure and contentment as they made out, their hips beginning to rock together.

Anders' lips tingled by the time he pulled away, kissing across Kelly's jaw to press against his throat. "Let's go in the bedroom," he whispered against his skin.

Kelly scrambled off his lap, then helped Anders by grabbing his crutches. He led the way, his body practically vibrating with eagerness. Anders smiled at his enthusiasm.

In the bedroom, Kelly shut the door behind them, then rummaged in his bag, pulling out the condoms and lube he'd mentioned earlier. Anders gave them a cursory glance but they were good choices.

Anders took a seat on the edge of the mattress, trying to decide how he wanted to proceed.

After Kelly had closed the curtains and turned on the lamps beside the bed, he looked at Anders and licked his lips. "I think I'm gonna hop in the shower and uh, clean up a little, okay?"

"Of course." Anders settled against the headboard, reaching for the book he couldn't focus on.

If Anders' ankle wasn't killing him, he'd get in the shower with Kelly but he could all too easily imagine slipping and injuring it more. That was not a conversation he wanted to have with Dr. Gardner or Coach Daniels.

Thankfully, Kelly was quick.

His skin was pink when he came out of the bathroom. He didn't wear a towel this time and Anders stared, mouth dry as Kelly walked to the bed. The room was dim and quiet. It felt like a private sanctuary where no one existed but the two of them.

Anders set his book aside, watching Kelly crawl onto his bed. Anders had already stripped out of everything but his underwear and Kelly raked an appreciative gaze across him.

Kelly knelt beside Anders' hip, his tongue darting out. He held out a hand. "Can I touch you?"

"Of course."

Kelly's touch was surprisingly soft and gentle as he skimmed his fingers across Anders' chest, tracing along his pecs before sliding up to his shoulder and down his arm. The honest appreciation in his gaze was heady and Anders reached out, pulling him closer, wanting to touch him too.

Kelly settled on his lap and Anders smiled. "You seem to like this spot. Are you trying to tell me something?"

Kelly grinned but his ears went pink. "Um, not really. I don't want to hurt your ankle though."

Anders ran his hands along Kelly's back. "I don't mind. It's a good starting point."

He liked Kelly's weight against his thighs and the way it put their faces at nearly the same level. Most of Anders' height was in his legs so in this position there was little difference between them, their mouths lining up perfectly.

Kelly stared into his eyes, absently playing with Anders' hair. "Kiss me?"

Anders pressed his mouth against Kelly's, warmth spreading through him when Kelly opened with a soft sigh and let Anders inside.

Anders had missed the warm give and take of a kiss, the way it felt like the perfect way to get to know someone. It was like being on the ice for the first time with a new teammate, learning the way they moved and beginning to anticipate their play.

Anders discovered that Kelly moaned when he pulled him closer, laughed breathlessly when he skimmed his hands up his sides, and went soft and pliant in his arms when he cupped his neck.

Kelly ground against his lap while they kissed and Anders hardened, moaning when Kelly reached between their bodies to rub him through the fabric of his underwear.

Anders dipped his head, mouthing along Kelly's neck as he gripped his ass.

"Can you reach the lube?" he whispered.

Kelly stretched out, snagging it from where he'd placed it on the bed earlier. Anders slicked his fingers, warming the lube between them for a moment before he reached behind Kelly, looking intently into his eyes. He slipped a finger between his cheeks, resting there, not pushing inside. "This okay?"

"Yeah, yeah it's good," Kelly said breathlessly. His eyes shone and his lips were so pink and biteable that Anders had to close his teeth over the lower one to see how Kelly would respond.

He let out a squeak but Anders wasn't sure if it was the bite or that he'd also circled Kelly's rim with a slick finger.

It made Anders smile. "Good?"

"Mmm." Kelly's eyes were bright, and his hips shifted restlessly.

Anders teased Kelly until he panted softly and whined. He tapped at his entrance, gently sliding one finger in.

Kelly tensed for a second before he let out a big breath and softened, his body drawing Anders in deeper.

His lashes fluttered, his head tilting back as Anders rocked in and out, carefully tugging at the rim to open him farther.

"Anders," Kelly whispered, gripping the top of his shoulders, his chest flushing a splotchy shade of pink.

Kelly moved restlessly, pushing back on Anders' finger. Anders added more lube, kissing along Kelly's collarbone to keep him occupied when he switched to two.

Kelly's breathy gasp was gratifying, and Anders teased him for a few moments, lightly grazing his prostate with the pads of his fingers while he used his free hand to toy with Kelly's nipples.

They were hard and apparently very sensitive, because Kelly writhed in his lap at the attention, panting, lips parted in the most obscenely gorgeous surrender Anders had ever seen.

"Kelly," he whispered, his own urgency growing with every minute that passed. He spread his fingers wide, scissoring them until a sharp cry fell from Kelly's lips.

Anders paused but Kelly's lashes fluttered and he whimpered, "Need you."

All Anders could do was add a third digit, wanting to be sure Kelly was ready.

But Kelly let out a pained sound, gripping his shoulders.

"Too much?" Anders stilled, ready to slide out if it was too uncomfortable, but Kelly shook his head, clamping tight around him, his breathing harsh and strained.

"I need a minute. I might not last if you keep that up and I don't want to come yet."

"Sure." Anders smiled, nudging at his cheek with his nose. "Whatever you need."

Kelly dipped his head, tucking it against Anders' neck. It was an oddly tender gesture given the situation they were in but Anders wrapped his free arm around Kelly and held him close, rubbing his back soothingly while he took a few deep breaths.

When the tension seeped out of Kelly's body, he lifted his head. "Okay. A little more, then I want you to fuck me."

Anders nodded, capturing Kelly's mouth in a deep kiss. He worked him open, distracting him with little bites and nips until he absolutely writhed on top of him.

"Now, now," Kelly begged against his mouth eventually. "I need you. *Please*."

"On your side. Facing away from me," Anders instructed, guiding him into position before he eased his fingers free of Kelly's clenching body.

Anders had spent most of the time Kelly was in the shower thinking about the best position for this and he'd decided spooning Kelly would be most comfortable for both of them. Anders settled on his uninjured side, smiling when Kelly passed a condom to him, fingers trembling a little. Anders suspected it was more from excitement than nerves.

It took longer than Anders would have liked to fumble the protection on—maybe *he* was the one who was nervous—but after he did, he took a moment to admire the view of Kelly's body. He ran an appreciative hand along his hip, skimming over the freckled pale skin, Kelly's body shivering with the sensation.

Anders dipped his head to kiss Kelly's shoulder and watched the muscles soften. He slid closer, guiding Kelly's leg up and out until his knee was bent at an angle, resting against the sheets.

"You ready?" he whispered against his skin.

"Please."

Anders had to close his eyes as he used a hand to guide himself into Kelly.

Kelly only tensed for a moment before he relaxed into the pressure, and Anders sank in slowly. Kelly let out a small, choked sound when Anders was buried deep and he nibbled at Kelly's neck, rubbing his hip to soothe him.

"Oh God." Kelly's voice was breathless and almost awed. "That's ... wow."

"Good wow?"

"Is there any other kind?" Kelly asked, laughing a little. He craned his neck to look at Anders.

He smiled helplessly at the happiness in Kelly's eyes, and he cradled Kelly's jaw, gently turning his head to kiss him more easily.

They didn't need words after that, their bodies attuned enough to each other that it only took little nudges and soft sounds to find their rhythm.

Anders had to close his eyes and rest his forehead against Kelly's shoulder as he rocked in and out, pleasure spreading across his skin and tangling deep in his core, igniting him from the center.

He roamed his palm across Kelly's body, needing the contact but struggling to make the moment last. It would be so easy to give into the instinctive urge to thrust until he spilled inside him.

Instead, he listened to Kelly's soft moans and breathy gasps of pleasure. He let Kelly set the pace, feeling Kelly's pleasure grow with every shudder and grip of the sheets in his fist.

Eventually, Kelly grabbed Anders' hand, guiding it to his cock. He was hard, wet at the tip, and Anders smoothed his fingers down his length in a gentle stroke. He'd never been with someone who was cut before, so he had to reach for the lube, but it only took a few slick strokes before Kelly let out a desperate noise, trembling, right on the edge.

Anders tightened his grip and focused on the head for a moment before Kelly's body curled in on itself, breath leaving his lungs in helpless choked-off pants when he shot into Anders' fist. He tightened around Anders for a few moments, small tremors wracking his body as he rode out his release. He clutched at the sheet until his knuckles went white, burying his face against the pillow with a final bitten-off gasp before all the tension left his body.

Anders let go of Kelly's cock, dimly cursing himself for not being prepared with a towel. He wiped his hand on the sheets with a grimace, but his own orgasm rushed toward him too fast to care.

He gripped Kelly's hip, pain flaring in his shoulder and his neck when he used those muscles to get some leverage, thrusting harder and deeper into Kelly for a few desperate moments. When he let go of that tightly wound spiral, he came with a blinding white haze of pleasure that lit up the back of his eyelids, his groan muffled against Kelly's shoulder.

For several long moments after, they breathed, still joined, spent and satisfied.

"Kelly," Anders whispered in a ragged tone, his head still swimming.

Kelly pulled away, wincing a little, and Anders had to grab for the base of the condom to keep it in place when he eased out.

"Was that okay?" Kelly asked, eyes wide and worried. He flipped onto his side to face him.

"Was it——" Anders choked out. "Yes, Kelly. It was perfect."

163

Kelly gave him an oddly shy, pleased smile before wiggling close.

Anders smiled, wrapping an arm around his back to hold him in place. "How are *you* feeling?"

"Never better," Kelly whispered against his chest, his contented sigh so heartfelt it made Anders squeeze him tighter.

The intensity of what Anders felt was nearly overwhelming, but the moment was so perfect he couldn't risk spoiling it with the wrong words. He merely curled his head and pressed a kiss to the top of Kelly's hair, breathing in his scent.

Kelly's pleased hum was answer enough.

CHAPTER FOURTEEN

Kelly lay in Anders' arms, trying to hold back a weird flood of emotions he hadn't expected. It was like everything inside him had been turned up to eleven, his emotions going haywire as he bounced between thoughts of "holy shit that was awesome" and "oh my god I'm in bed with Lindy", with a few "can we do that again?" moments thrown in.

He was a little sore and a lot fucked out and a happy buzz sang in his veins. This wasn't going to change anything. Anders wasn't going to suddenly fall in love with him but after wanting this for so long, it felt amazing to be in bed with him, naked and sweaty from sex.

Kelly wanted whatever little bits Anders would give him. Would it suck whenever this ended? He didn't want to think about that.

But he had this for now and it was so amazing he hugged Anders tighter.

"Are you sore?" Anders asked, his voice low and concerned in Kelly's ear.

"A little," Kelly admitted, skimming his fingertips across Anders' chest. "But like, in a *good* way."

"I know what you mean. I like that sometimes too. It reminds me of that post-workout ache."

Kelly lifted his head. "Wait, you mean you—"

"Yes. If you want to try it the other way around, I'd be happy to."

"Oh fuck," Kelly said, his eyes widening. He'd never imagined *that*.

Anders gave him a crooked little smile and Kelly lay back, pillowing his head on Anders' bicep, his mind swirling with images of sliding his dick into Anders. He felt light-headed at the idea.

"No pressure. I'm fine either way," Anders reassured him.

"No, I like the idea. I mean, I'm not going to stop wanting *this* too but …"

Anders brushed his thumb across Kelly's lower lip. "Tell me what you're in the mood for. We'll have to be careful because of games but—"

"Oh God, you aren't a 'no sex the night before a game kind of guy' are you?" Kelly asked, horrified.

Anders chuckled. "Generally, no. It depends on what happens in the postseason though. We both may be too wrecked to manage more than hands or mouths but I'm confident we can make it work."   .

"Oh, good." Kelly flopped on his back, hating the loss of Anders' skin against his, but too warm to tolerate it any longer. "You had me worried there for a minute."

"I won't leave you frustrated. I promise."

Kelly grinned at the ceiling. Well, that sounded encouraging. Anders definitely didn't sound like he regretted what they'd done so far. If he was thinking about how they'd manage it in the post-season, he clearly wasn't looking for it to end any time soon. That was promising.

"I need to get this condom off," Anders said. "And we're going to need to change the sheets."

"I should like … shower and stuff," Kelly agreed but he didn't move, just lay there, half-dead and happy as Anders shifted to sit on the edge of the bed to deal with the condom, Kelly managed to roll over, flopping onto his stomach so he could stare at Anders' long, toned back. He tied the rubber off, then neatly dropped it in the trash.

"You *should* shower, yes." Anders smiled, turning to glance at Kelly. "But you look too relaxed to move. I'll get you a cloth. Wait right there."

Anders patted his butt, kissed his shoulder, then reached for his crutches. The moment Anders left the bedroom, Kelly buried his face in the pillow and grinned.

He was sticky and sweaty but his whole body hummed with residual pleasure sparking through him like fireworks.

Kelly let himself lie there for a moment before he dragged himself from the bed, not wanting Anders to have to juggle a washcloth and crutches.

The bathroom door was open, so Kelly stepped inside, the room filling with steam from the running shower. Anders glanced at Kelly in surprise.

"I would have brought it out to you."

"Thanks. I figured I'd save you the trouble of hobbling in. Your ankle okay with the shower?"

"Yes," Anders said. "Want to join me? Carefully, of course."

Kelly would never turn *that* down, so he nodded. "Want me to take off your compression wrap for you?"

A look of surprise crossed Anders' face. "Thanks."

Kelly knelt, aware of the stickiness between his ass cheeks and his face warmed.

Anders had fucked him.

The realization felt both more and less real as time passed. He wondered what fifteen-year-old Kelly would have thought of that.

Current Kelly gently worked the compression wrap off and winced at the bruising on Anders' ankle, then laughed a little at himself.

He was *so* gone for Anders.

Trevor's ankle had been so much worse, and Kelly had relentlessly chirped him about being a baby in the weeks after his injury.

Over the years, Kelly'd had his own share of gnarly bruises he'd shrugged off without a thought, because that was the price of hockey. But seeing Anders injured was hard to bear.

Kelly was tempted to gently kiss the blue and purple splotched knob of Anders' ankle but he rose to his feet instead, placing the wrap on the edge of the nearby tub.

He didn't want to make it *weird*.

In the shower, Anders stood on one foot. He quickly rinsed off, standing in front of the massage jets mounted in the wall tiles to let the hot water pummel his back, shoulders, and thighs.

Kelly cleaned up too, hoping he could blame his suddenly hot face on the warmth of the water as he soaped between his cheeks.

"Feeling okay?" Anders' gaze was sharp, watching Kelly intently.

"Yeah." Kelly stepped forward, gently brushing his fingers across Anders' chest. His nipples were brown and a little bit of hair sprinkled across his pecs, his and Astrid's wedding rings glinting against his golden skin. "You?"

"Yes." Anders dipped his head, pressing his lips to Kelly's cheek.

"Okay, good."

The warmth in Anders' voice made a little tension Kelly had been holding onto disappear.

They were both pretty quiet as they finished their shower, and it wasn't until Anders dried himself off on a fluffy white towel that he spoke.

"Are you sleeping in my bed again?"

"If you want me." Kelly held his breath.

Anders nodded. "I slept well last night."

"My mom's trick works every time," Kelly said with a wink.

"Oh God, your *mother*." Anders closed his eyes for a moment.

Kelly shot him a confused look. "Yeah? What about her?"

"I was thinking that your father and brothers would murder me, and I somehow forgot about Catherine. She won't just dump my corpse in the Charles. She'll take her time and make me *suffer*."

"Why is my family going to go on a homicidal spree?" Kelly asked, puzzled.

Anders sat on the edge of the large, jetted tub with a groan, crossing one shin over the opposite thigh so he could work the compression wrap on over his foot. "If they find out about us."

"So, we make sure they don't," Kelly said with a laugh. He *could* kind of imagine his mom using her kitchen knives to go after anyone who hurt him. But surely his family would go easy on Anders. Hell, Kelly was pretty sure they liked Anders better than they did him.

Kelly felt disloyal as soon as the thought crossed his mind. His family loved him, but they didn't think he could handle himself without their meddling.

It was too early to go to bed yet, so they migrated to the living room. Anders pulled up the documentary they'd been watching earlier, and Kelly wandered toward the kitchen.

"Can I raid your refrigerator?"

"Yes. Help yourself."

Kelly browsed through the cupboards and let out a disgusted noise when he realized Anders had no delicious snacks. "Oh my God. Everything is so *healthy*."

"Sorry," Anders called.

"You don't sound very sorry." Kelly made a face and opened the refrigerator. It was neatly organized and everything was equally good for him. He wanted *junk*.

"There's ice cream in the freezer. Help yourself to it."

Kelly grinned triumphantly at the pint. It wasn't even frozen yogurt or something bland and boring like organic free-trade vanilla bean.

"Chocolate with salted caramel and almonds?" Kelly asked, waving his spoon at Anders. He carried the pint and some ice packs into the living room. "Lindy, you've been holding out on me."

Anders grinned. "I'm not *always* boring and healthy."

"So I see." Kelly got Anders situated with the ice packs, then plopped onto the couch next to him, unashamedly pressing himself against Anders' side. He lifted his arm, stretching it along the back of the couch, and Kelly wriggled into the embrace.

"Oh fuck." Kelly let out a garbled moan after he took his first bite of ice cream. "Damn, this is good."

"Glad you like it."

"Like it? I want to do nothing but eat this and fuck you for the rest of time."

Anders let out a little cough. "No more hockey?"

"Fine. Hockey, sex, and this ice cream. Maybe some pizza too."

Anders chuckled. "I'm glad to hear you'll have a balanced diet at least."

"Ehh. Overrated." Kelly stuck his spoon into the carton, then held it out to Anders. "Want some?"

Anders raised an eyebrow but took it.

"You're vaguely disgusted that I'm eating from the carton and that we're sharing a spoon, aren't you?" Kelly asked with a laugh.

"Yes. You know me well."

"You're a little tightly wound, Lindy." Kelly patted his thigh, then took the spoon back. "Don't worry. I'll get you to untwist."

"It *could* go both ways, you know. What if *I* make *you* think before you leap into a decision?"

Kelly gave him a shocked face. "What now? That's madness."

"Oh, Kelly." Anders ducked and pressed their temples together as he wrapped his arm around Kelly and pulled him close for a moment. "You do make me laugh."

"Good." Kelly smiled around the spoon, then made a show of licking it clean. "I try."

Later that night as they made the bed with clean sheets, Kelly felt awkward crawling in beside Anders without any excuse or reason other than wanting to.

But Anders was nonchalant when he flipped back the covers, lay on his back, then held out his arm. Kelly scrambled into place beside him and pressed his cheek to Anders' broad chest.

Kelly got comfortable, then tapped out the passcode on his phone.

Anders picked up his book from the nightstand.

"You do know they have these things called ebooks, right?" Kelly teased.

Anders swatted his ass, sharp enough to sting, but not enough to hurt. "Yes, I know what ebooks are."

"Just checking, Grandpa."

Anders let out a choking noise. "Don't you *ever* call me that in bed again."

"On the ice is okay then?" Kelly tilted his head and grinned.

"*Nowhere.*" Anders glowered, clearly channeling his Viking ancestors into the ferocity of his glare.

Jesus, Kelly was glad he'd never had to be opposite Lindy in the face-off circle. He'd pee his breezers.

But he pretended like it hadn't had any impact as he flippantly replied, "Well, you have to be specific if you're going to make rules like this."

Anders sighed. "What on earth did I do in my life to deserve having you in my bed chirping me?"

"Lots of good things," Kelly said with a happy little hum. At least one of them had done something very right.

"Is that so?" Anders glowered again, but this time it held no heat.

"Yes. Now read your old-fashioned book, Gramps, and let me check my social media." Kelly patted his chest.

Anders let out an aggravated noise. "My *mother* sent me this book. She's the one who isn't great with technology, not me."

"*Suuure.* That's what all the old-timers say."

"Do you think just because we've had sex, you can be a brat?"

"You like it," Kelly said, thumbing through his notifications on Instagram. Hmm, he'd gotten a lot of likes on his last video. He wasn't sure why. It was only him dicking around on the acoustic guitar he liked playing sometimes.

"So help me I do like your brattiness," Anders muttered.

Kelly grinned against his pec, then placed a smacking kiss on it. "I knew it."

———

Anders did, in fact, like having Kelly in his bed. He liked his chirps and yes, even his brattiness. He also liked the way Kelly wound himself around Anders' body and snuggled close.

Last night, Anders had fallen asleep smiling with Kelly's fingertips gently stroking his forehead and this morning he'd woken a few minutes before his alarm was set to go off, well-rested and content.

The contentment was possibly because Kelly was stroking something else. Although he hadn't started in earnest until Anders had begun to stir.

"What are you doing?" he asked, amused.

Kelly craned his neck though he kept stroking. "What the fuck does it feel like?"

"Like you're terrible at keeping your hands to yourself."

"Why would I want to do that when I'm in bed with you?" Kelly sounded mystified. "Seriously, man. That makes no sense."

"You make a—a good point." Anders' breath hitched when Kelly's thumb swirled over the tip of his cock. So sensitive.

Kelly grinned. "Look, you woke up hard for me. Clearly you need some attention."

"You wouldn't get anything out of this, right?" Anders asked, rubbing his hand across Kelly's shoulder blades, enjoying the warmth of his skin and the shift of his muscles beneath.

"I wouldn't be mad if you got me off too."

"I suppose I could."

"Okay, you're way too coherent right now. I think I better up my game."

Before Anders could process that statement, Kelly ducked his head under the covers and slithered lower.

In moments, Anders' cock was engulfed in wet warmth. Kelly was far less tentative than he'd been the previous time, teasing the tip of his tongue along the crown and gently playing with his balls. Anders shifted, creating more space between his thighs for Kelly to work.

Coherence went straight out the window when the blowjob got sloppy and wet, the suction increasing. Anders gasped, flattening his hand against Kelly's back. "Your *mouth*," he managed.

Kelly hummed and the sensation was so intense, Anders almost kneed him in the face. "Fuck," he managed.

Kelly pinned Ander's thighs down with his forearm, then rolled Anders' balls in his palm, tugging as he worked Anders harder.

"Coming," he warned but Kelly merely let out another pleased little hum and Anders closed his eyes as his toes curled and everything in his body went hot and tight.

He rode the wave of his orgasm until something in his ankle twinged and he swore under his breath.

Kelly popped his head out from under over the covers, wiping his mouth on the back of his hand. "What's wrong? Did I hurt you?"

Anders grimaced. "I tensed and it sent a weird little pang through my ankle. Nothing serious."

"Shit." Kelly's face was flushed, sweat dotting his brow and darkening his hair. He bit his lower lip and knelt beside Anders' hip.

"I *really* don't want to have to tell Coach I broke his top line center with a blowjob."

Anders snickered. "I wouldn't throw you under the bus, Kelly."

"Phew."

"Come here." Anders hooked his hands under Kelly's arms, then hauled him up. "Kiss me."

Kelly braced himself on the mattress, resisting. "You okay with morning breath and tasting your own cum?"

"I'll survive," he said drily.

"Damn, you are wilder than I expected, Lindy." Kelly leaned in.

Anders made a noise of disgust and pulled Kelly into a kiss. It took a moment but Kelly softened into it and Anders ran an affectionate hand down his back. Kelly was splayed across his chest, now straddling his uninjured leg. He was hard, either for the usual early morning reasons or because he'd enjoyed giving Anders a blowjob.

The head of his cock was slick as he rubbed against Anders' thigh.

"What do you want?" Anders asked when Kelly finally pulled away, flushed and needy.

Kelly bit his lip. "Would you suck me?"

"Of course."

Anders urged Kelly to roll onto his back, then settled between his splayed legs, shifting him on the bed until he had him where he wanted him. Kelly's eyes were bright as Anders stared at him, his entire body tight with anticipation.

Anders scooted back, then pressed a leisurely kiss to Kelly's inner thigh. He smelled like warm skin layered with the scent of Anders' bodywash lingering from his shower last night. Cedar and lime mingled with Kelly's natural scent and Anders let out a pleased hum at the combination. Kelly's thighs were lean and strong, and he whimpered when Anders dragged his thumb along the crease of his groin.

He squirmed when Anders pressed his mouth to the same spot, whimpering when he followed that with a lap of his tongue.

"Lindy," Kelly whined.

"Yes." He glanced up to meet Kelly's gaze.

"*Please.*"

"Be patient." He buried his nose in the tangle of ginger curls, right where his scent was strongest, and breathed deep. Kelly squirmed, trying to get him to move and Anders smiled against his skin. Anders licked and kissed his way to Kelly's balls, mouthing at them until Kelly made soft panting noises.

When Kelly whined, Anders circled his cock, enjoying the hot pulse of his blood as he kissed his way up the shaft.

The relieved sigh Kelly let out as Anders dropped his head made him smile around his cock. Kelly tangled his fingers in Anders' hair, gently urging him to move.

Anders did, sucking him slow and deep, moving with precise, teasing motions that wound Kelly tighter and tighter. His breath was raspy, his thighs twitching every time he let out a soft cry.

Anders shoved a hand under Kelly's thigh, draping it over his shoulder so he could get better access. He didn't want to pull away long enough to get lube so he licked his finger and circled

Kelly's entrance. His skin was a little reddened, possibly sore, so Anders merely teased the outside rather than pushing in.

When Anders worked his way up again and lapped at the sticky fluid at the tip of Kelly's cock, Kelly dug a heel into Anders' back, tightening his grip on Anders' hair.

A few strokes and hard sucks brought Kelly to the edge until he whimpered and writhed beneath Anders with delicious desperation. Anders backed off to give him playful little licks.

"Oh my God, you're a *tease*," Kelly huffed, his voice laced with frustration.

"And you're a brat." Anders dipped his head to bite his inner thigh, smiling against his skin. "Quite a pair we make, huh?"

He didn't torture Kelly too much longer and when Kelly tugged at Anders' hair hard enough to hurt, he took pity on him and took him deep, working him with a few firm strokes until Kelly shouted his release and shook under him, filling Anders' mouth with his cum.

"Holy fuck, Lindy," Kelly panted as Anders shifted to lie beside him. He curled into Anders' arm, plastering his sweaty chest against Anders'.

Anders kissed his hair. "I *did* tell you to call me Anders, right?"

"Yeah. But sometimes you're still Lindy in my head."

"Okay. Whatever makes you happy," Anders said, patting his hip. "Now, I think we should get ready for this road trip."

Kelly let out a whine. "Nooo. I don't wanna."

Anders glanced at the clock. "We need to be at the airport in less than two hours and the traffic is usually terrible."

"I know." Kelly flopped onto his back. "I'd rather stay in bed with you."

"Well, Coach wants us both there."

"At least you're going too." Kelly rolled out of bed and Anders sat up more carefully. "I would be bummed if you had to stay home."

"So would I," Anders said drily. He made the bed, mindful of his injured ankle. "Sitting at home and doing nothing is incredibly frustrating. Do you remember when I was out for a few weeks with the wrist issue last season?"

"You were about to start climbing the walls."

Anders tugged the covers into place, Kelly doing the same on his side.

"Exactly."

Anders froze, realizing he'd thought of the far side of the bed as Kelly's. That had always been Astrid's. It helped knowing it was a different bedroom, different bed, nearly different everything, but Anders shouldn't be thinking like that.

Kelly had only spent two nights in bed with him. It wasn't *his* side of the bed.

Anders straightened the pillows and shook his head at how ridiculous his thoughts were. He liked the sex and companionship. He wasn't looking for a new relationship. He'd loved deeply in the past, and love like that only happened once in a lifetime.

He wasn't foolish enough to believe it could happen twice.

"Anders?" Kelly's tone was concerned.

"Yes?" He fluffed a pillow and settled it into place before he met Kelly's gaze.

"You okay?"

"I'm fine. Just lost in thought." He reached for his crutches. "Could you grab my suitcase? It'll be difficult to manage with these."

"Of course."

Kelly dragged on a pair of shorts and Anders showed him to the walk-in closet. It was roomy and Kelly whistled under his breath. "I shouldn't be surprised that this is so well-organized, but every time I walk in here, I'm blown away by what a fucking nerd you are."

Anders grinned and opened a wardrobe door to reveal his suitcase and garment bag. "Do I want to know what your closet looks like?"

Kelly huffed and shot him a look over his shoulder, reaching for the bags. "It's a mess. Dumb, huh? Since I have to live in there."

Anders' shot him a confused glance before realizing Kelly had meant both his literal closet and the more metaphorical one he had to exist in.

"I wish you felt safe enough to come out."

Kelly shrugged, carrying the bags. "I probably could. It just feels like a huge fucking hassle. Although I guess it hasn't been too bad for you, huh?"

"No, not at all. Then again, I'm at the tail end of my career and my family has known for years."

"They're good with it?"

"They are. Sweden is generally more progressive though." He gestured to the luggage rack and hook nearby. "You can put them there."

"Yeah." Kelly did as instructed. "My mom will probably cry, and it'll be a big thing, and the thought of dealing with it sounds exhausting. I always figured I'd come out after. But now, I dunno."

"After hockey?"

"Yeah. Retirement's hopefully a long time from now but I guess we'll see." Kelly shrugged. "Okay, I'm going to go pack my stuff too."

Anders nodded, already scanning his suits to decide which he'd bring on the three-game road trip. It didn't take him long to pack. He was decisive and years ago, on the advice of a teammate, had learned to leave as much packed as possible. He had duplicates of his toiletries, and he carried extra charging cables tucked in his laptop bag so he had little to think about when it came time to leave for a road trip.

Anders left the bags in the closet, figuring Kelly would be willing to grab them for him, but when he walked into the bedroom, Kelly looked distressed.

His suits hung in a bag in the entryway but the rest of his clothes and belongings were spread out across the bed. He chewed at his lip, staring at everything strewn across the crisp white duvet. He shrugged, then began stuffing things into his bag again.

Anders winced. "Is that how you pack?"

"It's how *I* pack, yeah." Kelly looked up, laughing as Anders approached. "You really want to show me everything I'm doing wrong, don't you?"

"*Yes*," Anders said fervently.

Kelly held up his hands and backed away. "Have at it."

Anders grimaced at the lack of packing cubes and directed Kelly to fetch some of his. "Remind me to buy you a set," he said absently, rolling Kelly's undershirts and tucking them into the first cube. They could probably go into the center compartment of his rolling luggage.

Kelly stuffed his laptop charger into his backpack. "You don't have to do that."

"It'll make packing easier," he pointed out.

"Well, I was in kind of a rush when we stopped by my place the other day. I'm not usually *quite* this bad." He hesitated. "Um, I think I forgot my charging cable for my air pods though."

"Go in my office," Anders said. "The third drawer down on the left side of the storage cabinet behind my desk has spare cables. There should be one in there."

"Thanks!" Kelly disappeared and Anders turned his attention to Kelly's luggage. It was zipped and ready to go by the time Kelly returned.

"Got it!" Kelly said, holding up the cable. His gaze landed on his bag. "Hey, that was fast. Thanks!"

Anders narrowed his eyes. "Was this a ploy to get me to pack for you?"

"Maaayyybe." Kelly grinned.

"Brat," Anders said affectionately, swatting Kelly's ass as he passed him on his way to the bathroom.

He yelped and gave Anders a wounded look. "I was kidding!"

"Sure, you were."

Kelly caught his arm, pulling him in for a kiss. "Thank you. Seriously, I was joking but I appreciate that you did it for me."

"I'm happy to help."

Anders liked taking care of Kelly. Not because he thought Kelly couldn't manage but because it made Kelly smile and look at him with soft, fond eyes. Because Kelly deserved to be taken care of.

He pressed a kiss to Kelly's temple. "Anything else you need?"

"Not that I can think of."

"Okay. Let's get ready. We should have plenty of time to eat before we head out."

CHAPTER FIFTEEN

Anders was boring and made Kelly take the Mercedes to the airport. Kelly pouted the whole way, refusing to give in to Anders' friendly teasing, although he didn't push Anders' hand off his thigh.

They arrived at the terminal far earlier than Kelly usually got there, and Coach Tate shot him a surprised glance. "You're early, O'Shea," he said as they boarded the plane.

Kelly shrugged. "I drove Lindy. He's like … obnoxiously early to everything."

Coach Tate shot a smile at Anders over Kelly's shoulder. "See, good things are coming from this injury. You have the opportunity to teach Kelly what a clock is."

"Rude," Kelly said with a laugh. "I'm only late when Underhill's running behind and we drive together."

Kelly dropped into his usual seat, and Anders went to his, a few rows back and across the aisle. Too wound up to sit still, Kelly turned to Theriault and Walsh, who sat behind him.

"How's your dad doing?"

Theriault blinked, cocking his head as if trying to figure out where the question came from. "*Bon.* He's—he's doing as well as can be expected."

"You and Coach are moving soon, right?"

"After the season ends. We recently bought a place and met with an interior designer about furnishing it."

"Nice. Have any pictures?"

Gabriel nodded and reached for his phone. "One moment."

"How are you liking Charlie?" Walsh asked.

Gabriel hummed, smiling a little. "He's, uh, enthusiastic. Quite good though. Lance and I give him vague ideas of what we like, and he magically turns it into a design board."

Kelly grinned. He'd met Charlie Monaghan a few times and he was hilarious. He was best friends with Walsh's new boyfriend Taylor, and he'd had the locker room laughing their heads off when he snuck in after a home game one night a few weeks ago.

Gabriel handed over his phone, and Kelly was relieved to see the pictures were on the real estate listing website. He had a horrible mental image of accidentally coming across half-naked pictures of Coach Tate or something.

Kelly was happy for the two of them but damn, he did *not* want to think about his coach that way.

"Nice digs," Kelly said after he scrolled through the photos and returned the phone. The house was modest by most NHL standards, but it was a great place and it looked like it would be perfect for them.

Kelly couldn't imagine living with his father, but he couldn't blame Theriault for wanting to keep his dad close when he had a condition like CTE.

Tate was a hell of a guy for being unconditionally supportive of it all though.

Kelly glanced at Tate, who had his head down, staring intently at Coach Daniels' iPad along with Coach Horton and Coach Briggs.

He wasn't bad-looking but nope, Kelly didn't see the appeal. He glanced at Anders, watching him get settled into his usual seat and absently gather his hair into a bun, laughing at something Murphy said.

Was it Kelly's imagination or did Anders seem happier? Lighter than he had a few days ago?

Had Kelly's crazy idea to give Anders some stress relief actually worked?

It hit Kelly then, how insane it had been to strip down and tease Anders and hit on him. At the time it had seemed perfectly natural but Jesus, he'd really taken a risk, hadn't he?

Anders would never be cruel about it. Even if he hadn't been interested, he would have let Kelly down gently. He would have been kind, because that was who he was at his core.

But Kelly had risked the awkwardness and the ease of their friendship.

He was damn lucky it had worked in his favor.

Anders glanced up then, shooting Kelly a small smile, and Kelly felt something go soft and gooey in his chest.

Shit. No.

He looked at the front of the plane, ruthlessly stomping the feelings down. That wasn't what this was about. He couldn't let himself get all mixed up about this.

Anders had been clear about what he wanted. This wasn't going any further.

This was a chance for Kelly to learn what it was like to be with a guy and an opportunity for Anders to not feel so alone. It could benefit both of them if Kelly remembered the rules.

It would fucking suck when it all came to an end, but in the meantime, it could be good if he let himself enjoy it without hoping it would be something more.

Kelly had finished his useless little internal pep talk when he realized everyone had boarded the plane except Malone and Underhill. A glance at his phone told him they were supposed to take off five minutes ago.

Daniels grew increasingly annoyed, while Murphy left messages on the guys' voicemails. Kelly pulled up their chat and sent a message.

The fuck r u??

But a moment later, Malone sauntered onto the plane, Underhill on his heels.

"Nice of you to finally join us, gentlemen," Daniels said drily.

Underhill looked vaguely embarrassed as he slid into the seat beside Kelly, but Malone swaggered down the aisle to his usual spot with the rookies.

It was interesting. He was definitely losing his entourage. Kelly hadn't spent any time with him since the mess in Montreal. And for all of Malone's bitching about his suspension and fine, it certainly hadn't changed his attitude any.

"Why are you so late?" Kelly asked his roommate. "Was it 'cause I wasn't there to get you up in time?"

Underhill flipped him off. "No, fuckface. I wasn't home. I hooked up last night and I got stuck in traffic on my way to our place this morning to grab my shit."

"You spent the night?" Kelly was surprised. Underhill was definitely the love 'em and leave 'em type.

Underhill shrugged. "Malone and I were out last night so I didn't leave the club until like three. I dunno where he ended up but I was in bed with a hookup when my phone went off. We sure as fuck weren't sleeping though."

"Oh." Kelly smirked. "Got it."

"You're in a weirdly good mood," Underhill said, tone amused. "Especially when we're flying to Dallas."

Kelly shrugged. "I slept well last night."

Underhill snorted and hooked up his Switch. "So, what's her name?"

"I'm staying with *Lindy*," he protested.

Underhill raised an eyebrow and Kelly waved him off, hoping his face hadn't turned stupidly red. "No, he just has comfy beds. It's a great guest room, you know?"

Underhill nodded, suspicion fading from his expression although Kelly felt a little guilty about the white lie. "Oh yeah, I remember. We sacked out there after his housewarming party."

"Yeah, that's right." Kelly had shared a bed with Underhill that night, though they'd both been wasted, and he'd woken to the sound of Trevor puking in the bathroom in the middle of the night.

It was much more fun staying in Lindy's bed now.

Kelly smiled to himself as they got ready for takeoff, and once they were at cruising altitude, he and Underhill got a game going.

A while later, when Kelly got up to use the bathroom, he passed Lindy. He was deep in conversation with Murphy but his gaze was warm as it flicked over Kelly for a moment before he returned his attention to their captain.

Kelly had the oddest urge to reach out and touch him, trail his fingers along his shoulder or something, but he held back.

When he returned to his seat a short while later, he winced, a bit sore from his fun with Lindy last night.

Underhill gave him a quizzical look. "You okay? You strain something in the last game?"

"No. I'm fine," Kelly assured him. "Just a weird little twinge. Must've been from a workout."

Anders certainly *had* given him a workout, though he'd been surprisingly sweet and gentle. Well, maybe not so surprisingly. He was the kind of guy who always wanted to take care of people. Especially Kelly.

He glanced at Anders again. He was looking forward now and he gave Kelly another soft smile. Kelly smiled back, then ducked his head before anyone could see their interaction.

Damn, he would have to be careful before he made a total fool of himself in front of the team.

———

Anders watched the game against Dallas from the team suite. He hated it. It felt wrong to watch his teammates play without him. He would have to get used to it though. Retirement was creeping up on him and he couldn't stave it off forever. Meticulous training only went so far.

He'd been blessed with good health and good luck—at least as far as injuries went, he thought with a touch of bitterness—and he'd had an incredible run. But this injury had shaken him. Reminded him it couldn't last forever. A wrong hit, a problem with his equipment, and it could all be over.

Anders would have to get used to the idea and get over his fear of an empty future.

The game against Dallas was a tight one.

Although they won 3-1, it felt like they were playing from behind. They needed to be pushing now, grabbing every possible point they could get. But it was a win and hopefully that energy would carry them to a bigger victory against Phoenix.

On the plane from Texas to Arizona, Anders closed his eyes and rested a little. He didn't sleep, just let the quiet murmurs of Zane and Ryan across the aisle mingle with the louder noises of the guys playing cards or video games as they flew through the inky night sky.

Anders smiled every time Kelly's voice rose above the team's chatter.

After a while, he realized he'd slipped his necklace out from under the collar of his shirt and he'd been rubbing his thumb across the smooth, warm metal of his and Astrid's rings.

Anders wondered if the sight of them bothered Kelly.

He hadn't commented on them. Hadn't even looked twice at them. But was that intentional? Was he being polite?

Anders opened his eyes, tucking the necklace behind his shirt again.

Across the aisle, he caught Hartinger's curious glance. "You okay, man?" he asked quietly.

Anders nodded. "Yes. Just hated being out of the game tonight."

"We'll be glad to have you back soon," Hartinger said.

Keegan Truro turned around, peering over the top of the seat. "I wanted to talk to you about that, Lindy."

"Hmm?" Anders gave his teammate a curious look.

"I mean, I'm not here trying to steal your top line slot," Truro said. "But I was wondering if you'd be willing to work with me a little on my skills. Coach Tate is awesome but he's got a dozen of us to worry about. You're the best around. I thought maybe you'd be good with sharing some of your wisdom. You see stuff I don't in games, and I'd be happy to take any suggestions you've got on what I can work on."

"Sure," Anders said, surprised. "Why don't you grab an iPad and we'll go through tonight's game."

"Absolutely." Truro stood and walked to the coach's area, speaking quietly with Tate. His gaze flicked up to meet Anders' and he shot him a smile before he handed the device to Truro.

When Truro was seated beside him, Anders pulled up the game footage, then retrieved some notes he'd taken during the game.

"Wow. You already have notes?"

Anders shrugged. It was such a long-standing habit of his, he didn't think twice about it anymore. "After a game, I usually watch footage on my own and jot down my thoughts. Sometimes I pass them along to Tate or Greene but mostly it's for my personal use."

At first, Anders had worried he was overstepping but their offensive coach and video coach always welcomed his feedback.

"Huh. That's dedication."

"*That's* how he's so damn good," Murphy said drily, leaning around Hartinger.

"Yeah, he makes the rest of us look like lazy fucks," Hartinger chirped.

"Hey, I review footage after games too," Murphy said, sounding a little offended.

"Yeah, but you got the obsessive need to do it from Lindy. Although at least you know how to turn it off. He doesn't."

Anders smiled, acknowledging the truth of his words, and pointed to the screen. "Okay, Keegan, do you see this turnover here in the second period?"

Truro nodded as Anders pointed out where he'd gone wrong. After a few minutes, he dug his phone out. "Can I take notes on all this too? I don't want to forget anything."

"Of course," Anders said. He was pleased Truro was taking it seriously. At twenty-three, he was on the young side but he did seem focused on improving his skills. He'd made some errors tonight but overall he'd done well.

"Hey, can I get in on this too?" Walsh asked, sliding into the empty row behind Anders.

"Of course."

The remainder of the flight passed quickly enough and when they arrived at the hotel and waited for their keycards, the three of them were still talking plays and skills Truro and Walsh could work on.

"Could we do this again?" Truro asked eagerly as they rode the elevator to their floor, Walsh carrying Anders' bags so Anders didn't have to deal with them and the crutches. "I like the way you explain stuff. Something just clicks with me. Like, there's nothing wrong with Coach Greene's tape review but …"

"Yes, of course," Anders said. "Maybe after practice tomorrow?"

"Awesome. Thanks, Lindy." Truro patted his back and walked down the hall to his room.

"Yeah, seriously," Walsh said, setting Anders' bags inside his door. "That was helpful tonight."

"Glad to hear it." Anders smiled.

"Need anything else?"

"No, I think I'm set. Thanks for your help with my bags."

"Sure. No prob. I remember when I was on crutches a few years ago it was a giant PITA." He glanced at his phone. "Okay, well, I hate to rush off but I do need to get to my room."

"No problem. Skype date with your little one?"

"Yeah." Walsh's grin turned soft. "She's with Taylor tonight and I'm looking forward to talking to both of them. It's hard to be away."

"I bet. Night, Jamie."

"Night, Lindy."

After the door swung shut behind Jamie, Anders got his room in order, hanging his suits in the closet and plugging in chargers.

He thought about Jamie Walsh as he unpacked. He was glad Jamie had found someone like Taylor Hollis.

Jamie deserved it. He was a better player than he gave himself credit for and seemed like a genuinely good man. His daughter was special too. Strong and feisty and the kind of girl he thought Elia would have been when she was a little older.

Anders' throat thickened with grief, as always, at the thought of losing Elia. But over the years it had gotten easier to spend time with his teammates' children. To be happy for the guys instead of raw with envy. Going to Ava's birthday party earlier this month had been good for him, despite Kelly's worry it would be too difficult for him to bear.

After a quick shower to rinse off the grimy feeling that always clung to his skin after a flight, Anders settled on the bed, surprised to realize how quiet the room seemed. He clicked on the TV but even after he found something to watch, the sensation didn't ease.

After noticing he wasn't paying any attention to the screen, he turned it off and read for a while, willing himself to feel sleepy. It didn't work. Eventually, he tossed the book onto the nightstand and set his alarm for the morning. He clicked off the light and settled on the pillow.

Maybe some meditation would do him some good. His routine was off from not playing and having Kelly stay with him.

He brought up his meditation app and lay on his back, closing his eyes and following the gentle guidance, the soft murmur of white noise filling his ears.

But it did nothing to soothe his mind and help him wind down. Long after it ended, he lay there still and quiet, itching to move.

After a while, Anders gave in to the urge to shift into a more comfortable position, stretching his shoulders for a moment before flipping on his side. The bed seemed uncomfortable and not quite right. He frowned at the dark ceiling and swore under his breath when he admitted to himself why the too-quiet room and empty bed seemed all wrong.

How had he gotten so used to having Kelly around?

On the way to the airport, they'd discussed sleeping separately. Kelly had lobbied hard for sneaking into his room but Anders had dismissed the idea. It was too risky.

When Zane and Ryan had first come out, management had quietly told them they expected them to sleep separately. They'd gone along with it, and so had Gabriel and Lance, but management had loosened up on it recently and a few weeks ago Anders had spotted Ryan coming out of Zane's room in the morning without a hint of shame.

It wasn't unusual for guys to crash in each other's rooms anyway. Late-night movies or card games sometimes led to players sacked out platonically on each other's beds, especially as they got deeper into the regular season. No one would have thought twice about Kelly coming in to watch a movie, then leaving in the morning.

But Anders was wary of the accompanying questions if it became too much of a habit.

And yet, he regretted it with every fiber of his being now.

In a very short time, he'd grown accustomed to Kelly's sleepy murmurs and the sensation of their skin pressed together. Anders craved the comfort of Kelly's body tucked tight to his, his fingertips on Anders' forehead sending him drifting off to sleep.

He shifted onto his other side and reached for his phone. He had a message waiting from Kelly.

I don't remember these beds sucking so much. I like yours better.

Anders stared at the screen, unsure of how to respond. He liked his better too. But he suspected that was only with Kelly in it. But how could he say that? They weren't supposed to be getting more attached. It seemed like everything he wanted to say would only lead Kelly on more.

When they were together, everything seemed easy and uncomplicated but alone, his thoughts went wild, conjuring up possible pitfalls and complications.

Was he thinking clearly when he was alone or simply giving in to his deepest fears?

Anders grimaced and shut off his phone without replying, turning it facedown on the nightstand again.

Anders couldn't grow reliant on Kelly any more than he already had.

Not without hurting Kelly, and that was the last thing he wanted to do.

CHAPTER SIXTEEN

"You're looking good." Dr. Gardner patted Anders' shin. "I think you can say goodbye to the crutches now."

"I can't tell you how glad I am to hear that." Anders' tone was heartfelt.

The team doctor shot Anders a small smile. "I bet."

"What about playing?"

"Always so eager," he joked, but when Anders stared at him, he grew serious again. "You're cleared for practice today. Let's see how it goes, but unless there's a problem, I think you'll be good to play in the game against Nashville."

Anders let out a huge sigh of relief. That was the news he'd been waiting to hear but did he have to miss the game against Arizona?

"Not tonight?" he asked hopefully.

"No." Dr. Gardner leveled him with a serious look. "You *know* how tricky ankles are. I want to see how you do with some easy practice skating first. That'll give it time to show us any issues before you play a full game."

"Okay," Anders agreed, disappointed but able to see the wisdom in his approach.

"Think about it as a short-term investment for a long-term payout. We need you in the postseason." Dr. Gardner stepped away with a smile.

Anders bit back the urge to knock on wood or ask if he was sure they'd make it to a playoff run without him. But Truro had done well. If the team could hold it together again tonight, hopefully they'd have a chance. They were so *close*.

Anders slid off the training table, thanked Dr. Gardner, and walked down the hall, elated to return to practice.

Thankfully, his ankle still felt great after, and he was in a good mood as he ate lunch with the team at the hotel.

He'd slipped his keycard into the card reader for his room when he caught sight of Zane.

"Hey, I know you'll probably be grabbing a nap soon, but do you have a minute?" Anders asked.

"Sure." Zane turned back and gave him a concerned look. "Anything wrong?"

"No. I wanted to talk to you about the upcoming game."

The tension in Zane's shoulders eased as they stepped into the room. "Yeah, of course."

"First of all, I'm officially cleared to play so I'll be back in the lineup against Nashville."

A relieved smile crossed Zane's face and he held out his hand. "That's great news. We'll be glad to have you back, man."

They went through their usual complicated pre-game handshake ritual that ended with a backslapping hug.

"Truro's played well," Anders said thoughtfully. "He's stepped up when we've needed him."

"He has," Zane agreed. "But he's not you."

"You'll have to get used to that eventually. I can't play forever," he pointed out.

Expecting a chirp about him playing forever, Anders was surprised when Zane grew serious. "I'd like to talk to you about that."

Anders blinked at his captain. "Oh?"

"Well." Zane leaned against the wall. "Ryan and I are retiring after the end of the season."

Anders stared blankly. "Even if …" He couldn't say the words.

"Whatever happens in the postseason, we're hanging up our skates. Obviously, we both want another Cup this year." Zane let out a deprecating little laugh. "I mean, there's no question about *that*. But we're both in agreement that it's time."

"You're still young," Anders protested. "And healthy."

Zane grimaced, stuffing his hands into the pockets of his hoodie. "Honestly, my hip is starting to cause some problems."

He'd had issues with it two seasons ago and it had nagged him during their playoff run last year.

Anders frowned, concerned. "Do you need surgery soon?"

"Not yet. It's just a matter of time though."

"You don't want to go that route? Get a repair done, then play a few more years?"

Zane sighed, a weary expression crossing his handsome face. "I considered my options for a long time. A part of me wanted to go balls-out until they had to take me off the ice in a stretcher. But a bigger part of me decided it was time to start thinking about a different future."

"And Ryan feels the same?"

"He does. We've talked a lot about it. We want kids and we don't feel like we can juggle it while we're both skating."

Anders considered the idea and nodded. "It's different when one parent is home, isn't it?"

"Exactly."

Although Astrid's work in the hospital had been demanding, she'd still been in the same city in case of an emergency. Their nanny had been Astrid's younger cousin who'd come over from Sweden to stay with them and take care of Elia.

Zane and Ryan's families were both out of state and they'd probably have to rely on a stranger. During the season they'd both be away more than they were home. That wasn't an ideal way to raise a child.

"I understand," Anders said thoughtfully.

"I did suggest retiring while Ryan kept playing for a few more years but he didn't want to."

Anders nodded. He wasn't surprised. Ryan loved hockey every bit as much as the rest of them but his passion had always seemed to come from playing with Zane. When Ryan had the option to become an unrestricted free agent, he'd never considered playing for another team, despite the offers that would have given him his own captaincy.

The three of them had talked about it at length, Ryan stubbornly saying, "I don't *want* it. My place on the ice is beside Zane. It's Hartinger and Murphy until the end. If Zane is done, I'm done."

They hadn't even been dating at the time.

"What are your plans for after retirement?" Anders asked quietly. "Besides raising hockey prodigies."

Zane chuckled but his amused expression quickly fell. "Honestly, I want to get a position in the head office."

"With the Otters or are you thinking elsewhere?"

"With the Otters, if I can. I'll take whatever position I can to get my foot in the door here. Maybe something in marketing or scouting. Ultimately, I'd like a GM position though."

"You'll be good at it," Anders said honestly. Leadership rested easily on Zane's shoulders and Anders knew how much it chafed that he didn't have more say about problematic players like Malone.

"If it goes the way I hope, a lot of people will probably hate me."

"Oh?"

"I want to change the culture around hockey," Zane said flatly.

"You already have."

Zane shrugged the praise off. "Some, yes. Ryan and I coming out made a difference but there's still so much to do." He let out a frustrated sound. "There's so much that still needs to *change*. I want to carve out a space for guys who don't fit elsewhere. The head office has handled the coming out issues better than I thought they would, but we all know there's a long way to go with so many things."

Anders nodded his agreement.

"The league needs more players of color, more LGBTQ guys, and a hell of a lot less good-old-boy attitude." He scowled. "I want a place where the bullshit that happens over and over again with guys like Malone isn't tolerated. Where the people in charge don't look the other way when a guy is a good player but a piece of shit off the ice."

"It's a lofty goal."

Zane sighed and adjusted his snapback, tugging at the brim of the hat. "Maybe an impossible one. Maybe I'll get drummed out before I can get in a position to make a difference, but I have to *try*."

Anders squeezed his shoulder. "You've already made a difference. I believe you can do more."

"Thanks, man. That means a lot coming from you."

"It sounds more like you're gunning for commissioner of the entire NHL."

Zane let out a snort. "Talk about lofty. I doubt that'll happen but never say never, I guess."

"What is Ryan considering for his retirement? Or will he be a stay-at-home dad?"

Zane chuckled. "We seriously considered it and he might for a while, but he's also looking into some media stuff. He's been talking to his—*our*—agent about it. There's some tentative interest for him to do some work as a color commentator for one of the networks or the local market. We'll see how it all shakes out, but he's definitely got the knowledge and the charisma."

"He does," Anders agreed with a smile. "Samantha certainly has taken full advantage of that."

Zane laughed. "She has. That's kind of what got him seriously pursuing it."

Their Director of Marketing and Digital Media had used Ryan's on-camera talent for their social media campaigns in the past few months and fans had eaten it up.

"What about you?" Zane asked. "I know you're planning to skate until you're at least a hundred but surely you've considered your options."

"My future has been on my mind the past few weeks," Anders admitted. "This ankle issue ... it scared me."

"A minor tweak in two decades of an overall healthy career?" Zane scoffed.

"I feel like I'm living on borrowed time."

And Zane's statement wasn't entirely true. Anders had been out with plenty of injuries before. But he supposed Zane had a point. They'd been relatively minor, and he'd never been plagued by the recurring injuries so many of his teammates had suffered. "It scares me to think of what *could* have happened."

Zane frowned. "You okay?"

Anders lifted one shoulder in a shrug. "Yes. Just feeling my age, I guess. I have started considering my options for after hockey, but I don't have any clear plans." He'd been putting off thoughts of what he'd do after for as long as he could, but they seemed abruptly real and urgent now. Especially now that he knew his wingers were retiring.

"Your contract goes through next season though, right?"

"Yes." Anders frowned. "They'll have to buy me out if I leave. I never thought I'd have to consider doing my final season without you guys though. I always assumed you and Ryan would keep going for a while after I was gone."

"They'll find you some good wingers," Zane said confidently. "I mean, Tremblay will probably slot into Ryan's spot no problem. He's a Swiss Army knife."

"He is," Anders agreed. He was the kind of player who could adapt to playing with anyone. A flashy skater with the kind of innate hockey sense that couldn't be taught and the ability to set up scoring for everyone around him.

"They'll probably offer you the captaincy once I'm gone," Zane said more seriously.

Anders blinked at the idea. He struggled to imagine playing on this team without Zane and Ryan. He'd had other wingers over the years, of course, but since he'd been with the Otters, they'd had such a solid core for so long it was difficult to picture having to relearn all their systems and break new guys in.

And the idea of leading them …

"I honestly don't know if I want that position," Anders admitted. "I wonder if there's someone else who might be better suited."

Zane made a thoughtful face as if he was considering the idea. "This is going to sound crazy, but I think Theriault might be a good option."

"No, I don't think it sounds crazy at all," Anders said slowly. "He's not the player he was when he came from Toronto."

"No, he's a hell of a lot better. He's steady, thoughtful …"

"You don't think that would cause problems because of Tate's position as assistant coach?"

"I don't know. Maybe. I was mostly thinking out loud. He's come such a long way though. He's thoughtful and he knows the game so well. His hockey sense is unmatched, and he's been great with Kelly this season."

"He has," Anders agreed.

Zane paused. "That's something I've been meaning to talk to you about. Has Kelly seemed different to you lately?"

Anders tried not to flinch. "Different how?"

"I don't know exactly. He seems to be settling into his skin, shifting away from Malone and his little crew." Zane shrugged. "It's a good thing, I just wondered if you'd noticed something since he's been staying with you."

"We did talk about the Malone situation recently. He agreed staying away was good. Otherwise, I haven't noticed anything specific."

"I might be imagining things," Zane said with a shrug. "Then again, being away from Malone might be more than enough."

"I wish the league had done more after the altercation at the club."

"Yeah. A fine and a stern warning hardly seems like enough. But if the woman isn't pressing charges …" Zane scowled. "I don't want to think about what the franchise did to make sure that happened."

Anders winced. "No, me neither."

Zane let out a frustrated noise. "See, *that's* the kind of shit we need to change."

"You do have a daunting task ahead of you," Anders said.

To his surprise, Zane grinned. "Yeah, but when have you ever known me to back down from a fucking challenge?"

"Great point," Anders said with a smile. "Well, I wish you the best of luck with it."

"Thanks, man. I think I'm gonna need it." He slapped Anders' shoulder. "Now, I've gotta let you go. I need to get some rest in and win a game tonight. We've got a playoff spot to clinch, and we only have two games to do it."

"One step at a time," Anders said, knocking on a nearby wood panel and muttering the familiar Swedish phrase to dispel bad luck under his breath.

"One step at a time," Zane echoed and let himself out of the room, leaving Anders alone with his thoughts of the future.

CHAPTER SEVENTEEN

Kelly chewed his lip as he knocked on the door of Anders' hotel room. After the win in Phoenix, they'd flown to Nashville. He was wound up after tonight's game and the one against Nashville wasn't until the day after tomorrow. He'd turned down Malone's invite to drink and play cards in favor of seeing whether Anders wanted to hang out.

He'd been distant and distracted for a couple of days and Kelly was a little worried.

"Kelly." Anders looked surprised when he answered the door, his dress shirt unbuttoned, showing off a white undershirt clinging to his chest and abs. "Everything okay?"

"Yep. I thought maybe you wanted company for a bit. I ran across a documentary you might like." He held up his laptop. "Thought we could hook up to the TV and watch if you're interested."

Anders hesitated a second. "Yes. Okay. Sure. Come in." He held the door wide open, and Kelly stepped inside.

Kelly tried not to watch as Anders stripped out of the clothing he'd worn on the plane and hung it neatly in the closet.

"How's the ankle feeling?" Kelly asked. He set his laptop on the dresser next to the TV.

"Good. I'm in the lineup against Nashville."

"That's great," Kelly said with a smile. He looked away, afraid if he kept staring, he'd make Anders uncomfortable. After feeling so sure of where they stood, he was confused. Anders had been oddly distant the past few days and he didn't understand *why*. "It'll be good to have you on the ice again."

"I'm looking forward to it."

Kelly bit his lip, plugging in the HDMI cable with more care than was really warranted. "So, you didn't reply to my text last night."

Kelly half-expected Anders to say he'd fallen asleep before he could answer but instead, he let out a big sigh.

"I'm sorry. I thought it would be better if we slept apart."

"I get that," Kelly said carefully. "But it doesn't feel great to be left on read. You could have talked to me and explained it."

"I was afraid if I texted you, I'd change my mind."

Kelly smiled over his shoulder. "I am pretty hard to resist."

Anders chuckled. "You are."

Kelly turned to face him, trying to ignore that Anders was sitting on the bed wearing nothing but an undershirt and snug briefs. "So, you want to watch this documentary or what?"

"Yes."

Rather than turn on the power for the TV, Kelly set the remote on the bed and turned to face Anders.

"Or maybe we could do something else first?" Kelly offered.

"Like what?" Anders asked, like he didn't know perfectly well what Kelly had in mind.

"Like this." Kelly leaned down and pressed their lips together in a kiss that quickly turned hungry.

"Is this why you actually knocked on my door?" Anders asked a few minutes later, chuckling against his mouth, his palms warm where they hooked around Kelly's thighs.

Kelly gave him a sheepish little shrug as he drew back, straightening. "Maybe. I hoped, anyway. I *really* missed having you on the bench with me the past few games."

Not to mention sleeping beside him. But talking about hockey was easier.

"I missed being on the bench with you too," Anders said, reaching up to brush his thumb across Kelly's lower lip. "You and your incessant mouthguard chewing."

Kelly gave him a surprised glance. "You *miss* that? You always seemed disgusted by it."

"I find it annoyingly endearing," he said with a sigh. "Despite knowing it's unsafe and unsanitary."

Kelly smirked, rubbing his hands across Anders' chest, annoyed by the fabric getting in the way of his exploration. "I think I might be a terrible influence on you."

"Probably," Anders agreed. "But it would be a lie if I said I minded."

"Good." Kelly beamed. "Now, what do you say we burn off a little energy from the game?"

"I don't have any to burn off," Anders said, forlorn. But when Kelly hooked a finger in Anders' shirt, he lifted his arms to let Kelly strip it off him. "I sat in the box and watched."

"Ehh, fine. *I'm* worked up. Did you see the check I got against Phoenix's center tonight? That guy's so fucking cocky and I'm sick of him getting in my face." Kelly ripped off his T-shirt and flung it onto the nightstand.

"I did see your check." Anders hooked a finger in the waistband of Kelly's sweats, tugging him closer until he stood between Anders' splayed knees. "I also saw your assist. Now, what reward would you like for your contributions to the team?"

Kelly grinned, lighting up at the idea. "I get to choose?"

"Yes."

"Hmm. Lot of things sound tempting." Kelly stepped out of his sweats and kicked them away, his cheeks warm. "Maybe your mouth?"

"Would you like me to suck you?" Anders asked, nudging Kelly's boxers over his hips until they hit the floor. "Or eat you out?"

Kelly's breath hitched and he blinked at Anders a moment. "Um, both, now that I know I have those options."

"All you ever have to do is ask me for what you want." Anders smiled, gently wrapping a hand around Kelly's cock.

Kelly was already getting hard at the thought of what Anders had suggested. He looked down and gently pushed a lock of Anders' hair behind his ear. "It doesn't matter what we do, I just want you."

Anders tugged Kelly forward, skimming his nose across his abs, his warm breath leaving goosebumps in his wake. He ducked his head to press a kiss below Kelly's navel. "Then you'll have me."

At that, Kelly had to push him back against the mattress and kiss him. Anders gripped him tightly and rolled them over, pressing him into the sheets with his big body. Kelly went happily, smiling at Anders and winding their legs together.

"Kiss me again," Kelly begged, and Anders did, his tongue delving deep in a slow, intense kiss that sent Kelly's head spinning.

They made out for the longest time, Anders' weight trapping him against the mattress until Kelly felt both caged in and floating.

Anders rocked his hips against Kelly's, the slightly rough abrasion of the fabric of his underwear against Kelly's bare cock sending little shivers of pleasure through his body.

But Anders seemed determined to drive Kelly nuts. He wouldn't go any further, even when Kelly squirmed and begged. But he hadn't used his hands or his mouth on anything below his waist yet.

"Anders," Kelly whined, bucking his hips in a needy little gesture that would have made him embarrassed with anyone else. But it was Anders, so he didn't care. As long as it *worked*.

The bastard laughed against his neck, mouth warm and wet as he pressed his lips to a thousand sensitive spots Kelly had never known existed. "Yes, Kelly?"

"I thought you were going to suck me off or eat me out." He sounded petulant. Damn it, he *felt* petulant. Anders was being a tease. "This isn't much of a reward."

"No?" It sounded like Anders was smiling against his skin. "You aren't enjoying yourself?"

"I am but—"

Anders rose onto one elbow, the movement pushing their hips together. They were both hard and Kelly resisted the urge to rut against him. "I suppose I *have* made you wait a long time."

"*Yes.*"

Kelly held his breath as Anders flipped onto his back, smiling.

"Up here," Anders said, patting his chest.

Kelly eyeballed him. "Like, straddle you?"

"Yes. You'll have to do a lot of the work, but I think it's a good position for this."

"Oh, right. Okay. Yeah, I'm fine with that," Kelly said fervently, shifting to his knees, then swinging one leg over Anders' torso. "Tell me what to do."

Anders smiled, looking so happy and at ease that Kelly froze, staring at the light in his eyes.

Anders was rarely this relaxed except on the ice. It gave Kelly pleasure to think that maybe what they were doing was *good* for Anders. Not merely allowing him to get off but allowing him to be happy.

Obviously having sex with Kelly wasn't going to magically fix what Anders had lost—Kelly tried not to wince when he felt the brush of metal rings on a chain against his inner thigh as he walked forward on his knees—but it made him so pleased to see Anders looking alive again.

Anders wrapped his big, warm hand around Kelly's dick and Kelly stopped thinking of anything but how good it felt.

He had to brace himself against the headboard when Anders licked at the tip of his cock. He made a pleased little humming noise as if he liked the way Kelly tasted, then took him into his mouth, his tongue doing something to the underside of his shaft that made Kelly go lightheaded.

"Fuck, do that again," he begged.

Anders did, reaching out to grasp Kelly's ass and urge him to move. Kelly shifted his hips, trying to figure out what angle to thrust at.

When he did, Anders let out another encouraging noise, his mouth forming a tight, wet tunnel around Kelly's dick.

Kelly fucked in slowly and shallowly at first, testing how much Anders could take in this position. Kelly couldn't watch. It was too much to see Anders' mouth on his cock, so he tipped his head back, eyes closed, gripping the headboard because it was the only thing keeping him upright and anchored to the planet.

Without it, he'd spin off into outer space, the pleasure launching him into orbit.

Anders' hands were large and strong as they kneaded his ass, encouraging him. Heat spread through Kelly's body, settling into the pit of his stomach, winding him tighter with every stroke.

When Anders grazed a finger between his cheeks, teasing him, Kelly gasped. He bucked his hips and Anders let out a choked little sound, so Kelly drew back. "Sorry, sorry."

Kelly glanced down in time to see Anders slide off his cock with a final flick of his tongue that made Kelly twitch. He was so damn sensitive already.

"You're okay." Anders rubbed his hip soothingly. "Now, I want to taste the rest of you."

Kelly trembled, the tightness in his belly growing as Anders pressed Kelly's dick flat against his belly and dragged his tongue across Kelly's balls. He gently sucked one into his mouth and a punched-out sound left Kelly's lips, the wet heat surrounding such a sensitive part of his body almost overwhelming.

Anders did it to the other one, lapping and sucking with hungry little sounds that wound Kelly tighter and tighter. He had both hands on the headboard now, every muscle in his arms going rigid when Anders urged him forward.

Anders traced lower, gliding the tip of his tongue along the secret place behind Kelly's balls, sending little shocks of pleasure through him. He dragged the flat of his tongue into that space, then teased farther back.

Kelly shifted, planting one foot on the bed above Anders' shoulder.

And then Anders' tongue was *there*. Gently circling Kelly's hole and sending more sparks through Kelly's entire body.

A whine left his lips and Anders' hand tightened on his ass, rocking him over his tongue. Kelly let out a sputtering noise when Anders teased the tip of his tongue inside. The feeling was incredible, washing over Kelly in a wave of pleasure that had him slamming his eyes shut again, completely overwhelmed.

After a few moments, Anders guided him to lift, taking in a few gulps of air before pulling Kelly down against his mouth again.

Kelly whimpered when Anders grew more aggressive, alternating licks with what felt like suction, only stopping long enough to breathe before diving in again, coaxing Kelly to move with his big, strong hands.

Kelly gripped the headboard hard enough it hurt, his eyes tightly clenched while he rode Anders' tongue.

Strangled little whimpers fell from his lips and he was too lost in pleasure to fight them. His entire body trembled as Anders went deep and the gentle rasp of Anders' short beard made everything more sensitive.

After another quick break for Anders, Kelly blindly groped for his cock, no longer able to ignore the insistent throb of it. Anders let out a pleased sound and worked harder, spearing his tongue into Kelly's hole.

Kelly fucked himself over Anders' tongue for a moment, jerking his cock until the pleasure became a sharp, desperate need he couldn't hold back anymore.

He came with a choked-off cry, body curling in as he trembled through his orgasm, catching his release in one fist, his other hand gripping the headboard to keep himself upright.

———

Kelly flopped onto the bed, panting, his upper chest and face flushed red. Sweat darkened his hair and beaded on his forehead, his arm hanging off the mattress, his hand nearly touching the floor.

"Holy. Shit."

Anders wiped at his mouth and carefully knelt beside Kelly, his hand flying over his cock in a few short, hard strokes, the memory of the sounds Kelly had made while Anders ate him out fueling his urgency.

"Can I come on you?" he asked roughly, and Kelly groped for his hip, squeezing hard.

"Yeah, yeah. I want it on my face."

Anders let out a desperate sound and shifted so he was aimed at Kelly's mouth. "Keep your eyes closed," he urged.

It only took a handful more strokes before he came with a bitten-off groan, the first splash of cum landing across Kelly's lips, the second hitting his chin. The remainder dribbled onto his chest.

Kelly let out a pleased hum, licking his lips. Anders groaned and worked himself through the final moments of his release, his body trembling with the aftershocks.

"Oh, Kelly," he whispered. He shifted to the side and brushed his thumb across Kelly's lip. Kelly sucked it into his mouth for a moment, gently swirling his tongue around the tip.

Helpless and overwhelmed, Anders let out a desperate sound. Kelly released his thumb and smiled, cheeks flushed, expression peaceful.

"Don't open your eyes," Anders reminded him as he shifted to get off the bed, still mindful of his ankle. "I'll be back with a cloth in a moment."

Kelly nodded, his body slack with pleasure, smile still curving his lips at the corners.

Anders stood there, staring at Kelly and drinking in his obvious contentment for a moment before he shook himself out of his stupor.

He wet the cloth with hot water, then made his way into the bedroom again. Anders took a seat on the edge of the bed near where Kelly was sprawled and gently wiped him clean.

After they were both presentable again, Anders discarded the cloth, then settled on his side, sliding his arm under Kelly's bicep, throwing his leg over Kelly's thigh to pull him close.

"You okay?" he asked quietly.

Kelly's eyes fluttered open, the corners of his mouth lifting again. "You killed me, Lindy."

Anders smiled. "And to think I'm the one who's been injured."

"Oh God." Kelly draped his forearm across his eyes. "I can't even think about what it's going to be like to have you fuck me at full power."

Laughing, Anders pressed a kiss to his pec, the cooling sweat leaving his skin clammy, his natural scent mingling with the deodorant he wore.

"You're still a rookie. I suppose it'll take some time for you to get used to this level of intensity."

Kelly lowered his arm and squinted at him. "Did you call me a sex rookie?"

Anders tried not to let his grin widen. "Mmm. I think I did."

"Rude!" Kelly playfully shoved at his uninjured shoulder, laughing. "Jerk."

They tussled a moment, before Anders pinned him to the bed, their fingers wound together, their mouths inches apart.

Kelly let out a breathless little sound, lifting his head to kiss Anders. He pulled away immediately. "Sorry. Just realized where your mouth has been."

Anders shrugged, realizing he should have brushed his teeth or used mouthwash while he was in the bathroom. "I don't mind if you don't mind."

Kelly shrugged. "Some time I'll return the favor so, no."

They kissed again, slow, almost lazy pecks and brief tanglings of their tongues that left Anders wishing he was as young as Kelly so he could get hard again.

He said as much to Kelly, who looked at him like he was nuts. "I don't know if *I* can get hard again this fast. Jesus, between the game and you … I'm wrung out. I don't have the energy to get out of bed and go to my room, much less go another round."

Anders rolled onto his side, taking Kelly with him. He splayed a hand across Kelly's ass, enjoying the feel of it in his palm. "Was that a hint you want to sleep in here tonight?"

Kelly rose on one elbow, expression startled. "No. I mean I *would* like to sleep in here, but I wasn't angling for it. If you want me to go back to my room, I will."

"Stay." Anders pressed their foreheads together. "I sleep better when you're here."

The words were more nakedly open than he'd intended, but Kelly only went quiet for a moment before he nodded. "Yeah, okay."

Anders smoothed his thumb across the little dimple that appeared in Kelly's cheek, so faint he'd never noticed it before. Just like he'd never noticed Kelly's auburn lashes were tipped with gold, or the faint scar near the corner of his eye.

Anders lay there for the longest time, staring into Kelly's face, tracing every feature with eyes that felt like they were newly open.

Eventually, they dragged themselves up long enough to get ready for the night, then migrated to the bed again.

"I set my alarm for ass o'clock so I can sneak back to my room before anyone else is up," Kelly said with a yawn. He slipped under the covers. "Hopefully no one will notice me creeping down the hall."

Anders turned out the light, tempted to say he didn't care if they did but that wasn't entirely true. Whatever this was with Kelly that made his chest full and almost tender wasn't something he wanted to share with the team.

Anders trusted them—most of them anyway, Malone being the notable exception—but this was something private.

Not because he had any shame about having Kelly in his bed but because it felt too fragile to speak of aloud. Too flimsy to withstand the incessant chirping that would come with it.

Everyone had been extremely respectful of his mourning. No one—until the fight with Kelly in the Pittsburgh locker room when Kelly had angrily flung it at him —had told Anders to his face it was time to move on.

But what would their teammates think of Anders moving on with *Kelly?*

Especially when it was casual. The guys who had already come out to the team were in serious relationships. Deeply in love and determined to make a future together.

But he and Kelly had no future.

Anders felt an odd pang in his chest at the thought.

Absently, he dragged his hand along Kelly's flank, drawing a quiet, sleepy sigh from his lips.

The team knowing would change things.

Anders thought of the playoff run just within their grasp. They were so close. One more game to determine their chances.

What could be Anders' last shot at a Cup.

No need to upset the delicate balance they'd achieved. No need to strain an already tenuous cohesion.

This season, the team felt like a house of cards. They were stable for now, but a breath of air might be enough to send it all toppling over.

And Jack Malone was a bowling ball.

CHAPTER EIGHTEEN

"All right, Lindy." Underhill smacked his shoulder as he slipped into the open seat between Kelly and Anders the following morning at breakfast. "Way to go, man."

Kelly glanced at him, puzzled. The expression was mirrored on Anders' face. Clearly, he didn't know what Trevor was talking about either.

"I'm sorry?" Anders lifted a mug of green tea to his lips.

"I knew you had it in you." Underhill gave him a crooked grin, scooping up a forkful of eggs. "Who was she? Or, uh, he, I guess. Since you're not fussy either way."

Anders' mug clinked against the saucer. "Excuse me?"

"Dude, it's cool," Underhill said with a shrug. "You're allowed to, you know, enjoy yourself. I mean, I didn't need to overhear it but whatever. I'm happy for you."

Kelly looked down at his plate of food, willing his entire body to not flush.

Trevor had heard them last night. *Fuck.*

Kelly glanced up to see Anders hadn't turned red. But no. If anything, he looked a little green.

Underhill looked around at their teammates as if belatedly realizing he'd made a mistake.

"Sorry, dude," he said awkwardly. "If you don't want to talk about it or whatever, that's cool."

Anders cleared his throat. "I do prefer to be private about my personal life but you're right. I, uh, had someone in my room last night. I apologize if we kept you up."

The entire room went completely still, not even the usual clink of silverware on plates interrupting the quiet.

"Hey, that's great news, man," Hartinger said after a moment, a wide grin spreading across his face. "Glad to hear you're, uh, enjoying yourself."

The other guys chimed in with their congratulations. Kelly knew they meant well but he could see Anders growing more uncomfortable by the moment. Kelly desperately wanted to change the subject but he wasn't sure how to without drawing attention to himself.

Instead, he shoveled suddenly tasteless food in his mouth and tried to ignore the comments flying around the room.

Thankfully, breakfast ended eventually, and Kelly left, making a beeline for the elevator. He was halfway there before Gabriel caught up with him.

"Is everything okay, Irish?" he asked quietly.

"Yeah. Yeah, I'm fine," Kelly said. "I needed to grab some um, toothpaste from downstairs. I wanted to get it before the bus leaves for practice."

Gabriel gave him a searching look. "Want some company?"

"Uh, sure," Kelly said after a momentary pause. He couldn't think of a reason to turn Gabriel down and a group of their teammates were heading toward them. Kelly didn't want them to get dragged into whatever this was.

Gabriel was silent until they reached the stairwell. He pulled open the door and gestured for Kelly to go ahead. "Let's take the stairs."

Kelly grumbled under his breath but stepped inside. When they were halfway down the first flight, Gabriel caught his upper arm with a gentle grip, stopping him in his tracks.

"Are you upset at Anders for moving on from his wife?"

"What?" Kelly spun around and stared at Gabriel, shocked.

"I know he's a friend of your family and you knew her. You looked upset at breakfast when Underhill said he'd overheard Anders with whoever he had over last night and …"

"No," Kelly protested, swallowing the helpless laugh trying to bubble up. Gabriel had definitely jumped to the wrong conclusion. "God, no. I'm not mad because I feel like he should have some sort of loyalty to Astrid or whatever. She was amazing but the *last* thing I want is for him to be miserable forever."

"*Bon*," Gabriel said, his dark eyes intent as he searched Kelly's face. Kelly had spent enough time with French-Canadians to know that meant good, but he couldn't figure out what the fuck he was trying to see on Kelly's face. And the longer he looked, the more guilty Kelly felt. He wanted to squirm under the serious gaze but he forced himself to meet Gabriel's eye with a steady glance.

"So why were you upset then?" Gabriel asked.

Kelly looked away. "I wasn't upset. I, uh, well Lindy seemed uncomfortable. I was worried about how he felt about everyone knowing. That's all."

"Ahh." Gabriel's tone was filled with understanding. "Because if it's anything else … if you … you have anything else you want to talk to me about, Kelly, I'm here—"

"I have no idea what the hell you're talking about." Kelly turned and jogged down the stairs. Shit. Maybe Gabriel *had* figured it out.

"*Non?*" Gabriel was right behind him. "You have no other reason but friendly concern about Lindholm's wellbeing?" His tone was pointed.

"Leave it, Frenchie," Kelly snapped. "Seriously. I am not having this conversation."

"Okay, Irish," Gabriel said, his sigh audible. "But if you need to talk, I'm always around."

"No, I'm good. But thanks."

Gabriel didn't say anything else, just followed Kelly to the first floor. Kelly got the toothpaste he didn't need while Gabriel disappeared into the gift shop.

Kelly bolted for the elevator before Gabriel was done, afraid he'd get sucked into another conversation he absolutely didn't want to have.

Up on their floor, Kelly ran into Anders. Down the hall, two rookies disappeared into their shared room and Kelly slowed when he approached Anders' door.

"Are you okay?" Kelly asked under his breath.

"Yeah, I'm fine, Kelly." Anders' voice was quiet and a little distant. He reached for his keycard.

"I know you don't want the team to know and—"

"It's fine." Anders' mouth was turned down at the corners but he didn't seem upset otherwise. His motions were careful and controlled as he slipped the card into the reader. The door beeped and Anders pushed it open.

"Are you sure?"

"Yes." He paused, glancing at Kelly. "Go on, get ready to head to the rink. We have a big game tomorrow and we should be focusing on that."

Anders' voice was gentle, and he seemed okay so Kelly nodded and turned away, his stomach churning with a sick, sinking feeling this would come back to bite them in the ass.

———

Zane Murphy lifted his glass in a toast. "Whatever happens tomorrow, boys, it's been a hell of a season."

Zane had picked the team's favorite steakhouse in Nashville for the final dinner of the regular season and the mood around the table was loose and happy.

One final team event before they slunk away from Evanston to lick their wounds for the summer or settled into the grind of the postseason.

Knowing what Anders did about Murphy and Hartinger's plans for retirement, Zane's words became barbed, digging into the soft spot behind Anders' sternum, unexpectedly sharp.

It made him acutely aware time was winding down. After this season, things would shift fundamentally for the team.

Since Anders' conversation with Zane yesterday, he'd thought about his own future, the specter of it looming over him, the tick of an invisible clock resonating in his bones.

Was he ready to be done with hockey?

Anders looked around the long table at his teammates. He'd played with the Otters, with this core group of guys for so long he'd been spoiled. Other teammates came and went but Anders had been able to count on Zane since the beginning and Ryan for over a decade. Dean Tremblay had been with them nearly as long.

As always, Anders' gaze came to rest on Kelly, lingering, taking in his bright smile, laughing at something Underhill said in his ear. Anders felt a sudden sharp ache in his chest at the reminder that one way or another, he wouldn't always play with Kelly.

The nudge of Gabriel's elbow against Anders' made him realize the guys were all staring at him, waiting for him to raise his glass.

Anders fumbled for it, unusually clumsy, and he lifted his water as he joined in the toast to a hell of a season.

With such an important game tomorrow, about half the team had stuck with non-alcoholic drinks. The rest had ordered one or two glasses of wine or beer along with their meals.

Malone was the notable exception, though after he'd ordered his third double shot of whiskey, Zane had spoken to him quietly but sternly. He'd sneered, looking like he was about to argue, but from the coaches' table, Daniels had leveled him with a look they were all familiar with.

If Malone didn't behave, he'd find himself out of the lineup tomorrow night.

Malone had looked pissed, but he'd switched to water. It was more than he would have done in the past and Anders wondered if Jack was aware of how precarious his position on this team was getting.

With Gabriel's addition and Kelly's increasing skill, the team needed Malone less than they had a few seasons ago. The team's owner and GM might be willing to keep paying out his hefty salary but it had become clear he was no longer necessary to the team's success.

But he could bring about its downfall.

The public was beginning to turn on him. In the wake of the altercation at the club, there was escalating pressure on the organization. More fans wondering what the hell he contributed to the team.

Anders looked away in time to see waitstaff appear, ready to clear away their appetizer plates, and he focused on his team, glad the friction with Jack Malone was the only mar on what had otherwise been a great evening so far.

A few moments later, their entrees were served. No one put away food like a team of hockey players and the table nearly groaned with their laden plates.

Anders cut into his salmon and lifted a forkful to his mouth, chewing with a soft sound of pleasure. Though the restaurant's focus was steak, they knew their way around fish equally well and the spring vegetable barley risotto melted in his mouth.

Anders would miss nights like this. Private dining rooms in gourmet restaurants with the team, laughter and talk about hockey.

Cooper chirping Tremblay about the bad game of golf he'd played a few weeks ago.

A burst of laughter from the coaches' table, the team's equipment manager holding his side as he gasped out his amusement over whatever joke had been told.

Murphy bumping shoulders with Hartinger in silent thanks when Ryan slid a few extra stalks of asparagus onto Zane's plate, while Zane continued to talk to Hajek about something Anders couldn't hear.

These were his people. His team. His family.

Anders' eyes stung when he imagined this ending. What would it be like to no longer have that? To go home alone to an empty apartment and having *nothing*. Not even Kelly.

"What do you think about it?" Gabriel asked, his voice cutting through the static in Anders' head.

"Hmm?" Anders asked, turning to look at him.

He smiled but concern lurked in his brown eyes. "We were talking about your plans for the summer. Wondering if you'd ever thought about doing private training."

"I usually go home in the summers," Anders said automatically. "There's a private coach I work with in Sweden and—"

"*Non. Je suis désolé.* I meant you running the training."

"Me?"

Gabriel laughed. "*Oui.* You, Lindholm. You have the knowledge and the skills. I think a lot of guys could learn from you."

Anders considered the idea. "I've never thought about it but yes, I suppose I could fit in a week toward the end of the summer, maybe."

"I mean, why not?" Walsh said. "I've never played with or against anyone like you before."

Anders demurred but Truro leaned in. "He's right, you know. No one can see plays like you do."

"Yeah, share some of your wisdom with the boys," Ryan said with a laugh. "God knows I wouldn't be where I am now if you hadn't done that for me over the years."

"Me neither," Murphy said.

"Hmm."

Anders supposed that was true. He'd shared suggestions with his wingers a lot but it had never been a formal thing. Something he'd said to Ryan about keeping his head up through center ice during his rookie year had gotten through when their previous head coach's suggestions hadn't. He'd helped Zane fix the strange position he'd held his elbow at early on in his career. There were a handful of other things he'd likely forgotten. They'd seemed small enough at the time but Anders supposed the cumulative impact was helpful.

"Like an informal skills camp?" Anders offered.

Gabriel nodded. "That sounds great to me."

"I'll—I'll consider it."

"Great, man," Truro chimed in, like Anders had already agreed to it. "Let us know when you'd like to do it."

Anders glanced over to see Kelly looking at him with a small smile.

Anders looked away, focusing on the final few bites on his plate, but he did feel a spark of excitement in his belly at the idea.

As they returned to the hotel, Zane fell into step beside him. "Making post-retirement plans tonight, huh?" he asked with a nudge of his elbow.

Anders shook his head. "No, the guys were talking about something this summer …" But his voice trailed off as he considered the idea. He looked at Zane. "Do you think I could?"

"Could run skills clinics or a camp?" Zane asked, laughing. "Hell yeah, dude, I know you could. You're a future Hall of Famer. Guys across the league would flock to work with you."

"Hmm." Anders rubbed his jaw as they waited for an elevator. They'd missed the big crush of guys heading up and it was just the two of them from the team waiting. "I'd never considered the idea."

"Well, maybe it's about time. Whenever your retirement is, it's a good idea to have a plan for it, right?

"It is," Anders agreed. Having something to look forward to was the surest bet to keep himself from getting depressed.

When the elevator arrived, they stepped inside, and Zane studied him thoughtfully. "Are you okay with what happened this morning?"

"This morning?" Anders asked blankly, then remembered Underhill had called him out for having someone in his room last night. "Oh. Well, I wouldn't have chosen to have my personal life discussed over breakfast but I'll survive."

"Is it someone on the team or someone you met here in Nashville?" Zane's eyes widened as if a sudden thought had occurred to him. "It wasn't someone *from* the Nashville team, was it?"

Anders chuckled despite his discomfort with the conversation. "No. I'm not sleeping with someone on an opposing team. I promise."

"Well good. Because that sounds like a mess I do *not* feel like dealing with right now." Zane rubbed his head.

Something about the gesture reminded him of Coach Daniels and his exhaustion at the many changes that had happened with the team recently. Anders suppressed a smile.

"It's nothing you'll have to deal with," Anders promised Zane, confident he could keep what was going on with Kelly under wraps, despite their mistake last night. "I ... I've been lonely and it's helped. But it's not going to become something serious." The words felt bitter on Anders' tongue.

"I am glad you're ... finding some comfort," Zane said. "And you certainly don't have to tell me who it is or how you know them if you don't want. I just wanted to check in and see how you were doing."

"I appreciate that," Anders said honestly. He had no desire to discuss his sex life with his teammates—except the one he was sleeping with, he mentally corrected—but Zane's concern came from a good place.

They arrived on their floor and Anders held the door for Zane, who paused between the open elevator doors. "Just, as your captain speaking, I'm obligated to warn you to keep it down tonight and don't wear yourself out too much. We have a big game tomorrow."

Anders chuckled at the reminder. "I promise I'll be on my best behavior."

"Well"—Zane shot him a crooked little grin—"maybe enjoy yourself a *little*."

"Goodnight, Murphy," Anders said with a laugh.

"Night, Lindholm."

They went their separate ways and Anders let himself into his hotel room, mentally running through his nighttime routine.

He'd shower and relax for a while. It wasn't terribly late. He could watch TV or read for a couple of hours before he needed to be asleep.

He'd hung his suit jacket and tie in the closet and was working a cufflink loose when there was a quiet knock on his door.

He was unsurprised to find Kelly on the other side.

The moment Anders stepped away, Kelly slipped into the room, speaking as soon as the door was firmly closed. "Before you say anything else, I want you to know Trevor doesn't know it was me last night."

Anders nodded. "Okay."

"You don't have to worry about it, all right? I know this morning wasn't great for you, but I won't say anything to Trevor."

"You *are* friends with him," Anders pointed out, walking toward the dresser where he'd left the small jewelry case he used to store his cufflinks. He'd been thinking about this situation with Kelly all day. It seemed unfair to ask him to keep things a secret from his closest friend. "It's up to you if you want to share. Obviously, we want to keep this from Malone because he'd have a meltdown if he found out about us, and we don't need any more stress on the team right now."

"I *know*." Kelly sounded vaguely annoyed.

"I'm sure you already considered all of the concerns," Anders said soothingly. He pressed the gold squares into the velvety cushioned lining. "It's been on my mind."

"I definitely have. And I don't think Trevor would say anything to Malone. But I'm still gonna keep quiet on it."

"Okay."

"I mean, that's what we agreed was best, right?"

"Yes. I wanted to let you know I would understand if you wanted to come out to Underhill about us but it's your choice."

"Nah. Thanks though." Kelly studied him intently. "I hope you don't mind me barging in like this now. I know you said you wanted to wait to talk but I couldn't stop thinking about it and I wanted to clear the air."

Kelly looked uncomfortable and fidgety, so after Anders finished unbuttoning his shirt, he hooked an arm around Kelly's waist and pulled him close, pressing his lips to Kelly's hair and breathing him in a moment.

"I'm glad you came to talk." He didn't like when things were awkward between them either.

Kelly held himself stiffly for the briefest second before he softened and pressed a kiss to Anders' jaw. "Good."

Anders pulled away, shrugging out of his shirt. Sometimes he felt like he spent ninety percent of his time dressing or undressing.

"Do you want me to go to my room?" Kelly asked quietly when Anders got down to his underwear.

"No," Anders admitted. Was it risky to spend another night together when they were terrible at keeping their hands off each other and their teammates knew Anders was involved with someone? Yes. But Anders knew he'd sleep better if Kelly was beside him. But that was up to Kelly. "Would you rather stay in your room because—"

"No." Kelly laughed and flopped onto the mattress, sprawled out in his suit. "I'd rather be here with you. You know that."

"I don't like to assume …"

"Maybe you should," Kelly said, coming up to rest on his elbows, his gaze intent as his expression turned serious. "When it comes to spending the night with you, the answer is always *yes*."

"We should be quiet though," Anders cautioned.

"Well, *obviously*." Kelly bounced to his feet, kicking off his shoes and wrestling his jacket off, like he couldn't stand being dressed any longer. "And we need to get to bed pretty early. Captain's orders and all."

Zane had given the entire team the reminder as they entered the hotel lobby after dinner.

"Yes. Sleep is important." Anders tugged Kelly's button-down shirt from the waistband of his trousers to coax him along. "But I know I sleep better after an orgasm."

Kelly grinned and took over, his fingers flying across the buttons. "Me too. What are you thinking?"

"Well, is there something we haven't tried that you'd like to do?"

"I want to fuck you," Kelly said as his trousers came off and joined his other clothing on the nearby chair. "But maybe not tonight. I don't want to be worrying about if Underhill is going to overhear something."

"Fair enough." Although Anders had been thinking a lot about that too.

When Kelly was naked, Anders stepped close and skimmed his lips across the edge of Kelly's jaw. "Anything else you've thought about?"

Kelly drew back, his lower lip clamped between his teeth, his gaze a mix of uncertain and hopeful. "Just one thing. And it's probably kind of dumb."

"Tell me."

"You ever tried docking?"

Anders blinked.

"It's when—"

"I know what docking is." Anders gently cut him off. "I just hadn't considered it. No, I've never tried it with anyone."

"I mean, it's fine." Kelly's cheeks were pink, and he couldn't quite meet Anders' gaze. "It's a stupid idea really. I saw it in porn once and thought it looked hot."

"We can try it," Anders offered.

"Would it work with the height difference?" Kelly asked, his tone doubtful. "I've only seen guys standing and …"

He gestured between them, pointing out that Anders' cock was roughly level with Kelly's navel.

"I am sure we can figure out a way to work around it," Anders said with a smile, pulling Kelly close. "It might be easier lying down."

When they were both naked and lying face-to-face on the bed, Kelly pressed a palm to Anders' chest. "You're not doing this to humor me, are you?"

"To humor you?" Anders murmured, amused by the idea. "No, Kelly."

"Because if you don't enjoy it—"

Anders pressed their lips together, licking his way into Kelly's mouth to quiet the anxious, rambling words falling from his lips.

"I'm always willing to try something new with you," Anders said firmly when he pulled away. "If one or both of us aren't into it, that's fine. We can decide if we want to try it again or do other things. There's no pressure though, Kelly."

"Okay."

Kelly still looked a little apprehensive, but he let out a happy sigh when Anders wrapped a hand around his cock.

"Let's start with this." Anders stroked Kelly from root to tip, using gentle pressure to tease him into hardness. It wasn't long before Kelly was panting against his mouth, Anders doing his best to muffle the quiet little groans falling from his lips.

Anders pulled away long enough to retrieve the lube he'd tucked under his thigh to warm, and he spread some across his palm and worked Kelly for a few strokes. Anders slicked himself and teased a finger into the small opening of his foreskin, coaxing it to widen. The sensitive ache heated his body further, pre-cum helping slick the way when he slipped two fingers in.

His breath caught in his throat at the intent way Kelly watched him, lips parted, eyes desperate and needy.

"Hold your cock out straight," Anders whispered.

Kelly nodded and did so. Anders shifted his hips forward and Kelly let out a quiet little gasp when their cocks lined up, the heads kissing. Carefully, Anders stretched his foreskin, tugging it until it covered the head of Kelly's dick and a few centimeters down his shaft.

"Shit," Kelly said breathlessly, his tone awed.

"Good?" Anders asked.

"Yeah. Weird, but good. You?"

"It's strange," he agreed. "But it feels …"

Intimate, he thought. But he wasn't sure how to express everything he wanted to say so he kept it simple. "It feels good to me too."

"Okay." Kelly shifted so his cheek rested against Anders' bicep and their mouths were inches apart, so close Anders struggled to focus. Instead, he closed his eyes, nudging Kelly's nose with his own until their mouths met.

They kissed slowly, almost leisurely, as Anders gently thrust, using his palm to masturbate them both. It really was oddly intimate, much more than Anders would have expected, like something done in secret. He'd been inside Kelly's body in a myriad of ways but this was like he was wrapping Kelly up tight, sheltering him.

Ignoring the ridiculous, fanciful image, Anders turned off his mind and focused on how he felt. His skin heated as he stroked carefully, feeling out what made Kelly press closer and what made him tense.

A swirl of his thumb across the ridge of Kelly's head made Kelly let out a gasp against his lips. Anders kissed him more deeply, concentrating on making Kelly feel good.

But the slippery friction of the head of Kelly's cock rubbing inside his foreskin sent shuddery tingles through Anders' body and after a few minutes he was unexpectedly close to coming.

He froze, panting against Kelly's mouth, struggling for control.

"Too much," he said with a gasp.

"Yeah?" Kelly pressed his forehead against Anders', sounding pleased.

"You?"

"Not yet." Kelly rubbed his hand along Anders' back. "I need something more."

"Take over," Anders coaxed as an idea popped into his head. "Slick your hand and place it where mine is so I can finger you."

Kelly carefully cradled their cocks in his hand, his grip gentle. Anders' hand was already slick, so he reached behind Kelly, coaxing him to throw his thigh over Anders'. He slipped a finger between his cheeks, teasing at his opening.

Kelly gasped, his hips jerking, making the heads of their cocks bump together, sending a quiver of pleasure through Anders once again.

"Oh yeah," Kelly said breathlessly. "Fuck that's good."

"Stroke us a little," Anders coaxed, and it was clumsy at first but when Kelly found the right rhythm, Anders had to bite the inside of his cheek to keep from losing control

He got lost in the feeling, his eyes closed, his world narrowed to Kelly's hand on their joined cocks and Kelly's hole clenching around his fingers. Their movements were slow and almost lazy, not chasing pleasure so much as sinking into it like warm bathwater.

Nothing existed except Kelly's lips against his and the soft huffs of air he let out every time Anders hit a good spot. Anders' skin was cool everywhere they weren't touching, warm and slick from sweat where their bodies rubbed together.

Kelly was sweet and pliant in his arms, but not passive, gently rubbing their cocks together, stroking slick fingers along Anders' foreskin and making him shudder.

"Kelly," Anders whispered roughly, the small frissons of pleasure shuddering through him so close to being too much.

"I want to feel you come," Kelly begged, his voice a quiet, hoarse sound that wrapped around Anders and settled somewhere deep inside him. "Please."

The *please* did it, tearing at the final fraying threads of Anders' control until they snapped. He let out a quiet cry against Kelly's lips when he came, the pleasure overwhelming, the sudden rush of liquid adding heat and slickness to an already sensitive area.

Anders pressed his forehead against Kelly's and despite the instinct to slam his eyes shut, he kept them open, staring at their joined cocks. Cum welled up, slipping messily down their shafts, too much to be contained, the sight beautiful and overwhelming.

Anders panted desperately, small shocks of pleasure zinging across his skin. He pushed his fingers deeper into Kelly's ass and felt as much as heard Kelly's choked-off moan.

Kelly stroked Anders until the aftershocks were so intense he had to pull away.

Cum spilled onto the sheets when he eased away from Kelly, the final catch of his foreskin on the flared head of Kelly's cock sending one last shiver through his body.

He slipped his fingers out of Kelly and slid down the bed, wedging himself between Kelly's thighs, licking his cum from Kelly's cock. He did it until all he could taste was skin, then took him all the way in, pressing three fingers into Kelly's body, his thighs clamping tightly around Anders' shoulders.

Anders sucked hard and deep, twisting his fingers, grazing the sensitive spot that made Kelly curl upward, whimpering, clutching Anders' hair in a tight grip.

Anders slid off long enough to remind Kelly they needed to be quiet before he took him to the root again, his gaze never leaving Kelly's face. Anders stared up the length of Kelly's body when he bottomed out, Kelly's pale skin flushed pink.

Kelly reached for a pillow and covered his mouth with it, soft cries muted now.

Anders worked him over until Kelly came with a muffled sob, thighs trembling against Anders' ears, flooding his mouth with his release.

Anders eased him through it, then slid up Kelly's body. He pulled the pillow away from Kelly's sweating red face and wrapped him tightly in his arms.

CHAPTER NINETEEN

"Thank you." Kelly let out a shuddering breath, pressing his lips softly against the corner of Anders' mouth.

"For what?" Anders gently knocked their foreheads together, the way he did when they were on the ice.

Kelly's throat clicked as he swallowed. "Never making me feel silly or stupid for not knowing what I'm doing. For letting me try things to see if I like them."

Anders hesitated a moment. "Kelly, you should never be with someone who makes you feel silly or stupid for any reason."

"I know." Kelly traced his fingers across Anders' chest, following the contours of his muscles. "I won't. I promise, I won't."

But that made Kelly think about the time when *this* ended, and he hated the idea. Didn't Anders see how *good* they were together?

Kelly tucked himself close to Anders' chest, afraid Anders would see his feelings for him written all over his face. "Tell me about the guys you were with before."

"Where did that come from?" Anders sounded surprised.

Kelly shrugged. "Dunno."

"Are you sure you want to know?"

"I mean, if you don't want to talk about it, that's cool. I'm just curious. You seem comfortable with being with a guy and ..."

"I am." He went silent long enough Kelly was starting to think he didn't want to talk about it. Eventually, he let out a sigh. "It was ... easier in Sweden in some ways. There are bigots every-where, of course, but same-sex relationships were so much more normalized when I was growing up. None of this strange puri-tanism America has."

Anders absently brushed his fingertips across Kelly's shoulder blade, and it sent a shiver down Kelly's spine. Anders pulled the sheet over their bodies.

"It wasn't perfect. Even in Sweden, hockey players who were attracted to men were quiet about it. Discreet. But it seemed quite normal to me to see same-sex couples. My uncle Johan was gay. He was open about his relationship my whole life and he and his partner were always around at the holidays and family celebrations. It seemed perfectly natural to me. Though Johan didn't play hockey. He worked in real estate."

"That's good you had a role model or whatever. And that your family was cool with it." Kelly had a huge-ass family, and he couldn't think of a single person who was gay. Although the one story about his great, great aunt who'd never married and had a female roommate for most of her life had always made him wonder ...

"It was," Anders agreed. "So, when I was growing up and real-ized I was attracted to boys too, it seemed perfectly normal, and my family was supportive."

Kelly felt a stab of envy.

His family had said things that made him shrink away from letting them know who he really was. It wasn't anything worse than the usual chirps on the ice or in the locker rooms that most guys tossed around without thinking about twice. But it was bad enough.

And they were Catholic.

His parents and his brothers and their families went to church every Sunday except when hockey interfered, and Finn always said they had a special dispensation from the Pope for that.

It was a conservative parish too. One of the big ones with a bishop who was always going on about faith and choosing the right path.

Kelly was pretty sure his parents went to that parish because their families had always gone there.

At least he *hoped* it was more about tradition than strictly believing everything the Church taught. But how could he be sure? The nice priest who'd baptized all the kids in the family was the same guy whose homily after gay marriage was legalized was all about "homosexuals being called to chastity".

Because it was okay to be gay as long as you didn't *act* on that.

What exactly his parents and brothers believed was something Kelly had never dared ask about because he was terrified of finding out the truth. What if they believed that too? They loved him, but what if they wouldn't accept him being with a man?

Kelly wouldn't claim to be the most educated guy about LGBTQ stuff, but some of the shit that got thrown around in conversation when he was growing up had hurt deeply.

He thought—hoped—it was more ignorance than mean-spirit-edness, but he wasn't sure. Which was exactly why he'd kept his fucking mouth shut about himself.

But now, when he was naked in bed with a guy he was in love with, it was hard to imagine spending the rest of his life hiding.

What if Anders *did* want more? Would Kelly ask him to hide it? Would Kelly be able to? He felt like his heart was in his eyes every time he looked at Anders. His family was loud and some-times acted idiotic, but they weren't dumb. If they saw them together, they'd figure it out eventually.

"Did you have a boyfriend in school?" Kelly asked, before he started thinking too much about a possible future with Anders that felt so close, yet out of reach.

"No. Just boys I had crushes on and kissed."

Kelly tried to imagine a young Anders and his brain shut down. He'd seen pictures of him from his draft day and even then, he'd looked mature.

"You came to Canada for hockey when you were what, sixteen?" Kelly asked.

"Yes."

"How was that?"

Anders shrugged. "Much more hidden but I knew of a few guys who were so inclined. The family I billeted with, their son was around my age and gay, I think, and we explored a little. Mostly awkward teenage exploration but we managed. Even in the NHL, I knew a few guys who were open about their sexuality. Again, it was discreet but it wasn't difficult to find."

"You never hooked up with La Bouche, did you?"

Anders laughed. "No. I liked Noah, and we got along well the few times we met at All-Star games, but I never slept with him."

"Just wondering."

"Mostly I kept it outside of hockey. Boston was a big place. I could occasionally go to a discreet gay bar and find someone to go home with. And there were always road trips. It wasn't only men, of course, but casual sex wasn't something I did often with anyone. And it ended when I met Astrid, of course."

"Of course," Kelly said.

Anders was the absolute last man Kelly could imagine cheating.

Kelly realized his fingers had strayed close to the chain Anders wore around his neck. He nervously licked his lips and tapped on Anders' collarbone until Anders glanced down with a puzzled look.

Kelly hovered his fingers over the chain, wanting to touch but afraid it would upset him. "May I?"

Anders looked at Kelly for a long moment before he swallowed hard. "Yes."

Kelly gently traced along the fine gold chain, treating it with the reverence it deserved. Anders' face tightened for the briefest second but then it smoothed out, so Kelly didn't stop.

"Would you prefer I take it off while we're in bed together?" Anders asked after a minute.

Kelly shook his head. "No. Not unless you want to. *I* don't mind it. Even if we were … more than what we are now or whatever, I wouldn't try to take that away from you."

"I know." Anders smoothed his thumb across Kelly's cheek. "Nothing you've ever said or done has made me think you would."

"Tell me more about her?" Kelly had known Astrid, of course, but he'd been a teenager when they first met, and he hadn't known her *well*.

Anders' gaze flicked to Kelly's face, brow furrowed.

"If you want," Kelly hastily added. "It's okay if you don't. I just wanted you to know I'm okay with it if you do. But——"

"I understand." Anders placed a finger against Kelly's lips and Kelly quieted.

Anders took a deep breath, so deep it pressed his chest more tightly against Kelly's as they lay together under the sheet. "Astrid was … a spring thunderstorm."

Kelly gave him a soft, quizzical smile and Anders shook his head. "That sounds ridiculous, I know."

"No, it's romantic sounding. No one has ever compared me to anything like that."

An emotion flickered across Anders' face too fast for Kelly to identify.

"Astrid was many contradictions. Fierce but soft. Bright. Lively. So fucking smart. So much smarter than me. Not just her medical degree but she absorbed *everything* she read like a sponge. Unbelievably driven. If she'd lived, she'd have taken over the hospital."

Kelly smiled, because he could definitely picture it.

Anders continued. "But she was gentle too. Kind. Tender-hearted. Sad animal stories made her cry. She lit up every room she was in. And her laugh …" Anders' breath stuttered. "For the longest time I would have sworn I could hear an echo of it sometimes in the air, out of reach whenever I turned to find it."

The naked longing on Anders' face made Kelly's eyes prick with tears and he shifted until they weren't looking each other in the eye anymore. It made Kelly ache to think about Anders losing her. It mingled with the little sliver of hurt that Anders might never feel that way about *him*.

But Kelly had this. It was enough. It had to be.

"I remember her laugh," Kelly whispered. "It was special, wasn't it?"

"Yes." Anders brushed his lips across Kelly's hair, pulling him closer.

"She was so beautiful too."

When Anders drew back to shoot him a surprised glance, Kelly shrugged. "Look, I might not be into women that way but I'm not fucking blind. She was *gorgeous*."

Kelly didn't have to be straight to see *that*.

"She was," Anders agreed, the corner of his mouth turning up in a smile. "But I think it was her mouth that made me fall in love with her."

"Oh?" Kelly gave him a puzzled look.

"Not her lips but the way she spoke to me. Do you remember how we met?"

"In the emergency room at Northwestern Memorial Hospital, right?"

"Yes." Anders smiled. "I remember the first sight of her in her white lab coat, snapping on a pair of blue gloves, eyeing me up and down like an alien species. She told me hockey was a stupid sport."

Kelly laughed, muffling the sound against Anders' collarbone.

"I'd had a laceration from a skate." Anders held out his arm and Kelly smoothed his thumb over the faded scar. "It was deep enough the team doctor sent me to the emergency room. They wanted to check for tendon damage. The tendons were fine, so a young, beautiful resident stitched me up."

"I guess I can see why she thought hockey was a stupid sport," Kelly joked.

"Exactly." Anders said with a wry smile. "I asked her out for coffee, and she laughed and told me she didn't have time for romance and even if she did, she wouldn't date a hockey player."

"What made her change her mind?"

"Nothing that night. I walked out with no hope of getting her number."

"So, what happened then?" Kelly had ignored most of this story when Anders had told it in the past, too jealous to listen to the guy he'd been crazy about gush about the woman he loved. But Kelly wanted to hear it now. Wanted to understand everything about Anders.

"I got injured again. Broken hand. They sent me for x-rays."

Kelly chuckled. "Did you do it intentionally so you could see her again?"

"No! But she asked me that too."

"So, you got her number then?"

"No." Anders' mouth curved up at one corner. "She turned me down *again*. I was getting desperate, so I sent her and her coworkers an open invitation to come to a game. Promised there would be free tickets waiting if they did. I think if I'd only sent it to her, she absolutely would have blown me off but her co-workers finally dragged her to a game."

"Smart."

"I also left her my jersey at the will call box. And flowers."

"Romantic," Kelly teased.

"I liked to think so. It was nearly a month before the tickets I left there got used though so the people working in the will call office got to take home pretty bouquets until she finally arrived." He shrugged. "It was expensive but worth it to me."

"Oh wow. You had some there *every* home game, just hoping she'd show up?" Kelly was impressed.

"Yes." Anders sighed. "I was absurdly smitten with her. In hind-sight, it seems ridiculous. Maybe crossing the line into being too much, but the moment I laid eyes on her, I—I knew she was it for me."

"It's sweet," Kelly said, his throat catching.

"You don't know how it felt to finally see her in the stands."

"Wearing your jersey?"

"No." Anders laughed. "Absolutely not. She wore the opposing team's. Just to prove I hadn't won her over completely."

"Wow. Harsh," Kelly said, but he couldn't help but chuckle at the idea. God, Astrid had made Anders work for it. Kelly kind of loved it. He was pretty sure he was way too gone for Anders to play it that cool but he respected that she'd somehow managed.

"Yes." Anders' smile widened. "It made me want to impress her though. I scored four goals that night."

"Damn."

"Nearly made it a five-goal game but the puck didn't quite make it in."

"Jesus," Kelly breathed.

Five-goal games were insanely rare. In over a hundred years, fewer than fifty players had accomplished it. To even come *close* was incredible.

"Is that when it started?" Kelly asked. "The thing you did where you scored goals for her?"

"Yes."

"I wish …" Kelly's eyes burned as he thought about the way Anders' face fell whenever he looked into the stands and didn't see Astrid there cheering for him. "I wish you hadn't lost her. Lost them both."

He meant it too. He loved Anders enough that he'd give up every moment they'd had together if Anders could have Astrid and Elia back.

Anders' smile was tinged with sadness. He pulled Kelly close, brushing his lips against his forehead. "Thank you. Me too."

Kelly tucked his head against Anders' neck, breathing him in, letting the emotion settle. Anders stroked the back of his neck, soft little caresses that made Kelly shiver and flush, but made him feel safe too.

"Kelly," Anders whispered against his hair. "I don't want you to think *this* doesn't matter to me too. What we have now. It's … important in its own way. I hope you know that."

"I do," Kelly said, his eyes watering. He pressed his fingertips to the rings resting against Anders' chest, his throat painfully tight.

It felt strangely okay to be naked in bed with Anders and talking about the love of his life. Kelly's heart broke for him but it didn't hurt Kelly in the way he would have expected.

He didn't feel unimportant or like he was some sort of weird placeholder for Astrid or something. He couldn't undo the past but he'd be here for Anders in whatever way Anders would let him.

"I want to be good for you," Kelly said fiercely. "Whatever you need, I want to give you."

"Oh, Kels." Anders' voice was soft. "You are. You *have*."

CHAPTER TWENTY

Anders woke from his afternoon nap alone, but the sheets still smelled like Kelly and after Anders shut off his alarm, he turned his face into the pillow to breathe in the scent.

He thought about the conversation they'd had last night, and his heart felt oddly full.

He'd been worried he'd say something to hurt Kelly but he'd seemed so open to hearing more about Astrid.

It had been nice. More than nice. Comforting.

Despite Anders' fears, it had felt *good* to reminisce about his late wife. To think of his past without it hurting for once. For the first time in four years, it hadn't felt sharp and acutely painful to think of her.

It had been easier to bear the sadness of his loss with Kelly's leg slotted between his thighs and his fingertips gently rubbing along the chain Anders wore. His sweet reverence of the symbols of Anders' marriage and his willingness to listen had soothed the raw edges of the wounds Anders carried around.

For the first time, Anders hadn't felt like his heart would crack into a thousand pieces when he thought about Astrid being gone. And if it did, he thought Kelly would be there to cup his hands around those shattered fragments and carefully slot them into place again.

But was it fair to Kelly?

Anders rolled onto his back, staring at the hotel room ceiling.

Anders thought of the way Kelly had bitten his lip and said no one had compared him to anything like a spring thunderstorm. It made Anders sad for him. He deserved someone who saw him as something awe-inspiring and earth-shattering.

He *was*.

Kelly was no spring thunderstorm. He was more of a hot summer day, melting the ice inside Anders' chest, warming the chill he'd carried with him so long.

Anders hadn't realized how much he'd needed that. How cold and lonely it had been to carry the grief with him without anyone to share it with.

After the accident, Anders had seen a grief counselor. They'd helped. They'd gotten him back on his feet—and on his skates— and eased him through the worst of it.

Anders' family had flown over immediately from Sweden and stayed with him for weeks, feeding him and pushing him to shower and sitting with him while he wept until he had no tears left.

Pat had stayed up late with him on the phone, talking nonsense while Anders gripped the phone and tried to hold himself together. A touchpoint in the darkness when Astrid's side of the big bed was too empty, and Elia's elephant blanket no longer smelled of her sweet baby scent.

Anders' team had done everything they could as well. They'd stood beside him at the funeral and cried with him. Held him upright when his knees buckled as the tiny casket was lowered into the ground.

After his parents left, the guys had taken shifts staying with him as often as they could, both when he was home and on the road. Refused to let him be alone. Bullied him into eating and showering. They'd given him the support he'd needed. More than he would have asked for.

Their wives and girlfriends had cooked for him, sat with him, held his hand, and cried with him.

He'd had so many people who'd cared, but after a certain point Anders had begun to pull away from his team and stopped speaking so openly about his loss. Tried to show them he was okay. Tried to hide the ways he was falling apart.

Zane, Ryan, Dean, and the rest of the guys would have been there for him any time he'd asked. Their loyalty and support had been endless and he was grateful for everything they'd done for him, but he'd felt guilty constantly dragging down the mood of the room.

There might be no timeline for grief but it had felt like his was never-ending and he hadn't wanted to burden them with it.

But Kelly was special.

Kelly was the one person who had understood that sometimes Anders didn't want a distraction, he just needed to talk about Astrid and Elia. He could tell Anders needed to reminisce and sit with his feelings. Kelly seemed to intuitively grasp exactly what it was Anders needed.

Astrid would have been pleased. She'd always liked Kelly.

They weren't dissimilar, actually.

Astrid had hated the freckles sprinkled across her nose. Kelly had often complained about his too, groaning when a day in the sun on the golf course made them stand out. It was more than freckles and curly hair that they shared though. It was the bright spark in their eyes. Their compassion. Their intelligence and humor and the way they lifted Anders' mood.

Though where Astrid had been soft and willowy, Kelly was all tight, hard lines.

Either way, they both felt right in his arms. And that worried Anders.

His phone buzzed again with his reminder alarm, and he put away thoughts of the night before. He got out of bed and smoothed the covers. He dressed for the game, mentally running through his pre-game ritual.

On the bus to the arena, Anders watched Kelly laugh and joke with their teammates. He was in a good mood, clearly pumped for tonight.

Anders wasn't fired up in the same way but he felt good too. Eager to get on the ice again and with a calm certainty that tonight he'd be able to give the team anything they needed.

Anders went through his warmups like usual, anticipation thrumming in his veins as he lined up in the tunnel afterward, ready to go out onto the ice.

Kelly grinned, bouncy and excited, his brown eyes sparkling when he and Anders went through their usual routine.

"You've got this," Kelly said, tapping their helmets together in the final part of their pre-game ritual. Kelly smacked Anders' ass with his glove and winked. "Now, go win us a game, Lindy."

Anders headed down the tunnel toward the ice, the oddest sense of déjà vu washing over him.

He could hear Astrid say, "You can do this, Anders," and feel her soft palms cupping his cheeks, her vibrant blue eyes staring straight into his. "You are a talented player, and you are going to lead your team to victory. Now, go win me a game."

He could feel the gentle slap of her hand against his ass and the soft press of her lips against his when he dipped her and kissed her deeply.

Anders had never realized how similar his ritual with Kelly was to the one he'd had with his wife, but the little overlaps couldn't be denied. Kelly had never been around for his pep talks from Astrid. Never been in their home when Astrid did it in person or in his hotel room when they'd done it via video chat.

Had Anders initiated it? He didn't think so.

He thought the ritual with Kelly had developed organically. And even now that he'd noticed the similarities, the familiarity felt soothing rather than jarring, settling his raw nerves.

When Anders lined up for the anthem, a sense of calm blanketed him. He pulled out his necklace and closed his eyes, pressing the rings to his lips, the phantom echo of Kelly's touch against his chest overlaid with memories of Astrid.

He took a few deep breaths, the jittery energy that had coursed through him in the tunnel smoothing out as he pictured their success tonight.

This was their final shot at a playoff berth. If Anders did decide to retire and they lost tonight, this could be his very last game.

He couldn't go out with a loss. Couldn't stand the idea of not winning.

His team needed him.

Astrid might be gone but deep inside him, Anders still held her faith in his ability to carry the team to victory.

Kelly believed in him too. Kelly was counting on him.

Anders' heart beat slow and steady by the time the anthem ended and he tucked his necklace away and skated into position for the puck drop. He got low, staring into the eyes of Nashville's center.

He sneered at Anders. "We're going to beat your fucking ass tonight, Lindholm."

"I wouldn't bet on it," Anders said with a smile.

And then the puck hit the ice and Anders had it, shooting it blind off his backhand to Hartinger, gone before his opponent could blink.

The boos of the opposing crowd filled Anders' ears as he skated to the net, knowing Hartinger would pass to Murphy, who'd shoot it back to him.

Seconds later, the puck hit Anders' tape and he feinted around Nashville's D-men, sniping the rubber past their goaltender. It pinged off the crossbar for a beautiful bar down goal that made Nashville's tendie swear in frustration.

Anders grinned at him, then tapped gloves with Hartinger in celebration as the crowd roared their displeasure.

"That might be a new Otters' record for fastest opening goal," Murphy hollered. "Nice one, Lindy."

"Fucking *beaut*, man," Kelly said, eyes bright when he skated up.

"It's just the beginning," Anders promised, and Kelly's smile gleamed before he wheeled away.

They racked up two more goals in the first period and they were all flushed and happy as they left the ice.

The good feeling carried through to the second period, although Nashville tried to rally. On the bench, Kelly chewed his mouthguard. When he caught Anders watching, he winked again, and Anders felt the strangest flutter of warmth in his chest.

He caught a sly, amused grin from Theriault at the two of them but chose to ignore it.

Anders was over the boards again for his next shift, flying high on hockey and playing with Kelly.

He cursed when the opponent's D-man took the puck from Malone, who seemed slow on his skates tonight. Anders winced when Nashville scored a goal off it, but the team was still up one.

From the bench during the next shift, Anders watched Underhill rile up their opponents, goading their winger into shoving at his chest with his stick.

The ref called a penalty and Underhill grinned at the bench when he came off the ice.

"Nice one, Undertaker," Murphy called out.

"Just doin' my job, boys."

Hartinger laughed and slapped Underhill's shoulder. "That's what we like."

The power play was flawless, working exactly like they'd practiced hundreds—if not thousands—of times.

Anders moved the puck high into the offensive zone, then shot a forehand blind pass straight onto Murphy's tape. Murphy fired it in low through the five hole with an easy flick of his wrist that made the shot look effortless.

"God, I fucking love you," Hartinger yelled, shaking Murphy's jersey in celebration and Anders grinned and left them to it.

Kelly's gaze was heated as they tapped gloves and skated toward the bench in tandem. Once there, Kelly kept glancing at Anders out of the corners of his eyes and the sweep of his tongue across his lips was nearly pornographic. Anders had to shift on the bench to relieve the pressure of his jock against his hardening dick.

He squirted some water on the back of his neck and sucked down some Gatorade, pointedly ignoring Kelly's smirk.

Nashville managed to score twice more, leaving them tied at the second intermission and Anders quickly snapped into game mode, refusing to let anything distract him from the win.

He listened intently as Coach Daniels ran them through a few plays in the dressing room and gave them a pep talk.

"We're this close, boys," he said, his voice hoarse from the shouting he'd done on the bench. "Don't let me down."

The final period ticked away without a goal from either side and Anders' legs burned when he collapsed onto the bench after a long shift. He was soaked in sweat and breathing hard as he watched Malone make a stupid play that led to a turnover.

"What the fuck are you doing, Malone?" Daniels bellowed. "Get it together."

Thankfully, Tremblay stole the puck from Nashville, but they were all tense as the next few shifts passed with no goals.

With barely a minute left in the game, Anders knew it was up to him now and the hits came hard and fast as he shouldered his way past one of Nashville's D-men.

He swept the puck out of the corner, wheeling around the net and passing to Murphy. Murphy to Hartinger, then back to Anders, and he scanned the ice for an opening, the slightest thing that would give him an advantage. He passed the puck again, then Kelly and Gabriel were in the mix, going at it with Nashville's wingers and the puck was on his stick again.

The goalie blocked the shot but Ryan was there on the rebound, shooting it to Anders again. Nashville intercepted the pass, but Kelly went to one knee, shoving the puck toward Anders. It was crude and ugly but it *worked* and Anders chipped the puck in, watching it glance off the goalie's catcher.

With micro-seconds left in the game, time stretched and slowed, the puck tumbling through the air, seeming to take forever to cross the goal line. Anders held his breath for agonizing heartbeats, waiting to see if it would go in before the clock ran out.

When it tumbled in to land on the ice, safely in the net, Anders let out his breath in a noisy exhale. The rush sweeping through him was unmatched and the game horn sounding a fraction of a second later was the most beautiful noise Anders had ever heard.

He threw his stick away and turned to find Kelly. He was already skating toward him, throwing himself at Anders and wrapping his legs around his waist.

"We did it! We fucking did it!" Kelly hollered.

Their teammates slammed into them, joining in the celebration but Anders' world had narrowed to the feel of Kelly in his arms and all he could do was hold on tight.

CHAPTER TWENTY-ONE

Kelly's hands shook as he gripped the wheel of Anders' Mercedes and stepped on the accelerator.

Kelly had spent the entire plane ride squirming in his seat, worked up by the team's win and Anders' gorgeous hockey. Every single guy had played all out, and Kelly should be exhausted but he wasn't. He was too energized, too desperate and needy to get his hands on Anders.

Kelly slid through a yellow light he probably should have stopped at but Anders didn't comment, merely squeezed his thigh tighter, fingers biting into Kelly's sore muscles.

They didn't speak as they got out of the SUV and rode the elevator to Anders' condo. They didn't say anything at all until they were in Anders' bedroom, stripping out of their clothes as quickly as possible.

"Fuck." Kelly went up on his toes and pressed his naked body against Anders', his heart beating fast with anticipation. He kissed Anders hard and deep before pulling away with a groan.

"Fuck that was so fucking *beautiful* tonight. Your hockey makes me so fucking hot, Anders."

Anders let out a rough sound, sliding his palms along Kelly's back. "Yours too. Playing with you …"

Anders was getting hard too, and Kelly moaned against his mouth, grinding their bodies together. With every inch of their skin that touched, Kelly's body lit up with another shivery little spark of need, and he kissed his way down Anders' neck, pushing his hair off his shoulder to mouth at his collarbone.

"Kels …" Anders whispered, and the nickname made something go soft and molten within Kelly's body. He pressed desperate wet, open-mouthed kisses to Anders' pecs before dragging his tongue across the hard little nub. Anders hissed, gripping tightly, his hands hot as he roamed them across Kelly's body.

Kelly sucked and licked at Anders' nipple for a minute before switching to the other side. With a groan, Anders' slotted their thighs together but the height difference made it awkward.

Kelly straightened and pressed his palm against Anders' chest.

"On the bed," he whispered. "I want to make you feel good."

Anders went without a word, sprawling on the sheets. He looked so incredible Kelly had to grip his cock at the base for fear he'd come right then and there. He dropped to his knees between Anders' splayed thighs and gently kissed a bruised spot from the game, kneading the muscles around it. He dragged his nose up Anders' shaft, the scent of him filling his head, arousing and already familiar.

Anders' cock was warm and velvety soft, and Kelly took him in his mouth without teasing any further. Anders cupped the back of Kelly's head, showing him the rhythm he wanted, and Kelly lost himself in the motion for a few minutes, drunk on the feel of him.

When his head was swimming with the smell and taste of Anders, he slid off, lips wet and tingling. He wiped at his mouth with the back of his hand and dug in the bedside drawer for the lube and condoms. He gave Anders a questioning glance and he nodded, bending one knee up and reaching for a pillow to prop under his hips. Kelly let out a shaky sigh as he covered himself and slicked his fingers.

The desperation to fuck hard and fast crawled urgently along his spine but he wanted it to be good for Anders, wanted to do this *right*, so he watched Anders' face while he carefully explored his entrance, sinking a single finger in with a slow press of his hand.

Anders let out a soft groan, the twitch of his cock telling Kelly he was enjoying it. Kelly carefully opened him, stretching him for a few minutes, remembering the care Anders had taken with him.

Time slowed until all he could feel was the eager beat of his own heart and the slick grip around his fingers. Anders' hips rose with every careful thrust Kelly made and when Anders reached for the lube and slicked Kelly's cock, he eased his fingers out and let Anders guide him in.

Kelly moved slowly, afraid of hurting him, but Anders reached for Kelly's hips, pulling him in tight.

Kelly groaned, his gaze locked on where they were joined, and his dick throbbed when he watched Anders take him all the way inside, his body swallowing him until Kelly was as deep as he could go, red curls pressed against gold, Anders' cock leaking against his belly.

With a shaky breath to center himself, Kelly used his slick hand to caress Anders' balls and stroke his dick, afraid he'd shoot the second he moved.

Anders encouraged him and Kelly rocked slowly in and out, building up speed after he found the pace and rhythm that made Anders groan low in his chest, his abs clenching.

It was surreal to see Anders' big body stretched out on the bed, muscles tensing, golden skin sheened with sweat as he moved against Kelly's thrusts.

Anders lifted one leg higher, pulling his knee toward his chest, and Kelly helped, his palm against the back of Anders' thigh.

He'd never again see him stretching at the arena without thinking of this moment. Without remembering what it was like to be inside him.

Fucking Anders was everything Kelly had ever hoped for, intense and overwhelming in the best of ways. Pleasure spiraled through him until sweat built up on his forehead and dotted his shoulders, the strain of holding back his release taking all his concentration.

Even through the condom, the heat and the slickness were so intense it made Kelly's head swim.

"Do you like that?" Kelly whispered and Anders let out a throaty groan, muscles clenching as he encouraged Kelly to go harder and deeper.

"You feel amazing, Kels," he rasped. That sent another rush of heat through Kelly. All he wanted was to please Anders, so he tightened his grip, thrusting harder.

Anders' lashes fluttered and when their gazes met, a spark of connection shot between them. Kelly's chest went tight, full of something beautiful and scary he couldn't quite name, and he could see it echoed in Anders' eyes.

Kelly didn't look away, just wrapped his hand around Anders' cock again, desperate to make him come before Kelly lost all control of the pleasure spiraling inside him.

The air was filled with slick strokes, the sound of their ragged breathing, and the soft slap of their bodies coming together. "Are you close?" Kelly whispered.

"Almost there. Just a little more."

Kelly's palms were sweaty where he gripped Anders' body, their skin sliding together as Kelly drove in harder. He bit his lip until he could taste copper in his mouth, shaking with the urge to let go.

When Anders' head fell back, and he grabbed at the sheets, coming with a desperate groan, Kelly let out a sudden, strangled cry. Anders clenched around him, and pleasure rushed through Kelly, so sweet and overwhelming he came with a shocked gasp, shuddering through the orgasm before he could process it had hit.

His hips stuttered, his whole body jerking with helpless spasms of pleasure. He closed his eyes and rode out the final moments of his release, head swimming.

For the longest time they stayed joined, Kelly too overwhelmed to do anything but hang on tight.

He trembled when he finally let go of Anders' sweat-slicked skin and eased out of his body. He staggered toward the trash can and got rid of the condom before collapsing on the bed. He should probably get something for them to clean up with but it was all too much.

Anders reached for Kelly immediately and he buried his head against Anders' shoulder, his lips pressed to his neck, overwhelmed.

I love you, he thought, the words so clear he wondered for a moment if he'd said them aloud.

Anders wrapped his arms tightly around Kelly and Kelly clung to him, his mind a hazy wash of pleasure and contentment, his body aching with fatigue.

Even after Kelly's breathing slowed and he stopped trembling, Anders didn't let go.

Kelly lay there, eyes growing heavier as he silently wished that this, that *Anders*, could be his to keep.

———

Anders groped for his vibrating phone, eyes half-closed as he swiped his thumb across the screen and brought it to his ear. "Lindholm."

His voice sounded rusty and unused, a little hoarse from last night.

"Did I *wake* you?" Pat's incredulous voice filled his ear and Anders squinted at the clock, vaguely noticing the light coming in around the edges of the curtains and realizing how late he'd slept.

"Yeah. Late flight home after the game." He glanced at Kelly, concerned he'd wake him but he was sprawled on his stomach, dead to the world.

"Huh." Pat sounded shocked. "Want me to let you get back to sleep?"

"No. It's okay." Anders sat up and rubbed a hand across his face. "I'm awake now. What did you want?"

"Just wanted to say congrats."

Anders' thoughts immediately turned to Kelly, and he stared blankly at his sleeping form, horrified. Had Pat somehow found out about them?

"For what?" he asked hoarsely.

Pat let out a huff of a laugh. "Jesus, you are tired, man. For clinching the wildcard playoff spot? For being up against us in the first round."

"Oh." Anders let out a relieved sigh. "Right. Yes, that'll be a good series."

"Did you go out with the team and drink last night or something?"

"We had a few drinks on the flight to celebrate," Anders admitted. Though Kelly had only had one, wanting to be sober enough to drive them home, encouraging Anders to let loose. "Why?"

Pat laughed. "Because you haven't been this out of it since the time we got plastered in Back Bay your rookie season."

"Which time?" he croaked. He'd been a lot less rigid about his training then.

Pat snorted. "Fair point."

"I had a lot less on the plane last night than I did back then but I got to bed late and I'm still waking up." He didn't want to think too closely about why he'd been awake so late. Not while he was on the phone with Pat. Anders threw back the covers on his side of the bed, intending to pull on some pants and leave Kelly to sleep in peace. "Let me start some tea and maybe I'll be able to form a coherent thought."

"Shh. Why are you talking so loud, Anders?" Kelly whined, pressing his forehead against Anders' back. "I'm sleeping."

Anders jerked and whirled around, clapping his hand over Kelly's mouth. *Quiet*, he mouthed, watching confusion steal across Kelly's face and he tried to convey with his gaze how important this was. *Don't move.*

"Anders? Who is that?" Pat asked in his ear. "Do you have someone *over?*"

"Yeah, Pat." Anders grimaced at Kelly. "I, uh. I do."

Kelly's eyes went wide and panicked at the sound of his brother's name and Anders lifted his hand away.

"You … well damn." Pat laughed. "I didn't think you'd take my advice but that's great news. Who is she?"

"He," Anders corrected automatically. Though it wasn't like it was news to Pat. He'd known about Anders' bisexuality for decades. But maybe he'd forgotten.

"Right. Well, uh, who's he?"

Anders hesitated. He couldn't say no one. He could *never* say that when Kelly was sitting a few inches away, his face bleached white with worry. But Anders couldn't tell Pat who Kelly was without it blowing up into a messy argument.

Anders' stomach knotted, hating the entire situation and the way it felt like a lose-lose no matter what he did.

"Look, if it's a teammate and you don't want to out them or something, you don't have to tell me. And hell, I get it if you just don't want to talk about it or whatever," Pat said, clearing his throat when the silence stretched on, turning awkward. "I'm, uh, happy you're moving forward with your life."

"Thanks," Anders said, wishing he was a lot more awake for this conversation. The burst of adrenaline at nearly being discovered should have been enough to wipe away any lingering sleepiness. He didn't feel clear-headed at all though. "Was there anything else you needed?"

Pat let out another huffing laugh in his ear. "Well, no. Not really. I just called to congratulate you. I assumed you'd already be up doing your six hours of yoga and meditation while drinking kale smoothies but …"

"I'm getting old," Anders said automatically. "Even *I* need some time to recover from a late night."

"Far be it from me to complain about you acting like a human," Pat teased. "And apparently in more ways than one."

"It happens occasionally."

"Good for you, man. I'm glad. You just took me by surprise."

Oh, if he only knew … But no, it was better he didn't. Better if he never found out.

After an awkward goodbye, Anders ended the call, hand trembling.

"Fuck." Anders' heart still beat madly. He tossed his phone on the bed and turned to look at Kelly.

"Why the hell was Pat calling so fucking early?" Kelly groused, a worried groove appearing between his eyebrows.

"He wanted to offer his congratulations on the playoff spot. He assumed I'd be up …" Anders glanced at the clock, grimacing. Any other day, he would have been. "And it's pretty late. Good thing Coach gave us a break and told us to sleep in and rest up today."

"True." Kelly glanced at him and placed his hand on Anders' shoulder, gently tugging until Anders shifted on the bed. "Are you okay? You seem super stressed."

"I had a small heart attack at the thought of your brother discovering us."

"Well, it wouldn't have been the end of the world if he did, would it?"

Anders stared. "It wouldn't be good. We already talked about this. We agreed we wouldn't tell your family and you haven't come out to anyone, Kelly."

"Well, yeah." Kelly's cheeks flushed a little. "But that was *before*, right?"

"Before what?" Anders asked slowly.

Kelly shrugged, not quite meeting his gaze. "Before we … you know, got closer."

"We are closer," Anders agreed. "But nothing's changed since we talked about it, Kelly."

Kelly swallowed, the sound audible in the quiet room. "Hasn't it?"

"No. You know I care about you but we discussed this at the beginning. We agreed it would get uncomfortable and messy if anyone found out. Underhill already figured out I'm sleeping with *someone* and it's far too likely he'll put together the pieces if we're not—"

"I think Gabriel might have figured it out too," Kelly said, his tone hesitant.

Anders froze. He'd thought maybe but to have Kelly confirm it was concerning. "Why didn't you say something?"

Kelly shrugged, his shoulders hunching. "I didn't want to make a big deal of it."

Anders took a deep breath, his heart beating too fast, an odd shaky sensation building inside him. He rubbed a hand across his jaw, the whiskers of his beard rasping against his palm.

"I don't like lying to our teammates and friends."

"Well, I don't either," Kelly said. He scooted closer. "So maybe this is a sign."

"That we should end things?"

"No!" Kelly rested his hand on Anders' forearm. "That we should give this a real shot. Maybe we should think about actually being together."

Anders stared. "Kelly …"

"No, hear me out," Kelly said. "You don't want to be dishonest to the people we care about, right?"

Anders nodded and Kelly pressed on.

"I know you wouldn't feel good about keeping things a secret if we started dating so I should come out. I can do that for you, I swear. It'll be a little tough with my family but they already know and like you. They'll be surprised and it'll probably be a bit of a mess for a while but I'm sure they'll accept us eventually."

"You can't be serious," Anders said, struggling to understand where this had all come from. "You can't *come out* for me, Kelly."

"Why not?"

"This was supposed to be casual," he protested. "I told you from the beginning ... I can't do this."

This was exactly what he'd tried to avoid. Astrid had been right. He was going to break Kelly's heart.

"Okay, okay." Kelly held up his hands. "Dude, don't panic."

"I'm not panicking," Anders snapped. "I just ... we talked about this. We were on the same page."

"I know. Forget I said anything." Kelly drew his knees up to his chest, looking away.

"I was on the phone with my best friend trying to come up with a lie about what we were doing!" Anders picked up his phone and waved it.

"I never *asked* you to."

"What else was I supposed to do?" he protested. "Pat freaked out when you got a small cut in a game. What is he going to think of us *dating*?"

"I don't think you can compare a hockey game to our relationship." Kelly sounded stiff.

"We don't—" Anders bit back his instinct to tell Kelly they didn't have a relationship. But was that true? He wasn't sure anymore. Things that had seemed so clear were suddenly murky. "Kelly, this isn't ..."

"Yeah. I get it, Anders. You don't want things to change between us. It's fine. We'll keep doing what we're doing. Forget I suggested anything else."

"Maybe it would be better if we cooled off and went back to being friends sooner rather than later." The words felt wrong on Anders' tongue but he didn't know what else to say to Kelly.

Anders didn't want Kelly to blow up his relationship with his family for him. He didn't want to wreck their team with one more coming out. He didn't want to unleash Malone's fury on Kelly or add any pressure to what was already an unstable situation.

And most of all, he didn't want to promise Kelly something he wasn't sure he could deliver.

Kelly drew away, his expression closing off. "Cooled off sooner rather than later? You say that like you already had an end date on this."

Anders shrugged. "Well, I assumed when the season wrapped up …"

"So much for spending some time together during the off-season," Kelly said bitterly.

Anders sighed. He'd forgotten they'd talked about that. If they'd spent parts of the summer together, would he have been able to keep his hands off Kelly? If they toured Boston together and Kelly visited him in Sweden, their situation would have become less clear, not more.

"Well, if not then, after," he admitted.

"And what about after? We'd *ignore* each other next season?"

"I don't know if there will be a next season for me. I'm thinking about retirement."

"What?" Kelly gaped. "When the fuck were you going to tell me *that*?"

"I don't know. I haven't decided anything." He rubbed his forehead. "It's been on my mind a lot."

Kelly narrowed his eyes. "Is that why you were talking about skills camps and shit?"

"Sort of." He wasn't sure how to explain his thought process and that it had all started because of Zane and Ryan's retirement.

Would Zane care if he told Kelly? Anders wasn't sure.

"I thought you wanted to play as long as you could. I mean, I know your contract ends next year but …"

"I did want to play another year or two. But it sounds like Zane and Ryan are talking about retirement too and I'm not sure I want to spend my last season breaking in new wingers and—"

"So, we'll lose our whole top line in one go? How is that better?"

"I'm not sure what I want to do. I haven't made any final decisions. I'm considering my options for my future," Anders argued.

"A future that clearly doesn't include me." Kelly definitely sounded bitter now and Anders' heart twisted when he realized how hurt Kelly was.

Kelly got out of bed and picked his boxers up off the floor, the knobs of his spine showing when he bent over, making him look oddly vulnerable.

"Kelly …" Anders said, hating that they'd gotten to this point. Hating that he'd hurt Kelly. Hating that they'd landed right where he'd wanted to avoid. "Talk to me."

"Give me a day or two," Kelly said, sounding tired and distant. He rummaged through his overnight bag and pulled out sweats. "I'm going home. I haven't been there to sleep at all since you got injured and I think we could use some time apart."

Anders swallowed hard. "Are you ending things?"

Kelly straightened. "No. That was what *you* wanted."

"I …" Anders felt helpless. He knew the words Kelly wanted to hear but he wasn't sure he could say them. He felt like everything in his life was spiraling out of his control, spinning and whirling and he didn't know which way was up anymore.

He cared for Kelly so much but they'd only been intimate recently. Yes, it was built on years of friendship and trust but it was so fast. It felt too big and overwhelming.

Whatever he felt for Kelly, he still loved Astrid and he didn't know how to … move on.

Kelly deserved to be loved and treasured and Anders didn't trust that he was ready to do that.

"I'm going to go, okay?" Kelly's voice was soft, and Anders blinked, realizing he was fully dressed and standing in front of him with his bags slung over his shoulder.

Helpless, afraid he'd already screwed up and hurt Kelly, but unsure of how to fix it, Anders reached out and grasped Kelly's waist.

Kelly gave him a weak smile and tucked Anders' hair behind his ear, skimming his fingertips across Anders' short beard before he pulled away.

"I don't want to lose your friendship, Kelly." Anders' voice cracked. He didn't want to lose everything else they had but he didn't know how to say that. Not right now when his head was a mess.

"You won't. I'll always be your friend." But a shimmer of something in Kelly's eyes made Anders' heart ache. "Give me a few days to figure out some stuff and we can talk more when our heads are clearer, okay?"

"Okay," Anders whispered, afraid if he spoke louder, he'd break down completely.

Kelly turned away and Anders let his hands fall into his lap, listening to the sound of Kelly's footsteps growing quieter and quieter before the front door closed and the apartment was silent again.

CHAPTER TWENTY-TWO

Furious, Kelly stomped into his apartment, slamming the door behind him. "Stupid fucking idiot Swede," he muttered under his breath as he walked toward the kitchen.

He unceremoniously dumped his bags next to the refrigerator, belatedly remembering his laptop was in one of them and winced, hoping the bag was padded enough to protect it or he'd be buying himself a new laptop.

Underhill, who was slumped over the island staring blankly into a cup of coffee, straightened, squinting. "Dude, what the fuck? What's your damage this morning?"

"Nothing. Everything's fucking fine." Kelly glanced around the kitchen. "Jesus, have you even cleaned anything since I've been staying with Anders?"

Annoyed, Kelly grabbed a trash bag and shook it out, using his arm to sweep the pile of junk off the counter into it. God, he was turning into his mother. Cleaning when he was upset.

Underhill clutched his coffee mug to his bare chest, his eyes bleary, his hair a little greasy and standing on end. "Jesus, you're in a shitty mood. Did Lindy break it off with you or something?"

Kelly froze, staring at his roommate. "*What?*"

"Oh, come on, man. I'm not a fucking idiot. *You're* the one hooking up with him, aren't you? I mean, you've been staying at his place since he twisted his ankle. Until you stomped in now, you were both happier than I've ever seen either of you. And c'mon man, I'm not the brightest bulb in the drawer but when practically the whole team was talking about going out to celebrate and you two booked it off the plane last night like you were on fire, it isn't hard to figure out you wanted to fuck like bunnies."

Kelly's shoulders slumped. "Guess we weren't that subtle."

"Uh, no."

"Do you think everyone else knows?"

"I'm sure most of the rookies and call ups are oblivious. Murph, Frenchie, and Trembles probably put the pieces together though."

"As long as Malone didn't, I can live with that."

"Nah, you're fine. He was busy making plans and paying no attention to you two." Underhill took a sip of coffee. "So, what the hell happened between when you got off the plane last night and now?"

Kelly sighed and jammed some more trash into the bag. "We were—we were in bed this morning and my fucking brother called. Anders got all weird and cagey about stuff and now he's talking about retiring next season and—fuck!"

"Shit, that sucks."

"Apparently Murphy and Hartinger are retiring too."

Underhill gaped at him. "We're losing our entire top line?"

"I wouldn't make that shit up," Kelly said with a scowl. He tied off the bag and set it on the floor to take out later. "And I don't know for *sure* so don't say anything to anyone else about it, but it sounds like that's the idea."

"No, I know you wouldn't make it up. But damn. I thought they'd all play at least a few more years."

"Yeah, I didn't see it coming either." Kelly dragged himself over to the couch and slumped on it with a groan. Between the game last night and the fucking, his muscles were killing him. He should have stolen one of Anders' coconut waters on the way out. He'd been too hurt and pissed to think straight though. "It just sucks, you know?"

"Yeah, for sure."

"I mean, we've had a such a great team and …"

Underhill shrugged. "Dude, that's how hockey *goes*. There's always retirements and trades and shit. It hardly ever looks the same two seasons in a row."

"I know." Kelly flailed mentally, trying to explain why it bothered him so much. "But we had this core together for so long. This is only my fourth season but man, it's been great."

"It has," Underhill agreed. "But that's hockey, man. You know that."

"Ugh. Maybe I don't like it," Kelly whined.

Underhill laughed. "Dude, you don't have to. But it doesn't change shit."

"I know."

"Are you freaking out about the team or the shit with your boyfriend?"

"He's not my boyfriend," Kelly muttered. Much as he'd wanted that, it was never going to happen.

"Well, why the fuck not?" Trevor wandered over, still clutching his mug like it was a lifeline.

"Cause he's still fucking in love with Astrid. And he's like … convinced we have no future together."

"Hmm. I mean, a dead wife *is* a problem."

"Jesus." Kelly shook his head. "You are such a tactless asshole."

"What?"

"Never mind."

"Is it a dealbreaker though? Him being in love with her and all?"

"Well, not to *me*," Kelly said. "I know he's always going to love her. I don't want that to stop. I just want him to, you know, love me too."

"I get that."

"*I'm* not the problem. He's being a stubborn asshole."

"Why?"

"I don't know. Probably some stupid self-sacrificing nonsense about not deserving to find love again or some bullshit."

"Yeah, that sounds like Lindy. Any dude who gives up fried food and beer completely would totally be the type."

Kelly snorted. "Exactly."

"Are you gonna let him go without a fight?"

"No!" Kelly protested. "But I don't know how to get him to see what's right in front of his fucking face."

"Yeah, me neither. You're asking the wrong dude for advice on your love life if you're talking to me."

Kelly shoved his palm against Trevor's nose in an imitation of the kind of face wash he'd give him on the ice if he was wearing sweaty gloves. "Thanks, asshole. I already knew you were useless."

Trevor shoved his hand away. "I'm just sayin'."

"Yeah, I got it. Fine. I'll talk to someone who actually knows something about relationships."

He didn't know *who*. He could probably talk to Gabriel about it or Zane or Ryan but he wasn't sure if he wanted to talk about his personal shit with Anders with them.

He was kinda surprised by how well Trevor had taken the news.

Kelly glanced over to see his roommate absorbed in something on his phone, mug balanced precariously on the edge of the couch arm.

"You don't care?"

"Huh?" He lifted his head. "About what?"

"Me being into dudes."

Underhill made a face. "Why the fuck would I?"

"I dunno." Kelly fiddled with the strings on his hoodie. "I mean, I should have said something to you before now, right?"

Underhill grimaced. "I mean, yeah. Probably. It's shitty to keep secrets from your best friend."

Kelly squinted at him. "Are we best friends?"

"Well, I thought we were, asswipe. But maybe not anymore."

Kelly laughed, despite his shitty mood. "Yeah, fine. I was a jerk. I should have told you. I—I didn't tell anyone, okay? My family doesn't know. Anders is the only person I told."

"'Cause you wanted to bone him."

"Well, I did," Kelly admitted. "But it wasn't just that. He asked and I'm shit at lying to him."

"Well, it kinda hurts that you didn't trust me, man." Trevor shoved at Kelly's thigh with his foot.

"I'm sorry. I should have said something. I've been pretending so long and—"

"Wait, so you aren't into women at all?"

Kelly shook his head. "No. I'm really not."

"But what about the chicks you went home with?"

Kelly shrugged, staring at his hands. "You do what you gotta do to make things convincing, right?"

"Yikes. Glad I never had to do that."

Kelly looked up. "Huh? Oh, you mean fake an interest in women? Well, why would you? You're straight."

Underhill grimaced. "Yeah. Not so much."

Kelly gawked at him for a moment. "The hell?"

"I'm, uh." He cleared his throat. "Definitely not straight. Into both but … yeah."

"Wow." Kelly blinked. "And you gave *me* shit for hiding stuff."

"Well at least I didn't pretend to be something I wasn't!"

"Yeah, fair." Kelly slumped. "So, like … when did you realize it?"

"That I was into both?"

"Yeah."

"I dunno. I was probably in Juniors, man." He shrugged, a sheepish smile on his face. "The bro-job is a thing."

"I'm starting to regret going to college."

"Why? When did you realize it?"

"I guess I've known a long time," Kelly said slowly. "But like, I kinda fell in love with Anders when I was fifteen."

"Shit."

"Yeah." He swallowed hard. "He's the only guy I've ever been with."

"He fucked you when you were fifteen? Dude, that's sketchy as shit!" Underhill looked furious.

"What?" Horrified, Kelly realized how that had sounded. "Oh. God no. He didn't look twice at me until this spring."

"Shit. You had me worrying Lindy was a perv." He made a face. "He didn't seem like the type but there were some real creepy older dudes lurking around in Juniors, so it wouldn't surprise me."

"Eww." Kelly made a face. "No, Anders has always been a good guy. I had a huge crush on him, but he treated me like a little brother until recently."

"Good." Underhill gave him a quizzical look. "But wait, you said he's the only guy you've ever been with, and he didn't look at you until recently. Does that mean …"

"Yeah, I was pretty much a twenty-two-year-old gay virgin until a few weeks ago," Kelly muttered. "Get the chirping in now."

"It is pretty lame," Underhill said with a laugh.

Kelly shot him the finger.

"Seriously though." Underhill sobered. "You really saved yourself for him?"

"Ugh." Kelly stared at the ceiling. "Not like, *purposely*. I was never super into anyone else, and I was already fooling around with girls I didn't want. I didn't want to do it with guys too, you know? I wanted it to mean something, and he was the only person I felt like it would mean something *with*."

"Huh."

"Yeah, weird I guess."

"I mean, whatever." Underhill shrugged. "You do you."

"I was trying."

"So, you really think this is it for you and Lindy?" Trevor's expression was surprisingly sympathetic.

"I don't know. I hope not but unless I figure out some brilliant way to get through his stupid, thick skull, I probably am out of luck." Kelly's stomach growled and he sighed and heaved himself off the couch. "You want breakfast?"

"Sure. If you're making it."

"You're an asshole."

"Yeah, I know." He grinned at Kelly. "But like, you kinda owe me for lying to me for so long."

Kelly chucked a nearby remote at him. "You are not playing that card from here on out, dude."

Trevor batted it away. "I figure I've got about a week though."

"Yeah, probably," Kelly agreed. "Asshole."

"Hey, you apparently like those."

Kelly groaned. He'd given Trevor so much new ammunition to chirp him. "Yeah well, so do you."

"True that."

"So why didn't *you* say anything before now?"

"I dunno. This is the first time I've been with a team who wasn't going to care. And even then …"

"Malone?" Kelly finished.

Underhill grimaced. "Yeah. I mean, you're not going to say anything to him about me, are you?"

"Fuck no," Kelly said. "You're not going to tell him about *me*, right?"

"No. What about the rest of the guys? Like, I know some of them have their suspicions, but are you planning to confirm it?"

Kelly shrugged. "I don't know. I hadn't really thought about it. Probably not."

What was the point if Anders wasn't going to go for a relationship anyway? Why kick up a hornets' nest for no reason?

"I'm not gonna push you or anything. Maybe something to think about though." Trevor frowned. "So, you said you didn't tell your family?"

Kelly shook his head. "Nope."

"Damn. Y'all seem tight too."

Kelly shrugged. "We are but it's complicated."

"Sure, I get that. But like, they love you. They'll come around even if they're weird about it first, right?"

"I think so. I just have to pull the trigger on it, I guess."

Kelly sighed. He probably *should* do that. Because if shit was over with Anders he'd probably want to move on someday. It seemed unfathomable now but it would be stupid for him to spend the rest of his life moping about someone. He'd probably date someone eventually. And he was tired of lying to his family.

"Good luck with that. Now what did you say about breakfast?"

"We literally have no food 'cause I haven't been home and you never shop." Kelly closed the refrigerator door. "Want to go out and grab brunch?"

"Sure, why the fuck not? Let me put on some pants."

"Good call," Kelly said with a laugh. "'Cause I don't think any place around here is going gonna let you in without them."

"Shit, they need Waffle Houses around here. You can show up in *anything* to a place like that."

Kelly smirked and leaned against the counter. "There's that diner over on Chicago Ave. The one we've been to a few times. We could go there if you want." It was a greasy-spoon type that wouldn't care if they looked rough around the edges.

Although Kelly needed to look halfway decent because he had a volunteering thing later today. He groaned when he remembered Anders would be there too. So much for getting some space.

Trevor hopped up. "*Yes*. I am in. Give me two minutes to piss and brush my teeth."

"You still need pants though," Kelly called after him.

"God, you're the worst."

"Tell me about it." With a sign Kelly heaved himself off the counter to go get ready.

Sure, he was heartbroken. But eggs, bacon, and chocolate chip pancakes wouldn't make it any worse.

———

Anders jogged away from the shore, turning toward his condo, filled with regret over what had transpired with Kelly.

Not what had happened in the past few weeks, or last night, but the words that had come out of his mouth this morning.

What had he done?

Anders wouldn't say he felt any clearer than he had when Kelly left, but what he lacked in clarity he had in certainty. He'd reacted hastily and he didn't like the way he'd left things with Kelly.

What that meant or how he was supposed to deal with it were still a large question mark in his mind, however.

He muted the Swedish-language history podcast he'd only been half-listening to and removed his earbuds, greeting the doorman with a smile that felt forced.

He rode up to his floor in the elevator with his elderly neighbor, asking after her health and giving her small dog a scratch behind the ears before he stepped off on his floor.

His condo was still and quiet as he let himself inside, the silence oppressive.

But of course it was. It always was.

Except for when Kelly was here.

Anders' heart clenched at the thought as he tucked his earbuds into the case and plugged in his phone. He shouldn't have let Kelly walk out this morning.

Anders didn't like the way they'd left things. They should have showered and had breakfast together. *Hydrated* before they tried to have a conversation. It was never good to have a fight when both people were tired and hungry. Empty stomachs and pounding heads led to short tempers and even shorter words.

He and Astrid had learned that quickly enough.

His teammates had joked about them having the perfect relationship and seemed to imply they'd never argued, which wasn't true at all. They'd fought. Sometimes they'd said things they'd regretted.

But they'd learned from it. Gotten better at communication. Worked at saying, "This hurt me. Is it something you're willing to work on?" instead of "I hate the way you always do this."

They'd both had demanding jobs.

Astrid had come home from the hospital, drained from trying to hold together bodies torn apart by car accidents or vicious beatings. Some nights she was wrecked from seeing overdoses and tragic deaths and he'd guiltily stuffed down his petty whining about a lost game.

Sometimes he'd wished she could just be there for *him* but it had felt selfish and small when he thought about what she'd been up against.

They'd snapped and snarled at each other before learning to be gentle. Learning that it wasn't healthy to measure hurt against hurt. Mutual comfort was all that mattered.

Anders could wrap her in his arms and let her cry about the fourteen-year-old who was dead from gunshot wounds, and it didn't take away from the way she held him after a big loss.

On the scale of human tragedy, one of those things was significantly worse than the other, but that didn't mean they couldn't grieve them both. Together.

They weren't *competing*. They were a team.

So why hadn't Anders viewed the situation with Kelly the same way?

Anders sighed.

Because he was trying to hold Kelly at arm's length. Because he wasn't ready to admit they were already in a relationship. Because he was terrified if he let Kelly in all the way, he'd lose someone he loved again.

Anders closed his eyes, gripping the edge of the marble countertop, jaw clenched and tears wetting his lashes.

He loved Kelly. He knew it. He'd known it for a long time, probably.

Sleeping together had changed things between them of course. But it hadn't started anything that wasn't already there.

Anders had been too afraid to admit it.

He unclenched his hands and turned away, going through the motions of making a protein shake and drinking coconut water, enough to tide him over until he could shower and cook breakfast.

He thought about Kelly while he washed his hair, remembering the look on his face last night as he'd come apart inside Anders, the sweet way he'd wrapped around Anders in his sleep, the pain in his eyes when Anders had rejected him this morning.

Anders liked to think of himself as an intelligent, thoughtful man but he'd proven that was a lie.

He'd hurt the one person he cared most about.

Because he was *scared*.

And he would have to live with that. Learn from it. Do better.

How, he didn't know. The path forward to fixing it was murky. But perhaps, in time, he'd figure it out.

He'd never backed down from a challenge before.

CHAPTER TWENTY-THREE

"Great to see you!" Justin Lamb's handshake was warm as he shook Anders' hand. "So glad you could make it today."

Anders smiled. "It's a fantastic cause. I didn't want to miss out."

The Evanston Otters and the minor league baseball team, the Skokie Cougars, had both been partnered with the Evanston Youth Sports League for years.

Today, the baseball team was hosting an equipment drive to provide new and gently used sports equipment to children in need.

The joint event regularly brought in tens of thousands of dollars in equipment and scholarships to cover the costs of registration and other sports-related fees at the center and Anders had always enjoyed taking part.

He was grateful the fundraiser was intentionally held in the small gap between the regular season ending and playoffs beginning so the Otters' players could participate.

Justin was the volunteer coordinator at the EYSL and a former physical therapist for the Cougars organization. His husband, Micah Warner, was the first out minor league baseball player and now worked for one of the big talent agencies in downtown Chicago.

Through volunteer work, Anders had gotten to know both of them over the years.

"So, same as usual?" Anders asked a short while later as he and Justin set up one of the tables where people could drop off their donations.

"Yeah. Why fix what isn't broken, right?"

Anders nodded. With so many regular volunteers, the event usually came together like clockwork.

Nearby, a friend and former teammate of Micah's named Mike Berrera was carefully setting out bins to collect used equipment.

Zane and Ryan were around here somewhere as well, along with a couple of other guys from the Otters and Cougars organizations.

Kelly was at the table across the lobby with Micah. Kelly had offered Anders a tentative smile when their paths crossed earlier this afternoon, but they hadn't spoken otherwise.

It left Anders with a strange achy feeling in the center of his chest.

"Hey, congrats on the playoff spot," Justin said as he shook out a tablecloth and draped it over the folding table. "And great game last night. Micah and I watched it along with some friends."

"Thanks. It was a good one," Anders said absently, distracted by the flex of Kelly's shoulders in the snug gray T-shirt he wore, biceps popping as he lifted a tote.

"You okay?" Justin asked.

"Yes," Anders smiled reassuringly. "We had a late flight last night. I'm sure you remember what the travel is like."

Justin laughed, tucking a lock of curly blond hair behind his ear. "Minor league baseball is worlds away from what you do, Lindholm. We took buses everywhere. None of the cushy chartered flight stuff."

Anders' smile widened. "I suppose I shouldn't complain. How are things with you?"

Justin and Anders talked as they finished setting up but once the doors opened, the rush of people dropping off checks and equipment or taking info cards about where they could donate online kept them both busy.

It wasn't until the crowd cleared that they had a chance to speak again.

"You're bisexual, right?" Anders asked, trying not to let his gaze linger on Kelly as he laughed at something Micah said.

Justin nodded. "I am. Why?"

"I am too," Anders said. "It's nothing I've spoken about publicly but …"

But what? He had no idea how to finish the thought. Only it felt like it was important to say for some reason.

"But you have a reason for speaking out now?" Justin asked, his tone careful as he neatened a stack of cards scattered by eager hands.

"Possibly." Anders cleared his throat. "It's complicated."

"These things often are." Justin nodded toward the table across the lobby. "But sometimes it's worth the complications."

"Just before a playoff run?" Anders asked doubtfully.

Justin winced. "Not ideal, no."

"What if I hurt him and the team trying to figure out what I want?" He'd been speaking fairly obliquely but if Justin hadn't already put together that Anders was in love with someone who was a part of the organization, he certainly would now.

"A wise friend once asked me if I saw a future with Micah."

Berrera, who had wandered back from Kelly's table said, "That *was* pretty wise of me. I swear to God, if you and Micah hadn't had me around you two never would have gotten your heads out of your asses."

Anders smiled as Berrera walked away to check the other tables. The former baseball player was handsome, in a rough, craggy sort of way. Anders had met him at EYSL events a few times and liked him and his wife and teenage kids.

"Clearly you did see a future with him," Anders said.

"I did," Justin agreed. "And that question made me consider what I was willing to risk. In our case, it came at a high cost. I lost my job with the team here. And Micah decided to retire. It was unquestionably worth it, but we had to make sacrifices to do it."

"It's a terrifying thing, choosing to love someone," Anders said, his throat thicker than he'd anticipated.

Justin's gaze flicked to his face, his blue eyes kind. "Is it ever really a choice?"

"No, maybe not," Anders said, looking across the lobby at Kelly.

———

"What made you decide to come out?" Kelly asked.

Micah glanced at him. He wasn't Kelly's agent—that guy was in Boston and Micah only handled baseball—but they sort of knew each other through the EYSL. Probably not well enough to prompt that question though, especially when they'd been talking sports for most of the afternoon.

"Sorry." Kelly gave him a sheepish grin. "That was out of left field."

"Busting out the baseball metaphors, huh?" Micah's bright grin was mesmerizing.

Kelly laughed and tried not to stare at Micah. He was no Anders, but Kelly was starting to think he maybe had a thing for older men.

Micah's dark hair was streaked with silver—although he was probably around Anders' age or a little younger—and the corners of his eyes creased whenever he smiled. He carried himself with an innate confidence Kelly envied.

"Yeah. You know, figured I'd better since none of you guys ever seem to know hockey."

"Excuse me." Micah looked a little offended. "I'll have you know one of my close friends was the first out college player in the nation and our buddy Brent was a college hockey player too. We go to plenty of your games. Gotta support the queerest team in the NHL."

Kelly laughed but then his earlier words sunk in. "You know Nathan Rhodes?"

"You know who Nathan Rhodes is?" Micah looked surprised. "He's quite a bit before your time."

Kelly had been thirteen years old when Nathan came out.

"Well, it was a pretty big deal," Kelly pointed out. "It kinda made an impression on me."

"True." Micah smiled. "Sports are definitely changing."

"Not fast enough," Kelly muttered.

Micah's frown darkened his face. "Your team having problems? I know there have been a lot of new same-sex relationships in the organization lately but it seemed like it was going pretty smoothly." He chuckled. "Of course, I should know as well as anyone that good PR can spin anything."

Kelly sighed. "No. I mean, not really *problems* exactly. A few people on the team aren't super cool with it and one guy is actively against the whole thing but overall it's been fine."

"And you're getting adequate support from your organization? Because I can put you in touch with—"

"Oh, I'm not ..." Kelly suddenly felt flustered. But he was. That was the truth of it. And why had he started this conversation if he didn't want to talk to someone about it. "Um, that's not true. I am."

"Are?" Micah arched an eyebrow.

"Gay." Heat rushed into Kelly's cheeks, and he turned his back to the table across the lobby, not wanting Anders to see. "There's a teammate I've been ..."

"Screwing?"

Kelly turned even redder. "Screwing with feelings, I guess?"

"God have I been there." Micah laughed, his expensive-looking watch glinting in the light as he crossed his arms over his chest, his forearms tan and toned against his white polo shirt. "He wouldn't happen to be the handsome Swede across the lobby glaring daggers at me right now, would he?"

"What?" On instinct, Kelly turned to look but Micah kicked at his ankle.

"Don't *look*."

Kelly turned the motion into reaching for his discarded water bottle. "Why would he be glaring?"

"Jealousy, maybe?"

"Of you?" Kelly's tone was skeptical.

"Ouch."

"No, you're good-looking." Kelly's cheeks were practically nuclear now. "I don't think he cares enough to be jealous of me talking to anyone though. Besides, you're *married*."

"Happily, in fact." Micah smiled, leaning casually against the cinderblock wall behind him like he was posing for a photoshoot. "But trust me, kid, that looks like jealousy to me."

"Maybe?" Kelly said doubtfully. "We had a fight this morning though."

"About what?"

"About having a relationship." Kelly swallowed hard. "He lost his wife and baby girl in an accident a few years ago."

Micah sobered. "I remember hearing about that. It was awful."

"It was," Kelly agreed with a lump in his throat. "I don't think he's ready to move on."

"Maybe he's scared."

"Of what?"

"Losing you too."

Kelly sucked in a breath. He'd never quite considered it that way. It did put a different spin on things. "Oh."

"I'm just speculating, of course. Most of the conversations we've had in the past were about the EYSL or sports. We haven't spoken about anything very personal."

"Neither had you and I until now," Kelly pointed out.

"Yeah, but I have some experience with this." Micah sighed. "You would not believe how many closeted athletes slide into my DMs needing to talk. And I mean, some are dumb offers to suck my dick but most of them are about messy relationship shit. I can never decide which is worse."

Kelly laughed at the dick-sucking comment. Some guys were way braver than he'd ever be.

"Still, I dunno how I got the rep for being the go-to guy for gay dating drama," Micah said with a grimace. "I never wanted to be the person everyone looked up to. I just wanted to play baseball, for fuck's sake."

"Do you regret it? The coming out and all."

"God no. I've got Justin and three beautiful girls."

"You have kids?"

"Oh yeah." Micah laughed. "*Triplets*, in fact."

"Huh."

"It wasn't the plan, but we went with a surrogate. Did the whole artificial insemination thing. Multiples are pretty common with those procedures. We were prepared for twins but when they said three had stuck, I had a fucking heart attack. They said they could do what they called a "selective reduction" so there would only be two. It was so early, and I knew it wasn't a big deal but I didn't want to go that route, you know? Catholic upbringing and all, so it didn't sit right with me. We all sat down and talked about it. The surrogate was okay with the risk of carrying all three and Justin was okay with the idea too, so ... we went from zero kids to three in no time at all. It's insane but we're happy."

"Wow." Part of that caught Kelly's attention though. "So, you're Catholic?"

Micah shrugged. "I grew up that way. Now? I don't know. The Church isn't so supportive of my family so I'm not exactly supportive of them."

"How did your family—your parents and siblings and stuff— take all this?"

"My dad's not a factor but my mom was cool. So was my sister." He looked down, the first real trace of vulnerability appearing on his face. "Telling them was hard as hell though. I thought they might pick the Church over me."

"But they didn't?" Kelly clung to the hope his family wouldn't either.

Micah shook his head. "No. My mom told me it could never be wrong for two good people to love each other."

"That's ... that's good to know," Kelly said. "I hope my family feels that way."

"I hope so too." Micah clapped a hand on his shoulder. "But it looks like we've got some people coming through. We can talk more later, okay?"

"Okay," Kelly agreed, turning to face them with a smile that wasn't even faked.

The conversation with Micah hadn't magically fixed everything, but it did give him a little hope.

Whatever happened with Anders, Kelly knew it was time to come out to his family.

CHAPTER TWENTY-FOUR

The following day passed in a blur for Anders. He got up, he worked out, and he went to practice where the coaches ran them through game simulation play. It was basically like playing a game, with points and penalties, only it was the guys up against each other.

Anders could play in his sleep, and he'd perfected his ability to turn off his personal life and focus on hockey years ago but worries about the situation with Kelly sprang to life whenever he wasn't thinking about the game.

Things between him and Kelly were okay. Not great and they hadn't spoken much but Kelly seemed normal enough in the locker room and on the ice.

Kelly stuck to his fellow defensemen and Anders hung out with the forwards and none of their teammates commented on anything to Anders, so he assumed no one spotted the awkwardness between them.

After, Anders went home and ate alone at his dining room table. The weighted silence stretched until he felt as taut as a trebuchet pulled back as far as it would go.

Where he'd land once it launched, he had no idea.

He was tired, but too restless to nap, and unwilling to risk potential injury from overtraining, so he went out for a walk. He headed toward Lake Michigan, the wind ruffling his hair until he tied it back.

It was a gorgeous April day, sun-drenched and windy, reminding him of the time he'd spent along Lake Mälaren with Astrid and Elia one summer.

He remembered small arms wrapped around his neck and blonde curls tickling his nose. He could feel the press of Astrid's cheek against his upper arm as they pointed out boats and listened to Elia laugh delightedly at the swoop of the gulls on the air currents.

Now, Anders leaned against the railing and looked out over the water, the breeze churning it into choppy little waves that made him wish he had a boat to take out. Maybe he'd buy one after he retired.

He once again considered Zane's suggestion of opening a skills camp.

If Anders stayed in the US after retirement, he'd have plenty of players to work with during the off-season. Money was no obstacle and Anders' name was well known in the league. His reputation would be a draw. As long as he partnered with the right people to work out the logistics, this idea was doable.

Guys might come from anywhere and video or phone consultations were always an option.

This area wasn't a bad place to set up something. With two NHL teams in the city and ones nearby in Minnesota and Michigan, he'd be able to work with developing players or guys working on injury rehabilitation during the season.

And best of all, it *did* excite him. It made retirement seem like something to look forward to. He could still spend his time on the ice, but without the grueling schedule. Skate without fear of injury. Wake up without his bones aching.

He'd miss the excitement of the games, the rush of competition, honing his skills to always be a tiny bit better. But the idea of teaching other players how to improve had its own thrill.

It would still be doing what he loved but in a different way.

Anders knew why the idea of his retirement had upset Kelly but it was a shame. This was something Anders would like to discuss with him. Maybe once they talked …

Anders straightened, too restless to stay still, and he walked along the shore for a while, heading north. He was at a crossroads in his life. The pressure built within him like a storm gathering over the lake.

It had begun long before his relationship with Kelly shifted, but the changes in his personal life had given him a different perspective on what his future might look like. Those feelings had come to a point yesterday at the equipment drive. The sight of Kelly laughing with Micah Warner had driven him out of his mind.

Anders *knew* Kelly wasn't interested in Micah and vice versa. Micah was a happily married man and Kelly was probably being his usual friendly self. But the sight of Kelly laughing and talking with an attractive guy had sparked an ugly feeling inside Anders' gut and left him with a headache from his clenched jaw.

There were men all over the world who would give anything to be with Kelly. Anders had seen the comments on his social media accounts, noticed the signs gay fans held up at games, knew there were guys who would happily sweep in if Kelly let them know he was available.

They wouldn't have the history or the bond Anders and Kelly had now, but if Anders was out of the picture, Kelly would eventually meet someone else.

If Anders walked away from Kelly, he'd always wonder what could have been.

Kelly had said this wouldn't end their friendship, but Anders had his doubts. Not about Kelly, but about *himself*.

Could he watch Kelly fall in love with someone else someday? Could he be as selflessly supportive of Kelly as Kelly had been of him?

Could he watch Kelly marry another man and be happy for him?

The thought sent a shudder of distaste through Anders.

Even if he returned to Sweden, he'd always know what he'd left behind.

He had a chance at a new life now and Kelly was so good for him. But was *he* good for Kelly?

Could he give Kelly the kind of love he deserved?

Anders knew it was time for him to make two very important decisions about his future and he couldn't put either off any longer. But he wasn't used to making life-changing choices without someone to bounce ideas off.

And Astrid was the one person he'd always done that with.

As wonderful as Anders' parents were, they had so little to do with his day-to-day life they couldn't offer much in the way of advice. They'd love him no matter what he chose, which was always appreciated but not terribly helpful.

Anders could talk to Pat about his possible retirement but not about dating Kelly. He could probably talk to Zane or Ryan or Gabriel about either topic, but they were too close to the situation to be objective.

He needed Astrid.

Frustrated, Anders stopped in his tracks and nearly got hit by a kid on a scooter who had to zip around him.

"Hey, watch where you're going, man!" the kid called out.

But that was the problem. Anders didn't *know* where he was going.

He looked around, deciding it was probably time to head home. He'd gone pretty far north, and it would take him a while to get back. He turned and caught sight of the name of the cross street and shook his head, his mouth curving up in a rueful little smile.

He should have known. He'd asked for Astrid, and a literal sign had appeared, reminding him that she wasn't far.

Anders turned left, heading away from the lake, and walked a few blocks until he found himself in front of the cemetery.

"Very clever, *älskling*," he whispered. "I needed you and here you are."

Anders followed the winding path through the lush green lawns of the non-denominational cemetery, the route as familiar as the drive between his condo and the practice rink. He didn't visit as often as he had at the beginning, but he still tried to drop by regularly.

It was a lovely place. His mother had arranged for the secular service and burial when he'd been too submerged in grief to make a decision beyond burying his family in Chicago, hating the idea of taking Elia from the only home she'd ever known.

So his mother had chosen beautiful adjoining plots, on the rise of a small hill with a glimpse of the lake in the distance.

Anders took a seat near the two headstones, wishing he'd brought flowers. He rubbed his thumb affectionately across Elia's name.

"Miss you, little one," he said, letting a few tears fall. "So much."

He bowed his head and spoke quietly to her for a few minutes, telling her about the dog Cooper had gotten recently, with floppy ears and big feet, and the gold-striped stray cat he'd seen skulking outside of the practice rink. He told his little girl how he'd wished he could bring it home for her and he was sorry he'd never bought her the kitten she'd begged for in the months leading up to her death.

After Anders was done, he pressed a kiss to his fingertips, then touched Elia's name again. He'd never be quite whole after losing his child but in some ways the grief was simpler. More straightforward. It was an ache he'd carry with him forever, but less complicated than losing his wife.

A different type of loss.

Anders wiped his eyes, then shifted on the soft green grass, leaning his shoulder against Astrid's headstone. The closest he could get to the talks they'd often had in bed, shoulder-to-shoulder, fingers intertwined.

"We need to have a talk, *min kärlek*," he whispered.

His love, but maybe not his only one. Just as Anders had to think about a future after playing hockey, he needed to think of a future after losing her. Difficult as it had been to imagine after her death, now he had to face it head-on. If he waited too long to decide, the decision might be made for him.

"I'm dating Kelly." His throat went a little thick at those words. Whatever they'd called it, whatever it had been at the beginning, they had been dating. Anders could admit it now.

He closed his eyes, thinking of the gentle, reverent way Kelly had touched his necklace. The words he'd spoken in the quiet of the bed they'd shared.

"I loved you so much," Anders whispered hoarsely. "I always will but … But maybe it's time for me to let someone else in."

Anders drew one knee up and rested his forearm on it, letting out a soft sigh. "It's terrifying though. What if I lose him too?"

He looked at the sky, watching white clouds scuttle across the vast expanse of blue.

"I know what you'd say. You'd tell me that if I don't tell him how I feel, I'll lose him anyway." He cleared his throat. "But maybe it's less terrifying to love him from a distance. If something happens to him and we're not together I'll be devastated but …"

But if Anders let Kelly all the way into his heart, how would he survive a crushing loss *again*?

"I know, I know." He sighed. "Kelly and I might live happily together for many, many decades. The odds of something terrible happening to him too are so small, but even the thought of it …" His throat closed for a moment.

"Am I really supposed to risk it all again?" he whispered.

The breeze ruffled a piece of his hair, and he automatically tucked it behind his ear, remembering the way Kelly had done something similar before he left the other morning.

Anders closed his eyes and replayed every moment they'd spent together lately.

Every soft word and passionate touch. The way Kelly had spoken about Astrid. The way he'd listened. The way he'd quietly, steadfastly loved Anders. Looked out for him. Supported him whenever he faltered.

Tears prickled Anders' eyes.

Kelly was such a good person. He understood and respected Anders' past in a way that was far beyond his years and life experience. He'd given Anders far more than Anders had given him. If Anders took this leap, if he let himself be vulnerable again, love again, he would have to do far better.

Kelly deserved Anders' best, not merely the few scraps he'd shown him so far.

Anders would have to prove to Kelly how much he mattered. How *important* he was. Lately, Anders had kept his emotions locked down so tight he'd barely acknowledged them to himself, much less to Kelly.

Kelly deserved to know how cherished he was.

Anders closed his eyes and pictured what their future together would be like. He could readily imagine Kelly slipping into his life with ease. Not at all a filler for the hole losing Astrid had left in his world but working together to carve out new and different spaces in each other's lives.

More than friends. More than teammates. A deep, true, abiding love.

The type Anders had thought he'd only get a shot at once in his life.

He wanted it so badly he ached with it.

He drew in a deep breath, picturing what Astrid would tell him about the situation.

He smiled, eyes watering with tears.

It was so easy to imagine her soft little smile and the brightness in her eyes as she said, "Love him, Anders. Love him and don't let him go for anything. Live as long as you can and as fully as possible and whether you have five years or fifty together, make the most of every single second of it."

"Even if I'm scared?" he whispered.

"*Especially* if you're scared." He remembered the whisper of her fingertips against the shell of his ear and the press of her lips to his temple as if it was happening now. "You can do this, Anders. I know you can. You deserve love."

Tears spilling over, he pressed his lips to her headstone, letting it linger for a long moment before he rose to his feet. "Thank you, *älskling*," he whispered as he wiped the wetness from his cheeks.

For the first time, those tears felt healing instead of raw.

His heart was lighter as he walked down the path toward the exit, the ties to his past unraveling and floating free behind him, a tug in his breastbone urging him on toward his future with Kelly.

It was almost overwhelming to admit how much he needed to do to build that future.

Anders had to talk to Kelly. Apologize. Show him how deeply he cared for him and discuss what it would mean to be together.

They needed to tell Kelly's family.

Win a Cup.

And yes, Anders needed to retire.

In order to build a new future.

Anders smiled as he passed a park and spotted a couple sprawled out on an old quilt, picking at the remnants of their picnic lunch. He walked on, excitement building in him as an idea began to form.

It was nearly formed by the time he got home, and he didn't bother to hang up his jacket, just laid it over the back of a chair and made a beeline for his office.

He found a pad of paper and pen, booted up his laptop, and began working on a plan to show Kelly exactly how much he meant to him.

It would take a few days to pull it together and he had no time to lose.

Anders had set his sights on the future he wanted, and nothing would stand in his way.

————

Kelly trudged across the parking lot toward the practice facility, his steps heavy. Everything ached. He was worn down physically of course. By this point in the season there were always vague aches and pains.

But what hurt the most was missing Anders.

Maybe Kelly *should* be angry, but he wasn't. He ached with the fear that this was the end for them. After the playoffs ended, they'd go their separate ways.

Kelly wanted to believe they could be friends. That they'd spend time together in the off-season and Anders would play again next year and …

Actually, what Kelly fucking wanted to believe was Micah's comments about Anders being jealous. He wanted to believe it was true. That Micah had been an impartial observer who had seen what was really there. That Anders wanted him and was too scared of losing him to make the next move.

But what if Micah was wrong? What if he'd imagined it?

Kelly had been so sure all he and Anders needed to do was talk and they could work through anything, but doubts were beginning to creep in.

Should he give Anders more space? Should he confront him?

For the first time since they'd started sleeping together, Kelly regretted that he had no relationship experience. He didn't know what the fuck he was supposed to do now. It had seemed kind of romantic that Anders was the only guy he'd ever been with but now it left him totally out of his depth.

What the fuck did he know about what to do after a fight? Was this a fight? How the hell was Kelly supposed to know how to fix it?

He greeted a couple of guys absently as he walked into the dressing room and sat in his stall with a heavy sigh. He could dress for practice in his sleep, so he went through the routine as he let his mind wander.

God, he wished he could talk to his parents or one of his brothers. Much as they all drove him nuts, at least they knew what the hell to do in a situation like this.

Kelly glanced at Zane and Ryan. They were discussing something, heads bent together like maybe it was a private conversation. If anyone would understand what it was like to date a teammate, it was them.

Surely, they'd argued about stuff before. They'd been careful in the past two seasons to keep it from bleeding out into their hockey though. If they'd been mad at one another, it hadn't impacted their on-ice relationship.

Kelly felt a sudden stab of envy watching them bump shoulders, eyes filled with love, Zane playfully shoving Ryan away as he made exaggerated kissing noises in Zane's direction like he planned to lay a big one on him right there in the dressing room.

They didn't hide their affection for each other—and why the fuck should they?—but Kelly had never seen them anything but mildly annoyed with each other either.

But it wasn't possible to *always* be happy with your partner, right? Kelly had seen his parents argue enough times to know that.

They had a good marriage. It was clear they loved each other. But they still fought.

His mom still got exasperated at the way his dad constantly talked through the TV shows they watched together, and his dad was always irritated when his mom left silverware next to the sink, swearing she'd come back and use it later.

They probably argued about bigger stuff too, though Kelly hadn't seen it often.

They didn't fight about money much. His mom had plenty from her own family and his dad's NHL salary had been well invested so they'd always had a nice house and plenty in the bank.

They *had* fought about his dad's job after he retired from playing hockey though.

His dad had become a university coach and his mom had been *pissed* because she'd wanted him to get a job that didn't require any travel.

But they'd figured it out. Kelly hadn't seen exactly how but he knew they talked a lot. He knew they had date nights and that they'd surprise each other with little presents that made them think about one another and Kelly *knew* he was lucky to have a great example to look up to.

But that still didn't give him a fucking clue how to fix stuff with Anders.

"You okay?" Malone asked and Kelly jerked his head up.

"Huh?"

"Are you okay? You seem weird today."

Jesus, it must be bad if the most self-centered guy on the team had noticed.

"Yeah, fine. Just tired," Kelly lied.

Anders glanced up from his stall, his fingers stilling on the elbow pad he'd been securing. His gaze searched Kelly's face with so much intensity Kelly nearly flinched away from the scrutiny.

Anders looked good. Kelly stifled a sigh. He *always* looked good, but something in his expression was peaceful. More settled than he'd been in a long time.

Kelly swallowed, wondering if maybe it was for the best that they'd put a pause on everything. Maybe it would be better for both of them if they let what they'd had fizzle out and fade away.

It hurt, God, it *hurt* to picture his life without Anders in it.

But Kelly had been an idiot to think he could sleep with Anders without getting all twisted up inside over him. It was way too fucking late for that. He was in this mess and ignoring it didn't seem like the right call. Which meant they needed to talk sooner rather than later.

Kelly looked away and caught a glimpse of Malone glancing between them with narrowed eyes. He didn't say anything but Kelly knew this probably wouldn't be the last of it. Kelly realized with a sudden rush of clarity that he didn't *care* what Malone thought of him.

He didn't care what *anyone* thought of him being gay anymore. Things had gone better with Trevor than he'd expected.

Yeah, he wasn't looking forward to the conversation he needed to have with his family. He wasn't looking forward to hearing fans' taunts—better now than it had been a few years ago—but still not gone.

Whether Kelly was with Anders or not, he was gay. And a hockey player. And people were going to have to deal with it. Kelly was so fucking tired of hiding. Tired of pretending to be someone he wasn't. Tired of lying.

As soon as the time felt right, he'd come out. Not just to his family but to everyone.

The decision felt like a weight lifting off his shoulders and he smiled involuntarily.

Anders looked up again, smiling back with a helpless, puzzled little lift of the corner of his lips like he didn't know why Kelly was happy but he was glad he was. That made Kelly want to march over and plant a kiss on him in front of their whole team so he looked away, bending to grab his skates and tug them on with a renewed sense of determination.

Maybe he could discuss it with Anders after practice. They needed to sit down and talk now that neither of them were quite so worked up. Together, they could fix this. They had to. Because Kelly wasn't ready to give up on the future they could have together.

Kelly finished dressing, lighter than he'd been in days as he hit the ice.

Theriault was already out there, warming up with the weird, impossible trick shots he was so fond of. Kelly shook his head in amusement and took a lap. Halfway around, he caught a glimpse of a group of people in the stands on the opposite side of the practice rink. That wasn't so unusual lately, but this was a big crowd.

They'd always had closed practices in the past, but Samantha had convinced the club that fan engagement was crucial, and they'd recently opened some practices to the public, with the plan to do it more regularly next season.

Kelly *was* surprised by the cluster of fans holding O'Shea signs. When he approached, they let out a loud cheer and he groaned when he realized those people belonged to *him*.

With three days to go before the first game of the playoffs, the O'Shea family had descended on Illinois. His mom, his dad, his brother Finn and his wife and kids were there. And Pat and Con's wives and kids were there too. A whole gaggle of the red-haired menaces.

Presumably, Pat and Con would be traveling with their team. God, the thought of facing both of his brothers in the first round of the playoffs was not something Kelly was looking forward to.

They didn't take it easy on him. If anything, the hits were even harder.

"Mom?" Kelly said skating to the nearby Zamboni door, simultaneously happy to see everyone and mildly horrified they were making such a spectacle of themselves.

"Kelly!" Catherine O'Shea beamed and set down her sign to wave. "Surprise!"

"Uhh, big surprise, Ma," he agreed, flustered. "What are you all doing here?"

"Is that any way to greet your family?" Finn jogged down the bleachers toward him, engulfing him in a hug before Kelly could fend him off.

"When they're annoying, yes," Kelly muttered against his shoulder. Even in skates Kelly was a good half a foot shorter than his eldest brother. Finn's beard and hair were neater than the last time Kelly had seen him. He had narrow features and looked the least like either of their parents. He still had the red hair the rest of them had though.

The fictional all-ginger NHL team Kelly had invented popped in his head and his smile widened as he imagined Finn wearing an orange Charlestown Carrots jersey. He should get some made for prank Christmas gifts.

"Is that any way to talk about your favorite brother?" Finn grinned and palmed his helmet, jostling him in a familiar, affectionate gesture. "Missed you, runt."

"Oh my God," Kelly muttered. "You have to be shitting me. I told you *never* to call me that."

"What was that?" Ryan Hartinger buzzed by, grinning. "Did I just hear you called runt? Oh, that is priceless, dude."

"I fucking hate you all," Kelly called out.

"Language, Kelly!" His mom admonished as she walked toward him.

Her smile was wide and the light brown eyes he'd inherited from her sparkled. He'd gotten his freckles from her too, though she was more of a strawberry blonde than her children.

In college, Kelly had punched a friend who'd called her a MILF and threatened to sic his father and brothers on them until the guy begged for mercy, but even Kelly knew she was gorgeous and turned a lot of heads.

So awkward.

Kelly groaned internally, knowing he'd probably have a rookie or two making comments about her after practice today, although the rest of the team here knew better by now. It wasn't like this was the first time his family had come to visit. Though not usually so many at once. Then again, the O'Shea family kept getting bigger and bigger every year.

"Hi, Ma." Kelly hugged her and kissed her cheek. "I didn't know you were coming in this early."

He'd gotten a text from her a few days ago saying they'd be coming to Evanston for the first two games of the playoffs but he'd thought they'd show up the day before or something.

"Well, The Harriers fly in today, so we thought we'd do a big dinner tonight with everyone. We rented out the back room of the restaurant we went to last time."

Kelly groaned. "Has it occurred to you I might already have plans?"

She smiled and patted his cheek. "Sweetheart, I know you too well. You're either here practicing or playing video games with Trevor. Where is he, by the way?"

Kelly glanced around. "Over there by the goal."

He was talking about something with Cooper, Malone, and Coach Horton at the moment. Kelly would worry he was missing some important meeting about defense but Gabriel was off doing his own thing so Kelly was probably fine.

"Well, make sure you invite him," his mom continued. "And where is Anders? He needs to come tonight too."

Kelly bit his tongue against the protest it might be awkward. He sure as hell didn't want to explain why. "I'm sure he's around."

"Oh, there he is. Anders!" She called out, waving in his direction.

"Catherine!" He sounded genuinely happy to see Kelly's mom as he skated up and Kelly felt like an asshole for being more annoyed than happy to see his family. Anders only got to see his parents a few times a year.

She gave Anders a warm hug. "Great to see you. You're looking well."

"Thank you. You too. As lovely as ever."

She turned as pink as Kelly did when he got a compliment. "Oh, I have missed you."

Anders chuckled.

"What are we, chopped liver?" Finn asked, holding out his arms for a hug.

Anders smiled at his former teammate and hugged him. "Good to see you too."

"Kelly! Kelly!" Noel, one of his nephews, tugged on his jersey. "Will you take us out on the ice?"

"Not right now, bud," he said. "Practice is about to start."

Declan O'Shea sauntered up and ruffled Noel's hair. "Remember, hockey comes first."

"Hey, Dad," Kelly said with a smile.

"Hey." Declan gave him a tight, hard hug. "I was starting to think you'd dropped off the face of the earth. I can't remember the last time I got a text from you."

Kelly winced. "It's been busy."

"Mmhmm." His dad gave him an assessing look that made Kelly want to squirm in his skates. Declan O'Shea was an intimidating guy, even when you were related to him. His red beard might be flecked with silver these days, but he looked as fit and tough as ever.

Kelly had not inherited his height or build. Finn was more slender, like Kelly, but even he was tall. And Connor and Pat were giants in every direction. Even if Kelly was the smallest, he still resented being called runt.

"You sure you didn't meet a girl or something?" his dad asked, narrowing his eyes. "That's usually what happened with your brothers."

"I am one hundred percent sure of that," Kelly said with an awkward little laugh.

Just fell in love with my male teammate who isn't over his dead wife. No big deal, he finished silently in his head.

Kelly groaned. God, it sounded *so bad* when he put it like that.

Thankfully, the whistle blew a moment later, and Kelly was able to excuse himself.

"Did you know your family was coming into town this early?" Anders asked under his breath as they both skated toward Coach Daniels.

Kelly shook his head, trying to hide the little pulse of happiness that leapt in him at Anders talking to him. "No. It was definitely a surprise."

"They invited me to dinner tonight," he said quietly. "I wasn't sure how you felt about me coming but—"

"You should go," Kelly said. "They'll be glad to see you."

"And you?" Anders' gaze was oddly intent.

"Of course. I want you to be happy and you're close to my family so you should be there."

Anders nodded. "I'll plan on it then."

"Great. See you then."

Anders opened his mouth like he was going to say something else, but Kelly skated away before he could get it out. Like his dad always said, hockey always had to come first and with the playoffs a few days away, Kelly couldn't afford to let his team down.

With his family here, it would be difficult to manage some time alone to talk.

Kelly would have to wait and figure it out when they weren't about to start a playoff run.

CHAPTER TWENTY-FIVE

Anders walked toward the restaurant, smoothing the pale gray button-down he wore. He'd dressed carefully for the dinner with the O'Shea family, despite knowing he was unlikely to get much of a chance to speak to Kelly tonight.

Anders had wanted to talk this morning at practice but between Coach keeping them to a strict schedule and Kelly's family demanding his attention after, Anders hadn't been able to get a word in edgewise.

He checked in with the hostess who directed him to a private event space on the upper level. When he stepped inside, he could see why. Where it was just Anders, his parents, and a few cousins in Sweden, Kelly's family was enormous.

His three brothers were all married with multiple children and tonight there were kids everywhere. They ranged in age from their young teens to a tiny baby that Connor's wife, Vivian, was cradling.

Anders didn't recognize all the kids—most he knew through social media or texts from his former teammates—but he greeted everyone he knew and quickly found himself in conversation with Declan and Finn.

"Quite the season you've had this year, huh?" Declan said.

"It's been good," Anders agreed.

He'd always liked Kelly's father but he felt a stirring of nerves as he looked Declan over now. He was an intimidating man, tall, barrel-chested, with big, meaty hands. Those hands had been surprisingly deft at puck-handling but Declan had spent more than his share of time in the penalty box when he'd played.

For someone who hoped to officially date his son, it was daunting.

"It's hard to believe you're nearly forty and you're still playing like that." Finn let out a low whistle. At thirty-five, he was the eldest O'Shea brother, the most serious of the four.

"You retired last season," Anders countered.

"Yeah, but I'd slowed way down. I don't know where you found the fountain of youth, but I wish you'd shared it."

"Seriously," Declan grumbled. "I'm on my third knee surgery now."

Anders chuckled and fell into easy conversation with them about hockey and their lives as everyone mingled, sipping drinks and enjoying the appetizers the staff had set out.

"How's work been?" Anders asked Finn.

He had left the NHL and gone on to work in investment banking, though he was a program coordinator for a youth hockey league, and he spoke enthusiastically about both.

They sipped their drinks and talked as the kids ran around, but one guest was notably absent.

"Where on earth is my brother?" Finn asked after a while, glancing around the room.

"I'm not sure. I'm not his keeper."

Anders' tone was level but Finn still arched an eyebrow, his blue eyes cool as he regarded Anders. "Still annoyed we asked you to keep an eye on Kelly?"

"Pat passed that message along, huh?" Anders asked, taking a drink of his lemon water.

"What did I pass along?" A heavy arm settled onto Anders' shoulder, and he glanced over to see Patrick O'Shea grinning at him, Connor only a few steps behind.

"Anders' annoyance at being made Kelly's keeper."

"Yeah, I got quite the dressing down."

Anders narrowed his eyes. "That wasn't a dressing down. I merely said—"

"Yeah, yeah." Pat was clearly refusing to get sucked into the familiar argument. "Good to see you, buddy."

"Good to see you too," Anders said with a smile and hugged him.

"Hello? I'm here too," Connor protested and Anders chuckled.

Anders hugged Connor. Aside from Kelly, of course, Anders thought he was the best-looking of the bunch. His hair and beard were more auburn than Finn or Pat's and his eyes were the deepest blue Anders had ever seen.

In the past, he'd had a stray thought or two about Connor but that was information Anders hoped he'd never have to share with Kelly. Anders was a big believer in honesty in a relationship but he didn't need to dig a hole and hand Kelly the shovel.

Kelly had always been sensitive about his stature and his freckles and Connor was tall and broad, without a freckle in sight.

Anders knew which *he* preferred but he wasn't sure if Kelly would believe it.

And if Anders didn't get his shit together soon, there wouldn't *be* a relationship.

"How is my brother doing?" Connor asked with a frown.

"Good," Anders said. "He's had a great season and we're both excited about the playoffs."

"I don't know why." Connor's eyes twinkled merrily. "We're going to knock you out in the first round."

The conversation devolved into trash talking, occasionally interrupted by the guys wrangling their kids.

Finn had wandered off to mediate an argument over a toy when Kelly and Trevor arrived.

"There he is!" Pat called out as everyone broke out into claps and whistles. "Nice of you to join us, runt."

Kelly groaned and shoved at Trevor's shoulder. "I *told* you we were going to be late, you jerk."

"It is actually my fault," Trevor said with a grin. "You can blame me."

"But it's so much more fun to blame Kelly," Connor called back.

"Fuck!" Kelly wrestled out of his coat and dropped it onto a nearby chair with an annoyed grunt. "You're all the worst."

"Language!" Catherine called, shooting them an impish grin over the rim of her drink.

Kelly rolled his eyes. "Yeah, because no one here has *ever* sworn." He gave Connor a pointed look.

Connor grinned and covered the ears of the toddler he was carrying, pressing her face against his shoulder. "Let them at least get to first grade."

Anders wasn't entirely sure if the kid was Connor's or someone else's. The O'Shea family seemed to take a communal approach to raising children. Which made sense when the adults were so outnumbered.

Anders felt a familiar stab of longing for Elia, missing the warm weight in his arms and the soft hair brushing his skin. The new baby smell.

"It's always something with you guys, isn't it?" Kelly muttered and Anders forced his thoughts away from what he'd lost to what he hoped to gain.

Kelly got dragged into hugs and a flurry of back pounding and chirping from his brothers and cheek kisses from his sisters-in-law, while Anders hung back, watching them interact.

Kids were pressed into Kelly's arms, and he cooed over them and praised the toys and dolls the children proudly showed off. At one point, softly jiggling a fussy baby in his arms, Kelly glanced at Anders with a nose-scrunching smile.

Kelly had the look he always did when he was around his family, vaguely annoyed but content, and something passed between them. A spark of hope mingled with worry. *I miss you*, Kelly's gaze said.

When he turned away, Anders rubbed at his chest. God, he hoped so.

But they'd never discussed this topic. Kelly would likely want to have kids someday. Anders had been so focused on the other parts of their potential relationship he'd never considered that.

Anders' stomach flipped anxiously as he watched Kelly take a bottle from his sister-in-law and hold it to the baby's mouth, cooing at the little boy when he latched on.

Kelly was great with children.

Despite his love for Elia, Anders had felt awkward with her at first. He'd been unsure of what to do, his family so small that he'd had little experience with newborns.

Fatherhood would come naturally to Kelly when he was ready to take that step.

But was Anders willing to risk that loss again?

It was hard enough to open his heart up to Kelly after losing Astrid. But opening his heart to children of his own after losing Elia …

That was something he'd never contemplated.

And it was something he and Kelly would have to talk about before they could plan their future.

———

Anders was oddly quiet tonight.

Maybe not *so* oddly, Kelly corrected himself. It was difficult to keep up with the general volume of the O'Shea family as they took a seat at the long table and servers came in bearing trays of food.

Kelly's mom had hosting parties down to a science. Ones in Boston were always held in the roomy brownstone in

Charlestown, but on the road, she rented out a private room in a restaurant. Somewhere the kids could run around and shriek without bothering other patrons, and she could order a variety of foods to be served family-style. It kept things running smoothly and the waitstaff didn't have to do much beyond refill drinks and stop in to see if anyone needed anything.

Spending an evening in the midst of a dinner like this was a lot for anyone to handle though.

Especially for someone on the reserved side like Anders.

So, Kelly didn't blame Anders for being quiet when faced with the general chaos of getting kids fed and quieting crying babies and trying to eat and talk all at once. But Anders had gotten the oddest look on his face when he'd seen Kelly holding his new nephew and Kelly wasn't sure why. It worried him.

Was he missing Elia? He'd seemed okay at Ava Walsh's birthday party but maybe it was hitting him hard tonight for some reason.

"Yo, take the damn plate, runt," Pat said, bumping Kelly's hand with his.

Kelly glared at his brother. "Uhh, kinda wrangling a kid at the moment." Kelly patted Brendan's tummy and jiggled his knee before zooming a spoonful of food into the fussy toddler's mouth.

"You better get used to it," Pat teased. "It'll happen to you too one day or another. Just gotta find the right woman."

Or not, Kelly thought with a pang. But he couldn't exactly tell his brother that over dinner.

"Oh, I'll take it," Aubrey said with a laugh as she took the platter from her husband. "Honestly, Pat. Be grateful your brother is helping out."

"He'd be more help in Boston."

"I'm happy *here*," Kelly said automatically. "The Otters are a great team."

Aubrey nudged his shoulder and smiled. "I'm glad you're happy here. You're doing well this season, no matter what your brother says."

Pat gave him a skeptical look. "You're doing okay but your forecheck could use some work."

"And your gap control!" his dad added from across the table.

Kelly stifled a groan. "Always with the helpful tips."

"Always!" Connor said, baring his teeth in what was probably supposed to be a grin.

"You are all the absolute worst," Kelly muttered.

"You know it!" Pat said. He didn't sound remotely ashamed.

"More, more!" Brendan chanted.

Kelly tuned the rest of his family out for a few minutes as he focused on his nephew. He was a cutie, all chubby cheeks and curly hair and a strong appetite, if the way he pounded his fists on the table was any indication.

By the time his family had finished eating and Aubrey had taken Brendan from him, Kelly was wearing some of Brendan's dinner and had only managed to eat a few bites of food himself.

"Thanks, Kelly." Aubrey's voice was soft as she rubbed her baby bump. "I appreciate the help."

"Sure. No prob."

"Some girl really will be lucky to snag a guy like you." She squeezed his upper arm. Her voice was filled with nothing but warmth and she meant well but it was like a stab to the heart as he was reminded of the way everyone saw him.

How differently would they look at him if they knew?

"Let's get you some more food. I made sure these pigs didn't eat *everything*," she said with a cluck of her tongue, her pink nails flashing brightly as she handed him a platter.

"Thanks," he whispered, placing some of the chicken onto his plate with a numb, sick feeling. He got food and ate without tasting it as the voices of his family washed over him; words meaningless when thoughts whirled in his brain and crowded them out.

Part of him wanted so badly to jump up and blurt out the truth. He'd thought about it earlier while he waited for Trevor to return from wherever he was, then again on the drive over.

Kelly should wait to tell his family, right? He should definitely put it off until after the playoffs. He shouldn't say anything now and upset the delicate balance of things. At least not when he'd be facing off against his brothers in a few short days.

He should wait until he was home for a few weeks in the summer … or maybe before he returned to Evanston.

Kelly winced. He knew himself. If he waited, he'd keep putting it off forever and ever. There would always be a better time around the corner. Ugh. No, he needed to bite the damn bullet and tell his family before he chickened out.

Before Kelly could second-guess himself, he rose to his feet, clinking his fork against his glass to get everyone's attention. "I have something I need to say."

The table fell silent, even the little kids quieting as they stared wide-eyed. Butterflies tumbled through Kelly's stomach like they were on a rollercoaster doing loops and he glanced involuntarily at Anders.

He was wide-eyed too, but he nodded as if he knew what Kelly was going to share.

I'm here for you, his gaze seemed to convey. *Whatever happens.*

Kelly took a deep breath and cleared his throat until he was sure he could get the words out. "I'm gay."

The room went abruptly silent.

After a few moments that felt like lifetimes to Kelly, Connor spoke.

"Since *when?*" His brother sounded equally confused and stunned.

Kelly tried not to roll his eyes.

Pat did it for him, hitting their brother's arm. "That's not how it works, dumbass."

"Language!" Catherine said absently, like it was a rote response, but her gaze was trained on Kelly, her expression soft and confused. Worried. But he wasn't sure if she was upset with him or not.

"Since always," Kelly admitted, looking at his plate. He couldn't look at his dad. "I wasn't honest about stuff before."

"So, the girl you took to prom in high school …" Finn said.

Kelly shrugged. "A friend. I wanted people to think I was normal." He finished the word on a whisper, his deepest secret laid out for everyone to judge.

"Oh, honey." His mom was on her feet and hurrying around the table before he could blink. She wrapped Kelly in a big hug and

Kelly sagged against her, his throat working as he swallowed back tears at the comfort she offered. "You *are* normal. We had no idea you were gay, but we love you. You know that, right?"

Kelly shrugged, breathing in the scent of her hair. "Yeah, but I mean … we're pretty fucking Catholic, so …"

"Oh, sweetheart, come here." She wrapped her arm around his waist and guided him toward the door leading out onto a deck. When the door closed and the loud voices faded into a distant hum, he was relieved to have a place to flee to.

She led him over to a lounge area and took a seat, smoothing down her dress. She took his hands and looked him in the eye. "I love you, Kelly. You're perfect just the way you are."

Kelly's eyes burned. "Ma …" he said helplessly.

"I mean it. I will fight the Pope if he says otherwise, okay?"

Kelly let out a wet laugh. "Okay. I'll keep that in mind."

"Yes, we're Catholic but that doesn't mean I believe everything the church teaches. I mean, to look at us, you'd think this family didn't believe in birth control, but it could be a lot worse if we didn't."

Kelly let out another sputtering laugh and wiped at his face. "True."

His dad had always made sure he and his brothers had the sex talk and access to condoms and all that so yeah, they weren't *that* conservative but … But being gay was a lot different from birth control. Lots of people were okay with one but not the other.

"Did we do anything to make you think we wouldn't support you?"

Kelly shrugged, looking at his mom's hands, still clenched tightly around his. "I dunno. There's a lot of talk thrown around and I wasn't *sure*."

She let out a sad little sigh. "We'll all work on that, okay?"

"Okay," Kelly agreed, too overwhelmed to say more.

"Is there someone special?" his mom asked hopefully, and Kelly laughed, unsurprised but unsure of how to answer.

"I thought maybe but I dunno. I'm still figuring it out. I know it looked like I wanted to make a big deal out of this tonight, but I don't," he muttered. "I just couldn't hold it in any longer."

Restless, Kelly rose to his feet and walked to the railing. It over-looked a tangle of buildings, so it wasn't like it was a particularly inspiring view, but he stared out at the lights anyway, realizing they'd grown blurry.

"Tell me what I can do for you right now. Do you need some time away? Do want me to tell everyone to leave you be?"

Kelly chuckled. "I'm not sure even *you* could manage that."

"Well, I'll *try*."

That was his mom. Fierce as any hockey player at half the size.

"No, it's okay." Kelly chewed at his lip. He could deal with the inevitable questions from his brothers. His dad was the one who worried him most. "What about Dad though? Is he going to be okay with this?"

"Oh, honey. Of course he is. He loves you."

"Yeah, well, I was pretty young when he called a guy a—" Kelly's throat closed and he couldn't get the word out. "A pretty nasty slur when he was on the ice."

His mom's sigh was audible. "He has said things. I don't think he meant them but that's no excuse, is it?"

"Not when you're fourteen and pretty sure you're the *thing* he's talking about."

Her heels clacked on the wood as she walked toward him but he still jerked in surprise at the press of her hand on his back. He settled when she rubbed her palm in soothing circles. "That must have felt pretty terrible."

"It wasn't great," Kelly admitted. He rested his elbows on the railing, throat tight with the lump that didn't want to go away.

"Does it help that he's cleaned up his language since?"

"A little." But it would always hurt, even if it was buried deep now. Kelly would always carry with him that moment of pure fear and self-loathing that had washed over him then. The way he'd cringed and wanted to hide, curl in a little ball so no one would see he was like that too.

"Oh, sweetheart, I'm sorry we didn't do better by you."

Kelly wet his lips. "Me too. I know it wasn't intentional but …"

"It doesn't take away the sting."

"No. It doesn't."

She sighed. "Your brothers look like they're about to break down the door. Can I let them come out and talk to you? Or do I need to tell them to get lost?"

Kelly straightened, blinking away any moisture from his eyes. "Yeah. Sure. Let them out before they cause any damage."

"Okay. And you tell them to fuck off if they're assholes."

"Ma!" He said, a little shocked as he turned to look at her. It wasn't like she never swore herself, but he still hadn't expected it.

"Well, this time you have my permission." Her smile was impish and amused.

Kelly chuckled. "I'll keep that in mind. And thanks."

He turned to face her and pulled her into a hug, pressing a kiss to her temple, so grateful for her easy acceptance.

"Of course. Just know I wouldn't change anything about you for the world." She squeezed tight. "I love you, always."

"Love you always too," he whispered. He hadn't heard her say that since he was little. She told him she loved him, of course, but 'love you always' was something special she'd said when he was small.

Always was unconditional. He should have remembered. Should have trusted in that.

Kelly let her go, relieved by her support but apprehensive about what was to come next. Oh God, why had he thought it was a good idea to come out like this?

She slipped into the restaurant, saying something under her breath to his brothers. A moment later they joined him.

Kelly leaned against the railing, crossing his arms, staring at his three older brothers as they formed a half-circle around him, shifting apprehensively, their gazes not quite meeting his. Kelly was pretty sure there had been a hasty conference inside, an office huddle as they talked strategy.

"We want to say we're sorry," Finn finally said. He'd always been the self-appointed spokesman for them.

"For?" Kelly arched an eyebrow.

"For making you think you couldn't tell us before now."

"Oh." Kelly uncrossed his arms. "Well, I didn't tell *anyone*."

"Really? It sounded like Lindy and Underhill knew. Neither of them looked surprised and they admitted you'd told them already."

"It was pretty recent."

"I guess it probably came out now that your team is uh, a little more …" Pat glanced furtively at him as if unsure of how to finish the statement.

"If you say fruity, I will punch you in the nose," Kelly warned.

"Diverse?" Finn supplied.

"Yeah. That'll work," Kelly agreed, a chuckle slipping out. "And that's kind of why I came out. I mean, having a team who gets it does help, but I'm not out to them yet. It hasn't been worth it with Malone being …"

"Malone?" Connor supplied.

"Pretty much." Kelly sighed and rubbed his head.

"God, when is the league going to do something about players like him?" Connor grumbled.

"Probably when hell freezes over," Pat said drily. "But that's not the issue right now. The issue is our baby brother came out and we need to support him."

It took a moment before Kelly could breathe, much less speak. "You guys don't care?" he finally whispered.

"Oh, for fuck's sake," Pat said, pulling him into a hug and smooshing Kelly's face against his pec. "Of course, we don't care. We just feel like shit that you didn't tell us until now."

335

"I kind of care," Connor protested.

Kelly wriggled away from Pat to look him in the eye, stung. "You do?"

"Yeah, you denied me years of chirping, dude. You were so into Anders when you were growing up it was embarrassing. I mean, I thought it was just a hockey crush but maybe not."

"Shut up." Face burning, Kelly punched his brother in the arm. It was kind of like punching a tree but it made him feel better. "He's a fucking amazing player."

"He is. But you still used to follow him around, staring like a creeper."

"I did not!" Kelly protested, although he was pretty sure Connor was right. "And like you should talk. I remember you constantly talking about your captain your rookie year. What was his name again?"

"We're not talking about that," Connor said loudly. He yanked Kelly in for a hug and Kelly laughed and hugged him back, feeling lighter.

But his stomach flipped with apprehension when Finn nodded toward the door. "Pat, Con, why don't you head in? I want a moment with Kelly."

They both nodded and disappeared inside after a final slap to Kelly's shoulder, leaving him alone with his eldest brother. Finn wasn't the one who was physically scariest. But he was always the one Kelly had looked up to the most. The one whose approval mattered more than anyone except their father's.

"Were there things I did that made this harder on you?" Finn asked, brow furrowing.

"Probably," Kelly choked out, overwhelmed by the emotional gut punch of his brother's words. He really did care.

"Shit." Finn raked a hand through his hair. "I'm sorry. If I'd known——"

"Yeah, that's just it," Kelly said, annoyance washing through him and pushing away everything else. "You can *never* know. You'll never know if a guy is gay or bi or whatever. You have to be a decent person and maybe not say shitty things ever, no matter who's around."

"Fuck." Finn's expression grew pained. "When did you get so smart?"

Kelly laughed and punched him in the shoulder. "I've always been smart, asshole. You never noticed."

Finn pulled him close and for a moment, Kelly could feel the beat of Finn's heart against his cheek. "Apparently there's a lot I should have noticed," he muttered against Kelly's hair.

"Apparently." Kelly's words were muffled by his brother's shoulder but he stood there a moment, his eyes stinging, grateful for his family. They were assholes but they were pretty great assholes, all things considered.

"I really am sorry." Finn let out a sigh and finally let him go. His eyes looked a little watery when Kelly pulled away.

Kelly nodded, staring at his toes again. "I know. I know nothing you guys have said or done was intentional but ..."

"Still made you feel shitty though, huh?"

"Yeah. Yeah, it did," Kelly admitted.

"Is that why you kept quiet about it?"

"It's a big part of it." He scuffed his shoe along the boards of the deck. "I didn't want to let the family down. And no one was out in pro hockey when I was growing up, so I assumed I'd have to be quiet about it until I was retired or whatever."

Finn whistled lowly. "That's a big burden, Kelly."

"Yep."

"I'm sorry you had to carry it alone."

Kelly's mouth twisted up. "Me too."

"You don't have to anymore, okay?"

"Okay. Thanks."

Finn tilted his head toward the door. "You want to head in?"

"I think I'm gonna take a moment out here," Kelly admitted.

"Okay." Finn turned to go inside but he paused halfway there. "Um, Kelly?"

"Yeah?" He glanced up.

"Would it help if I had a talk with my team? Worked on some LGBT stuff with them?"

Kelly's breath caught. "That would be … that would be great, actually."

It wasn't like anyone could go back in time and undo the hurt done to kids like Kelly. But if the people in charge would *educate* kids when they were young, maybe shit would be a lot better in the future.

"Then I'll do that. I promise."

"Thanks," Kelly whispered.

"I'm going to make you come talk to them too though," Finn added.

Kelly groaned. "You're a jerk."

"Yeah." He shrugged a little. "But I'm your brother. So, you've gotta love me anyway."

Kelly made a face. "Do I?"

"Yep. O'Shea family rules!"

"Damn it," Kelly swore, knowing he couldn't argue, and Finn laughed as he pulled the door open and disappeared inside.

Kelly was alone for a while, listening to the sound of the city around him as he breathed and tried not to cry.

He felt weird and shaky. Relieved and tired all at once. But tension still threaded through him as he wondered what came next.

Wondering if this would change anything between him and Anders.

Kelly hadn't done it for Anders. It was just a secret he couldn't keep any more. Even if Anders was done with him as everything but a teammate, Kelly hadn't wanted to keep silent any longer. It was the right time.

But what did Anders think of him? Kelly winced, feeling a little bad that he'd dragged both Anders and Trevor into his family's already chaotic celebrations, then dropped a bomb in the middle of it.

That hadn't been his goal.

Oh well, after the way their teammates kept coming out, they should both be pretty used to shit like that by now.

Behind him, a door creaked open, and the sounds of the party spilled out for a moment before the air fell silent again.

His shoulders tensed at the heavy thud of steps approaching before his father appeared at his elbow, matching his posture to Kelly's, leaning against the railing.

They didn't look at each other.

"Is this why you left Boston?" Declan eventually asked.

Kelly sighed. "Partially. It's always been hard. I'm so different from the rest of you and—"

His dad nudged his elbow. "Different how?"

Kelly shrugged. "I dunno. I'm smaller. I'm a defenseman. I know I didn't make any of the decisions you wanted me to but—"

"Do you think we're unhappy with you because of it?"

"Disappointed, maybe?"

"Oh, Kelly." Declan leaned against Kelly, pressing their arms tightly together as he let out a sigh. "We're not disappointed in you."

"Aren't you?"

"Do you *want* to play hockey or did we assume that was the right path for you?"

"I did!" Kelly protested, straightening and turning to look at his dad. "I mean I do. I love it. I've never really wanted to do anything else."

"You're sure?"

"I'm sure," he promised. "I swear on the signed Yzerman stick you have."

Declan smiled a little, a quirk of one corner of his mouth, nearly hidden by his red beard. He leaned a hip against the metal railing. "Did you think maybe we wouldn't be okay with you being gay?"

"Well." Kelly scuffed his toe on the ground. "Maybe. I mean, the church stuff ..."

"You're my son. I want you to be happy. Nothing the church could ever say would be more important than that." His tone was grave.

Kelly didn't look at his dad. "I wasn't totally sure."

"*Fuck.*" Declan dragged a hand through his hair, not quite as thick as it had been a few years ago. "That's on me, I guess. You should have known."

"I mean, after I left, you didn't text me much except to talk about hockey so ..."

"Damn it. I fucked up all around, didn't I?"

Kelly shrugged. "We're different people, I guess."

"I never know what you're into. You don't talk to us about anything. You shut us out. You have for years."

"I ..." Kelly looked at him, perplexed. "I don't, do I?"

"It seems like you do. Even if you don't mean to."

"Maybe I was afraid you'd find out the truth."

Declan sucked in a sharp breath. "Oh, boy. I guess that makes sense then, huh? You pulled away when you realized you were— were gay."

It sounded forced.

"Yeah, probably," Kelly admitted. "Plus, you know, you said some stuff on the ice and around the locker room when I was at the rink and …"

"Fuck!" He rubbed his forehead. "I let you down."

Kelly shrugged. "I didn't think you meant it really, but it still hurt. A lot."

"Oh God. Kelly. I am so sorry. I never knew …" He grimaced. "But I guess that's the point, huh? Whether it was you or one of my teammates, the stuff I said hurt people, didn't it?"

Kelly nodded. "Yeah."

"Shit." Declan leaned against the railing. "I'm going to have a lot to think about."

Kelly didn't answer because what could he say? He hadn't done this because he wanted his family to feel guilty. But he was glad it had made them rethink some of the stuff they said and did.

"Maybe we can do a little better from here on out?" Declan offered. "Like … talking more. Maybe this summer we can do a fishing trip or something. Just the two of us."

"I'd like that," Kelly whispered.

"Good."

They both fell silent.

"You, uh, dating anyone?" Declan asked.

"You really wanna know?"

"Yeah. If you want to talk about it, I'd like to hear it."

"There's … honestly, I don't know." Kelly sighed.

"Don't know if you want to talk about it, or …?" His dad raised an eyebrow.

"Don't know if it's going to be anything," Kelly admitted, his throat tightening. "I thought maybe. For a while. But now I'm not sure. We kinda had a fight and he's not sure what he wants."

Kelly hoped Anders offering him silent support before he blurted out his news meant something, but he could have just been being a good friend. Kelly couldn't be sure they'd be on the same page about a future together.

"Your mom and I have had a lot of fights over the years."

"Yeah?" Kelly snuck a glance at his dad. "Really? I never saw it much."

"We used to go out in the garage and fight in the minivan so you kids wouldn't know."

Kelly snorted. "We always assumed you were … uh, doing something else."

"Well, sometimes that too." His dad shot him a crooked smile. "Make-up sex isn't all bad."

"Eww. I don't need to think about that," Kelly protested.

His dad chuckled. "I wasn't planning to go into details. I'm just saying … fights are normal. Not being sure of what you want is too. Sometimes big decisions mean big feelings. You gotta learn when to listen and when to push."

"I think maybe I've been kinda pushy."

"Do you love him?"

Kelly's breath caught. "Yeah. Yeah, I do."

"Well, if he's the right one, he'll come around."

"I hope so." Kelly chewed at his lip a moment. "I'm afraid I pushed *too* hard though."

"Maybe he needs a little time to get his head on straight. Not everyone dives in the way you do, Kelly. From the second you came screaming into this world, you were ready to take it on."

"With three big brothers, I had to be," Kelly muttered.

"Yeah, probably true. You've never let anyone push you around, that's for sure."

"I don't want to push him *away*, you know?"

"I know." His dad squeezed his shoulder. "But don't give up yet. That's not what you're about."

"What do you mean?"

His dad huffed out a laugh. "You never let a single coach tell you that you were too small. Not a teammate or an opposing player or even your brothers or me. You put your head down and pushed forward and proved them wrong."

"That's what I should do now?" he asked, feeling doubtful.

Sure, it made sense in hockey but in the relationship he had with Anders, he wasn't so sure.

"That I don't know. I don't know him."

Oh, but you do, Dad, Kelly thought, but he kept his lips tightly mashed together so those words didn't slip out.

Declan sighed and continued. "You're not the type to be easily defeated. Don't let a setback get you down."

"Thanks, Dad," Kelly said roughly. "I needed that."

"Any time. And I mean it. You text or call if you want to talk about anything, you hear me?"

"I will," he promised.

"And maybe you can reply to some of my texts sometimes? I'll lay off on the game notes, I promise."

"I'll do better," Kelly promised.

"Okay, I'm gonna go in and make sure our crazy family hasn't burned the place down. You comin'?"

"I think I'll stay out here a minute. It's nice out."

"Okay. Love you, kid." His dad wrapped a thick arm around him and squeezed, pulling Kelly in close. Kelly held on tight, feeling like a little kid again, safe and protected.

"Love you too," he whispered thickly.

"Never forget I'm proud of you."

Kelly couldn't speak at all after that, so he just nodded and squeezed tighter.

After his dad left, Kelly stood in the spring night for a little while, listening to the sound of traffic and watching the lights, overwhelmed but still more peaceful than he'd been in years.

God, what a night.

CHAPTER TWENTY-SIX

Finn nudged Anders' elbow. "Would you go out and check on him?"

"What happened to me not being the intermediary?" Anders asked mildly, but he set his glass of water on a nearby table. He'd wanted to check on Kelly anyway. He'd just been concerned about overstepping.

Trevor stopped him when he was halfway to the door. "Hey, uh, I think I'm gonna bail. Tell Kelly I'll have an eye on my phone if he needs me though, okay?"

"I will," Anders promised. "See you at practice tomorrow?"

"Yeah. See ya, man." With a nod, Trevor made his escape and Anders pushed the door to the deck open.

Kelly glanced over his shoulder, a flicker of surprise crossing his face. "Oh, hey," he said quietly.

"Are you okay?" Anders leaned against the railing, staring at Kelly's profile. There were decorative lights strung over the patio area, waving a little in the breeze, leaving some parts of Kelly's face in shadow.

Kelly let out a shaky breath. "I think so. It's been a bit of a wild ride but … yeah. I'm gonna be okay."

"Good."

Kelly gave Anders a wry smile. "Sorry I dropped a bombshell on dinner."

"If that's what you needed to do, I support you."

"I know." Kelly chewed at his lip. "Are *we* okay?"

"I hope so," Anders said truthfully.

"I didn't do this because of you. It was just time."

"I understand." Honestly, it didn't matter to Anders one way or another, as long as Kelly felt good about it. "Do you have plans tomorrow?"

Kelly gave him a puzzled look. "Just practice. Why?"

"Don't eat at the rink after we're done with practice, okay? I want to take you somewhere."

"I don't know, Anders," Kelly said slowly. "We should talk …"

"I plan to," Anders said with a smile. "But I want to do this too. It'll be private enough that we can eat and talk."

"Is this because of me coming out?"

"No," Anders said truthfully. "In the past few days, I took some time to think about us and what I want and I'm ready to figure it out with you, if you want that too."

"Oh." Kelly let out a sigh, relief filling his voice. "So, you do want …"

He didn't seem to know how to finish his thought, so Anders did it for him. "I want to take you on a date and talk about our future."

"Oh. Okay," Kelly said, almost breathless sounding, his smile pleased. "Yeah. I'd love that."

Anders smiled and reached out, gently taking Kelly's hand and squeezing. It was shadowy enough that even if someone looked out at them, they wouldn't see their intertwined fingers. "Good. I'll see you tomorrow."

"Yeah, tomorrow," Kelly said faintly, his lips curving up in a puzzled but happy smile.

———

Kelly was floating on air as he walked into the restaurant, the private room warm and cozy after the cool night breeze outside. Everyone was eating dessert and although a small lull in the conversation fell over the room, no one did more than shoot a quick glance at him.

It was honestly kind of a relief. The *last* thing Kelly wanted was to be the center of attention right now.

Kelly dropped into a chair between Patrick and Connor and dragged a slice of chocolate cake toward himself. He lifted a big forkful to his mouth. *Mmm, salted caramel buttercream.*

Pat nudged Kelly's leg with his knee. "You okay?"

"Yep. I'm great." He meant it too.

"Ehh, you won't be after this first round," Connor teased. "You'll be crying into your beer and moping about how you got robbed by the ref's calls after we beat you."

Kelly shook his head, relieved to see things were normal again. "Maybe *you'll* be doing that after *we* win."

Connor let out a disgusted noise and made a snarky retort, while Kelly happily ate his cake and tossed chirps back.

After the cake was gone and the trash talking was done, the little kids were clearly too restless to stick around much longer and everyone dispersed.

Kelly said goodbye to his parents, then Finn's and Pat's families but as they all streamed out into the parking lot, Kelly looked around, confused.

Trevor had left already—which Anders had told him about before *he* said goodnight and headed out—but apparently so had Kelly's sister-in-law and some of the kids. In fact, he hadn't seen them since he came in from the patio.

"Where's Viv?" he asked Connor.

His mouth flattened into a thin line. "She, uh, took the kids to the hotel a little early. They were getting squirrely." But he didn't meet Kelly's eyes.

"Connor," Kelly warned. "Don't bullshit me."

He sighed. "She's … we, uh, had some words about your coming out."

"*Viv* has a problem with it?" That was a gut punch. Kelly was closer to Pat's wife Aubrey, but he'd always thought he and Vivian got along well.

"I think in a few days she'll come around," Connor said gruffly. "You know what her family's like."

Kelly thought back to Connor and Vivian's wedding and grimaced. "Yeah."

There had been a big fight over the open bar the couple had planned.

Vivian's parents were religious and conservative, and adamantly against drinking. While Kelly knew there were people out there who abstained for a variety of reasons, Kelly sure wasn't related to them.

After a big fight, Connor had finally smoothed things over with her parents and paid for the open bar himself as a compromise. But his brand-new in-laws had still left the reception early, clearly disapproving.

Apparently, Viv was more like her parents than Kelly had realized.

"Shit. I don't want to cause any problems for you guys," Kelly said weakly.

"Hey, that's not on you, I promise." Connor pulled Kelly into another bone-crushing hug. He'd had softer hits from opponents.

Jesus Christ, sometimes love in this family was exactly like playing hockey.

"I know," Kelly said as he finally extracted himself. "I just …"

Connor punched his arm. "Hey. You're my brother. O'Shea family rules, right? We gotta love each other and stick up for each other always."

Kelly nodded, a lump in his throat. He hoped his brothers would still feel that way if—*when?*—they found out about him and Anders.

CHAPTER TWENTY-SEVEN

As Anders drove to the park where he'd directed Kelly to meet him, he realized he'd never been so nervous in his life. Proposing to Astrid had been easy by comparison. He'd known where they stood and never doubted she'd say yes, but Kelly he was less sure of.

Anders wasn't proposing today but this conversation was equally important to him. Whatever came of it would shape the direction their futures took.

So Anders heart beat fast with excitement and nerves as he parked the Bentley and carried a picnic basket and insulated bag toward a large tree he'd already scoped out.

He'd spread a blanket near its base and begun setting things out when Kelly approached. He was dressed nicer than usual, foregoing his usual athletic shorts and tee for fitted denim and a casual striped button-up. The guys had teased him about it at practice when he changed into it after his shower.

"Hot date?" Cooper had chirped.

Kelly had deliberately not looked in Anders' direction and said, "Maybe."

Now, his cheeks were pink, and his eyes sparkled as he looked at Anders. "You planned a picnic?"

Anders had to swallow the urge to drag him down onto the grass and kiss him until he was breathless. Instead, he patted the blanket. "I did. Would you like to join me?"

Kelly nodded, his eyes bright and pleased as he kicked off his shoes and took a cross-legged seat, his fingers toying with the small bouquet of flowers Anders had set on the top of the picnic basket. "This is nice."

"It gets better," Anders promised.

Everything was already prepared so he laid the food out carefully, watching Kelly's smile widen.

"Deviled eggs." Kelly sounded pleased.

"Those are homemade," Anders admitted. "The rest I bought."

"Yum." Kelly popped one into his mouth with a smile as Anders pulled out a foil container he'd heated at home and secured in an insulated bag to keep warm.

Kelly's eyes widened at the logo on the container. "Oh my God, is that roast beef from the place on the North Shore?"

Anders nodded.

Kelly blinked. "You had my favorite sandwich flown in from Boston for me?"

"Yes." Anders carefully set out buns and cheese and the special barbecue sauce the restaurant was known for. Everything had been overnighted and had thankfully arrived in perfect condition. Maybe not quite as good as when it was fresh from the restaurant's kitchen, but from Kelly's smile, it wouldn't matter.

"Oh my God." Kelly grabbed the front of Anders' shirt and tugged, hauling him in for a kiss.

Laughing against Kelly's mouth, Anders had to brace himself on the blanket, so he didn't tip over and crush the food Kelly was so excited about. "We *are* in public, you know," he murmured.

"I know." Kelly drew away with a sheepish grin, gaze heated. "But I couldn't resist."

Anders glanced around. Thankfully, on a weekday the park was nearly deserted. A woman with a stroller was nearby but she had a phone pinned between her ear and her shoulder and appeared much too distracted by that and the crying toddler to be paying any attention to them.

Anders returned his attention to sandwich assembly, but he looked up when Kelly hesitantly said, "Do you mind? I should have asked."

Anders shrugged. "About people knowing about us? Of course not. But I also don't want our team and your family find out because a picture of us kissing appears on social media. The likelihood of it happening here in Evanston is pretty small but …"

"Whoops." Kelly's cheeks turned pink as he reached for another deviled egg. "Yeah. Sorry. That's a good point. I'm blown away by all this though."

"I wanted to do something special for you," Anders explained. "Show you that I pay attention to you too. You've done so much for me in the past few years. Given me those tastes of home when I needed it and I wanted to do the same for you."

"It's really sweet," Kelly said softly. "I love it. Honestly."

"Good." Anders nudged a plate toward him. "Now, eat."

Kelly tucked into the sandwich, a pleased hum leaving his lips as he took his first bite, the sauce and juicy meat dripping down his arm.

"How is it?"

"Perfect." Kelly beamed as he absently mopped up the mess with a napkin. "God, I haven't had one since last summer, I think."

He took another big bite, his expression blissful, and Anders ate too. Roast beef sandwiches weren't his favorite food by any means, nor were they on his diet plan, but Kelly's pleasure was more than enough to make it enjoyable for him too.

When their sandwiches were gone and Kelly had licked his fingers clean, Anders held out a bakery box. "Open it," he coaxed.

Kelly's lips parted as he lifted the lid. "You got me a Boston Cream Pie from my favorite bakery."

"I debated between that and cannoli. I know you like both, but I thought this would ship better."

"Definitely. Cannoli have to be fresh. Besides, I can get good ones here at the Italian bakeries in Chicago." He looked up, clearly excited. "Can I have a slice?"

Anders grimaced. "I forgot a knife. I do have forks though."

"That's fine." Kelly placed the box between them and snagged the forks, holding out one to Anders. "We can share."

"I'll have a few bites."

Anders had been rather confused about why a cake was called a pie the first time he had one, but he found the dessert decadently enjoyable. The buttery yellow layers of cake had a vanilla custard filling between them and the whole thing was drenched in rich chocolate.

Anders took a couple of bites, enjoying Kelly's obvious pleasure, then set his fork down. To his surprise, Kelly paused too.

"This is amazing, Anders." Kelly looked him in the eye. "But I'm confused. You said we would talk and …"

"I know. Why don't you keep eating while I explain."

"Okay." Kelly licked chocolate off his fork.

"First, I want to apologize for the way I acted when Pat called." Anders cleared his throat. "I panicked."

Kelly nodded, his mouth full of cake.

"This is complicated for me. I … I've been wrestling with what my future will hold, afraid of what it would bring, all while clinging to the past."

Kelly wiped his mouth. "I don't expect you to forget about the past—"

"I know." Anders' tone was gentle, and he reached out to touch Kelly's knee to reassure him. "And I'm grateful. But if the past is holding me back from what I want now and, in the future, that's a problem."

Kelly nodded.

"I loved my life with Elia and Astrid. I've loved my life playing hockey here. And after the people I loved were gone, I kept clinging to this idea that if nothing else in my life changed, I could hang on to what I still had left and keep them with me somehow. But that's—that's not realistic, is it? Whether I retire this year or three years from now, that day will come eventually."

"Yes," Kelly whispered. "I'm not ready for you to leave the team though."

"I know." Anders swallowed hard. "But I think *I* am. My wife and child are gone. No matter how long I continue to play hockey, it won't bring them back. Nothing will."

Kelly's swallow was visible in the bob of his Adam's apple, and he set down his fork again.

Anders pushed on. "But they *are* gone. And it doesn't mean I should stop trying new things and finding out who and what else I might love in the future."

Kelly inhaled, a shaky little breath that made Anders reach out and twine their fingers together.

"I know I love you, Kelly. I think I've felt that way for a long time, but I was terrified of letting anyone in again. Of allowing myself to risk my heart."

"And now?" Kelly whispered.

"I'm still scared. But I'd rather be with you and be scared than go without you in my life."

Kelly opened his mouth but nothing came out. Anders smiled softly and continued.

"Kelly, you have been by my side this whole time. Always looking out for me. Always knowing when I floundered. In a thousand quiet ways you've kept me going. Made it easier to get up in the morning." He squeezed Kelly's hand. "Made it easier to fall asleep. Made it easier to find hope again."

"I don't think I've done much." Kelly's voice sounded thick. "But I love you too. You know that, right?"

Anders nodded, rubbing the pad of his thumb against the back of Kelly's hand.

"I've loved you since I was fifteen," Kelly continued doggedly. "That's a long time. But I didn't really know what love was then. I can see the difference now. And last night it hit me that I've never done this before. You're years ahead of me. You fell in love and had a kid and lost them both and I've never so much as dated anyone. I don't know what I'm doing, Anders. I want this but holy shit, I don't feel prepared. It's like being thrown into my first pro game without ever having played Junior or college-level hockey."

Anders took a moment to think about Kelly's words, letting the tweet of the birds in the background and the quiet hum of the traffic outside the park wash over him as he tried to pull together his thoughts.

"I don't feel prepared either," he finally admitted. "I'm terrified of losing you. Of trusting someone and letting myself be vulnerable to that kind of loss again. But I'm going to do it anyway. I know you think I have it all together, Kelly, but I don't."

"But you seem—"

"I know." Anders let out a rueful little laugh. "I know I seem pulled together and confident, but the truth is, so much of it is a show. As much for myself as for anyone else but it was my desperate attempt to hold my life together. I had experience playing hockey but my first game in the NHL, I still felt like I had no idea what I was doing. I was completely overwhelmed but I pretended like I was fine. And in a couple of games, I *was*. This is the same thing."

"Fake it until you make it?" Kelly offered and Anders laughed thickly.

"Yes. When my world was collapsing around me, the more I projected that I was okay, the more it felt like the lie was the only thing holding me up. And somewhere along the way it *did* get better. But there are still some days where the grief hurts so much it takes my breath away."

"I know."

Anders let go of Kelly's hand long enough to shift the plates and boxes out from between them until he could scoot closer to Kelly. So he could look into his eyes and see his reactions.

"Kelly, if we're together, you don't have to be perfect. You don't have to know what you're doing. I don't either, to be honest. No matter how it looked on the outside, my marriage to Astrid wasn't perfect. It was wonderful and every bit of it was worth it, but we fought and sometimes it was ugly. Sometimes she thought I took her for granted. And sometimes I did. But Kelly, no two relationships are the same. Knowing what worked for Astrid doesn't mean I know exactly what to do in my relationship with *you*."

"Okay," Kelly said slowly. "That makes sense."

"The one thing Astrid and I did well was that we kept trying. That's all I'm asking from you."

"It's okay that I don't know what I'm doing?" Kelly whispered.

"Yes. As long as you believe it's okay that I don't either. I need you to go into this knowing I don't have all the answers. I'm asking you to figure them out with me as we go."

"I can do that."

"And while I know you're okay with me talking about Astrid and respecting her place in my life, you need to know you're not a replacement, Kelly."

"I know." He shrugged like it was unimportant, but Anders wanted Kelly to understand what he meant.

"You're a new and exciting future I'm looking forward to discovering."

Kelly closed his eyes, emotions flickering across his face for a moment before he opened them again, tears glittering on his lashes, the sun catching them and turning them into pinpoints of light.

"Take me home, Lindy. Please."

———

An hour later, body humming with the satisfaction of reconnecting with Anders physically, Kelly snuggled into his side.

"I love you, Kelly," Anders whispered as he pulled Kelly more tightly to him.

"I love you too." Kelly buried his head against Anders' neck, overwhelmed still. "God, I never thought …"

Anders smoothed a hand along his back. "Never thought what?"

"That I'd get to *keep* you."

"I'm yours, Kelly, as long as you want me."

"Forever then?"

Anders kissed the top of his head. "That sounds perfect to me."

"Good," Kelly whispered.

Anders pulled back far enough to look him in the eye and Kelly flipped onto his side. "I am going to retire at the end of this season though."

Kelly sighed but he nodded. "Okay." He didn't love it, but if he'd have Anders outside of hockey at least, he could live with it. "Uhh, you aren't planning to move back to Sweden though, are you?"

"No." Anders smiled. "I'm going to look into starting a skills camp."

"Around here?" Kelly asked hopefully.

Anders smiled. "It seems like a pretty good location to me. There are plenty of hockey teams and I like being near the lake. Besides, there's someone I want to be close to."

Kelly smiled too. It felt good to be a part of Anders' decision-making.

"I'll have to figure out the visa situation, but I think it's workable," he said.

"Well, if the government tries to kick you out, I know someone who'd probably marry you." Kelly offered with a sleepy yawn, sort of kidding but mostly not.

Anders chuckled. "Good to know."

Kelly ducked his head, his face warm. "Not that I'm rushing things. I just wanted you to know."

Anders' smile widened. "It's good to consider all the options."

"What if I got traded?" Kelly asked, turning serious again.

"We'd figure it out. I don't see the Otters being in any hurry to get rid of you, but if that happens, we can talk about it and figure out a plan."

"Okay."

"There's one thing we haven't talked about though. Having children."

"Oh." Kelly wet his lips. "I mean, I would like kids someday. Way fewer than my brothers have but … I'd like to be a dad. I know that might not be something you're thinking about though."

"I'm going to need some more time," Anders said with a heavy sigh. He rubbed his thumb across Kelly's cheekbone. "I would like to give you that but it's going to take a lot of work on my part to get to a point where I'm ready. Losing Elia was …"

"It's okay. I know. I'm not in a rush. We have time."

A flicker of doubt crossed Anders' face but it smoothed away and Kelly wondered if that would take a while. If Anders' automatic reaction would be doubting they would have a future. Kelly didn't think it was because Anders doubted their ability to make it work, more that he was scared that something catastrophic would prevent it. And well, Kelly couldn't blame him.

"Is that hard for you?" Kelly asked. "Trusting we will have a future?"

"Yes." Anders rolled onto his back, resting his arm on his forehead. "I want it. I trust that you want it too. But trusting that fate will allow it to happen is harder."

"Okay." Kelly settled a hand on his chest. "We'll take it one day at a time then."

"Oh, I don't know. Let's be wild," Anders said, turning his head to look at him. "Let's at least think about a few months at a time."

Kelly laughed. "I can do that."

Anders levered himself out of bed and Kelly blinked, trying to figure out where he was going.

"Actually, there's something else I want to show you. Stay there."

Where else am I going to go? Kelly wondered. Now that he had what he was pretty sure was an open invitation to be in Anders' bed, he wasn't going to get out of it unless he had to.

Anders returned a few minutes later, carrying his computer. He seemed completely unselfconscious about his nudity and Kelly was glad. It was a hell of a view.

As Anders sprawled on the bed beside him, in all his sexy, Swedish glory, Kelly felt like he might need to pinch himself to believe this was all real. That Anders was real.

That his life included being naked in bed with this man and talking about their future together.

Fifteen-year-old Kelly was definitely psyched. Honestly, Current Kelly pretty much was too.

Anders fiddled with the computer for a moment, then pushed it toward Kelly. "Take a look."

Kelly flipped onto his stomach and scanned the screen for a few minutes before he turned to Anders with a smile. "You made plans for our summer."

"I put together a list of ideas, anyway. We'll have to see how the postseason goes and what I need to do to get this skills camp up and running. Depending on how much time we have, we can do more or less. But these are options we can choose from."

"That sounds perfect."

"I thought you could show me some places in Boston I might have missed when I lived there too."

"I'd like that." Kelly froze and turned to look at him. "How are we going to tell my family? *When* are we going to tell them? I mean, I assume we are going to have to, right? If we travel together all summer that's going to be a clue and honestly, I'm not sure I'm going to be any good at pretending like I'm not totally into you."

"I'd like to tell them, yes," Anders said. "But I was thinking we'd hold off until after the playoffs are done. However this first round goes, we probably don't want to complicate it with announcing our relationship in the middle of it all."

"Agreed," Kelly said without hesitation. "What about the team?"

"I'm thinking maybe the same thing, unless you want to tell them immediately."

"I'm okay with keeping quiet," Kelly said. "And honestly, with as much bullshit as there's been with Malone, I don't want to risk it."

"That was my thought too."

Kelly glanced back at the screen and scrolled through the list of ideas, smiling with helpless fondness. It was a *very* well-organized spreadsheet. "I'm excited about the idea of seeing Sweden."

"I'm excited about taking you there."

"I'll fucking miss having you on the bench with me next season," Kelly admitted, his throat tighter than he'd expected. "But I'm looking forward to everything else in our future."

Anders let out a contented sigh as he smoothed a hand across Kelly's back. Kelly shimmied closer and Anders pressed a kiss to his shoulder, his hair tickling Kelly's skin.

"I'm looking forward to our future too."

CHAPTER TWENTY-EIGHT

"God this feels weird," Ryan said with a huff.

Anders looked up from the sock he was taping to glance at him. "Your gear? I'm sure Jim can fix it if something's wrong."

Despite the skate blade issue Anders had experienced in March, he had absolute faith in Jim's ability to wrangle their equipment.

"No. My gear's fine. I mean playing Boston in the first round. The league reshuffle is weird," he said.

"It is strange," Zane agreed. "This season has been okay, I guess. But you're right, it is odd to be up against Boston now."

Tonight was the first time the Evanston River Otters had gone up against the Boston Harriers in the first round of the Conference Quarterfinals. Since the Otters team was created, they'd been in the Central division but the league reshuffle before the season started had put them in the East.

It had thrown Anders at the beginning of the season, but it hadn't bothered him much since.

"It makes me feel dirty," Ryan said with a shiver. "I don't like it."

Zane snorted. "Pretty sure that's all in your head, you weirdo."

"Hey, you love me. Pretty sure that makes you the weirdo."

"Pretty sure it does," Zane agreed with a resigned sigh. "Pretty sure I'm okay with that though."

"Aww, aren't you romantic," Ryan teased.

Anders smiled, winding more tape around his sock. Left before right, like always, as he listened to them banter.

The more wound up about hockey Ryan and Zane got, the more they flirted with each other. It used to make Anders laugh but when he glanced across the dressing room to see Kelly buckling his elbow pads, Anders definitely understood it. There was something unique about falling in love with your teammate.

He looked away before anyone saw it written all over his face.

"It'll be more romantic if you win me a Cup," Zane shot back.

"Me?" Ryan sputtered. "Why is it all on me? *You* could win me a Cup too, you know."

"I hate to interfere with your pre-game foreplay but I'm fairly sure we're supposed to all work together to win," Tremblay said mildly.

"Oh, is that how it works?" Cooper asked. "Damn, wish someone would have told me before now. I thought these guys were gonna flirt their way to victory."

"If anyone could do it, it would be them," Truro said drily. "Although if I have to hear one more time from my wife about how romantic it would be for them to get engaged on the ice, I'm going to barf."

Ryan gave him a disgusted look. "I'm not proposing after the *conference quarterfinals*." His tone was disparaging.

"Yeah, and I'm holding out for a second Cup," Zane said flippantly. "I won't settle for anything less."

Anders grimaced and knocked on wood, muttering under his breath. If his linemates didn't jinx them, it would be a miracle.

"You're both ridiculous," Tremblay said with a snort. "But thankfully, entertaining."

———

Malone was quiet as they got ready for warmups, glowering in his stall as he dressed in his base layers, clearly tuning out the rest of them. He appeared hungover, to be frank. Kelly didn't know if he was, but he looked like shit.

There were circles under his eyes and his dark brown hair—something he was normally incredibly vain about—was greasy and lank. When he disappeared toward the toilets, Kelly leaned into Underhill's stall.

"Dude, is Malone okay?" Kelly asked Trevor under his breath, under the pretense of stealing some tape.

He shrugged. "I dunno. We grabbed dinner last night with a couple of other people and I think he was a few drinks in before I got there. I cut out early, but they were still going pretty hard when I left."

"Who else was with him?" Kelly glanced around to see if the rookies who usually tagged along looked any worse for wear today. Jesus, how dumb was he to be hungover for a playoff game?

"No one on the team. I don't think you know them. There were a couple of influencers and some DJs or something. I don't know. I fucking hated them all, which is why I bailed quickly, but you know he likes sucking up to people who pump his tires or who he thinks will be useful to him."

"Yeah. Ugh." Kelly glanced at their captain and his alternates, trying to ignore the little flutter of happiness that went through him every time he saw Anders. "Should we say something to Murph or Coach?"

"I dunno," Trevor said doubtfully. "Maybe let's see how Malone does in the first period and let them decide."

"Yeah, okay," Kelly said reluctantly. It wasn't like he was happy at the thought of ratting out one of his teammates, but Malone had been playing like shit lately and he didn't want to see their play get hurt with Malone's sloppy turnovers and inability to protect their net. Not in a game like this.

Hajek was good, but he could only do so much when there was no one in front of the goal. Well, Cooper was there and doing his best, but he couldn't do it alone.

"I don't like this," Kelly muttered as he dragged on his jersey and hooked his fight straps, but a glance at the clock told him it was nearly time for warmups. He'd have to keep an eye on Malone and see what happened.

Warmups went fine. Kelly buzzed by where his parents' seats were and got a big cheer from them, which felt good. He didn't stop to see if Viv was part of that or not. He didn't want to know.

He met his brothers at center ice for their usual trash talk, then went and did his pre-game shin taps with Theriault.

"You feeling good?" Gabriel asked after, his dark brown eyes sparkling as he juggled a puck.

"So fucking good," Kelly shouted, sending a slapper into the net. Hajek was busy doing his stretchy goalie thing, so it was wide open.

The music was pumping, the crowd was already fired up, and the team was going to tear up the ice tonight.

Best of all, Anders loved him.

Kelly did a showy little spin to make Gabriel laugh before he wheeled away to bother Ryan.

Kelly was still buzzing when the first period ended. They were up 2-1 and Kelly had gotten an assist on one of the goals. Anders had gotten the other goal.

Kelly jostled Anders' shoulder as they walked down the tunnel. Anders smiled with a big, genuine grin and Kelly was so happy he had to look away before he kissed him right then and there in front of their teammates.

But as Kelly glanced away, he caught a glimpse of Anders' chain, hooked on the edge of his jersey, peeking out with a flash of gold.

"Oh, hey," he said, tugging off his gloves and tucking them under his arm to pull Anders into the side hallway. "C'mere."

Anders gave him a questioning look but did it, their teammates continuing on toward the dressing room.

"Something wrong?" Anders asked when Kelly finally stopped, partway down the hall.

"Just, your chain is a little funny. Let me fix it." Kelly lifted it, tugging it out from where it was tucked under the jersey and pads. He turned the clasp so it rested at the back of Anders' neck. "Wouldn't want anything to happen to something so important."

Kelly lifted the chain to slip the wedding rings safely under Anders' gear when he spotted something new on the necklace. "Anders?" he said a little breathlessly. "What …"

He gently shifted the rings to better see the charm. His heart raced with a sudden jolt at the sight of the gold #13. Absently, he touched the matching number on the arm of his jersey.

"You …"

Anders nodded. "It's for you, Kelly. I wanted to carry a piece of my future with me as we went into the playoffs."

"Oh God." Kelly was helpless to stop the sudden surge of emotion washing over him. "You can't *say* stuff like that, Anders."

With a quick glance around to be sure no one was in sight, Kelly grabbed the front of Anders' jersey and yanked him down into a kiss. It was awkward with the difference in height, but he didn't mind the strain in his neck as he told Anders without words what the gesture meant to him.

"What the fuck was that, Malone?" Coach Daniels bellowed and Kelly froze, slowly lifting his head. "You were fucking late getting out for warmups, your line changes were shit, and that icing call was—"

The abrupt cut off made Kelly turn his head toward the tunnel.

Both Coach Daniels and Jack Malone were frozen as they stared at Kelly and Anders, eyes wide.

Kelly let go of Anders' jersey and smoothed out the wrinkles, patting it against his chest like that would somehow hide that he'd been kissing his teammate. His lips were still wet from Anders' mouth and there was no denying what they'd been doing.

"What the fuck?" Malone shouted, lurching toward them. "Jesus fucking Christ, O'Shea. I can't believe you lied to me too!"

"Did you ever think about why?" Kelly hollered back, his irritation rising. Malone didn't exactly have the moral high ground here. "Maybe it was because I knew you'd be an asshole about it."

"I'm not the one—"

Coach Daniels grabbed Malone's jersey in his fist and shook him. "I don't give a shit who did *what* unless it impacts the play out there. You're the one sweating whiskey out of your pores like a cheap hooker. This is no way to act, and you know it. I wouldn't tolerate it in an exhibition game, but *this* is inexcusable."

"But he—"

"I don't fucking care," Coach bellowed. Several more people peered around the corner. Kelly caught a glimpse of a couple of the assistant coaches and some of the support staff. "The team can have a goddamn orgy in their free time for all the fucks I give. They're all still playing like winners. You're not. Get that jersey off your fucking back. You don't deserve to wear it."

The venom in his voice made Kelly blink.

"But the game …" Malone protested weakly.

"You should have thought of that before you got drunk. You're out."

"Who's going to take my place?" Malone sneered.

Daniels scoffed. "We've got plenty of Black Aces called up who are dying to prove they've earned a spot on this roster. Not that it would take much. I'd rather grab a goddamn fan out of the seats than have you wear our colors right now." He glowered. "Get out of my face, Malone. Call your wife to come pick you up. We'll talk disciplinary action tomorrow when you're sober."

He shoved Malone away from him and he staggered back, his shoulder catching the wall.

"This is all your fucking fault," Malone shouted at Kelly. "You and your goddamn—"

Daniels advanced on him. "So, help me God, Malone if you finish that sentence with a slur, I will fucking spend the rest of my career burying you so deep you will never see the ice again."

"Your career isn't going to last long if I have anything to say about it." Malone threw his gloves on the ground and turned to go.

"Then I'm taking you down with me." Daniels stared after Malone until he was gone, the other coaches and staff quickly scurrying away.

Kelly's heart thundered as he wondered what came next.

Daniels' face was red as he turned to look at Anders and Kelly but his shoulders slumped and the anger seemed to leach out of him. He dragged a hand through his thinning gray hair. "Jesus. This is a mess."

"I'm sorry, Coach," Kelly said miserably. Anders settled a hand on Kelly's waist and squeezed.

"You could have picked better timing but I honestly don't give a shit about you two," he said, his tone weary. "Just tell me if you're doing a press conference or a press release through your agents or what. I don't like being left out of the loop."

"Neither, I hope," Kelly said, taken aback. "We want to get through the playoffs before we come out to the public. Maybe something quiet during the off-season?"

"Thank fucking Christ," Daniels said with a relieved sigh. "Someone has some fucking sense around here."

"The team probably overheard this though," Anders said. "Or if they haven't yet, they will soon. We should at least talk to them so no one else is blindsided."

"Go then." Coach waved them forward. "Tell them and be quick about it. We have a game to finish playing, or has everyone forgotten?"

As Kelly and Anders walked into the dressing room, it was nearly silent. Malone was gone already, and pieces of his gear were strewn everywhere. A tipped-over laundry cart and trash can spilled their contents on the floor, like he'd thrown a giant tantrum on his way in or out.

A terrified look on his face, one of the rookies was hurriedly re-taping a stick like it was the only thing he knew how to do.

"So," Cooper said, clearing his throat after a moment of silence. "You guys are dating, huh?"

"Uhh, yeah," Kelly said. "That's the short version."

"Great. Happy for both of you." Cooper nodded decisively. "Malone's out for the game. Will someone fucking tell me who I'm partnered with now?"

That broke the tension and several guys laughed, as much from relief as anything, probably.

There were a few congratulations and supportive fist bumps from the team but there was little time for anything else.

Coach Daniels came in a moment later, his gaze zeroing in on Kelly and Anders. "We good?"

"We're good," Anders assured him.

"Okay. Malone is officially out until further notice. Underhill, we're keeping Burgess with you tonight. We'll be down a forward but Coop, you'll be paired with Kajota. We'll rotate him into the D-slot for tonight and I'll work out something for the future."

"It's pronounced Ka-YO-ta, sir," the call up squeaked. "It's Polish."

Daniels turned to look at him.

"But you can, um, say it however you want," he hastily added, withering under the weight of the glare.

"Kajota," Daniels said wearily, his pronunciation perfect as he stared at their Black Ace who had been skating as a fourth line forward. "Can you skate?"

Kajota looked confused. "Yes, sir."

"Do you know what a defenseman is supposed to do?"

He glanced around like it was a trick question. "Um, keep the puck out of our net and provide opportunities for our guys to score on the other team?"

"Great. And are you drunk?"

"No-o, sir."

"Perfect. We're already doing better than we were." He looked at the team. "I am going to make the world's quickest speech because we need to get our asses out there. Kelly and Anders have my support. Any of you who are gay or bi—or whatever the fuck you are—have the support of the team. Anyone who has a problem with it, you can get the fuck out of here too."

"Uhh, is this a good time to mention that I'm bi as well?" Underhill said.

"It absolutely is not but thanks for letting us know." Daniels gaze swept around the room. "Anyone else while we're at it? I'd like to get this out of the way."

One of the rookies held up his hand. "I'm kinda questioning things but there's a guy outside the team I'm already—"

"Great. Put your hand down, Bennett," Daniels said. "That everyone?"

They all nodded.

"Fantastic. Now, can we get the fuck out on the ice and think about hockey?"

"Yes, Coach!" they all shouted, tapping their sticks on the floor.

"Good. Now go win us a game."

For a moment, Kelly slumped against Anders with a sigh, then tromped down the hall to take the ice.

CHAPTER TWENTY-NINE

Later that night, as Anders dragged himself out of the shower following a painful 5-2 loss, he knew he'd let his team down.

He grimaced as he dried off. He couldn't remember the last time they'd had such a terrible game. Before he and Kelly had been outed, they'd had the lead. After intermission, it felt like they became a different team.

They'd played sloppily, with missed passes, off-timing, too many penalties, and Anders had been the cause of more than his share of it.

If he'd been able to put up a single point in the last two periods, they might have been able to turn it around, but with his game a mess, there was no way.

It was a rough start to the series.

Anders dressed robotically and had just finished tying back his damp hair when he felt a gentle smack against his hip.

"You okay, Lindy?"

Anders turned and blinked tiredly at Ryan Hartinger. "Disappointed in my performance tonight."

Ryan let out a rueful laugh. "Yeah well, none of us did anything that's going to make the highlight reels, bud."

"I know. It's just …"

"Hey, I get it." Ryan's expression turned serious. "Zane said you're thinking about retirement, and this could be your last run. Plus, you and Kelly got outed in a super weird way and that's a lot of pressure."

Anders slumped. It was true. He hadn't quite put it all into words, but Ryan made a good point. "I feel like I have so much to prove."

"I know. I get it, man." Ryan patted Anders' chest. "And dude, do you think Zane and I haven't felt the exact same way since we came out? We've had every damn person in the league and every fan watching us to see if we're going to fuck it up. Zane is beating himself up after every single loss and every time the team makes the press. Not to mention every bad decision the head office makes about the shit-stain of a D-man on our roster."

Anders let out a tired, rueful laugh at Ryan's description of Malone, but let Ryan continue, since it seemed like he was on a roll.

"Zane has been working himself to *death* for the past few years trying to prove we're good enough. That a team with a captain who is dating his winger can still be a winning team. It's grinding at him, and his hip is hurting way more than he lets on. But I think I finally got it through his thick skull that he can't take it all on. He can only do so much. And that's true for you too, okay?"

A wave of guilt washed over Anders. At times, he'd thought about the pressures on Zane, but it hadn't sunk in how much he'd taken on. How big the load he carried was.

"I should have done more," he said aloud.

Ryan grabbed Anders' shoulders and shook. He was one of the few guys on the team almost tall enough to look Anders straight in the eye. "Dude, that was *not* me telling you to beat yourself up *more*, you dumbass. It was me telling you to let up on the guilt, dude. Jesus."

Anders opened his mouth to argue, then closed it. "You're right."

"*Of course*, I am. Not just a pretty face, you know?" Ryan grinned, but he didn't let go of Anders. "So … go home with Kelly tonight. Make each other feel better. And come back for practice tomorrow with your head on right and determined to win. This was only our first game. We're not out of contention yet. Sucks that we lost our first home game, but we've got the next one to turn things around and even then, we could still battle our way back. We'll keep Boston fighting for it until the bitter end. If I have anything to say about it, we'll be bringing home a Cup for Evanston and proving all those assholes wrong, okay?"

"Okay," Anders said, the light of hope flickering on again, pushing against the darkness threatening to overtake him. "Yes. I'll do that. Thank you."

"Pffft. Any time."

Ryan pulled him in for a hug and Anders let his head drop to Ryan's shoulder in a gesture of camaraderie and exhaustion.

"Aww, buddy," Ryan said in a soft tone, squeezing harder.

Anders let himself soak in the affection for a few seconds, taking strength from his teammate. From one of the guys who had been there for him for so long. From someone who understood better than almost anyone what he was going through.

"Should I be jealous?" Kelly asked a minute later, but from his tone, it was clear he wasn't worried. He skimmed his fingertips across Anders' back, another grounding touch that allowed Anders to straighten and turn to face Kelly with a soft smile.

"Yes." Ryan grinned at Kelly, his arm still slung around Anders' shoulder. "I'm leaving Zane for your man, Shaysey. I can no longer resist his sad face and tight ass." Ryan smacked the body part in question and winked.

Truro, who had been walking by, did a double take. Anders opened his mouth to explain but Truro held up a hand. "I don't wanna know."

"Well, my work here is done," Ryan said cheerfully as he walked off, whistling.

Anders envied his ability to shrug off a bad game, but he was grateful for it. Ryan's jokes and playfulness were exactly what he'd needed tonight. Well, one of the things.

Anders turned to look at Kelly with a soft smile.

Kelly smiled back and slipped an arm around Anders. "Well, I know I'm second best to Hartinger, but do you think you'll settle for coming home with me tonight?"

"Oh, I don't know," Anders teased. "Think you can beat his offer?"

Kelly gave him a considering look. "Hmm. Are we doing a boyfriend swap or what? 'Cause I mean, Zane *is* pretty hot. Maybe I should go for him instead …"

Anders gave him an outraged look, then they were both laughing, punch-drunk tired and unreasonably amused by the whole exchange.

Eventually, when the mirth had faded, Anders kissed the top of Kelly's head. "You're coming home with me," he said. "And *only* me."

Kelly's smile was soft as he looked up. "Yeah, okay. Sounds good to me."

On the way out, a few more guys greeted them, told them congratulations, and wished them well.

But it wasn't until they were sprawled half-dead on the couch eating the food the team's chef had prepared that Kelly addressed the questions that had probably been swirling around in his head since he found Ryan and Anders hugging.

He nudged Anders' thigh with his knee. "So, what was that about with Hartinger?"

"I felt terrible about the game, and he offered me some ..." It took Anders a moment to find the right words for it. "Advice, I suppose. Or perspective, maybe."

"Yeah? What kind?" Kelly looked more curious than concerned.

"That I'm not at fault for the way the game went tonight."

"Anders!" The sharp snap of Kelly's voice made Anders straighten out of his tired slump. "Do you want to play the blame game tonight? Because if you do, I'm the one who fucked up."

"Kelly, you didn't—"

"I *did*." Kelly shifted to look at him. "*I* straightened your necklace, and *I* kissed you where anyone could walk by. And *I'm* the

379

reason we got caught. The reason Malone blew his stack and we got outed and the team was a fucking mess tonight. So, if we're getting into this whole thing, at least lay the blame where it belongs."

Anders sighed. "Okay, point taken."

Kelly poked at his brown rice and chicken. "I *am* sorry, you know."

"No. You misunderstood. I wasn't blaming you," Anders protested. He set his container of salmon and quinoa on the coffee table.

"Well …" Kelly's lips twisted in a frown. "Maybe you should. I fucked up."

"Hey." Anders took Kelly's container away too and pulled him close. "No. We're in this together. I could have told you we should be more careful but I didn't. And to be honest, in some ways, it's a relief that everyone knows. Now we don't have to worry about it hanging over our heads."

"I guess." Kelly shifted, settling so his head rested against Anders' chest. "I feel *terrible.*"

"Well, you shouldn't. Malone is the problem."

"I know *that.* But I didn't have to make a volatile situation *worse.*"

"Maybe it isn't the way we would have chosen to have this all happen," Anders said soothingly. "But it did. And Ryan made some great points. We're not out of the series yet. It's the first game. It was a terrible one but we have to put it behind us and move forward."

"True." Kelly let out a thoughtful hum. "Do you think there will be any more blowback from us coming out?"

"It's possible," Anders admitted. "But let's take it one day at a time."

———

The next morning, Kelly woke to Anders' lips tickling the back of his neck.

"Mmm. Morning." Kelly smiled sleepily and burrowed against Anders' warm, hard body, utterly content.

"Love you." Anders splayed a hand on Kelly's stomach, and Kelly had to close his eyes and breathe deep for a minute because he was so happy.

Yesterday had been a huge fucking mess. And Kelly hated that it had impacted the team.

But this … this was good. Kelly was lying in bed with a man who loved him. The man he had been half in love with since he was a stupid teenager with more breakouts on his chin than good sense in his head.

And while his coming out and the team finding out about him and Anders hadn't gone the way Kelly would have wanted, most of them were supportive. His coach had stood up for them. That was all Kelly had ever wanted.

"God, I love you too," Kelly whispered, overwhelmed by every-thing he felt. "Anders …" His voice broke.

"Shh." Anders petted his flank, coaxing him to roll onto his back. "I know. Come here."

Anders cupped Kelly's cheek, kissing him slowly, soothing him. When the heat between them built, Anders reached for the lube, slicking both their cocks, and taking them in his large hand.

They made out slowly, the lazy kisses and languid strokes slowly building in intensity until Kelly came with a soft cry against Anders' mouth and Anders followed a few heartbeats behind.

For a few minutes, they lay there together quietly, Kelly's forehead pressed against Anders' collarbone, Anders' chin resting against the top of Kelly's head, Anders rubbing soothing, aimless patterns on Kelly's sweaty back.

When the sweat and cum began to cool and grow uncomfortable, Anders patted his butt. "Come on, Kels, we need to shower."

Kelly smiled against Anders' clavicle, kissed it once, and stood. He wouldn't mind spending the day lazing in bed with Anders but rubbing soapy hands all over Anders' body was also a pretty good way to top off an already promising morning.

Over breakfast, they checked their phones and grumbled about the messages they had waiting for them.

"Looks like we have a busy day ahead of us. Samantha wants to talk media stuff with us," Kelly groused. "It's so dumb. We're not going to come out to the public yet."

"Yes, but it's good to have a plan in case it's leaked."

"I know." Kelly made a face. "Guess I better call my agent too."

"I should too. Both of them."

Kelly nodded, remembering Anders had one guy back in Sweden who handled his stuff in Europe and another here in Chicago for everything in North America. He had some sweet endorsement deals too. Kelly's favorite was the men's fashion brand because it meant there had always been plenty of ads with suit porn for Kelly to drool over in private.

Kelly had been able to see Anders in a suit before and after every game, of course, but he hadn't allowed himself to enjoy it. He'd snuck quick, furtive glances at the arena or on the plane, but the ads he could linger over in the privacy of his own bedroom.

Of course, now Kelly got to see the suit porn up close and personal in the privacy of Anders' bedroom, which was way better.

Kelly smiled goofily to himself as he stared at his phone. His life had improved a thousand percent in the past few months.

"Hey, you're with the guy downtown right?" Kelly asked a while later as he absently scrolled through his social media notifications. "The one Murph, and all the other LGBTQ players, are with, right?"

"I'm not with Wade Cannon, no, but I am with someone in Premier Talent's office."

"K. Well, I may need to contact them in case things get weird with my agent. He's always been a stuffy old guy so who knows how it'll go over with him when I tell him."

"Of course. Let me know if you need their contact information."

"Thanks." Kelly grimaced and pushed away his empty plate. "Can I use your office? I should get this over with and contact my dude before we have to head in to talk to Samantha."

"Of course. And I'll let Samantha know we'll be there about an hour before practice."

"Sounds good."

Forty minutes later, Kelly found Anders reading on his tablet in the living room. "Sorry, that took longer than I expected."

Anders set the device aside, then glanced at his watch. "It's fine. We have about ten minutes before we need to leave. How did the call with your agent go?"

"Pretty well," Kelly said, relieved. "He seemed totally fine with me coming out. He's preparing a press release in case anything leaks early but he was very chill about it all."

"That's good news."

"It is." Kelly dropped onto the couch beside Anders. "Frankly, he didn't sound surprised. I wonder if he knew."

Anders' expression turned doubtful. "I can't imagine how."

"Maybe it's because I'm on the queerest team in the league."

Anders chuckled. "Well, true."

"I mean, you have to admit, there's a lot of us," Kelly pointed out.

"There are. I'm sure other teams have gay or bi players though."

"Oh, no doubt," Kelly agreed. "They're less vocal about it but I suppose having Murph out from the beginning helped."

"It did." Anders patted his thigh. "Okay, let's get ready to go."

Kelly dragged himself off the couch, brushed his teeth, and got his stuff together. When he met Anders by the door, they did a little dance around each other as they put on their shoes. Anders grabbed a random set of keys from the table by the door and handed them to Kelly, but when Kelly went to take them, Anders grabbed his hand and held on, the cool metal pressed between their palms.

"You should have your own keys to this place," Anders said after Kelly gave him a perplexed smile.

"Oh. I ... Are you sure?"

"Yes. I hope you'll be around a lot in the future."

"Okay." Kelly's smile grew genuine. "Sure, that would be great. Thanks."

It wasn't until they were downstairs and walking toward the underground parking that Kelly asked him to clarify. "Was that you asking me to move in?"

"That's up to you. Would you like to?"

Kelly blinked and tried to coordinate breathing and walking at the same time. It was like the question had short-circuited his entire system. "Um ..."

"If it's too soon, I understand."

Kelly glanced at Anders. He truly didn't look upset by the idea of Kelly saying no.

"It's pretty fast," Kelly admitted.

Anders smiled. "It is. But I've seen how short life can be and I'd rather not lose any of the time I could have with you."

Kelly nodded. Knowing Anders, that made perfect sense. "I love that. Let's talk about it at the end of the summer. I know I'll probably be here pretty much every night we're not on the road until the end of the postseason anyway, then we're gonna travel together this summer, so is it okay if I decide then?"

"Of course." Anders' gaze held nothing but understanding.

Kelly reached out and took Anders' hand, a funny little thrill going through him at holding his boyfriend's hand in public, even if the area was totally deserted. He was allowed to do this now. Yeah, he needed to tell his family about them still, but he could be out about being with Anders and that felt so fucking good.

"I *want* to, but I want to be sure you aren't going to get sick of me, you know?"

Anders squeezed, his gaze warm as he looked Kelly over. "I could never get sick of you, but I have no problem waiting."

"I don't know," Kelly said doubtfully as they approached Anders' Bentley. "I mean, I'm kind of messy sometimes and I know how neat you like things. I don't want to drive you nuts."

"I'm sure we'll figure out a compromise." Anders pulled Kelly close, pressing a kiss to his temple. "But I know I'd rather have your mess in my apartment than not have you in my life."

Kelly sighed, those words chasing away a little of the worry. "You say the sweetest things."

"I mean them."

"I know." Kelly smiled to himself.

That was the best fucking part.

CHAPTER THIRTY

After a lengthy conversation with the team's social media director, a meeting with the coaches, and practice, Kelly was ravenous, but Zane pulled him aside. "Hey, if you and Anders don't have plans, Ryan and I would like to have you over for lunch today."

"Uhh, I'll ask but I don't think we have anything going on," Kelly said. He was quietly thrilled they were already getting couples invites to things. "Is this like some 'welcome to the gay side' lunch or something?"

Zane laughed. "Not exactly but I do like the idea."

Kelly grinned. "What's it about then?"

"We can't hang out with you guys because we want to?" Zane teased.

"Uhh, well you can," Kelly said, a little surprised.

Their captain had organized plenty of events for the team to do and Kelly had been invited to their place to watch football games and stuff with the other guys, but small group lunches were usually out at local restaurants, not their apartment.

"Except for team events, the three of us don't hang out a lot at your place," he admitted. "You guys don't really party and that was sort of my thing with Malone in the past."

Zane's expression turned uneasy, and he glanced around before he leaned in and lowered his voice. "We want to talk to you about the Malone situation."

"Ahh." Kelly nodded. "Sure thing. Let me check with Anders."

Anders agreed and they drove straight from the rink to their teammates' place in Evanston.

Zane and Ryan's apartment was nice. Less formal than Anders' but certainly cleaner than Kelly and Trevor's place had ever been.

Kelly thought about Anders' invitation to move in with him.

The more Kelly thought about it, the stupider his earlier concern seemed. He'd been surprised by the question, but if they were having conversations about what their future would look like and if they wanted to have kids, Anders wasn't going to dump Kelly because he was bad at unloading the dishwasher.

And Kelly loved the idea they'd be sharing a life someday. Not only during the postseason or this summer but years from now. He thought of the jingle of the spare set of Anders' keys he'd clipped onto his keychain earlier and the promise that this was the beginning. This was the start of building a life together.

Kelly, who had loved Anders with the fervor of a teenager for seven years, was learning to love him as an adult too.

It was deeper and more amazing than he'd ever imagined.

Anders smiled at Kelly as they walked through Zane and Ryan's apartment and a rush of affection for him washed over Kelly.

When he reached out and tangled their fingers together, he was rewarded with a soft look and squeeze from Anders.

"I thought we'd eat on the balcony. The weather is great," Zane said as he led them outside.

"Nice day for it for sure," Kelly agreed, but he was so happy he wouldn't have cared if it was hailing.

When they were all seated at the patio table with grilled chicken and whole wheat pasta salad, Ryan brought out cold bottles of beer. Zane raised an eyebrow at the sight, but he didn't argue, just dropped a kiss to Ryan's lips before he sat down and cracked one open.

Zane was usually as uptight about nutrition as Anders was but either this was about to be a way more stressful conversation than Kelly had anticipated, or he'd decided he'd earned it.

Kelly was pretty sure it was the first one.

They mostly talked hockey as they ate, and Kelly grew more anxious by the minute. Zane and Ryan had seemed totally cool with Kelly's relationship with Anders, but what if they were upset about the way they'd come out and how it had set Malone off and impacted the team?

"So." Zane drummed his fingers on the patio table after their plates were cleared. "What's the game plan?"

Kelly glanced at Anders, who looked equally baffled. "For?"

"Figuring out what the fuck we do to handle this Malone situation."

"Oh." Kelly grimaced, relieved. "Should I, uh, apologize, by the way?"

Zane waved it off. "No. You did nothing wrong. He can go fuck himself."

The venom in his voice took Kelly by surprise. "Uhh, *agreed* but you're usually more 'we need to get along for the good of the team' and all, Murph. What changed?"

Zane hesitated. "Well, first of all, I need you guys to swear that what we talk about here won't go any further than this, okay?"

After Kelly and Anders had promised to keep the information between them, Zane continued.

"Let's just say that this season, especially following the fight in Montreal, I got looped in on some stuff that made me realize this is more than Malone being a homophobic dick who may have hit on the wrong girl in a club. Some women working for the organization came forward and said he'd made some inappropriate comments, grabbed them. Propositioned them. Implied that if they didn't go along, he'd get them fired."

"Fuck," Kelly muttered.

"Yeah. HR is looking into it, and I *want* to trust them, but we know their desire to protect the franchise is often stronger than their willingness to fight for the people who work for it."

"I wish it were otherwise but you're right," Anders said, his mouth tightening. "We can't trust them to look into this very hard."

"Exactly. And let's be honest, guys, do we think that's *all* of it with Malone?" Zane leaned back in his chair, hands laced together at the base of his neck, his expression worried.

Reluctantly, Kelly shook his head, his stomach twisting with apprehension. "Probably not."

"If we start digging, I don't know how bad it'll get, but I'm bracing myself for it to be ugly."

Beside him, Anders let out a rough sigh.

Kelly pressed his knee to Anders' leg under the table and a moment later, Anders settled a hand on his thigh. He squeezed once and left his hand there.

The warm weight made the tension in Kelly unspool a little.

"This is the *worst* fucking time to deal with it too, of course," Zane said, scrubbing a hand across his face. "But I don't want to be the guy who puts a Cup win above taking care of the people in this organization. Maybe our GM and owner are willing to do that, but as long as I'm captain, this is *my* team too. A win will mean nothing if we let Malone get away with this shit."

Kelly nodded, unsurprised to see Anders and Ryan nodding too.

Zane tossed his snapback onto the table, then dragged a hand through his unruly hair to smooth it down. "We've seen the shit that's happened around the league over the years. The cover-ups. The refusal to discipline players for their behavior. And I'm not talking about crap like showing up hungover to a game. I mean the serious stuff."

The drug useand the drinking problems were the least of it. Those were guys who needed *help*.

But Kelly felt sick as he went through the list of other rumors that had come up over the years. The sexual assaults. The domestic abuse.

As players, they'd heard it all and there was an unspoken code of silence.

But what if a lot more existed that they *hadn't* heard about? What if staying quiet about guys like Malone had let terrible people get away with horrific things? A chill ran down Kelly's spine.

"It seems pretty obvious that the higher-ups won't change. They're too old and stuck in their ways. Which means it has to start *here*. With us." Zane glanced at Kelly. "But this is going to leave you the most vulnerable, O'Shea. If the rest of us are retiring from playing, we don't have as much to lose. Might fuck up our retirement plans, but Ryan and I can live with that."

"Me too," Anders said.

Zane nodded and continued. "You're still at the beginning of your career, Kelly. You have *everything* to lose."

Kelly was already shaking his head. "Yeah, but when people find out I'm with Anders, there will be blowback on me anyway, right? I'm in."

Anders leaned in. "We wouldn't have to—"

"Oh no." Kelly held up a hand. "Fuck that shit. I did *not* hide in the closet for this long to stay there for the rest of my career. We are going to travel together this summer and I am going to post stupid sappy pictures of us in love on Instagram like these fuckers." He waved at Zane and Ryan. "No one is taking that away from me. Especially not Jack Malone."

Despite his light-hearted words, the name tasted bitter in his mouth now, the knowledge that Malone was someone he'd used to call a friend turning his stomach.

Ryan chuckled but he let them continue.

"You could find yourself blackballed," Zane warned. "I don't know how bad it'll get."

Kelly took a deep breath. "If it happens, it happens. I ... I have to take responsibility for the times I didn't stand up to Malone in the past. If I contributed to him getting away with horrible shit, it's on me to help fix it."

Anders squeezed Kelly's thigh again, his gaze solemn but understanding.

The warm appreciation in Anders' eyes was nice but it wasn't why Kelly was doing it. He was doing it because it was the right choice. Because it felt like the *only* choice.

Kelly looked around the table. "What do we do next? I mean, what's our goal? Getting more dirt on him?"

"Yeah. I know a couple of people at the NHLPA who were pissed he's only gotten a mild reprimand in the past. They're in positions where they could move things along if we find something credible, but it's gotta be information that can't be refuted or hidden."

Kelly grimaced. "Shit, that won't be easy."

"No, it won't." Zane hesitated. "And I think we should decide if there's anyone else we should include."

"Well, Theriault, right?" Kelly looked around. "He's an obvious choice."

Zane hesitated, glancing at Ryan. "That's something we've been debating."

"What's the hesitation?"

"Well, he's dating our position coach. That complicates things."

"Sure," Kelly said slowly. "But Tate's a good guy. He's not going to go running to our GM. He doesn't like Malone any more than

Daniels does, and he was ready to play hardball to keep Cliff from trading Gabriel or something. We should trust him."

"I *do* trust him," Zane said, his tone thoughtful. "I know he's a standup guy. I don't want to put him in an awkward position, however. If he's stuck between the players and management, that could get ugly for him too."

"Isn't that *his* choice to make?" Anders asked.

"That's what I've been saying!" Ryan said.

"Okay." Zane held up his hands. "If that's the consensus, I'll meet with both of them and let them decide if they want to be a part of this."

"Tremblay would be in," Kelly said confidently. "I know Malone said some racist shit to him over the years."

Ryan looked murderous. "Yeah, don't get me started on that."

"I know Jamie can't stand him," Zane said. "So, I was considering him. And uh, Malone was kind of a dick to Taylor earlier this season when he was doing the skating lessons. They'll be on board, I think."

"Yeah, that makes sense to me," Kelly said, then added, "What about Underhill?"

"I don't know." Zane looked hesitant. "Can we trust him?"

"Yes. He was actually great when I told him I was gay. He found out a bit ago and he didn't say anything to Malone about it. I mean, that much is obvious from the way Malone reacted during the game."

"Hmm. I mean, if you trust that he'll be willing to help or at least keep his mouth shut, then I guess we should talk to him at least."

"How are we going to find out anything though?" Kelly asked doubtfully. "At this point, Malone doesn't trust *any* of us. It's not like he's going to let something slip."

"I know." Zane rubbed a hand across his face. "I don't know what to do."

"Have you thought about talking to your agent?" Anders suggested.

"About Malone?"

"Yes. I know agencies have people who do social media work. And that often involves digging up dirt on their clients to be sure they have a media plan in place for scandals getting leaked. Why don't we see if they'd be willing to help us expose him? It's at least worth asking. The worst they'll do is tell us they can't help us."

Zane's jaw dropped. "Lindy, you are a *genius*. I could kiss you right now."

"You better not," Ryan teased.

Zane gave him a fond smile, though he rolled his eyes. "Seriously though, that's the first promising plan I've heard. Let me get ahold of Wade. I think you may have hit on the perfect solution."

CHAPTER THIRTY-ONE

All thoughts of Malone were pushed to the background over the next few days as they focused on hockey.

They squeaked in a win in the second game at home, but partway through, Tremblay went out with a sprained wrist.

They lost the third game to Boston on the road, and Anders grimaced as he watched Kelly limp onto the team bus to the hotel, undoubtedly sore after blocking a puck with his thigh in overtime.

Thankfully nothing was broken, but the move hadn't been enough to get them a win. Immediately after, Boston had gotten possession of the puck and scored, Hajek diving to make the save a fraction too late.

"Sit!" Anders ordered later that night as he got Kelly situated on his hotel bed.

"Is that what I sounded like when you were injured?" Kelly grumbled.

"Probably." Anders laughed and carefully wrapped an ice pack he'd gotten from one of the trainers around Kelly's thigh. He settled on the bed beside Kelly and reached for the remote.

Kelly rolled his head to the side, leaning his cheek against Anders' shoulder and nuzzling close. Anders shifted, carefully sliding in behind Kelly and arranging their bodies so Kelly lay in the vee between his legs, and he could rest against Anders' chest.

"Comfy?" Anders asked when Kelly let out a contented little sigh.

"Mmhmm."

Anders ducked his head and pressed his lips against Kelly's hair, letting the kiss linger. It smelled of the shampoo from the Harriers' locker room. "I love you," he whispered.

"Love you too." Kelly dropped his head and kissed Anders' forearm, soft and careful, since it was right where Anders had been slashed by one of Boston's D-men, a stick-shaped bruise beginning to form. "You know what's funny? I thought about being with you so many times over the years but I never considered this."

"What do you mean?" Anders could feel the slow, steady thump of Kelly's heart against his wrist.

"The quiet moments, I guess. I mean I imagined what it would be like if we had sex or, you know, if you told me you loved me or whatever."

Anders smiled against Kelly's hair, knowing without looking that his cheeks were probably bright red. Anders was oddly charmed that Kelly seemed shyer about admitting he'd pictured Anders saying he loved him than fantasizing about sex.

Rather than comment, Anders squeezed Kelly a little tighter, letting him continue.

"But I never thought about stuff like *this*. Being tired after a tough game and coming back to the hotel and being happy to be with you. Like, I'm exhausted and sore and tonight's game sucked donkey balls but it's better because I have you. Because we're here together."

For a moment, Anders couldn't answer, because Kelly had so perfectly put into words how Anders felt too. And yes, he knew how good moments like this could be, because he'd experienced them before. But he hadn't realized how much he'd missed them.

Or how uniquely different they were with Kelly because of the passion for the game the two of them shared.

"Sex is …" Anders let out a small laugh. "It's wonderful. You *know* how much I want you. How good we are in bed together. But in the end, it's only one part of intimacy. These moments shouldn't be discounted. And even after we're too tired or beat up from a game to do much else, we always have this."

"It'll be hard next season with you gone," Kelly whispered. "You sure you don't want a job with the team or something?"

"Yeah, I'm sure," Anders said with a smile. "But there's no saying I couldn't fly out to see you sometimes, especially on longer road trips."

"You'd do that for me?" Kelly craned his neck to look him in the eye and Anders pressed his lips to Kelly's cheek.

"I would do anything for you," he said and the smile that bloomed over Kelly's face was so sweet it made Anders tighten his grip.

"Good. Then hand me the clicker. Whatever you put on the TV is terrible," Kelly said with a cheeky grin.

Anders smiled. "The clicker?" *Clickah*, with a Boston accent like Kelly's.

"The … the remote!" he said, poking Anders' thigh. "And you knew what I meant."

Anders laughed. "Yes, but I like teasing you more."

Kelly sniffed. "And you called me a brat."

Anders reached for the remote on the bed beside them, handing it to Kelly with a smile. "I stand by it."

Kelly sputtered and proceeded to put on a terrible movie.

Anders didn't complain. He was content to hold Kelly and feel grateful to have him in his arms.

———

They won game four in Boston.

Anders' knee twinged as he left the ice after the third period, sweat-drenched and as exhausted as if he'd spent the entire sixty minutes on the ice instead of the twenty-seven he'd actually skated.

Kelly slipped an arm under his shoulder, taking some of his weight as they walked down the tunnel. "You okay?"

"Knee hurts," he gritted out.

"You should have said something!"

Anders let out a quiet snort. "Like you would have?"

They'd been down to the wire, 2-2 until the last few minutes when Anders had scored the final goal to give them a win. They'd *needed* him.

"Yeah, okay," Kelly muttered. "Fair."

"What's up?" Cam asked. "Your knee's bugging you?"

"Yeah," Anders said with a sigh as the trainer took over. "I don't remember tweaking it or hearing a pop but it's pretty bad."

"We'll go take a look. I've got him from here, O'Shea."

Kelly gave Anders a mournful look but headed in the other direction toward the dressing room.

The media would have lots of questions for him tonight since he'd tussled with Pat to get the puck, which led to an assist on Ryan's second-period goal. The press were eating up the on-ice O'Shea Family rivalry and with the series being so tight, fans were incredibly fired up.

Anders had managed three points tonight, with two assists and a goal, so he felt good about his contributions. He only hoped he hadn't put himself out of the rest of the series in the process.

After the usual poking and prodding and concerned muttering, Dr. Gardner and Kirk, their head trainer, agreed it was a muscle strain. Anders could put weight on the leg, and bend the joint fine, the tenderness and swelling would go down with proper care and rest.

"Will I be back in for game five?" he asked hopefully.

Dr. Gardner patted his shoulder. "I'm not making that call yet but I think as long as you take it easy in the next few days, you should be able to."

Anders' relief was indescribable.

Ten minutes later, anti-inflammatories and painkillers on board, he lowered himself into an ice bath, biting his lip to keep from swearing. He'd done this how many times and he never got over how damn *cold* it was.

His penis and testicles had retreated so far into his body he might never manage an erection again. Of course, if anyone could coax them out, it was Kelly.

Zane gave him a weak grin from the adjacent tub. "Fun times, huh?"

Anders snorted. "Something like that. How's the hip?"

"Ehh." He grimaced. "Not great."

Anders nodded. Despite the cortisone injection, Zane was obviously in pain.

Then again, as Anders glanced around at the trainers and massage therapists running around treating their battered team, who the hell wasn't?

That was playoff hockey.

———

Despite the game four win in Boston, and currently tied series, the team was fairly subdued as they touched down in Chicago that night.

Kelly was grateful they had two days off between games four and five. The arena in Evanston was used for other big events and a concert scheduled for the following night gave them an extra day of breathing room.

Everyone badly needed the rest.

Kelly slept in, then enjoyed a lazy afternoon on the couch with Anders. That evening, he had dinner with his parents, and met up with his brothers for drinks after.

Anders' knee was better by the second day, and after a light skate at practice and a checkup from Dr. Gardner, Kelly drove them to Anders' place for a nap.

But Anders was restless that afternoon and he'd been cleared for mild exercise, so they took a walk along the lakeshore.

Kelly was about to ask Anders if he wanted to grab some ice cream from the nearby Scoops stand when Anders got a phone call from their captain.

Anders listened intently, then nodded. "Yes, we can be there in about an hour. Will that work?"

He went silent, then nodded again. "Okay, we'll see you then."

After he hung up, Kelly gave him a questioning look. "What's going on?"

"Zane wants us to meet him downtown to talk to his agent about our plan."

"Okay."

They headed straight to Anders' place, took quick showers, and traded in their athletic wear for something nicer. Of course, Anders looked like he'd stepped out of a magazine ad, but Kelly thought he managed to pull himself together okay too.

"So much for a relaxing evening," Kelly said with a rueful sigh as Anders drove them to the office in The Loop, the buildings getting taller and taller as they got closer to downtown Chicago.

"I know. It would have been nice." Anders parked in the nearby parking structure and Kelly got out of the car. "We could go out to dinner after though, if you want."

"Yeah?" Kelly grinned. "Our second date, huh?"

Anders gave him a small smile. "That's the idea. And hopefully you enjoy it as much as the first."

"I'm sure I will." Kelly nudged his side with his elbow. "But, you know, any time you want to send a Boston Cream Pie from my favorite bakery, you should feel free."

Anders laughed. "I'll keep that in mind."

———

Anders had been in the Premier Talent office numerous times since he'd signed with them, but he'd never met Wade Cannon before. He was an imposing man, with a tall, muscular frame and a strong handshake.

Zane and Ryan had already arrived. Gabriel, Lance, and Dean Tremblay walked in around the same time, and Trevor was a few minutes behind. Jamie had a scheduling conflict, but he'd asked them to keep him updated.

No one looked happy to be there, merely resigned.

After the greetings were done and the group of them were seated at a conference table and had been offered beverages, Wade cleared his throat.

"Well, this is certainly an unusual situation. I've never been approached about something like this before, but I understand your concerns that the league isn't taking discipline for problematic players seriously."

Zane, as their spokesman, nodded.

Wade continued. "I've quietly spoken to one of my investigators. Her role is typically to do a deep dive on our clients' social media and see if there are situations we need to contain. She's never done research with the intent to spread that information, but she's as concerned as I am about the situation and more than willing to make an exception."

"We appreciate that. Is this going to cause problems with your bosses?" Zane asked.

Wade's jaw tightened. "That's for me to deal with. This is too important to be ignored."

Zane hesitated, then nodded. "Okay, so what now?"

"Well, I'll need some time. Laurie has already begun her digital investigation but that's a lot of information to go through. She's thorough and meticulous. If there's something there, she'll find it."

Wade glanced around the room. "This could get ugly. And I want to warn you all that because of your particular demographics, if we find something and bring it to the media, whoever is working for Jack Malone will spin this as sour grapes. There will likely be a targeted campaign against you all."

Anders looked around the table. All of them were either LGBTQ or, in Tremblay's case, a black man.

"Won't that backfire on him?" Kelly asked. "I mean, call me naïve but I'd like to think the public would be more on our side."

"Some of them certainly will be," Wade agreed. "But if they're appealing to the more conservative contingent of hockey, they'll paint you all as the problem. You're flouting long-standing if unspoken rules, trying to change a sacred game, and Jack Malone is the guy who is protecting the traditions of hockey."

"Oh, come on, racism and homophobia isn't traditional to the game," Kelly protested.

Wade arched an eyebrow. "Really? Because I sure remember a lot of it when I played."

"Kelly," Lance said carefully. "We still have a lot of problems in the league, but you'd be appalled to see what was common ten years ago, much less twenty or more."

Kelly grimaced, remembering his father's thoughtlessly cruel remarks in the past. "Yeah, okay. I'll shut up. Continue, Wade."

"No, that's okay. It is different now. But because it's quieter doesn't mean it's gone. I respect what players like you have done. Hell, I wish I'd had the opportunity to come out in my day, but we weren't there yet." He cleared his throat. "While I understand your head coach's reasoning for benching Malone for the rest of the series, it's probably only making him angrier and more resentful. He'll likely claim Daniels is unfairly biased toward you."

"Daniels isn't biased toward us," Ryan grumbled. "It's not our fault Malone shows up late and drunk."

"Well, *we* know that," Wade said. "But that's likely how Malone sees it. From what you've said, he's a bigoted person filled with a lot of hate, and I doubt he can differentiate between the two. He's being held responsible for his actions for the first time and he's lashing out. You're a convenient target."

Several of them let out frustrated sighs that Anders could totally relate to. But he could see Wade's point as well.

"So, what can we do now?" Zane asked. "Other than wait to see what the investigator finds."

"Not much, I'm afraid. Unless you can somehow find proof of Malone's problematic behavior, we have to wait and let her do her magic."

"I sort of wish this had come up before Malone found out I'm gay," Kelly said with a grimace. "I might have been able to get him drunk and talking. I could have recorded it or something."

"That would have been ideal," Wade agreed. "But unless you think he'll come around …"

"No," Kelly said with a sigh. "I don't. He's barely looked at me since this happened."

Anders' squeezed Kelly's thigh, knowing the entire situation was eating at Kelly.

———

As they sat around the conference room table discussing their options for how to deal with Malone, a kernel of something began to grow in Kelly's mind, and he straightened out of the slouch he'd been in.

"I think I might have an idea."

"What's that?" Wade asked.

After Kelly ran through his plan, Trevor blinked at him. "You want me to do *what?*"

"I want you to apologize to Malone and see if you can find proof of what kind of shit he's been up to."

"How would that work?" Trevor asked. "I mean, I got in his face about the stuff he said about you and Anders being together when he was throwing his temper tantrum in the locker room. Besides, he must have heard I'm bi. Surely one of the call ups would have said something to him by now."

"Maybe not," Kelly said slowly. "The two guys who usually do that have been out and I don't think he's bothered to get to know the rest because they weren't willing to kiss his ass. He might not have heard about you."

"I mean, maybe." Trevor's tone was doubtful. "But I still bruised his ego in the locker room. He's not going to forget it."

"So find a way to stroke his ego," Wade said. A shrewd look crossed his face. "Make him think you need him for something. Flatter him."

"Dude, I don't think I'm that good of an actor," Trevor said.

"You're going to have to be." Wade leaned forward, staring at Trevor intently.

"Easy for you to say," Trevor sniped. A weird animosity vibrated between them. Kelly couldn't quite put his finger on it but clearly something was up. "You're not the one putting your neck on the line."

"I put my neck on the line every day I work with athletes like you."

"What's that supposed to mean?"

"Is there something we should know about here?" Zane asked, and Kelly was glad he wasn't the only one who had picked up on Trevor's attitude toward the agent.

"Underhill here is my client. He doesn't always agree with my suggestions for his career," Wade said calmly, never looking away from Trevor.

"And Cannon here wouldn't know a good endorsement deal if it hit him in the face." Trevor didn't look away either.

Zane cleared his throat. "Uhh, well, I think we have bigger things to worry about at the moment. This Malone situation isn't going to go away. He may feel driven to retaliate in some way. Trevor, if you're not willing to do this, that's fine. But we need to know so we can figure out a different approach."

That seemed to break Trevor from his focused glare at his agent. "You're right." He dragged a hand through his light brown hair. "I don't like this and I'm not sure I can pull it off, but I'll try. I'm not gonna sit here and let him be a creep to women in our front office if I can stop it."

Everyone seemed to let out a collective sigh of relief.

"That's great news," Wade said. "Looks like we'll be working together a lot more in the future."

The look Trevor sent him was filled with pure annoyance, but he nodded tightly. "Looks like it."

The meeting ended shortly after that and as Anders and Kelly left the building, Kelly grimaced. "I know we had to do this, but it really sucks."

Anders rubbed his back. "It does."

"I … I hate that he was my friend. Or at least I *thought* he was. That's what keeps bugging me."

"I think Jack Malone is ultimately a selfish person," Anders said, trying to word it carefully. He didn't want to unintentionally hurt Kelly more. "I'm not sure he's capable of true friendship."

"Yeah, I know he liked that I was always available to get drinks and go out, but we never shared anything personal. It's just feels shitty to realize how shallow it was."

"I'm sorry," Anders said, curving an arm around him and pulling him in close, his lips brushing Kelly's forehead. "I can tell this is hard on you."

"Yeah." Kelly settled against him with a sigh. "But that's enough of him. You promised me a date, Lindy."

Anders smiled. "Well, I certainly don't want to miss out on that opportunity. Come on, I know a great place not too far from here. How do you feel about dinner at the restaurant in the Park Hotel? Being tucked in a boutique hotel means it doesn't get a lot of street traffic and I've never been recognized when I've eaten there. I think we should have enough privacy."

"I've never eaten there," Kelly said, tilting his head to look at Anders. "But if you say it's good, I'm sure I'll love it."

Anders dipped his chin and pressed his lips to Kelly's. Despite the pressure and exhaustion of the playoffs and the chaos of the situation with Jack Malone, nothing felt more important than stealing a few hours to show Kelly how much he was loved.

CHAPTER THIRTY-TWO

"Hey, you got a sec?" Underhill called out.

Kelly glanced over. He and Anders had arrived at the arena early so Anders could speak to the trainers before the game and Kelly had been chilling in the players' lounge watching baseball on the flatscreen and dicking around on his social media. It had been forever since he'd posted anything, so caught up in hockey and his relationship with Anders that he hadn't thought to upload content.

A bunch of people were bugging him to post more videos of him playing his guitar, but he couldn't remember the last time he'd touched the thing. Probably before Anders had injured his ankle. The instrument had been sitting dusty and unused in his apartment with Trevor. He should bring it to Anders' place. Maybe he'd move in slowly, one trip at a time.

"Sure, what's up?"

"Just come with me." Trevor jerked his head to the side, indicating the door.

Kelly raised an eyebrow but followed. He grew more confused when Trevor wove through the hallways of the arena and out the door to the parking lot.

"What the fuck are we doing out here?"

"I need to talk to you and as you found out the other day, there's no privacy in the arena."

Kelly snorted. "Yeah okay, that's fair. So, what's the big secret?"

"I think something's up with Malone."

Kelly leaned against the wall, staring out over the players' parking lot. "Other than the usual bullshit?"

"Yeah. I mean, you got blocked on his burner social media accounts, right?" Trevor paced a little, looking way more stressed than Kelly had ever seen him.

"Yeah."

That had been a weird thing to discover.

Many players had private accounts to control what was shared with the public. Guys with kids shared videos of them doing cute stuff and single dudes often posted pics of their vacations and the boat they bought or whatever. Some had burner accounts so they could quietly keep up on hockey news or use them for being fun and stupid without it impacting their public persona.

Kelly had a few of his own, in fact.

But the other day, Kelly noticed he'd been blocked on every single one of Malone's burner accounts.

And, as much as Kelly hated who Malone was, it still stung.

"Well, he's been saying some weird shit," Trevor said, rubbing his hand along his other arm, smoothing over his sleeve of tattoos the way he always did when he was nervous or uncomfortable.

"Weird how?" Kelly asked quietly.

Trevor frowned. "I don't know. Just pissed off about being benched. And he's kinda hinting that you and the other guys who are out are the problem. That you've turned the franchise against him. It's like he's trying to drum up support or something."

Kelly made a face. Wade Cannon had definitely been right. "That's bullshit."

"Yeah, I know," Trevor said, sounding irritated that Kelly had implied otherwise. "I'm just saying, watch your back. I can't put my finger on anything in particular, but something feels off to me."

"Thanks for the heads-up," Kelly said, meaning every word of it. "Hey, could you send me screenshots of what he said?"

"Oh, yeah." Trevor dug in the pocket of his basketball shorts and pulled out his phone. "I should have thought of it."

"Nah it's fine. This whole situation is weird."

"Tell me about it." Trevor frowned at his screen. "Also, are you ever coming back to our place or are you like, permanently living with Lindy now?"

"Uhh. Well, he did ask me to move in with him, but we're gonna wait until the end of the summer to make it official. I'll probably be at his place a lot though and we're talking about doing some traveling together so … yeah, I won't be around our place much this summer. I'll keep paying my half of the rent though, so you don't have to worry about finding a new roommate or whatever."

"Thanks. I guess I'll have to like … start getting groceries delivered or something though." Trevor shoved at his shoulder playfully.

Kelly laughed and shoved him back. "I think you'll survive."

———

Kelly had looked oddly rattled as he dressed for the game. Now, as they stood on the ice, waiting for the anthem to finish, he shifted restlessly, his upper arm brushing Anders' elbow. Anders shot him a worried glance out of the corner of his eye, but his head was bowed as he stared at the ice at his feet.

Concerned, but knowing Kelly would talk when he was able, Anders took a deep breath, calming his mind and finding his focus. They needed another win tonight and Anders couldn't afford to be distracted.

As the final notes rang out through the arena, he lifted his necklace to his lips, pressing a kiss to the wedding rings and Kelly's charm. The gesture soothed him, allowing his head to slip into game mode, and by the time the puck dropped, Anders was more than ready.

He took control of the game from the beginning, slamming a shot into the goal within in the first few minutes.

The moment it was in, he turned to find Kelly, playfully shoving him against the boards with a roar and watching him beam up at him.

"That was for you," Anders shouted, hugging him tight. Astrid would understand he had a new tradition now.

Kelly didn't say he loved him aloud, but it was in his eyes and the way he tucked his head into the crook of Anders' neck for a moment when he hugged him back.

The team followed Anders' lead like they so often did, fired up for the entire first period as they chased the puck up and down the ice. Boston wasn't letting up either, battling hard to keep the puck away but the Harriers were having to defend more than creating offensive chances.

The Otters scored again in the first and twice in the second, Boston beginning to lag by the time it ended, leaving the ice tired and drawn.

"God that was hot. I am going to suck your dick so fucking hard tonight," Kelly said under his breath as they slid onto the bench after a shift in the third period where Anders scored a wrap-around goal that had hit the back of the net before the goalie knew it was there.

Kelly had blocked his mouth with his glove and stick so the broadcast cameras couldn't pick up his filthy words, but Gabriel let out a quiet snort on Kelly's left.

Zane glanced at them with a curious smile from Anders' right but he didn't press.

Anders shook his head at them, playfully knocking elbows with Kelly, who grinned at him.

"Hey, you always say positive reinforcement is important for motivation and optimal performance."

Anders laughed. He *had* said that numerous times.

They desperately needed this win and while Anders wanted it badly enough he might not need Kelly's reinforcement to motivate himself to score, it certainly couldn't hurt.

But the Harriers rallied, tying the game up before the end of the third period.

During intermission, Coach Daniels hoarsely talked strategy while Anders mopped at his damp hair, wiping the sweat from his face and neck with a towel.

Anders fueled and hydrated, then they were out on the ice again for overtime. The play was so fast and tight they could barely manage line changes and by the end of the second double shift, Anders' legs burned, and his knee ached.

Both teams looked equally worn, sweat-drenched and weary, but Luke Crawford had enough energy to board Gabriel and leave him swearing up a blue streak in French as he limped off the ice. The refs rarely blew the whistle in overtime but the hit was so egregious Crawford went to the penalty box with a snarl, breaking his stick against the bench.

Anders gritted his teeth, shouldered his way through Boston's defense, and hammered in an arm-wrenching goal from the top of the point to end the game. His team crashed into him and for a moment Anders wondered if the press of all those bodies was the only thing holding him upright.

He was wrecked.

By the time Anders stripped off his sweat-soaked pads in the dressing room after the game, he was shaking with exhaustion. They'd *won*, and he'd played as full out of a game as he'd done in maybe a decade.

The thought of napping in his stall seemed perfectly acceptable and he must have closed his eyes for a second because he blinked them open to see Kelly holding out a protein shake and a carton of coconut water.

"Vad är det?" Anders mumbled and it took a moment for him to process the confusion on Kelly's face before he realized he'd used the wrong language.

Which was odd because English felt every bit at home in his mouth as Swedish, if not more so. He must be depleted if the adrenaline of the win wasn't enough to keep him going.

Anders shook his head, sucked down the coconut water, and tried again. "What is it?"

Kelly's worried expression smoothed out as Anders traded the carton for the protein shake. "You nodded off. You feeling okay?"

"Exhausted," Anders admitted. "But yes, I'll be okay."

"Well, you need to drink up so you can do media and all your postgame stuff so we can go home. I don't want to sleep here at the arena." Kelly nudged him. "Besides, I believe I made a promise to you earlier."

That got Anders moving. Not particularly *fast*, but he dutifully drank the remainder of the shake and coconut water, then trudged toward the shower with more energy than he'd had before.

After work with the trainers and time in the sauna, Anders felt semi-human by the time they walked through the doors of the dressing room in their suits.

He jerked to a stop when he came face-to-face with a furious-looking Patrick O'Shea pacing in the hallway. "You asshole," he snarled.

"I can't believe you're such a sore loser, Pat," Anders teased, assuming it was a joke. "I mean, I know you take the game seriously but—"

"This isn't about the goddamn game! When the fuck were you going to tell me my *brother* was the guy you were sleeping with, Anders?"

Anders and Kelly both blinked in confusion.

"What?" Kelly sputtered.

"Don't even try denying it. I've *seen* the article and the pictures." Pat waved his phone at them. "They're all over JockGossip."

Anders stared at him blankly. "What pictures? What are you talking about?"

Pat thrust the phone in their direction. Kelly took it, looking as shell-shocked as Anders felt. Anders stared over Kelly's shoulder while he scrolled through the photos and article.

———

A Second Chance at Love for Anders Lindholm?

Yet another love match amongst the Evanston River Otters has recently been spotted in the wild.

We're not sure what's in the water at the arena in Evanston, but something clearly is and we at JockGossip are here for it!

Recently leaked pictures show veteran forward Anders Lindholm tenderly kissing defenseman Kelly O'Shea after a romantic dinner at the Park Hotel's restaurant.

Although the hockey world was saddened by the tragic death of Lindholm's wife, Dr. Astrid Sjöberg, and their daughter, Elia, in a horrific car accident four years ago, it appears he's found a second chance at love with his teammate.

O'Shea, who played for Boston University for two seasons until he signed with the Otters, has never been linked to dating anyone publicly, although he has been snapped in several fan photos with women over the years.

Neither man has previously spoken to the press about their sexuality.

Whether this relationship is new or has been flying under the radar for a while, we couldn't be happier for them.

Though rumor has it not everyone on the team is thrilled about the news and with a playoff series to win, this may be the final straw in an already tumultuous season for the Otters.

Kelly lowered the phone, exchanging a worried glance with Anders.

They couldn't deny the photos. It wasn't a blurry camera snap with hard to make out figures. The shot of them kissing was in profile, the image clear and their faces easily recognizable. Whoever had done it had been a pro.

Had someone been following them? An uneasy feeling stirred in Anders' gut, but he had more pressing concerns at the moment. Like his pissed-off best friend.

"Pat," Anders said in a measured tone. "I understand why you're upset but—"

"You lied to me! Both of you. I can't believe this."

"We didn't lie," Kelly protested.

"Oh, I'm sorry. You failed to mention it. Kind of an important detail." The sarcasm practically dripped from his mouth.

Kelly sighed. "We didn't want to create a big fuss during the playoffs."

"Yeah well, instead, I had to find out from *Viv*."

Anders frowned, perplexed as to why Pat and Kelly's sister-in-law would have cared.

"She made it pretty clear she doesn't approve of me being gay," Kelly said bitterly.

Anders felt like he'd missed something, but it wasn't important right now.

"I argued with her and Con. I told her she must be mistaken. That they were weird rumors because you two have always been close. Surely if you were *together*, you would have told me. You're only my fucking brother and best friend. You wouldn't have hidden this from me."

Kelly's shoulders slumped and Anders wanted to reach out and reassure him but touching Kelly right now wouldn't help the situation.

"What the hell, Anders? I asked you to look out for Kelly, not take advantage of him. You're almost twice his age. What the fuck, man?"

"I'm not twice his age," Anders reminded him. "That would make me forty-four."

"Fine." Pat scowled. "Still, what are you doing with someone who is *twenty-two*?"

"Kelly is a grown man. He's allowed to date whoever he wants," Anders reminded him.

But Pat's jaw tightened. "Just tell me how long this has been going on. Since his rookie year?"

"What? No. It just started," Anders explained.

Kelly held up a hand. "Shut up and listen to me for a minute. It was one thing for you to be protective when I was a kid. But I'm a grown man. *I* get to pick which team I play for and who I fall in love with and date. I don't need my brothers running interference in my life anymore."

Pat, who looked thoroughly chastised, nodded, the annoyance beginning to leach out of him. "Maybe I was out of line. But I don't get it. Why my brother?" He looked at Anders with a confused frown.

"Uh, 'cause I'm awesome?" Kelly said.

Anders smiled, though his words were serious. "Because Kelly was the only person who made me smile and feel truly happy for the first time in four agonizingly lonely years."

Patrick froze. "Oh."

Anders swallowed, surprised by how emotional he felt admitting this aloud. "I closed myself off after Astrid's death, swore I would never fall in love again. But Kelly … something about him thawed the ice in my chest, and made my heart beat again."

Kelly let out the softest little noise and Anders reached out, pulling him close, though his gaze never left Pat's face.

"I'm in love with your brother. He makes me happy. He makes me feel alive and hopeful for a future again. You know I loved Astrid with every fiber of my being and all I want is the chance to love Kelly as much. For as long as I'm able."

Pat sighed. "Fuck. How can I argue with *that?*"

Anders half-expected Kelly to respond with a snarky remark but instead he turned his head into Anders' chest and hugged him tighter.

"You love him too, Kelly?" Pat asked.

He straightened. "More than anything in the world."

"Guess that would make me an asshole if I have a problem with it."

"Guess it would," Kelly agreed.

"Well fuck." Pat let out an irritated-sounding sigh. "Can I at least tell Anders that he's dead if he ever hurts you?"

Anders looked him in the eye. "You can, but I'd rather hurt myself than hurt him."

"How about you both agree to not fuck this up?" Pat said, almost smiling now. "I don't want to have to hurt *either* of you or lose my brother or my best friend."

"Sounds good to me," Kelly said.

Anders nodded.

"All right." Pat let out another heavy, put-upon sigh. "C'mon. Bring it in."

Before Anders knew what was happening, Pat had pulled them both into a hug.

"God you're annoying," Kelly said, his voice a little muffled because he was trapped between two men who were half a foot taller than him.

"Good thing you both love me," Pat said, thumping Anders' back.

Kelly shoved him away. "That can always change."

But laughter filled both of their voices and Anders knew the worst of the storm had passed.

CHAPTER THIRTY-THREE

They flew out to Boston that afternoon and played game six the following night.

Despite the work the trainers had done, Anders was stiff as he warmed up for the game. The grind of the playoffs had begun to set in and with every game they played, he became more convinced retirement was the right choice.

But he had no time to think of the future or anything else when he skated out onto the ice. They had a game to win. It would be harder here in Boston's arena without the home ice advantage, but they could do it. Boston was good this year but they weren't unbeatable.

Hajek had been playing well, keeping the Harriers' scoring opportunities low, and if the Otters were tight and focused tonight, they could win this.

"So, you're dating my brother, huh?" Connor O'Shea muttered as Anders faced off against him.

"Yes."

"Do I need to have the Zamboni talk with you?"

"The Zamboni talk?" Anders asked, not quite following.

"The 'you hurt my brother and I throw you in front of a Zamboni' warning."

Anders chuckled. "Pat's already covered that. Although I think he was going to use his fists, not a Zamboni."

Connor grinned. "I like to be creative. Besides, my hands are too good to risk." He winked at Anders.

"I will do everything in my power to not hurt Kelly," Anders promised. "I'm lucky to be with him. I won't risk that."

Connor smiled. "Good. You passed the test."

"That was a test?" Anders asked. He'd known these guys for years but sometimes he still didn't understand the way the O'Shea family operated.

But Connor sobered. "I *am* sorry about Viv spreading stuff around to Pat and sending him on a tear. I don't know what she was thinking. Her reaction to Kelly coming out has been weird."

Anders opened his mouth, but the ref spoke first. "Guys, can we finish this conversation after the game? We have some hockey to play here, or have you forgotten?"

"Right." Connor snapped to attention and Anders did too.

The puck dropped but Anders was a fraction of a second too slow and Connor had stolen it before Anders could react.

It was a strange first period, with icing calls and more stops in play than usual. Neither team scored for several minutes with shots going wide for the Otters and Hajek blocking Connor's wrister and batting it away.

It made for a slow, frustrating game. More of a grind than the previous ones and they were all pissed when Connor scored for Boston four minutes in. The crowd went wild, the building nearly shaking with their enthusiastic cheers.

"Come on, guys, we can do better than this," Daniels shouted.

But they couldn't seem to get it together. After a tussle instigated by Luke Crawford, he and Gabriel were split up by the refs and told to watch it. Gabriel had done his best to hold his temper but Crawford had been goading everyone on the team and Anders was afraid if he kept it up, they'd wind up with a brawl on their hands.

A few minutes later, Tremblay scored with an assist from Truro and the Otters were able to breathe a sigh of relief as they ended the first period tied with Boston.

A pep talk from Murphy helped and they had better energy in the second period.

Crawford was relentless and eventually Underhill snapped. He dropped gloves and fought, landing a solid punch to Crawford's nose that left him bloodied and snarling by the time the linemen pulled them apart.

Down to four on four, the fight fired the team up and a few minutes later Cooper's assist to Kajota got them a second goal.

Unfortunately, the hits from Boston just got harder. Anders gritted his teeth and limped toward the bench from a particularly brutal one from Crawford.

"*Crisse!* I hate that guy," Gabriel muttered.

"I can't say he's my favorite," Anders agreed, knowing he would be aching tomorrow.

That was even more of a reason for them to shut Boston down to prevent the series from going to seven games, so Anders dug deep, pushing the pain away to get them another goal before the second period ended.

"God, I love you," Kelly said as they went off the ice for the second intermission and all Anders could do was grin despite the throbbing in his left shoulder and hip.

————

Kelly was about ready to murder his brothers and their team. Although the Otters were ahead 3-2 as they went into the third period, Boston was playing a hard, grinding game and it was clearly wearing on Anders.

He looked grim and drawn as he took the face off, but Kelly knew it wouldn't stop him from playing with everything he had in him. The fourth win was always the hardest to accomplish, but they were so close Kelly could taste it.

Although he wanted this win for himself and his team, he wanted it for Anders most of all.

Anders had won with Boston once, early in his career. The Otters win two seasons ago had given him a second. Kelly knew how hungry Anders was to win a third. Few players in the modern era managed that feat and if this was Anders last season, Kelly would do anything to help him achieve that.

But Boston was playing hard and dirty. Kelly got into it with one of his brothers' teammates until a lineman pulled them apart. He muttered under his breath on his way back to the bench, determined to keep it from happening again. They needed shots on goals, not a fight.

As the minutes of the third period ticked away with the score still tied, Kelly skated harder, looking for any opportunity to get in Boston's path and disrupt their play.

It wasn't until the final minute of the period when he got his chance. He put his shoulder down and slammed one of Boston's wingers into the boards. Before he could recover, Kelly stole the puck, racing through the neutral zone, legs burning as his focus narrowed to finding a passing lane.

He spotted it, sliding the puck in between two of Boston's players and straight onto Anders' tape. Kelly tensed as the puck flew from Anders' stick, barely grazing past Boston's goaltender.

It tumbled into the goal and when the end of game horn sounded, Kelly threw up his arms and raced to Anders, who was already skating straight for him.

Kelly threw himself at Anders, hugging him tightly as he clamped his legs around Anders' waist, screaming, "We did it! We're going to the second round, Lindy!"

CHAPTER THIRTY-FOUR

Because they'd won the first round of the playoffs in six games, the team had four days to rest and regroup before they moved on to the next round.

The entire team seemed grateful for the break, everyone as worn and weary as Anders had told Kelly he felt. They were all bruised and battered, though thankfully no one on the team was out with a major injury.

There were three more series to win. And the Malone situation to deal with. Not small things, but earlier Anders had reminded him it was good for them to focus on what they had accomplished so far.

Zane had organized a team dinner—Malone notably absent—to celebrate their first-round win and Kelly enjoyed the first night out with the boys they'd had since they were outed.

"To the queerest team in the NHL!" Ryan said, lifting his drink toward the end of dinner.

Kelly sputtered into his own beer—thankful they were in a private room—but he lifted the glass in a toast while the rest of the guys around the table did the same.

"Ryan." Zane looked a little pained as he clinked glasses with him. "C'mon."

"What, it's true," Ryan protested. "I mean, look how far we've come. This season we went from the two of us to nine—if you include Coach, Underhill, and Bennett."

"That's true but …"

"Aww, come on. It's all in good fun, right, guys?" Ryan looked around the table.

Kelly shrugged. He didn't care what Ryan called them. It just felt great knowing that he was a part of it.

Never in a million years would he have imagined a night like this. Being on a team like this.

They were a Stanley Cup winning team—two-time winners by the end of this run if Kelly had anything to say about it—who had a group of openly gay and bi guys playing. That was huge.

History-changing.

Life-changing. Or at least it had changed *his* life.

Kelly glanced at Anders, watching him laugh with the guys, his eyes crinkling at the corners as he pushed some of his hair behind his ear. His facial hair was a little scraggly since they were both growing playoff beards—though Kelly's had always been patchy and pitiful—but it was the brightness of his eyes that made Kelly's heart sing.

A sharp, intense surge of love took his breath away.

He wouldn't have come out without someone like Anders to help him find his courage. Anders might not have done it without Jamie telling the team about his relationship with Taylor. Jamie and Gabriel and Lance probably wouldn't have come out if not for Zane and Ryan paving the way.

And well, none of them would have done it without Noah Boucher being the first.

Without that, Kelly wouldn't be where he was now. His family wouldn't know who he was and know about him and Anders. And be *okay* with it.

He was so happy he didn't know what to do with himself.

"Do you want dessert?" Anders asked, nudging Kelly out of his thoughts.

"I dunno." He shot a glance at Zane. "Is Cap gonna be on my case about it?"

Zane laughed. "*I'm* ordering cheesecake. I put on a suit for tonight and it was looking a little loose around the waist."

Kelly laughed but he was feeling it too. He'd lost a few pounds of muscle mass already this season. And while his mother and the team nutritionist might tell him he should be focused on lean protein, he figured he could get away with being a little more indulgent tonight. But maybe just a little.

"We could split something," Kelly suggested to Anders.

"Who said I'm willing to share?" Anders teased.

Kelly faked a gasp. "Who are you and what have you done with Anders Lindholm?"

Anders grinned. "I seem to remember you saying that spending more time together would get me to untwist. It seems you were right."

Kelly thought back to that conversation. "Pretty sure you said you'd make me think before I leapt into a decision. I dunno about that."

"Oh, I think that's happened at least a little bit. Besides, we have time, Kels."

Kelly smiled. They did.

Kelly felt hopeful that there were good things waiting for them in the weeks and months and hopefully years to come.

They were both battered and tired and they had a long way to go before the season was over, but this was good. They were good together.

Anders seemed peaceful now. Content and happy in a way Kelly hadn't seen him since Astrid had been alive. Kelly was incandescently happy to be a part of that.

As much as Kelly hated to admit it, some of it was probably because Anders had officially decided to retire. But Kelly knew he'd played an important part in Anders' happiness too.

And no matter how many assists Kelly gave him on the ice, nothing could possibly compare to that.

Seeing Anders' joy and hope for the future and getting to share it with him was the one thing Kelly had always wanted.

So, he leaned his shoulder against Anders and smiled, utterly and perfectly content.

———

The following afternoon, after they were done with practice and recovery work with the trainers at the rink, Anders suggested they walk along the lake.

It was a warm spring day and Kelly eagerly said yes. Although Anders went with no destination in mind, he found himself drawn to the cemetery.

"Are you okay with going?" he asked Kelly. "We won't stay long, I promise. I just want to …"

He didn't know how to put it into words, only that it felt right to visit with Kelly. But Kelly seemed to understand.

He nodded and took Anders' hand. "Yes. I want to tell Astrid thank you."

That, maybe more than anything else, made Anders' heart feel full. Kelly *understood*. He and Anders would build a new life together but he would always respect the foundation that it was built on.

Whatever their future brought, the past wouldn't be forgotten, but gently and respectfully set aside to make room for what was to come.

As they walked to the graves, Anders told him about the talk he'd had with Astrid before he decided to go all in on their relationship.

"I know she's not really *here* and answering me," Anders said as they approached the grassy swell where the two gravestones sat. "But it helped me work through my fears about loving someone again."

Kelly squeezed his hand, his eyes watering. "I'm glad it helped."

Anders pulled him close, pressing a kiss to the top of his head.

Kelly knelt and laid a flower on each grave. He'd pilfered them from a nearby park on the way to the cemetery. While the park groundskeepers might not appreciate the gesture, the sight of it was so sweet it made Anders' heart fill with love for Kelly.

"Don't you worry," Kelly promised as he gently rested his fingertips on Astrid's headstone. "I'll take good care of him for you."

Anders knew without a shadow of a doubt that Kelly would.

At the end of the summer, they'd talk about moving in together.

When the time was right, Anders would propose, unless Kelly beat him to it first.

Someday they'd talk about having children.

Whatever the future brought for them, Anders' heart was in safe and loving hands.

THE END

sniffles I love Anders and Kelly. Theirs was a tough story to tell but I hope you adored it as much as I did.

Breaking the Rules is next. It is the final book in the Rules of the Game series and features Trevor Underhill, aka. *The Undertaker*, and his agent, Wade Cannon.

Trevor has a chip on his shoulder and a healthy grudge against Wade, but they're going to have to work together if they want to expose Jack Malone for the slimeball he is …

Learn more here.

BRIGHAM'S BOOKS

Rules of the Game

Join the pro hockey players who fight hard and love hard in the Rules of the Game Universe.

The chronological reading order is *Road Rules, Bending the Rules, Changing the Rules, Unwritten Rules, Rules of Engagement, and Breaking the Rules.*

Road Rules: Rule #1: Don't fall in love with your best friend.

(A 45 k series prequel. Available exclusively through Prolific Works.)

Bending the Rules: Rule #1: Never give up on love.

Changing the Rules: Rule #1: Don't fall in love with your coach.

Unwritten Rules: Rule #1: Don't fall in love with your family's sworn enemy.

Rules of Engagement: Rule #1: Don't fall in love with your brother's best friend.

Breaking the Rules: Rule #1: Don't fall in love with your agent. Coming November 2022.

All titles coming soon in audio.

———

Pendleton Bay Books

Visit the fictional small town of Pendleton Bay on the shores of Lake Michigan. All books set in this universe can be read as standalones but characters from other books/series may appear from time to time.

There are currently two series set within the Pendleton Bay Universe.

Naughty in Pendleton Series

A complete m/m romance series set in the town of Pendleton Bay with characters exploring the kinkier side of romance. BDSM elements will appear in all books.

Date in a Pinch: When chemistry teacher Neil gets an unexpected delivery at the high school where he works, he's mortified when his crush, Alexander, sees the contents. Curious but inexperienced with kink, Neil has no idea how to live out his fantasies until the hot lit teacher offers a helping hand.

Embracing His Shame: Forrest, the town's accountant, may look uptight but he's anything but. When he offers the local mechanic, Jarod, an indecent proposal to fulfill his shameful fantasies, Forrest will have to decide if he's willing to give Jarod a chance to show him that he can have love *and* the kink he longs for.

Made to Order: Donovan, head chef at the Hawk Point Tavern, loves to be in charge in the kitchen *and* in the bedroom. Tyler, a former solider, is pretty sure he's straight and definitely only into kink if he's the one dishing it out. Until he and Donovan start butting heads about who is calling the shots …

Flipping the Switch: When Logan, a silver fox Dom looking for *experience* on a kinky app, stumbles across Jude, a flirty switch who just so happens to be best friend's son, *and* introduces him to a sweet cinnamon roll of a sub named Tony, they heat between them will sizzle hotter than Jude's kitchen. But they'll have to decide if three is the perfect number.

Preston's Christmas Escape: When Hollywood actor Preston gets caught by the paparazzi in a compromising position, he flees to his home state of Michigan to hide out with his former best friend and ex. Reclusive potter Blake is reluctant to let Preston invade his quiet home in the woods but the heat between them can only be denied for so long … (BDSM)

Poly in Pendleton Series

An ongoing m/m/f romance series set in the town of Pendleton Bay.

Three Shots: Reeve, a local musician, and Grant, a computer designer, have fun in bed together but pursuing a relationship never feels quite right until they meet tavern owner Rachael and try to figure out how to be poly in the small town of Pendleton Bay.

Between the Studs: Coming soon

———

Peachtree Books

Visit the real life city of Atlanta, Georgia. All books in this universe can be read as standalone but characters from both series do crossover.

There are two series set with the Peachtree Universe.

The Peachtree Series

Complete, continuous m/m series featuring an age gap, light kink, and found family. *Also available in Italian.*

Off-Balance: Coworkers Russ & Stephen meet over a spilled cup of coffee and navigate the complexities of a nineteen-year age gap, a big difference in income, and the death of Stephen's estranged father.

Love in the Balance: Their story continues as Russ introduces Stephen to his family, searches for his absent mother, and asks Stephen to marry him.

Full Balance: They navigate new challenges as they take in a teenage foster boy named Austin and decide to make him a permanent part of their family.

Peachtree Place

Standalone m/m books in the same universe as The Peachtree Series

Trust the Connection: Evan & Jeremy find a love that will heal both their scars in this slow-burn, age-gap romance about living with a disability, believing in yourself, and building the family you always wanted.

———

The Midwest Series

Complete m/m series featuring four couples. Stories intertwine but can be read as standalones. Opposites attract m/m sports romance with numerous bisexual characters.

Bully & Exit*:* Drama geek Caleb is sure he'll never forgive Nathan, the hockey player who dumped him in high school, until he learns the real reason why in this slow-burn, second-chance new adult romance. Now available in audio.

Push & Pull*:* Lowell & Brent have nothing in common when they leave on a summer road trip, but by the end, the makeup-wearing fashionista and the macho hockey player will realize they're perfect for each other in this enemies to lovers, slow-burn story about acceptance. Now available in audio.

Touch & Go*:* Micah, a closeted pro pitcher, and Justin, a laid-back physical therapist, have nothing in common but when Micah blows out his shoulder, he'll have to choose which he wants more: baseball or love? An enemies to lovers, out for you romance. Now available in audio.

Advance & Retreat*:* When fate brings Ian and Ricky together, a college swimmer will have to figure out how to reached for the gold without losing the sweet hotel manager who lights up the stage as sizzling drag queen Rosie Riveting. An age gap sports romance with a gender fluid character. Now available in audio.

———

The West Hills

Standalone m/m series featuring three different couples

The Ghosts Between Us: Losing his brother in a devastating accident sends Chris spiraling into grief. The last person he expects to find comfort in is his brother's secret boyfriend, Elliot, in this slow burn, hurt/comfort romance.

Tidal Series – Co-authored with K Evan Coles

A complete, continuous m/m duology that takes Riley & Carter from best friends to lovers in this slow-burn romance featuring the sons of two wealthy Manhattan families.

Wake: After a decade and a half of lying to himself and everyone around him, Riley slowly come to terms with his sexuality and his feelings for his best friend, Carter, shattering their friendship.

Calm: Carter reaches his own realization and they slowly build the relationship they've been denying for so long.

Speakeasy Series – Co-authored with K Evan Coles

Complete, standalone m/m series featuring characters from the Tidal universe

With a Twist: After Will learns of his estranged father's cancer diagnosis, he returns home and slowly mends fences with him and falls in love with his father's colleague, David. Enemies to lovers, opposites attract, interracial romance.

Extra Dirty: Wealthy, pansexual businessman Jesse is perfectly happy living his life to the fullest with no strings attached, but when he meets Cam, a music teacher and DJ, he'll find that some strings are worth hanging onto in this age-gap, opposites-attract romance.

Behind the Stick: Speakeasy owner and bartender Kyle has taken a break from dating when he's rescued by Harlem firefighter Luka. Interracial romance and hurt/comfort.

Straight Up: When hot, tattooed biker chef Stuart meets quiet and serious Malcolm, they both have secrets they're hiding. Gray ace, bisexual awakening, lingerie kink.

―――

The Williamsville Inn

Standalone m/m holiday romances in a shared universe with Hank Edwards

Snowstorms and Second Chances: Erik and Seth don't hit it off at first, but when a snowstorm leads to them sharing a room at a hotel, Erik discovers a whole new side of himself and his feelings about the holidays. A forced-proximity, bisexual-awakening romance with a second chance at happiness.

The Cupcake Conundrum: Adrian comes face to face with the biggest mistake of his past, Ajay, a hookup who he ghosted on. He'll have to make amends and win Jay's heart back in this single dad, second-chance interracial romance.

―――

Colors Series

A continuous f/f series featuring a bisexual character and opposites attract trope

A Brighter Palette: When Annie, a struggling American freelance writer, meets Siobhán, a successful Irish painter living in Boston, the heat between them is undeniable, but is it enough to build something that will last?

The Greenest Isle: After Siobhán's father has a heart attack, she and Annie travel to Ireland to care for him. Their relationship is tested as they navigate living in a new place and healing old wounds.

———

Standalone Books

Baby, It's Cold Inside: Meeting Nate's parents doesn't go at all like Emerson planned. But there might be a Christmas miracle for the two of them before the visit is through in this sweet and funny m/m holiday romance.

Bromantic Getaway: Spencer is sure he's straight. But when an off-hand comment sends him tumbling into the realization he's in love with his best friend Devin, he'll have to turn a romantic vacation meant for his ex into the perfect opportunity to grab the love that's always been right in front of them in this best friends to lovers bi awakening m/m romance.

Cabin Fever: Kevin's best friend's dad is definitely off-limits. But he and Drew are about to spend a week alone in a cabin the week before Christmas. And Kevin's never been any good at resisting temptation. An age gap, best friend's father m/m holiday romance.

Also available in audio and in Italian.

Corked: A sommelier and a wine distributor clash in this enemies to lovers, age-gap m/m romance that takes Sean & Lucas from a restaurant in Chicago to owning a winery in Traverse City.

Inked in Blood: **Co-Authored with K Evan Coles** An unexpected event changes the life and death of a sexy, tattooed vampire named Jeff and Santiago, a tattoo artist with a secret. A paranormal, age-gap m/m romance.

Seeking Warmth: When Benny gets out of juvie, he's lost all hope for a future for him or his sister, but the help of his ex-boyfriend Scott will show him that hope and love still exist in this m/m YA novel about second chances.

The Soldier Next Door: When Travis agrees to keep an eye on the guy next door for a few weeks while his parents are out of town, he never expects to fall in love with a soldier heading off to war. An age-gap m/m novella.

ABOUT THE AUTHOR

Brigham Vaughn is on the adventure of a lifetime as a full-time author. She devours books at an alarming rate and hasn't let her short arms and long torso stop her from doing yoga. She makes a killer key lime pie, hates green peppers, and loves wine tasting tours. A collector of vintage Nancy Drew books and green glassware, she enjoys poking around in antique shops and refinishing thrift store furniture. An avid photographer, she dreams of traveling the world and she can't wait to discover everything else life has to offer her.

Her books range from short stories to novellas to novels. They explore gay, bisexual, lesbian, and polyamorous romance in contemporary settings.

Want to read more of her work? Check it out on BookBub!

For news of new releases and sales, follow on Amazon or BookBub!

If you'd like to become an ARC reader, take part in giveaways, and get all of the latest news, please join her reader group, Brigham's Book Nerds. She'd love to have you there!

Made in the USA
Monee, IL
14 January 2023

25045405R00267